The Unbegotten

To order additional copies, please contact us.
BookSurge, LLC
www.booksurge.com
1-866-308-6235
orders@booksurge.com

JAMES GORDON

THE UNBEGOTTEN

A NOVEL

2003

The Unbegotten

In loving memory of my mother, Henrietta P. Gordon.

CHAPTER ONE

Seattle, Washington. The once graceful skyline looked as if a nuclear bomb had been detonated in the heart of the city. The huge skyscrapers were gone and the Space Needle lay on the ground in pieces. A river of fire stretched into the horizon and the sky was as black as night. It was just before dawn, the day following Armageddon. The remnants of humanity burned and debris cascaded from the heavens. The screams of the slaughtered still echoed in the winds. Demons and gods had ravaged the land, and the evil beast that was imprisoned in the pit for eons had been released. Many died this day, and death's grip knew no boundaries.

Chaos and destruction were everywhere. Buildings that once housed thriving businesses were empty cracked shells that lay open like a festering wound. Streets that once carried the city's inhabitants to their destinations were destroyed, riddled with huge sinkholes and protruding rock formations. The bodies of gods, angels and humans littered the streets like confetti, dangling on the crumbled remnants of buildings or laying in pools of blood on the ground. I could see it all so clearly as I stood atop Mount Rainier. But as horrifying as these images were, the reason behind the cataclysmic events that led to this chaos was equally disturbing. All of this happened because I was allowed to live.

My name is Vanifera. I am the person responsible for all of this. I didn't actually destroy this world, but because of my existence, others did. Supernatural forces waged a war that left millions dead and this planet ravaged, all because of me. I am an entity called the Gaian, a being created for the single purpose of causing this destruction. This fate was something I never asked for. However, I wasn't given the option of choice. Regardless, innocent people lost their lives. I looked into the sky as tears rolled down my cheeks. The pain in my heart was so overwhelming that I couldn't find the strength to ask God why all of this had to happen. I used to believe that when someone died, they would find peace and exist in serenity. But I was wrong. The truth was that the afterlife was just another place of existence, another realm of misery and pain. There was no peace and there was no serenity. Only the continuing battle against evil awaited the unsuspecting soul that crossed into the next dimension. The only thing that provided strength and comfort was faith. Believing that there was a purpose for the suffering a soul went through was the only thing that helped it to continue fighting. It was like a carrot, dangling in front of a starving horse's face. To me, that analogy was quite appropriate. It symbolized the relentless pursuit for truth or perfection. It gave a purpose to one's life, even if that wasn't their true purpose. But what happens when you find out that faith is not enough? What if that rewarding future you believe will come, holds a less than optimistic outcome? What if your journey toward a life of peace suddenly takes an alternate route? Every soul is born with a purpose, waiting for its possessor to discover its true mission. My purpose, as unbelievable as it sounds, was to bring about the destruction of God's kingdom.

Morning had come to the land, but you wouldn't have known it. As the sun rose in the east, a dense layer of smoke blanketed the sky. A foul stench accompanied the rising sun, mingling with the frosty winds that swirled around the mountain's summit. The pungent odor was nearly suffocating and reeked of sulfur and burned flesh. Despite the sun's failing attempts to cut through the overcast, the presence of a new day was welcomed. The night was over and the end had come to the horrors of yesterday. A new day was coming, and for me, it couldn't happen soon enough.

Still, there was one major drawback that came with this morning. I was alone now. I, too, have suffered great losses and the anguish gripped my heart like a vice. Yesterday, my loved ones were alive. Today, they are not. Everything I ever loved had been taken from me. The loneliness I felt was unbearable. I wanted to talk to someone, perhaps commiserate with those who'd also suffered losses. But there was no one left. The entire city had been destroyed and everyone in it had been killed. Even if I had found someone to talk to, what would I say? Could I tell them that all of this was my fault? Would they understand and comfort me in my time of pain and loss, or would they curse me and add even more guilt to my already burdened soul?

I gazed at the shambled burning skyline, feeling more isolated than I'd ever felt. The pain squeezed my heart tighter and I dropped to my knees in the snow, too hurt to cry and too angry to think. It just didn't seem right. Why did all these people have to die? Why did those I loved have to die? I shook my head in disbelief as the bitter cold wind blew across the tears on my face. But, like any story, the truth and the answers are best found by starting at the beginning.

~~~

San Francisco, California. It was a day just like any other day. The alarm clock beeped and I slammed my hand on the snooze button. I turned over and draped my arm across the chest of my boyfriend, Angelo, who always seemed to awaken before the clock alarm sounded. I scooted up and kissed him on the lips.

"Good morning, bright eyes," he said.

I always got a kick out of his little comments.

"I don't feel like getting up," I said as I stretched and yawned. "Why don't we call in sick today? We can stay in bed and just cuddle."

"Sounds like a plan; just one problem. I have that budget meeting this morning and I'm the only one who has the presentation," he replied.

"You sure do know how to ruin a good idea."

Angelo rolled me over and began passionately kissing me. It was almost as if he suddenly got the hint. We made love as the morning sun gradually filled the room with light. After thirty minutes of passion, I got up and went into the bathroom to take my shower. Angelo turned on the television to catch the morning news, then went to start making coffee. I closed the door and turned on the shower, checking the water to see if it was warm enough. Suddenly, I heard Angelo's muffled voice screaming something from the other side of the door. However, the hiss of the shower was drowning him out.

"What?" I screamed back.

He opened the door and stuck his head in.

"I said it's going to rain."

"Oh, could you pull out my umbrella?" I asked.

"You've been in San Francisco for two years and you still use an umbrella?"

"Sorry, but I'm not like some folks who think they're waterproof. I don't like to get wet."

He shook his head and closed the door. As I held my arm in the water that had finally gotten warm, I suddenly saw the irony of my comment. I chuckled to myself, then hopped into the shower. I would've enjoyed a long shower this morning, but there never seemed to be enough hot water. That was one of Angelo's pet peeves. He always accused me of using up all the hot water. To avoid hearing him fuss this morning, I quickly finished my shower and stepped out on the floor mat. I dried myself and wrapped the towel around me. Angelo knocked and then barreled into the bathroom, placing a cup of coffee on the ledge of the sink.

"Let me know when you're done," he said.

"You could have joined me if you weren't so bashful," I replied, teasing him by pretending to unwrap my towel.

"Didn't I scratch that itch already?" he asked as he took a bite of his jelly toast.

I walked to him and also took a bite, then I pecked him on the lips. He began wrapping his arms around me, trying to entice me into another lovemaking session by kissing my neck. I pushed him back, shot him a smirk and patted him on his arms.

"We're going to be late," I said.

I hurried to the closet and pulled out the outfit I was going to wear. Angelo closed the door and began taking his shower. The muffled report on the television played in the background as I began getting dressed. Yes, this was the start of a day, more or less, like any other day. But I would soon find out that it wouldn't be for long. In fact, it would be a day I would long regret starting.

We took the BART into the city and then caught a bus to the west side. Angelo was the director of the St. Martins Rehabilitative Center. I worked across the street at the McClendon Family Practice Center as a nurse in the OB-GYN clinic. As we kissed goodbye, Angelo and I saw a young woman running toward St. Martins. She had bruises on her face and body, and her clothes were torn. Angelo and I looked at each other and hurried inside the building to see what was the matter.

As we entered, the woman became hysterical as tracks of mascara tears ran down her cheeks. She claimed that her boyfriend had beaten her and that she came here for help. Angelo quickly assisted her to the urgent care room. I followed.

"Barbara, could you get Dr. Stanton and tell him to come to the urgent care room," he said to one of the nurses.

"Right away," she replied.

As we entered the room, she instantly grabbed Angelo's hand and clutched his arm, holding on to him as if her life depended on it. The sight of her doing that made me feel a little uneasy, maybe even a slight bit jealous. He looked at me and flashed me the 'I didn't do anything' look. But I remained professional. She was the immediate concern right now, and Angelo was there for support.

"Miss, can you sit on the table for me? I need to examine you," I said.

The woman turned and looked at me with what appeared to be a scowl.

"And just who are you?" she asked with a snippy tone.

"My name is Vanifera. I'm a nurse," I replied.

She gave me a menacing glance up and down, which surprised me to say the least. Then, she released Angelo's arm and sat on the examination table. She placed her hands over her face and began crying once more. I glanced at Angelo, who still had a befuddled look on his face. I smirked and shook my head. I proceeded to the table and grabbed the blood pressure cuff. As I grab her arm to wrap the cuff around it, the woman snatched away from me and gave me another menacing glare. I was starting to get a little annoyed with her antics.

"I need to take your blood pressure," I said.

Just then, Dr. Stanton entered the room along with Denise, my best friend and one of the ER nurses. He pulled out his otoscope and flipped on the light. The woman glanced at him, then clung to Angelo's arm once more. Needless to say, I was almost ready to pop her one. Denise reached over and tugged on my sleeve. I turned and looked at her. She nodded and gave me one of those 'calm down' hand gestures.

"Hello, I'm Dr. Stanton. Who did this to you?" he asked.

"My boyfriend! He just flipped out, saying that I was fooling around!" she said tearfully.

The doctor performed a quick check of her ears and eyes, then looked at her bruises. She hissed as he touched one of the cuts on her forehead.

"Did we get any vitals on her?" he asked.

"No, I wasn't able to," I replied as I returned my own sneering glare toward her.

"Let's take her to X-ray and get some shots of her arms, head and torso," said Stanton.

Denise leaned toward me.

"You want me to handle this?" she whispered jokingly.

"That probably would be best," I replied.

Suddenly, the woman became panicky again.

"Don't leave me!" she begged, tightening her grip on Angelo's arm.

Angelo looked at the doctor and then back at her.

"I'll be right here, okay?" he said patting her on the arm.

At that point, I had to leave. I couldn't stand to watch this any longer.

"Well, I'll just leave you guys to your work," I said as I walked out of the room.

I left the building angrier than I'd ever been in my life. I wasn't sure whether I was angry with the woman or with Angelo. Frankly, I was surprised that he didn't follow me out. But Angelo knew me well, and I'm sure he realized that right then wasn't the time to talk to me. Besides, he had a job to do, and it was time for me to get to mine.

It took me the next few hours just to calm down. By noon I wasn't angry anymore, but I was still very disturbed by the way that woman glared at me. Another peculiar thing was the fact that Angelo never called me. Normally, when he knew I was upset about something, he would at least call a few times to make sure I was okay. But today, he never did. I was preparing to go to lunch when Denise called me.

"Hey girl, what's up?" I asked.

"Lots. You remember that woman that was here earlier?" she asked.

"Yeah?"

"Well, I just wanted to tell you that Angelo stayed with her the entire time."

"Oh really?"

"Yep. After we took her to X-ray, we brought her back to the urgent care room and cleaned her up. Stanton said there was nothing wrong with her, but she held on to Angelo the entire time."

"Then what happened?"

"Well, we cleaned and bandaged her up. Then we released her."

"What is this woman's name?" I asked with a slightly aggravated tone.

"Let me see...I had her file right here. Ah, here it is. DeVeaux, Candy DeVeaux!"

"Candy DeVeaux, huh? Sounds like a hooker's name to me."

"But wait, there's more. She would not leave. She hung around here talking about how she had no place to go, that she had no family here and her boyfriend threw her out," Denise continued.

"I'm sorry to hear that, but that's her problem. She can go down to the mission. They'll put her up for the night."

"That's just what Stanton told her. He said we aren't running a boarding house. But then, Angelo stepped in."

"What did he say?"

"He and Stanton walked into the hallway. Being nosy as I am, I stood by the door and listened. Angelo asked Stanton if he thought he was being a little strong back there when he told her this wasn't a boarding house, and Stanton said not at all. In fact, he thought she probably was fooling around and got caught. He said he saw this type of stuff every weekend, girls strung out on crack or crystal meth who end up having sex with someone in order to get money for more drugs. The boyfriend finds out, gets jealous and then kicks them out. They come here for a couple of days, use up our supplies for free and then go running back to their abusive sweethearts and their addictions. In many respects, he's right."

"What did Angelo say?"

"Well, not much after that. But he did ask if one of the staff members could put her up for the night. Stanton didn't feel right about that. I'm telling you, Vani, your boy was acting like he was sprung on this woman."

"Where is Angelo now?"

"I don't know. Last time I saw him was right after that woman left. He's probably at lunch or something. You want me to tell him to call you?"

"Nah, I'll catch him later."

"Vani, that woman was something else. And the way the two of you were staring down one another, you'd think you two knew each other," said Denise.

"Yeah. She just kept staring at me and snapping at me. I thought she was psycho."

"I hear ya. Well listen, let me get back to work. I just wanted to give you the 411 on little miss strange."

"Thanks, Denise. I'll call you later."

I hung up the phone and sat there for a few minutes. I wasn't so much concerned about that Candy woman as I was about Angelo. If what Denise said was true, he was acting rather peculiar. Then, for him to disappear like that and not call me was also concerning. Angelo was always level headed, and he'd never given me any reason to distrust him. But even when I met Candy, I knew something was odd about her. I decided to shake off my suspicions and go to lunch. I had about fifteen minutes left and needed to eat something. I hopped up from the nurses' station and walked to the lunchroom.

The rest of the day flew by and soon it was six o'clock. It was quitting time, and it couldn't have come any sooner. I finished my report and gathered my things from the desk. It was then I realized that Angelo hadn't called me all day long. I picked up the phone and called his office. There was no answer. I called the nurses' station to see if Denise was there. She was.

"Hey, you seen Angelo around there?" I asked.

"No, I hadn't seen him all day. In fact, come to think of it, I haven't seen him since this morning right after that woman left," said Denise.

"Alright. Well, if you see him, tell him I'm going home."

"Okay, I'll give him the message. Be careful, Vani."

I hung up the phone and made my way to the bus stop. Thirty minutes later, I arrived at the BART station and waited on the platform for the train. All the while, I kept wondering where Angelo was. He'd never done anything like this before and I was starting to get worried. Just then, an old bum stumbled into me. He startled me and I backed away from him. He looked at me with the same kind of stare that Candy what's-her-name looked at me, very menacing.

"Excuse me," he said.

"No problem," I replied with a weary expression.

As he walked away, I watched him until he'd gotten quite some distance from me. Just then, the BART pulled into the station and eased to a stop. The doors opened and out came a flood of people. I waited for them to finish exiting, too tired to fight against the flow. As the last person left, I attempted to board. Suddenly my path was blocked by a young boy who couldn't have been more than twelve years old. He, too, glared at me like the old bum had done.

"Excuse me," he said.

I looked at the boy with a puzzled expression on my face.

"No problem," I replied.

The lad walked passed me and in the same direction that the old man had walked. I looked at him and began getting a very eerie feeling. Suddenly, the announcement that the doors were closing echoed on the platform, and I ducked through them just as they were beginning to close. I made my way to a seat and released a deep sigh as I slumped down.

As the BART began pulling off, I turned and looked out of the window next to me. I expected to see the disappointed faces of the stragglers who'd just missed the train. But instead, I stared into the face of the old bum who'd bumped into me. Standing next to him was the young boy. They were both glaring right at me. As the train left the station, a very uncomfortable feeling came over me and a chill raced down my spine.

During the entire trip home, the bum and the kid were on my mind. Why were they staring at me? It also seemed weird that they both were standing next to each other. Their eyes possessed a bitter coldness as they leered at me from the platform. As I reflected on the rest of the day's events, namely Candy's antics and Angelo's disappearance, this was turning out to be the most disturbing day of my life.

Forty minutes later, the train came to my stop. I gathered my things and got off. I was extremely tired and couldn't wait to get home. I didn't normally go home by myself. Angelo would accompany me, but for some reason, he was nowhere to be found. My mind was beginning to run wild with all sorts of thoughts, ranging from kidnapping to him meeting that woman somewhere. I blamed most of my suspicions on the fact that I was tired and that it had been a long day. My mind kept going back to the old man and kid on the platform. It was odd how they just stood there staring at me. In fact, the whole episode involving the two of them was weird.

When I finally made it home, the streetlights were beginning to come on and the sounds of Mr. and Mrs. Johnson's nightly argument was starting. I pulled my keys from my purse and unlocked my door. Chloe, my little fluffy white terrier, trotted to me and began leaping all over my legs.

"Hey girl, how are you?" I asked in a child-like voice.

I used my leg to close the door and walked to the counter, laying my things on top of it. I knelt and scratched Chloe under her chin, her tail wagging wildly. As I looked up, I saw something I didn't expect. The shirt that Angelo had worn to work that morning was lying on the floor. I stood, walked to it and picked it off the floor. I detected a strange smell and sniffed the shirt. I'd smelled this scent before. It was that rancid perfume Candy wore when she was in the urgent care room earlier. Suddenly, I heard a muffled sound coming from the bedroom. My heart sank in my chest and I slowly began walking to the bedroom door. It was slightly cracked. I pushed it open and stood wide-eyed in the doorway.

There they were, lying on top of my bed. They were involved in an extremely passionate kiss, so passionate that a dim light seemed to emanate from between their lips. Angelo's arms were outstretched and Candy was straddled atop him, wearing one of his shirts. It was completely unbuttoned, revealing her naked well-defined body.

I felt as if I were going to vomit. I couldn't believe what I was seeing. He'd brought this woman back to our place and was in the process of having sex with her. It felt as if a knife was being pushed and twisted into my chest. I couldn't move nor speak. I just stood there, staring at the two of them. Finally, after a few moments, I turned and walked away. Tears began rolling down my cheeks, and I didn't know what to do. I felt as if my breath had been taken from me. My mind told me to leave the apartment, but I just couldn't do it. I couldn't just let this woman invade my home and get away with it.

I turned and walked back to the room. I marched toward the

bed and was about to push her off Angelo when I saw something strange. When I first saw it, I thought the light between their mouths was simply my imagination. However, as I stood there watching her kiss Angelo, I saw that the dim light was real. Angelo's eyes were wide and a pained expression was etched on his face. His body was tense and he appeared unable to move. I knew then that this was more than just a kiss.

"Get off of him!" I screamed.

Without so much as a thought, I pushed Candy as hard as I could. She slid off of Angelo and fell to the floor with a thud. From the look on his face, Angelo was in a lot of pain. He had trouble breathing, gasping as if he had been suffocating. I grabbed him around his shoulders and lifted him to a sitting position in the bed.

"C'mon baby, breathe," I said as I gently tapped the sides of his face.

Just then, Candy stood back up and glared at me just as she did in the rehabilitation center. I turned and glared right back at her.

"I don't know what you were doing to him, but you better get the hell out of here!" I said as Angelo coughed.

"Hell, an interesting choice of words. However, I'm not done here yet. The Seraph must die, and I will not leave here until he is dead," said Candy.

"If you don't leave right now, I'm going to call the police!"

"Go ahead, call them. I will kill them just as I am going to kill the Seraph."

Candy began moving toward me. I could see that there was no reasoning with her. I then saw a lamp that had fallen to the floor. I picked it up, held it in front of me and positioned myself between Angelo and her.

"I'm only going to tell you one more time; get the hell out of my house!" I screamed as I stood from the bed.

Candy leaped into the air and kicked the lamp from my hands. Before her feet touched the floor, she delivered a roundhouse kick to the side of my face and knocked me to the ground. I slid to a stop, stunned by the power of the blow. I'd never been hit that hard in my entire life.

"Stay down, Gaian. My fight is not with you. I am here to kill the Seraphim," she hissed.

I looked at her, trying to regain my bearings. That's when I really got scared. Her eyes suddenly turned serpent-like, slit pupils surrounded in yellow. She had a hungry look on her face and my bottom lip trembled with fear.

"What the hell are you?" I asked.

Candy smiled, then turned and looked once more at Angelo. However, he was no longer lying outstretched on the bed, but standing, glaring back at the woman with a look of anger.

"You will pay for your treachery, demon," he said, clenching his fists.

Suddenly, his eyes began glowing, turning completely white in color. Candy screamed and then crumbled to the floor, writhing in pain. She sounded like a witch. I sat there in disbelief, totally confused and frightened by what I was witnessing. Was I dreaming or was this really happening? I looked at Candy as she bucked on the floor. Then, I looked at Angelo as his eyes continued to glow.

"Vanifera, you need to get out of here," he said in an echoed voice.

I couldn't respond. I was too stunned to move. But, in speaking to me, he'd made a very careless mistake. He'd become distracted and gave Candy the break she needed. A huge tail sprang from behind her and struck Angelo on the side of his face, knocking him into the wall.

"Angelo!" I exclaimed.

He fell to the floor with a thud. I scurried over the bed and to his side to help him. When I got there, I saw that he was out cold. I tried shaking him, hoping that it would revive him. At that moment, Candy stood to her feet. Her huge tail wagged behind her, and her skin was now green and scaly. Her hair was no longer the long blonde colored locks that flowed to her shoulders. Instead, it was white and ratty. Her nails had become claws and fangs now hung from the edges of her mouth.

"How sweet. The little girlfriend is concerned. Don't worry, sweetie, I'll finish him off real quick," she said.

Angelo was still unconscious and Candy was ready to strike. I could not let her harm him, no matter the cost. I was the only thing standing between the two of them and I was determined to not let her lay one claw on him. I looked down and spied the lamp that she knocked out of my hands. I scrambled over to it, picked it up and charged toward her swinging. I struck her on the side of her face with everything I had. She never even flinched.

"What was that, a mosquito bite? Surely you aren't trying to challenge me, and if you are, I hope that wasn't the best you had!" said Candy.

My inability to inflict any damage to her caused the fear to swell inside of me. I stood there clutching the lamp and wondering what to do next. It was my best shot and it had no effect on her. Candy reared back and slapped me across the face. Like Angelo, I smashed into the wall and then fell to the floor. I lay there, dazed and hurt. The room was spinning, and I felt as if I were on the verge of blacking out.

"As I said, my fight is not with you. Now, stay down or I'll be forced to put you down permanently," said Candy.

She walked back to Angelo, turned him over on his back and placed her lips over his. I shook my head, trying to clear the cobwebs. As my senses returned, I saw another being standing next to me. It was a man dressed in a leisure suit. He knelt beside me and I instantly began backing away from him.

"Who are you?" I asked.

"You aren't going to sit there and let her kill him are you?" he asked, completely ignoring my question.

"What do you mean? I tried to stop her..."

"Not hard enough."

I looked back at Angelo and Candy. The light was starting to appear around the edges of their mouths again. I turned and looked at the man once more.

"Please, can you help him? She's hurting him." I pleaded.

"Only you can stop her, princess. Only you have that kind of power," said the man.

"How? What can I do? I hit her with everything I had and it didn't phase her."

"That's because you aren't using your true powers."

The man stood and looked at Candy as she continued to kiss my unconscious boyfriend. The light around their mouths intensified.

"She is devouring his soul. Soon he will be dead, and it will be all your fault," said the man.

I couldn't grasp the concept of what he was saying. But what I did catch was the fact that if I didn't do something soon, Angelo was going to die. I pushed myself off the floor and stood, glaring at Candy with one thought in mind. Somehow I had to stop her.

~~~

CHAPTER TWO

The light between their lips appeared to be growing weaker by the moment. I shook my head and regained more of my senses. My heart ached as I watched Candy continue to ravenously kiss Angelo, who began twitching. Suddenly, as if a switch had been flipped inside of me, something snapped. It was as if every emotion I had came rushing to my chest. I released a scream that seemed to come from the depths of my soul. All the anguish I was feeling exploded from my body in one huge cry.

I then felt a swirl of wind spinning around me and I was instantly cloaked in darkness. I could see nothing, hear nothing. The swirling wind dissipated and I felt the sensation of water being poured over my body, almost as if I was standing beneath a gentle waterfall. The air became fresh and the trickling sound of water echoed all around me. I felt exhilarated and panted heavily, trying to regain the breath I'd lost during my scream. Then, an abrupt silence came. All was quiet except for the sound of my panting. I lifted my head to see if I could find Angelo. Instead, I saw a massive golden pyramid shaped object rotating before me. It glistened like a jewel and its surface looked as smooth as ice. Hues of garnet, emerald and sapphire flashed across its surface. I was confused by the phenomenon, wondering what this object was. I looked around, hoping to see where Angelo was. But aside from the pyramid, all I saw was darkness.

"Where am I? Where did everybody go?" I asked.

I turned to look at the pyramid once more. I felt disturbed, yet at the same time intrigued. There was something familiar about this object, like it was somehow connected to me. To my knowledge, I'd never seen this object before and my curiosity was piqued. I lifted my hand to touch it. Just as I did, the massive object disappeared.

Another gust of wind whisked around me, and I found myself back in my apartment. Papers and other articles were whirling in the air. Lightning exploded all around me as I lifted my arms to shield my eyes from the flash. A page from the newspaper wrapped around my arm. I quickly grabbed it and looked at it. It was the front page and the headline read, 'Change is coming!'

"I'm afraid you don't have time to read," said the leisurely dressed man from earlier.

His reappearance startled me. Before I could say anything, he nodded toward the bed. I looked and saw that Angelo and Candy were still entwined. The spiraling wind had grown to its maximum intensity and the flashes of lightning were lighting up the room. Her blatant disrespect changed my anxiety into rage.

"Stop!" I screamed as I released the paper.

The sound of my voice startled Candy and she jumped from fright. She turned and glared at me with a look of bewilderment. I clenched my fists and assumed a fighting stance. Candy's expression loosened.

"So, you seem ready to give it another go. Well, I think it is fair to warn you that should I strike this time, I will show you no mercy," she said in a raspy voice.

"I wouldn't have it any other way," I replied.

In my chest, I could feel a simmering hatred beginning to develop. As I glared at Candy, all I wanted to do right then was knock her head off her shoulders. She was so full of herself that it was nauseating. From my earlier encounter, I knew that fighting her would be a mistake. But if I didn't do something, Angelo would be dead soon. If he had to die at the hands of this monster, she would first have to go through me. I saw the smug expression on her face and her arrogant demeanor. It worsened the anger I already felt. She slithered from over Angelo and stood a few feet in front of me.

"You sure seem confident! Are you sure you are ready to die?" she hissed.

"Are you?" I replied.

The gleam of blood lust was in her cold slit eyes, looking at me as if I were a wounded animal. But strangely enough, that seemed to enhance my now boiling contempt for her. As I was about to make my move, I heard a voice whispering in my ear. It sounded like the man who was here earlier.

"Focus your energy, Gaian! Concentrate! Use your anger and pain as your weapons!" he said.

The voice startled me and I looked around to ask the man for advice. To my surprise, he wasn't there. I scanned around me, frantically trying to locate him. He was here a few seconds ago and the voice sounded just like his. Candy growled, causing me to focus on her once more.

"What's the matter, Gaian, looking for someone to help you?" she asked.

Fear suddenly gripped my chest. I didn't know what to say; probably because that was just the thought I had in mind. But when I looked at Candy once again, my anger began to over-shadow my fears. It was like I'd somehow been transformed into someone else, feeling a surge of energy I never knew existed. All I could see before me was an animal that had no mercy or remorse, a ravenous bloodthirsty beast that had to be killed. She was a predator that fed on those that were unaware of her vile nature. To allow her to continue living was not an option. She had to die, and it would be by my hands.

I felt my anger peaking inside of me, empowering me with the strength and will to do what I needed to do. In my infuriated state, I lunged forward and grabbed her by the hair. I delivered a closed fist punch to her jaw that was filled with so much angry power that I felt the room vibrate when I struck her. A green discharge shot from Candy's mouth and drenched me, almost as if I'd ruptured a major artery. It was sticky and foul smelling. The fact that she'd sprayed me with her icky discharge infuriated me more, causing the energy I felt to increase. I swung again, this time connecting to her left temple. She screamed in agony and fell to the floor with a thud. She began scrambling and clawing in an attempt to get away. I grabbed her by the hair once again and slammed her face repeatedly into the floor. Then, I pulled her to her knees, glaring at her with pure contempt. My basic instincts had taken over, and I could feel the power from my anger cruising through my body. I stood over her, barely able to contain my rage.

As I looked at Candy dangling in my grasp, I felt something inside of me struggling to keep me from going over the edge. It was like a voice screaming from the darkness that had now engulfed my soul. But the urge to do damage was too strong, and the feeble attempt at restraint was getting weaker. I looked at her, still trying to fight my murderous desires.

"You animal! I should kill you for what you've done?" I said.

Candy lifted her head as she wobbled in my grasp. She knelt before me, covered with the greenish ooze that flowed from the wounds and lacerations I'd inflicted. Her eyes begged me to put an end to it all and finish her quickly. The truth is, I wanted to kill her so badly that I could taste it on my lips. She didn't deserve to live, and in a strange twisted way, I almost felt sorry for her, almost.

"Do it! Finish me off! I will not grovel for my life!" she said.

Her words struck me like a hammer.

"What?" I asked.

"You heard me! Finish the job!"

"You sound as if you want me to kill you," I said.

"Yes, that is exactly what I want," she said huffing.

"Why?"

"It would be more merciful than allowing me to live."

A look of fear blanketed her face. Her eyes seemed to hold an infinite amount of anguish. I was really thrown off by her comment and the way she was looking at me. It was as if she were pleading for mercy from a life of misery. I stood there with widened eyes and my mouth agape. What would make someone want to be killed? This was something I'd never encountered before and quite frankly it was starting to scare me. I released her hair and began backing away from her.

"No, I cannot do that," I said.

"Gaian, you must finish me off! I cannot go back to him! He will do terrible things to me! I can't handle that anymore!" said Candy.

"Who, Candy. Who's hurting you?"

"My master! He has ownership of my soul! If you have a shred of mercy, you'll kill me and release me from my bondage to him!"

I was really getting scared now and stepped back from her a little further.

"I'm sorry, Candy, but I will not kill you," I said.

"Gaian, please," she begged.

"Get out of here, right now!" I said frantically.

Candy's look of fear turned to a scowl.

"You are pathetic and weak, foolish and arrogant! You do not deserve the blessings of being the Gaian! Since you will not kill me, then I will kill you, and your boyfriend!" she hissed.

Before I could catch myself, the restraint I tried to maintain disappeared and the rage caused from her remarks consumed me. I drew back my fist and delivered an uppercut to her chin, knocking her through the air and into a bookshelf on the far wall of the room. She crashed into the wooden structure and slumped to the floor in a disgusting pile. Suddenly, her body began to shake and tremble, as if she were having convulsions. It was then I noticed the splintered stake protruding from her chest. When she crashed into the bookcase, one of the broken shelves was driven through her body. She lay on the floor shaking as the green ooze poured from the open wound in her chest. She struggled to lift her head and looked at me.

"Thank you, G-Gaian," whispered Candy.

Then, with a gurgle, her eyes stared straight ahead, her head dropped and her body relaxed. Candy was dead. As she lay impaled on the floor, her body began to smolder and hiss. Smoke seeped from her skin, and she began dissolving into a puddle of sludge. I watched as her remains fizzled away right before my eyes. I felt shocked and panicky. I'd never seen anyone dissolve before. But even though the sight of her dissolving shocked and scared me, I felt no remorse. As the moments passed, I actually began feeling a degree of satisfaction for what I'd done, perhaps even joy. She'd threatened the lives of Angelo and myself and deserved the fate she'd incurred. At least I knew now that she would never bother us again.

"Good riddance," I said.

I then remembered about Angelo. I turned to see that he was still lying on the floor. I raced to him and knelt beside him. He was still unconscious. I pulled a pillow from the bed and slid it beneath his head. I began stroking his face, hoping that he would soon awaken. It was then I saw that he had a rather large knot on his forehead, no doubt the result of his fall. I curled next to him and checked his pulse and respiration. I reached up to the nightstand and grabbed the phone to call for an ambulance. Suddenly, he opened his eyes.

"Hey," I said as his eyes fluttered open.

He was silent for a moment, scanning around the room trying to regain his bearings. I placed the phone back in its cradle and looked at him.

"What happened?" he asked.

I chuckled.

"Well, let's see. There was a green snake lady that almost killed you. But I stopped her. In fact, I killed her," I said.

Angelo sat up quickly and looked at me.

"Are you okay?" he asked.

"I should be asking you that question."

"Where is she?" he asked looking around frantically.

"Why? Do you want to kiss her again?"

"What? What are you talking about?" he asked, looking dumbfounded.

"Nothing."

"So, where is she?"

"Didn't you hear anything I said? I killed her!"

His eyes grew wide.

"You?"

I was almost offended by his remark.

"Yes, me."

Suddenly, the reality of what I'd done hit me. I'd actually murdered someone. Angelo had a look of worry. I instantly felt a huge degree of panic. Tears welled in my eyes as the reality of what I'd done continued to sink in.

"I killed her, Angelo! I actually killed someone!" I said sobbingly.

"Vanifera, calm down. Everything is going to be alright," he said hugging me.

"Angelo, what am I going to do? I don't want to go to jail," I cried.

"Don't worry, Vanifera. I don't think you'll have to worry about that," he replied.

"How can I not worry about that? I just killed someone!"

Angelo looked at me, as if he didn't know how to respond.

"Why did you do it, Angelo? Why did you bring her here? This is our home. She didn't belong here and now I'm a murderer," I said, now into a full-blown cry.

Angelo looked down at the floor.

"You're not a murderer and you aren't going to jail. That woman, well...she wasn't normal," said Angelo.

"And that's another thing! She melted into the floor! What kind of person melts into the floor?"

"Vanifera..."

"And she had these eyes, they were like snake eyes..."

"Vanifera..."

"And she had a tail. Who in the hell has a tail?"

"VANIFERA!"

"What?"

"She wasn't human!"

"Well no kidding! I kind of figured that out when she dissolved into the floor!" I said sniffing. "I'm so confused and scared right now that I don't know how to react. What is going on, Angelo? First, this woman is sucking out your soul and then..."

"How did you know she was devouring my soul?" he asked abruptly.

"There was this guy who appeared out of nowhere and he..."

"What did this guy look like?"

I sighed, annoyed by his constant interrupting. I wiped my eyes and continued.

"He was an older guy, I'd say about in his mid to late fifties."

"Was he short and well built?"

"Yeah, now that you mention it," I said nodding.

"Have a slight accent?"

"Yep."

"Barhim Hajj," Angelo mumbled.

"Barhim Hajj? What's a Barhim Hajj?" I asked.

"Not a what, but who," said Angelo as he pushed himself to stand.

"Are you sure you want to do that?" I asked as I also stood, bracing my hand against his back to steady him.

"I'll be fine in a few minutes," he said as he twisted and rotated his neck.

I looked at him to make sure he was okay. It was then I noticed that the lump that was on his forehead was gone.

"You had a lump on your head and now..."

"I know. That's what I need to..."

"Damn it! Will you quit interrupting me! Let me say what I have to say!" I exclaimed.

"Sorry." Angelo replied.

I folded my arms and walked to the other side of the room. I braced my back against the wall and tapped my foot in order to keep myself from losing it. Then, I slid down the wall and sat on the floor, curling my legs to my chest. Angelo sighed and sat next to me. We both stared ahead of us, not sure what to say. I couldn't believe I'd killed somebody. I wanted to tell him how I was feeling, but I just didn't know how to begin talking about it. It was too surreal and unnatural that words couldn't begin to describe what I felt.

"Shock, that's how I felt the first time I took a life," said Angelo.

I turned and looked at him with amazement.

"You killed someone?" I asked breathlessly.

"I've killed many. It's what I was made for," he replied.

I couldn't believe he was saying this to me. I'd known Angelo for two years, and I thought I knew him. This was the first time he'd ever told me anything like this, and honestly, I was beginning to fear for my life.

"Angelo, please stop, you're scaring me," I said.

He continued to stare ahead.

"The woman that you killed, her name was Caliestra. She was not a human but a succubae, a demon from the pit," said Angelo.

I gave him a skeptical look.

"A succubae? A demon?" I said disbelievingly.

"Yes. I'm afraid that the worst is yet to come," he said turning to finally look at me.

"Listen, I really didn't expect this today. I don't know what I've gotten myself into, but this is my stop and I'm getting off this ride right now," I said as I pushed myself from the floor.

Angelo leaped up and stood in front of me.

"Vanifera, you must listen. There is much to tell you and a very short time to explain," he said.

"I don't want to hear anymore. Just stay away from me, Angelo," I said pushing my way passed him.

I walked into the kitchen and grabbed my keys and purse.

"Where are you going?" he asked.

"I don't know. I just need to get away from here for a little while."

I opened the door and walked out. I ran out of the apartment building and began walking toward the BART station. I couldn't think, and I needed to place some distance between myself and Angelo. I knew that sooner or later, Candy, or whatever her real name was, would come up missing and I would have to turn myself in to the police. But how was I going to explain that she just melted into the floor when she died? I would surely be locked away in an insane asylum. The whole thing sounded like a bad plot to a horror movie. However, this was no movie and I definitely wasn't amused.

A few minutes later, I found my way to the BART station. The next train would be there any minute. It was starting to get cold, and I realized that I'd forgotten my jacket. In fact, I still had on my nurse's uniform. I folded my arms across my chest and marched in one spot. I kept peeking down the tracks to see if there was any sign of the train approaching. I did a quick scan around me and saw a handful of other people waiting for the train. Just then, a teenager startled me from behind.

"Pardon me, ma'am, but do you have any spare change so I can get something to eat?" he asked.

I turned and looked at the kid. I was sure he wasn't there a second ago, but perhaps he'd been in my blind spot. I reached for my purse and opened my wallet. I gave him a dollar.

"Here you go," I said.

The kid took the money and shoved it into his pocket. Then, he grabbed me by the arm.

"My master would like to see you," he said in a low, distorted tone of voice.

I stared at him with fright. His eyes glowed a bright red and his teeth were jagged-edged fangs. I tried to pull away from him, but his grip was too strong. I began screaming at the top of my lungs.

"HELP! SOMEBODY HELP ME!" I yelled.

Just then, another hand grabbed me on my shoulder. I turned to see that another being that looked just like the teen was standing behind me. I was frozen with fright, unable to mouth another plea for help.

"I don't have much money, but you can take what I have," I said.

"We don't want your money. We want you," said the creature.

He opened his mouth, almost as if he was about to bite me. I became so terrified that I simply reacted. I swung my purse and nailed the first monster in the face, freeing me from his grip. Then, I began running down the platform, screaming for a police officer or anyone who could help me. But all of the people I saw moments ago were gone. The two creatures began walking slowly after me. I didn't stop running. Within moments, I was at the end of the dock and had no place to run. I looked over the edge and saw that it was a twenty-foot drop. My only chance to get away was to go for it. I leaped over the edge and landed on the ground. My shins stung from the harsh landing. But that was the least of my worries. As I stood to continue running, I saw that another creature was standing before me.

"Going somewhere?" it asked.

I turned and looked back at the platform. The other two creatures had made their way to the edge and were looking down at me.

"There is no place for you to run," one of them said.

Then, the two that stood on the platform leaped to the ground behind me. I was surrounded. I tried looking around for something to defend myself with. The only thing I saw was a small pole left from the construction of the fence that lined the tracks. I grabbed it and lifted it before me. The creature in front of me swung and knocked the pole from my hand. It clanged to the ground on the other side of the tracks.

"Now, no more games. You will come with us," said the creature.

Just then, I heard the BART approaching. I lifted my hands like I was surrendering. The train roared down the tracks and was now mere feet from me. The creature reached out to grab me. Just then, I leaped toward the tracks and to the other side just as the BART barreled to a halt. It had created a barrier between the beasts and me. I quickly started running down the tracks with all the speed I could muster. If I could make it to the rear of the BART, my plan was to get on board and hope that the creatures didn't figure out that I'd gotten on. It wasn't a very good plan, but it was the only one I could think of.

As I got to the back of the train, I climbed the ladder and boarded. I opened the back door and crouched in the conductor's cabin. I was panting heavily, but I tried to calm my breathing as much as I could. All was quiet and still. After a few minutes, I wondered why the train hadn't started moving yet. Normally, the BART took only a couple of minutes between stops. Something must have happened to the conductor. *Those beasts must have gotten to him,* I thought.

As I sat crouching on the floor, I could see the image of one of the beasts through the window. I prayed that he wouldn't come in and that the train would hurry and leave. I couldn't help but to begin whimpering. I was so scared I couldn't control it.

Suddenly, the hand of one of the monsters pierced the side of the compartment and grabbed me. I began screaming and fighting with everything I had to get away. Then, the door was kicked in and the other creature entered. All I could do was cry in horror.

"NO! GOD PLEASE NO!" I screamed.

The beast that kicked in the door grabbed me by the collar and lifted me up. I continued to fight, but my punches weren't doing any damage. It pulled me from the compartment and back outside, down the ladder and to the ground. I was literally at its mercy, dragged like a rag doll behind the monster. After pulling me a little ways from the train, it dropped me on the ground and stood over me. The other two creatures joined him and they encircled me, glaring at me with looks of ill intent.

"Since you will not come easily, then I will swallow you whole and take you back to my master," said the first monster.

Then, it ripped open its shirt and revealed a huge mouth located in its chest. It began opening and a vortex began pulling me toward it. The suction was so strong that I had a hard time breathing. I grabbed a piece of electrical wire that was protruding from the ground, trying to keep myself from being pulled in. But it was no use. The vortex was too strong and I was losing my grip. My feet were lifted from the earth, and I was suspended in the air. Within moments, I would be sucked into its orifice and taken to wherever it wanted to take me. All I could hear was their laughter and the howl of the air rushing passed me. My grip finally slipped and I barreled toward the huge hole in the beast's chest.

Suddenly, the suction stopped as well as the laughter of the beasts. I fell to the ground hard, knocking the wind out of me as I landed. Although I was hurt, I crawled to the wall, still trying to catch my breath. I suspected the creatures would be coming to get me soon. But after a few moments, I noticed that they weren't surrounding me like they had done. I turned to look at them and see what they were doing.

Their backs were toward me as they stared at the platform. I looked up to see what had grabbed their attention. My eyes widened. Angelo was standing on the edge, glaring down at them. I quickly crawled to the train and hid behind it. I peeked around the corner to see what was going to happen.

"Be gone, Seraph, this is none of your affair," said one of the beasts.

"The woman is my affair. I suggest you leave her and go back to your master," said Angelo.

"We have our orders and they are that we retrieve the woman and bring her back to our lord. We will not leave here without her," said another beast.

"Then you will die here!" said Angelo.

"Not this day, Seraph."

The three leaped into the air and landed on the platform, surrounding Angelo on all sides. Angelo seemed unusually calm as the snickering monsters closed in on him. One tried to charge him from behind, but Angelo simply lifted his hand and backhanded the creature into one of the support walls on the platform. The other two creatures glanced at their fallen comrade and then charged Angelo simultaneously. One swung at him while the other blew flames from its mouth. Within the blink of an eye, Angelo vanished, causing the monster's blow to strike its partner and the flames to totally engulf the other. The two beasts fell to the ground, writhing in pain.

I glanced at the wall where the other beast was knocked into and saw Angelo nonchalantly standing next to it. After a moment of regrouping, the two beasts zeroed in on his location and charged once more. The creature that Angelo struck reached up and grabbed him by one of his ankles.

"Now we've got you," it hissed.

I felt that Angelo was in trouble, so I stepped from behind the train and prepared to help him any way I could, even if it was to simply distract them for a moment. But Angelo had everything under control. He kicked his leg upward and flipped the beast that had grabbed his ankle into the air. As it tumbled downward, he delivered another punch to the beast and sent it sailing into the two that charged toward him. The collision knocked all three into the side of the train where they then collapsed to the ground. The impact shook the train and knocked me to the ground. Angelo calmly began walking toward the incapacitated creatures. But just as he approached them, the creatures suddenly disappeared. Angelo stopped in his tracks, apparently surprised by the move. Then, he looked to his right and saw another being walking toward him.

"What are you doing here?" asked Angelo.

"I came to take back those demons you just beat up," said the approaching being.

As the man stopped a few feet from Angelo, I could see that he had dreadlocks and was cinnamon in complexion. He wore a long trench coat and was very conservatively dressed. Angelo never took his eyes off the guy, but then called to me.

"Vanifera, are you alright?" he shouted.

"Yes, I'm fine!" I shouted back.

"Come to me," he said while still staring at the man.

I stood and ran to the platform stairs, climbing them as quickly as I could. I raced to his side and wrapped my arms around his waist. He placed his arm around my shoulders, never once removing his eyes from the man.

"So, this was your doing, huh, Azreal?" asked Angelo.

I lifted my head and looked at Angelo, then at the man he called Azreal.

"I had nothing to do with this, Uriel. These demons were escapees, rogue hounds who tried to undermine the agency. I was sent to bring them back. That is why I took them before you could do any further damage," said Azreal.

"You were wise to do so. Otherwise, I would have killed them," said Angelo.

Azreal turned and looked right at me.

"Is this the Gaian?" he asked.

Angelo did not answer.

"She's pretty," Azreal continued.

"Listen, you have what you wanted. I suggest you leave now," said Angelo.

"You know what's happening, and you know why those hounds were here. I suggest you keep a closer eye on her," said Azreal with a nod toward me.

"I don't need for you to tell me what my duties are. Now go."

"I'll go, but I won't be far. Keep that in mind, Uriel."

He gave Angelo a smirk, then turned and began walking away. Angelo kept his eyes on him the entire time until he was no longer in view. Then, for the first time since he appeared on the platform, he looked at me.

"Let's get you home," he said.

~~~~

CHAPTER THREE

Within a few minutes, we arrived back at the apartment. I walked to the couch and laid down. Angelo went into the kitchen, poured a glass of water and brought it to me.

"Here, drink this," he said.

Chloe trotted to the couch and jumped on my lap as I sat up. I took a sip of water and placed the glass on the coffee table. I stared blankly into space. I was numb, not knowing what to make of all of this. It was like a nightmare I couldn't wake up from. I glanced at the clock. It was 11:30 p.m.

"I don't think I'll be going in to work tomorrow," I said, trying to act unaffected.

Angelo looked at me and chuckled.

"Tomorrow is Saturday," he replied. "You're off."

"Oh. Right."

I patted and stroked Chloe's fur a couple of times, then placed her on the floor. Angelo had walked back into the kitchen and was washing his hands in the sink.

"I guess I should be freaked out about all of this right now, but for some reason, I believe you have some sort of explanation for it all," I said.

I stood and walked to him. Angelo sighed, then turned off the water. He shook the residue from his hands and then dried the remaining water with the dishtowel. He turned to look at me, placing the towel on the counter. With watery eyes, I looked back at him. My emotions were once more getting the better of me. Fear instantly gripped my chest and the lump of emotions in my throat made it hard to breathe. I was shocked and confused. Angelo pulled me close and hugged me tightly.

"Damn it," I said as the tears started to fall.

Angelo hugged me tighter.

"Easy there, Vanifera. Everything is going to be alright," he said stroking my head.

"I'm scared Angelo. What is going on?"

He walked me back to the couch and we sat. He passed me the glass of water and I just held it in my hands. We sat quietly for several minutes. Angelo watched as I slowly regained my composure.

"Are you okay?" he asked

"Yes, I'm fine. I just want to know what's going on," I replied.

"Are you sure you want to know?"

I nodded and sniffed.

"What I'm about to tell you might sound too fantastic to believe. But after what you've seen tonight, I'm sure this will not seem too far-fetched," said Angelo.

"You aren't human, are you?" I asked flatly.

His brow hunched and his body tilted slightly away.

"No, I'm not human, Vanifera, and neither were those creatures you saw on that platform."

"What are you?"

"I am a Seraph, a high-ranking angel."

"An angel?"

"Yes. I was sent here to protect you."

"Protect me? From what?"

"A being too horrible to describe. Those creatures you encountered on that platform were Hell Hounds, lower-level demons." Angelo explained.

"Why were they after me?"

"That I'm not sure yet."

I stared at him with a blank expression. "Angelo, you're not making any sense."

He stood up, walked to the entertainment unit and paused in thought.

"Do you believe in Heaven and Hell?"

I shook my head, trying to think. "Ah, yeah. I guess."

"Do you remember the stories told about the war between Heaven and Hell?"

"You mean the one about Lucifer and his followers being cast out of Heaven? You mean that war?"

"Sort of. Only it wasn't a war, but a cleansing. What if I told you that the beliefs about good and evil are so distortedly wrong that it would boggle your mind?"

"My mind is already boggled. But, I'm listening," I said, wiping the tears from my eyes.

"There was a war, but not with Lucifer or his minions. It was a war with God. A war that shook the very foundation of creation," he explained.

"I'm not sure I follow you."

Angelo began pacing the floor. He stopped, placing his thumb between his lips.

"Long ago, before any recorded period of time, the entity the humans call God was composed of both benevolent and malevolent natures. But the conflicting natures caused our master to be merciful one instant and cruel the next. So, in order to create prosperity and to be a just ruler, our master exorcized the evil essence from his being. This essence was like a symbiote and required a host in order for it to survive. It came across Lucifer and merged with him. The evil tried to take over Heaven, which prompted Lucifer and his follower's to be exiled from Heaven. But Lucifer overcame the evil and he too exorcized the vile spirit. However, the Archangel Michael forbade Lucifer to walk the lands of Heaven, fearing that he may still be contaminated and controlled by the evil. He was quarantined in the bowels of Hell for a thousand years. With Lucifer confined to Hell and the rest of the angels protected by our master's divine hand, the essence of the evil was once again without a host. Unable to find a suitable vessel, it created a new host, one fashioned for its own purposes," Angelo explained.

"So, this evil is a parasite?" I asked.

"You can say that. Having an understanding of medicine, you should be aware of a condition known as mental illness."

"Yeah, I'm aware of the term. I'm starting to think you're quite aware of it also."

"If what you saw could be confined to simple mental illness, then I'm not the only one who is not well," he replied.

"Touché."

"This evil is like a spiritual illness, feeding on the souls of the unsuspecting. It contaminates the spirit and provokes it to perform all sorts of atrocities," Angelo continued.

"Can it be killed?" I asked.

"Well, that's what we're unsure of. Legend speaks of a being who will one day destroy the evil. But, the tale seems more like an urban legend. For eons, my brethren and I have fought to contain the spread of the evil essence. But its influence is far reaching. It's like a puppeteer, using whomever and whatever it can to accomplish its desires. Those creatures that I fought weren't acting on their own ambitions. They were being controlled."

"By this evil spirit?"

"That I don't know yet. The evil essence created a host of beings with the same seed of maliciousness and manipulation," said Angelo.

I sighed deeply and tried to comprehend what he was saying. It wasn't a hard concept to understand, but I wasn't totally convinced that I believed him, despite what I'd seen. There was, however, one question, the main question that needed to be answered.

"This is a very fantastic story and all, but I just want to know one thing; what does all of this have to do with me?" I asked.

Angelo shot me a very solemn look. It was almost as if he were debating whether to answer my question.

"Remember I told you that the evil required a host and that it had created one in order to carry out its purposes?" he asked.

"Yeah."

"You are that host, Vanifera."

My eyes widened and I slumped back on the couch.

"You're joking, right?" I asked.

"I'm sorry, but..."

"No, don't say another word! I don't believe this!" I exclaimed as I sat forward.

"I know this is..."

"No! I refuse to believe this. You're telling me that I'm some creation of an evil spirit? Bullshit!" I exclaimed.

Angelo tried to reach for me, but I hopped up from the couch and backed away from him.

"You stay away from me, Angelo!" I said, backing into the wall.

"Vanifera, you must calm down."

"Calm down? How dare you tell me to calm down! I may not know what the hell is going on, but I know I'm not some reservoir for some evil spirit! You lied to me! Everything has been a lie! I thought you loved me and I thought we had something! Now you tell me you're some angel who was sent here to protect me! I don't believe you! I don't believe any of this!"

"Vanifera! You must listen to me! How do you explain those demons that attacked you? How do you explain Caliestra? This is not a lie and it isn't a joke! You are in serious trouble and I am here to protect you!"

"Yeah, right!"

"Alright. I may have deceived you about who I was, but you must believe that I didn't lie to you about how I feel for you. I've loved you since the first time I saw you. It was hard at first, trying to keep my feelings separate from my duties. But the more I was around you, the harder it became. I needed to stay around you, not just because it was my duty, but because I loved you. You mean everything to me, and I never want you to forget that."

"How can you stand there and say that to me? You lied to me about who you are and then expect me to believe that you love me?"

"But, I do."

A look of frustration bloomed across my face. "I don't know what you angels believe, but down here you don't lie to someone you love, Angelo!"

I couldn't stand to look at him anymore. I was about to walk into my bedroom, when suddenly, I felt a sharp pain in my head. I crumbled to the floor and clutched the sides of my head.

"Vanifera, what's wrong?" asked Angelo, kneeling beside me.

"I just have a sharp pain in my head," I said with a grimace.

Angelo helped me back to the couch and I sat down. I hung my head between my legs and covered my head with my hands. The pain was excruciating and throbbing. Angelo sat next to me, placing his arm around my shoulders. I really didn't want him touching me right then, but I was in so much pain that I could hardly move. For several minutes, the pain was relentless and intense. I grew nauseous and dizzy, and at one point I almost passed out. Then, just as suddenly as it began, the pain stopped. I sat there, dumbfounded by the sudden absence of my migraine from hell. I wasn't ready to move just yet and kept my head lowered for a few minutes more. As I sat there, all sorts of thoughts raced through my mind. I couldn't help wondering how my life became so terribly screwed up in such a short period of time. This morning, I was a woman who had everything. I had a good job, a handsome boyfriend and a very simple and pleasant life. Now, I was in the middle of a war that was far beyond the realm of my comprehension. And to top everything off, I was told that I was the host for some demonic symbiote. Could things get any worse than this? After several minutes, I lifted my head and looked at Angelo.

"How are you feeling?" he asked.

"Confused," I replied.

"That's understandable."

"What am I supposed to be thinking right now?" I asked.

"That you aren't in Kansas anymore?" replied Angelo, trying to be funny.

"I'm serious. You lied to me. How do I know you aren't lying to me now?"

Angelo tucked his head. "After what you saw tonight, lies should be the least of your worries."

"But I am worried about it. If what you say is true, then I need to know that I can trust you. I need to know that I can believe in you and the things you say to me."

Angelo looked into my eyes. His expression seemed to indicate that he understood my question. "You're right," he said nodding.

"I mean it, Angelo. No more lies."

"No more lies. I was wrong for deceiving you and I promise it will never happen again."

I stared at him, unsure whether to believe him. But the look in his eyes seemed so sincere, and if there was ever a time I needed to believe in something or someone, it was now.

"I hope you're telling me the truth. I need to know that something about my life isn't a lie," I said.

"You have my word."

I rubbed my eyes and released a huge yawn. I was tired, both physically and mentally. I couldn't think anymore and all I wanted to do was sleep. I actually hoped that I would go to sleep and wake up to the knowledge that this was all a dream. For now, I just needed to have Angelo hold me and let me know that everything was going to be okay. Without me asking, he did just that.

"Let's get you to bed. You had one hell of a day today," he said.

I nodded. We both stood and walked to the bedroom. As I flopped on the edge of the bed, I began growing anxious. Despite his attempt at reassurance, I was worried and scared. Although his comment was very arrogant, he did have a point in saying that lies were the least of my worries. If everything he said was true, from this moment forward there was sure to be much pain and suffering in my life.

~~~

As Angelo walked Vanifera to the bedroom, a short man stood outside, braced against a long black limousine and staring at their

39

apartment window. His name was Moa Ding Huang. His hands were in his pockets and he tapped his foot with impatience. As the lights went off in the apartment, he pulled his right hand out and grabbed the cell phone from his inside coat pocket. He flipped it open and pressed a few numbers. Then, he lifted it to his ear.

"Yeah, its me. Seems as though our dearly beloved Caliestra has failed her mission as well as those three demons. The Seraph is still alive and the Gaian is with him. Yes, I know what that means. I don't know what happened, but I will get to the bottom of this. Its probably not safe to be here, but I'll keep you posted," he said.

He removed the phone from his ear and closed it. Then he stared at the darkened bedroom window.

"I don't know how you managed to escape Caliestra, Archangel, but I can assure you that you are going to regret the fact that you didn't die this night," he said with a menacing growl.

Huang nodded to the chauffer, who quickly opened the door. He entered the car and the door was secured behind him. The chauffer scurried around to the driver's side and got in. Within moments, the black limo pulled out from the parking space and disappeared into the steam exiting through the manhole covers.

~~~

When I awoke, the sun was bright and glorious. It was already well into the late stages of morning. Another day had begun, but to me this morning had a different air than yesterday. It marked the beginning of a new life, a new and uncertain life. I still had a hard time believing that the events that took place yesterday really happened. The disappointment of last night not being a dream caused a rush of anxiety in my chest. I sat up and looked around the room. The splintered bookshelf where Candy met her end instantly brought back images of the battle. It also reminded me of the run in I had with the demons at the BART station. It still seemed too fantastic to believe.

I slid to the edge of the bed and put my robe on. I felt sore and my muscles were tight. I looked to the side of the bed were Angelo normally slept, but he wasn't there. I looked around the room, then called to him.

"Angelo?"

There was no response. I stood, walked to the door and opened it. I entered the living room and continued looking around for him. The curtains in the kitchen were drawn apart allowing the sun's radiance to pour into the apartment. Yet, in spite of all the light, the living room as well as the rest of the apartment had a different feel this morning. It seemed cold and confining. Perhaps it was my imagination playing with my fears, but it just had a presence that was less like my home and more like a prison. I tried calling to Angelo one more time, hoping that I was just overlooking where he was. Once again, I was met with silence.

Just then, Chloe trotted to me, wagging her tail as she approached. I knelt and curled my fingers beneath her chin. Her tail wagged even more wildly with excitement.

"Hello there, girl!" I said with my childlike voice.

I stood and walked into the kitchen. I opened the refrigerator and pulled out the juice. I took a couple of sips straight out of the carton, which was very uncharacteristic of me. I placed the juice on the counter and walked back to the bedroom. I stood inside the doorway for a moment, thinking. I decided that I needed to get out of this apartment for a bit. Besides, Chloe needed to be walked. I went into the bathroom and turned on the shower. As the water began heating, I pondered Angelo's absence. Flashbacks of his rendezvous with Candy came to mind. I was still disappointed with him about lying to me and now my insecurities were filling my head with other reasons to be angry with him. Suddenly, I heard a voice behind me.

"You look rested."

I turned around, thinking it was Angelo. Instead, I stared into the face of the Barhim Hajj.

"Where did you come from and what are you doing here?" I asked, pulling my robe tighter around me.

"From a land far, far away," he said with a slight snicker.

"Cute, now get out!"

"Relax. I'm not here to cause trouble. I'm merely here to make sure you are okay," he said as he turned and walked away with his hands clasped behind his back.

"I'm fine," I said with a sigh.

Chloe was sitting by the bed, watching him. She wasn't a friendly dog when it came to strangers and her blasé attitude toward him struck me as odd. He knelt and petted her on the head. She never barked once. In my mind, if Chloe didn't view him as a threat, perhaps I shouldn't either. I turned off the water in the shower and walked into the living room. Hajj stood and followed.

"I understand you had a run in last night with some very nasty demons," he said.

"Yes, I did. Did you have anything to do with that?" I asked.

He turned and shot me a glance.

"No. I had nothing to do with that. Suffice it to say though, you probably have a ton of questions right now."

"I might. I don't know what your purpose is in all of this, but I'm sure it isn't good."

"And why would you say that?" he asked, scrunching his brow.

"Let's just say that was the impression I got when I spoke to Angelo."

Barhim Hajj bobbed his head.

"I would expect that from him. However, I can assure you, my actions are nothing less than honorable. I only want to make sure that you are okay."

"Why? Why are you so interested in my welfare, Barhim Hajj?"

"Ah, I see he has told you my name. No doubt he has also told you of your identity, yes?"

I tucked my head and didn't answer. Barhim Hajj turned and paced the floor a couple of times. Then, he stopped and looked at me.

"Maybe you can answer another question for me. Why are they coming after me now?" I asked.

"Think back, Vanifera. Do you remember a pyramid?"

I paused for a moment.

"Barely. I think I remember seeing one shortly after you appeared last night."

"That little treasure is one of the items they are after. It is an artifact called the Gate of Osiris. You are its guardian," said Hajj.

"The Gate of Osiris?"

"Yes. It allows free passage between the seven realms of the universe. Whoever finds that gateway will be able to pass from this dimension into the various other dimensions of creation."

"But I don't know anything about this gate."

Barhim Hajj walked to me and lifted his hand toward my forehead. I quickly pulled back from him.

"Don't worry, I'm not going to bite you," he said.

He placed his hand on my forehead, closed his eyes and tucked his head.

"Your memories are still intact. The Hierarchy will be pleased to know this," he said.

"The Hierarchy? What's that?"

"It's the council of angels. Your beloved Angelo is one of its chief members. They will be happy to know that you haven't regained your memories," said Hajj.

"My memories? What are you talking about?"

"Your past memories have been blocked."

"Blocked? Why would my past be blocked?"

"Why else would your past be blocked? There's something you aren't supposed to remember."

I began chuckling from confusion and disbelief.

"What's so funny?" asked Hajj.

"You and all of this. You come out of nowhere and start telling me that I'm some guardian of a gate. Angelo is telling me that I'm some vessel of an evil spirit. Next, you'll be telling me that the tooth fairy is real," I replied.

"Vanifera, this isn't a joke, and I wish I could make this a little easier for you to understand."

"Well, I don't understand and I don't believe you or Angelo! All of this is some twisted lie that I can't explain yet! I don't believe there is a gate! I'm not some guardian, and I'm not a vessel for an evil spirit! Now get the hell out of here before I call the police!" I exclaimed.

"Then what do you believe? Do you believe your eyes and ears? Do you believe what you saw last night was real? Turn on the television, Vanifera, and see what the news reports are saying about last night at the boarding station. Think back and search your feelings. You know that what I'm saying is true," Hajj replied.

"No, I will not give in to that! I don't care what you say! I will not believe it! Now get out!"

"Vanifera."

"GET OUT!"

In a flash, Barhim Hajj had disappeared. I was so irate that I hadn't noticed he'd left until a few seconds later. I was trembling with anger and began grabbing the pillows off the couch and throwing them across the room. I pounded on the cushions and knocked over some of the items on the étagère. I couldn't take this anymore. I wasn't what Angelo and Barhim Hajj said I was, and I was tired of this game they were playing with my head. I sat on the floor and pounded it with my hands until they were sore. Then, I slumped and began crying. My tears flowed like a river, and the anguish I felt was more than I could bear. After a few moments of crying, I felt a hand touch my shoulder. It was Angelo. He sat on the floor next to me as I continued to whimper.

"I don't want this. I never asked for all of this. It's too much. It's just too frickin' much," I said with clenched teeth.

"Yeah, I know," Angelo replied somberly.

I turned and looked at him with a tear-drenched face.

"Is everything about my life a lie?" I asked.

"No, not everything. My feelings for you are very real and true. I've loved you from the moment I first laid eyes on you. There is nothing that I wouldn't do for you," said Angelo.

"Then give me my life back! You're supposedly an angel. Isn't there something you can do about this? Can't you stop this?" I asked.

"If I could, Vanifera, I would have already done it. Unfortunately, there's nothing I can do."

"So, that's it, huh? I have to suffer because God was too much of a coward to deal with his own pain, is that it?"

"I don't have any answers. All I can say is that I will be here with you and help you through all of this," Angelo replied as he tried to put his arm around me.

"That's not good enough," I said pulling away from him.

"Vanifera."

"No, damn him and damn you! All of you!" I said as I stood up and walked away.

I went into the bedroom and locked the door. I walked to the bed, continuing to cry as I flopped across it. Even though I'd just awakened, I was exhausted.

"No, I'm not a monster. I just can't be," I said sobbing.

Suddenly, I had the feeling I wasn't alone. I looked up and saw someone sitting on the edge of the bed. It wasn't Angelo or Barhim Hajj, but the image of a woman. Seeing her startled me and I sat up quickly, pushing myself away from her. Her hands were clasped in her lap, and she looked at me with eyes filled with compassion.

"Who are you?" I asked.

"You must not be afraid, Vanifera. This task is one that only you can carry out," she said.

I still couldn't believe what I was seeing. Was she a ghost or another demon who'd come to torture me?

"Who...the hell...*are* you?" I repeated.

"Don't you recognize me?" she asked.

"No."

"I'm the woman you killed. I'm Caliestra."

"No, it can't be you. You're dead," I said in disbelief.

"Yes, I am. However, I was granted this opportunity to speak to you. You must accept who and what you are. The time grows short and many are depending on you," she said.

"Depending on me to do what, save them?"

"Yes."

I laughed sarcastically.

"Listen, I was told that I was some sort of monster. Now you're here telling me I'm some sort of savior. Which one am I?"

"You are both. Just like a coin has two sides, so do you. I was cursed to walk this earth as a succubae. I performed some of the vilest acts known to man, all for the cruel master I served. Last night, you freed me from my enslavement, and for that I am truly grateful."

"But I didn't ask for this. I don't want to be some vessel of evil."

"And I didn't choose my fate either. Some paths are chosen for us, and even though we may not wish to journey down the path, it doesn't lessen our responsibility to travel them. You have been chosen for a very important task, and just like so many other obstacles you've overcome in your life, you will overcome this one."

"But this is so big. It's too much for me."

"You have all the help you need. All you need to do is simply ask," she said motioning toward the bedroom door. She was referring to Angelo, who was on the other side.

I sighed and shook my head.

"I can't promise anything," I said.

"Then don't," she replied.

With that said, the image of Caliestra slowly faded away and once more, I was alone. I took a deep breath and wiped the tears from my eyes. Although I didn't want to believe that all of the things I'd witnessed and heard were true, there was no way I could justify what I'd just seen. The image of Caliestra was the clincher, and I had to finally admit that this was not a joke or some figment of my imagination. I slid to the edge of the bed and dangled my feet over the side. I took another deep breath and stared at the floor. My mind still didn't want to accept my fate, but it appeared that I had no choice. I stood, walked to the door and opened it.

Angelo was sitting on the couch watching television as I

peeked through the cracked opening I'd made in the door. I finished opening it all the way and stood in the entrance. He turned and looked at me. A depressing expression of acceptance covered my face.

"I don't want to cry anymore," I said.

Angelo didn't say a word. He stood, walked to me and hugged me. I did likewise, clutching him tighter than ever.

"You *will* be there with me through all of this, right?" I asked.

"Every step of the way," he replied.

I pulled back from him and looked into his eyes.

"I mean it, Angelo. Don't leave me hanging with this," I said.

"I won't, I promise," he said with a little more assurance.

I paused for a moment of thought. If I were going to deal with this, I needed some questions answered. The first one was about my past. I had to know what started all of this.

"Barhim Hajj said my memories were blocked. He said that you were a part of some organization and that you'd be happy to hear they were still blocked," I probed.

"This is true," said Angelo reluctantly.

"Why?"

"Because it spares you from remembering the horrors of the past and the atrocities you'd committed."

"My atrocities? What did I do that required the stripping of my memories?"

"You are the vessel of the anti-God, the most unholy entity ever known, and your actions were just as unholy. You committed vile acts of destruction, killing entire civilizations with the whisk of your hand. But it was your ultimate act of evil that was the most disturbing."

"And just what was this vile act?" I asked.

Angelo appeared reluctant to say.

"Tell me, Angelo! What did I do?"

"You tried to kill our master, the almighty God."

~~~

CHAPTER FOUR

I did what?" I asked.

"It's true. I was there," said Angelo.

"I tried to kill God? Are you serious?"

Angelo turned and took a few steps.

"I remember it like it was yesterday. The Great Battle is what it was called. The forces of Jehovah battled the forces of the Vul Paux," he said.

"The Vul Paux?" I asked.

"That was the name of the evil essence that possessed you. The war lasted many eons with neither side able to gain a true advantage. But the casualties were starting to mount and the war took its toll on both camps. Then, the crucial moment of battle came. The Vul Paux and Jehovah decided to meet on the battlefield to settle the war. It was an even battle with neither entity able to gain an advantage. Then, fate tipped the scales in our favor when the Messiah was crucified. When that happened, he absorbed the sins of not only this world, but that of all creatures in the universe. Sin was what the Vul Paux fed off of. It gave him strength and power to match that of our master. When it was absorbed by the Messiah, he soon grew hungry and weak. With his power diminished by the reduction of sin, the Vul Paux was quickly defeated and imprisoned in a place called the Omega Realm. Some of its minions were placed in the Shadow Realm, a barren parallel realm to this one. Others escaped and hid. One of the Hierarchy's jobs is to track them down and incarcerate them with their brethren."

"The Hierarchy. Hajj told me that you belonged to that organization."

"He talks too much. In any event, we'd heard through various sources that the gods, as they like to be called, have been planning a second war. It looks like that rumor was true."

"The gods? As in the Egyptian and Greek gods?"

"Afraid so."

"Amazing. So, tell me this. If the Vul Paux was defeated and imprisoned in this Omega Realm, why am I here? I mean, aren't I the vessel?"

"Yes, you are. Just before it was imprisoned, the Vul Paux teleported you through a gateway it created called the Gate of Osiris."

"The pyramid, right?"

"How did you..."

"Hajj."

"Idiot. Anyway, you landed here on Earth where you hid the gate and went into a hibernating sleep. You were supposed to be picked up and guarded by the Vul Paux's second in command, a being called the Contravexus. Within your memories are the secrets to the gates activation, as well as its location. The plan was to activate the gate and free the Paux. However, we got to you first. We tried to discover the location of the gate by probing your mind, but we were unsuccessful. During the probing process, we miscalculated and triggered something that caused you to awaken. You resumed your destructive ways, causing massive chaos and destruction. Eventually, you were stopped and your memories were sealed."

"So, all of this was done so that none of the Paux's minions would release him?"

"Right."

"And that's why these beasts and demons are after me?"

"Basically. I suspect the Contravexus is behind this. He might be trying to get you back and unlock your memories in order to release his master. That is something we can't allow."

"So, this is all a game. Whoever gets the info first, wins, is that it?"

"No, this is not a game. I have seen the evil that the Vul Paux is capable of, and I do not want it to ever be released. That's why

I chose this assignment. But I never expected to fall in love with you."

"Do you really love me or is this a part of your mission? Can a creature like me even be loved?" I asked.

"I've known the love of my master, and now, I know a new kind of love, one that rests comfortably in my heart. It is difficult to understand how something that housed such an evil spirit could bring such delight to my soul. I watched you for centuries and made sure that nothing happened to you. You were oblivious to all that had happened. Without the memories of your past, I believed that you should be allowed to pursue a new life, one that would bring you happiness. I chose to watch over you because I wanted to ensure that happiness. The more I was around you, the more I saw you blossom into something more beautiful than anything I'd ever imagined, not just in body, but in spirit as well. I do love you, Vanifera. You must always remember that," said Angelo.

I was quiet for a little while, not sure how to respond to his comments. I was skeptical of his feelings for me, but what I did know was that I loved him more than I could ever describe and I prayed that he was just as honest about his feelings.

"How do I know you're the good guys? I mean, after all, I used to work for the other side," I probed.

"As long as we are together, I will let nothing happen to you. That alone should tell you my allegiance," Angelo replied.

We sat quietly for a moment.

"Tell me about Barhim Hajj."

"What's to tell? At the conclusion of the war, some of the Vul Paux's minions sought mercy from our master. He pardoned them and allowed them to perform certain tasks for the Hierarchy. Barhim Hajj is a watcher. He reports events to the Hierarchy and records the information. You could call him an administrative assistant to the angels," said Angelo.

"You don't trust him do you?" I asked.

"Not particularly. Although, much to his credit, he's never betrayed the Hierarchy."

"Then don't you think you should give him the benefit of the doubt? After all, it was he that told me how to save you when that woman almost sucked out your soul."

"Perhaps."

Another long moment of silence fell in the room. My attempt to change the subject didn't make me feel any better. My eyes squinted as I tried to fight the tears.

"How am I supposed to handle this?" I asked.

Angelo flashed an uncomfortable glance.

"I'm not sure. I've asked myself how I would handle such information if I were in your shoes. But for the life of me I cannot imagine that heavy a burden," he replied.

"I want to die. I just want someone to kill me and get it over with," I said.

"Please, don't say such things. I know this is hard, but I will be here with you, just like I always have. I will not forsake you, Vanifera," Angelo emotionally replied.

"I just don't know if I can do this, Angelo. I don't think I can handle this."

"You can, and you will. We will," he said placing his hand on mine.

I looked at our hands, his atop of mine. I turned my palm over and entwined my fingers between his. I wanted to cry, but at the same time, I was tired of crying. I wanted to be strong, and I felt that with Angelo with me, I could.

"I know I've asked you this before, but you promise you won't leave me?" I asked as I looked into his eyes.

"You have my word," he replied.

We hugged each other for a long time. I felt safe in his arms, and I never wanted him to let me go. Then, Angelo sighed and pulled away from me. A very frustrated look was on his face.

"What's wrong?" I asked.

"I'm just wondering if anything I told you or any of these events brought back your old memories?" he asked.

"Not really," I said with a sigh. "Before I attacked that woman,

I remember seeing the gate, pyramid, whatever it is, but I have no idea where it is or how to operate it."

"You saw the gate?"

"Yes. It was as if I was having a vision. It rotated right in front of me. I tried to touch it, but then it vanished."

"Then what happened?"

"I was back in the apartment. Shortly after that, I fought that woman. However, I must say that after I had that vision, if that's what you want to call it, I felt stronger. It was like I'd gotten a boost of energy or strength."

Angelo looked disturbed.

"Is that a bad thing?" I asked.

"Not necessarily. But it is something we need to keep an eye on. Let me know if you have any more of these visions," he said.

"Okay."

I searched my thoughts, trying to see if there was anything else I needed to tell him. Then a question came to my mind.

"Why haven't you guys killed the Contravexus? I mean this whole thing could have been eliminated had you just killed him."

"The Contravexus cannot be killed by any of our master's creations. Only the Vul Paux and the Gaian can kill him. Besides, killing him would not eliminate the problem. Another would simply take his place," Angelo replied.

"You mean, I'm the only one that can kill him?"

"Correct. You or the Paux."

"Interesting. One thing puzzles me though. Why hasn't anyone tried to kill me?"

"You are in the same category as the Contravexus. Only the Vul Paux has the power and ability to do that."

"So, I'm sort of the first in his chain of command."

"In a matter of speaking."

Angelo's eyes indicated that he saw the frustration building in me and that all of this information was starting to overload my circuits, so to speak. He quickly jumped to another subject.

"So, which name do you prefer, Angelo Ramone or that other name?" he asked.

I scratched my head. "What was that other name?"

"Uriel."

"Uriel. Oh yeah, that man on the platform called you Uriel."

"Yes, he did," Angelo replied.

"I don't know. Whichever one you feel most comfortable with is alright with me."

"Then Angelo it is," he said.

Just then, I overheard the news report on the television about a presumed explosion at the BART station located near our apartment. I looked at the television and saw the camera shots from the scene. The gaping holes in the frame of the train brought back the fear I felt last night. The report stated that a few people got hurt, but it was nothing serious. I felt relieved to hear that bit of information. Angelo looked at me with a very serious expression.

"We have to stay sharp, Vanifera. The Contravexus and its minions may try again. With our location compromised, we're going to have to move," he said.

"Move? Move where?" I asked.

"Seattle. The Hierarchy sent the order this morning. That's where I was earlier. They gave us twenty-four hours to leave San Francisco."

"But what about my job, my friends?"

"The life you once knew is passed. We cannot stay here. We must leave, and you must promise me that you will never come back here, do you understand?" asked Angelo.

"But..."

"Do you understand?"

"Yes, I do," I replied somberly.

"Good. Now please, get dressed. We need to leave as soon as possible."

I stood and walked toward the bathroom. As I got to the doorway, I paused and turned to look back at Angelo.

"Can I, at least, say goodbye?" I asked.

Angelo looked at me. He saw the pain on my face brought on by the decision I was forced to make.

"Sure," he said.

I quickly raced to the phone and called the hospital. I left a voicemail for my boss, informing her of my resignation. I also spoke to some of the other staff members. All of them seemed upset because of my decision to leave and each of them wished me luck. I then called Denise. That was probably the one call that hurt me more than anything. We'd been friends for two years, and we considered each other best friends. Now, the true pain of what I was about to do kicked in. She was in tears and begged me not to leave. But I had no choice and told her that I would keep in touch. As I hung up the phone after saying goodbye, the tears had formed a stream down my face. Angelo walked to me and placed his arm around me.

"It's for the best," he said.

"Then why does it hurt so much?" I asked.

"I promise, some day you'll see her again."

I nodded.

"By the way...thanks for all your help," I said.

"Don't mention it," he replied.

I pulled a tissue from the dispenser on the nightstand and wiped my eyes. I tried to accept what I was doing and convince myself that it was for the best. But even as I pondered, the situation was still too fantastic to readily believe. I was being asked to abandon my life and blindly follow someone who was supposed to be an angel. Despite what I'd seen and heard, it was still too surreal. Each passing moment brought a greater struggle to following through with this decision. I stood and made my way to the bathroom mirror. I stared at my reflection, shaking my head in disbelief.

"Good lord, Vanifera, what have you gotten yourself into?" I asked.

I took a deep breath and began collecting myself. I stared at my reflection and was instantly appalled. My hair was mangled and matted. My lips were dry and my eyes were puffy. My mascara left dark tracks on my cheeks. I looked terrible and I felt just the same. However, I had to do something to make myself look more presentable. Perhaps that would make me feel a little better.

I turned on the faucet, scooping a handful of water and splashing it across my face. After doing that a couple of times, I grabbed a towel and dried the residue. I looked into the mirror once more. My eyes and lips looked a little more refreshed. The mascara tracks were gone, and I did feel better.

I began looking around for my comb or a brush so I could do my hair. I looked inside the shower and saw them both lying on the ledge. I picked up the brush and began detangling my matted locks. Soon, my hair lay midway down my back, shiny and jet-black in color. I quickly braided a long ponytail that rested on my shoulder. I glanced into the mirror once more and smiled, trying to force myself to be positive. I brushed my teeth and then hopped into the shower. After a quick rinse, I stepped out and wrapped a towel around me. I walked to the dresser and found a T-shirt I liked, some socks and some underwear. I pulled them out and quickly put them on. I then trotted to the closet and pulled out some faded blue jeans and a pair of my hiking boots. I put them on, then walked back into the bathroom. I started applying my lipstick and my eyeliner. As I did, I could feel myself getting anxious. I wanted to get out of here as quickly as possible. I'd said my goodbyes and there was nothing keeping me here. Despite my attempts to disconnect myself from my home and the life I'd made in San Francisco, I still found it extremely painful to leave this life behind. I paused for a moment and tucked my head. A huge sigh flowed from my lips. It felt as if it came from the depths of my soul. Just then, Chloe trotted in from wherever she'd been hiding and jumped up on the counter.

"Hey you!" I said.

She shook her head and then sat on her hind legs. Angelo's muffled voice resounded from the kitchen.

"You want something before we leave?" he asked.

"Could you fix me a bagel and a cup of coffee?" I yelled back.

"No problem," he replied with a slight chuckle.

I finished putting on my makeup and then clicked my tongue for Chloe to follow. We walked into the kitchen where Angelo was finishing up with my food. He seemed to be in good spirits; in fact, the best that I'd seen him in a while. He looked at me and smirked.

"You look great," he said.

"Thank you," I replied with a smirk of my own.

Suddenly, I heard a crash of thunder outside. We both jumped, then turned and looked out the window. While Angelo and I were getting ready, it had started raining. But it wasn't just raining, it was a full-fledged thunderstorm. We shot each other a befuddled glance.

"Thunder? In San Francisco?" I queried.

"Yes, that is strange," Angelo replied.

It was really pouring and I knew that it was unwise to leave right now. Something unnatural was causing this storm and it wasn't hard to figure out who was behind it. Less than an hour ago it was sunny. Now, the wind-driven rain pounded against the window, which gave me an idea. I would use the storm as an excuse to delay our departure a little while. I needed that time to allow my change of life to settle in. Besides, it would also give Angelo and I one last opportunity to spend an intimate moment together before we left our home for good.

We both ate our breakfast, then began packing. An hour later, we placed our bags by the door. The rain had stopped and Angelo called for a cab. I was a little disappointed it had stopped raining so soon, but I decided to make the most of the moment. As he hung up, I walked to him and wrapped my arms around his neck. He did the same around my waist.

"I have an idea," I said. "Why don't we use this time to enjoy our home one last time?"

I pulled him close and began kissing him passionately. The more we kissed, the more my body desired him with an urge that was hard to control. It was like stealing a moment of passion. As far as I knew, this would probably be the last time I would ever have a moment like this. All that was certain was right now. Angelo was here with me, and it felt comfortable and right. I felt excited by the spontaneity of the moment. A warm sensation raced through me. Angelo's hands gently caressed the sides of my body. His touch was as light as a feather and as gentle as a whisper. It sent a chill racing down my spine and through the rest of my body. I wrapped my arms under his and gripped his upper back. My stomach tightened with nervousness, and I shivered as I kissed him. I was thrilled and scared at the same time. Despite the countless moments I spent with him in the past, I was feeling something I'd never experienced before. I felt as if this was the first time I'd ever made love and I didn't want this moment to end. It felt magical and I wanted to stay there, holding him in my arms forever. It was as if we were the only two people in the world and that time itself had stopped.

We began making love on the couch. His hands seemed to massage my soul as he gently caressed my body. His lips were soft, kissing every part of my anatomy. The sweat on our bodies glistened in the dimly lit room. Our passion was intense as we rhythmically grinded against one another. He felt so good that I moaned in total ecstasy. I gripped his back and pulled him closer to me, feeling his warm body pressing against mine. Each stroke drew us closer and closer to ecstasy. Our hearts pounded as we pushed faster and harder against each other. I felt a tingling sensation all the way to my toes. Then, our bodies tensed. I couldn't move as I wrapped my arms around his neck and held him while I reached my climax. I panted and cooed uncontrollably. He grunted and buried his face into my shoulder. Our bodies shuddered. It felt like a release of all my tensions in one mighty rush. My nails were embedded into his back and his hands tightly gripped my hips. Moments passed and our bodies relaxed. My breathing returned to normal and the tingling sensation subsided.

As we lay on the couch enjoying the afterglow, my mind drifted, reliving the passionate interlude we'd just experienced. My body still tingled as I caressed Angelo's sweat-drenched frame. The experience left me feeling tired, but totally satisfied. The love

I possessed for him burned deeper than ever within my soul. It was the kind of love that completed the entire picture of my life. We laid there as the rain started to pour again. Just then, we heard the honk of the cab's horn outside. We both looked at each other and chuckled.

"We'll leave in the morning," he finally said.

"Sounds good to me," I replied breathlessly.

~~~

The next morning, it was sunny again. I sat up and looked around, a little disappointed by the rain's absence. Angelo was still sleeping. I looked at him and shook my head, wondering whether he was crazy for staying and helping me with all of this. I laid back down and began stroking the side of his face. He then placed his arm around me. His eyes fluttered open, and he quickly squinted.

"Good morning, sleepy head," I said softly.

"Good morning," he replied groggily.

"Sleep well?" I asked.

"I should be asking you that question," he said rubbing his eyes.

"As well as can be expected."

Angelo released a huge yawn.

"I love you," he said.

"I know. Either that or you are the craziest person I'd ever met, staying with me through all of this," I replied.

He smirked.

"So, you ready to get up?" he asked.

"Yeah, I guess," I replied.

A few minutes of lounging passed. Then, we got up, washed and put our clothes back on. Angelo called once more for a cab, and within ten minutes, it was there. We grabbed our things and Angelo opened the front door.

"Babe, cab's here," he said.

"I'm coming," I answered, walking out of the bedroom.

I stopped in the middle of the living room and took a moment to look one last time at the place I'd called home. I could never come back here again, and I wanted to look around and say my farewells. Tears welled and I found it so difficult to say goodbye. Angelo walked to me and grabbed my hand.

"Don't worry, sweetie. We'll make another home," he said.

I nodded and wiped the tears from my eyes. I wasn't sure whether I was crying because of the life I was leaving behind or the uncertain life that lay ahead. I took a deep breath and walked to the door. Chloe darted ahead of me. Angelo exited last. He closed the door behind him and we made our way downstairs.

The driver quickly packed our things in the trunk and got in the cab. I paused and looked up at the living room window of the apartment. This was my home and leaving it was just as hard as saying goodbye to Denise. I loved this place and cherished the memories those windows and walls held for me. However, I knew that I could never again gaze at the city through that window as I'd done so many times before. With one last deep sigh, I got in the cab and we drove away.

As we rode down the street, I noticed that we were headed toward the airport. I dried my eyes, then turned to look at Angelo with a questioning glance.

"Where are we going?" I asked.

"Oh, someplace special. You're really going to love it," he said.

His response bothered me.

"Listen, I've had enough surprises for one day or for one lifetime, for that matter. So, could you please tell me?" I insisted.

"Gosh, you sure know how to take the fun out of surprises, don't you?" he replied.

I shot him a very dirty look.

"Very well. But before I do, I have something I want to ask you," he said.

"What?"

"Close your eyes first."

I was starting to get a little perturbed and did not want to play this game. I looked at him sneeringly. He, on the other hand, continued to smile at me. But after a few moments and some prodding from him, I went along with his request just to see what he was doing. I closed my eyes and sat slightly slouched.

"Okay, you can open them now," he said a few seconds later.

As I opened my eyes, I saw something I never expected to see. Angelo's hand was extended slightly with his palm opened. In his palm was an opened ring box with an engagement ring inside.

I looked back at Angelo, who now had a huge grin on his face. He sat there staring, almost as if he were waiting for my response. I could see the nervousness in his expression as he tried to read my reaction.

My heart was flooded with so much shocked joy that tears welled without me even knowing they were there. I lifted my hands to cover my gaped mouth and looked back at the ring. It was the most beautiful thing I had ever seen.

"Oh...my..."

"Vanifera, will you marry me?" he asked.

I sat there trying to compose myself. I looked at him as streams of tears rolled down my cheeks.

"I don't know what to say. I-I really don't know what to say," I babbled.

"She doesn't know what to say," said the cab driver sarcastically.

Angelo chuckled. I looked at him disbelievingly.

"After everything you've told me about my past and with the uncertainty of my future, are you sure this is what you want?" I asked.

"With all my soul."

In that moment, my heart exploded with happiness. I wrapped my arms around his neck and hugged him tighter than ever. I kissed his cheeks, lips and his entire face.

"Yes. I will marry you, Angelo!" I exclaimed.

The airport was about a thirty-minute drive away, but we seemed to arrive there in a matter of moments. The cab driver unpacked our bags and Angelo paid him.

"Congratulations you two," he said.

"Thank you," I replied proudly.

We quickly checked our bags, made our way through the terminal and onto the plane. The entire time I kept looking at my ring, and every time I did, I kissed Angelo. Two hours later, we were landing in Las Vegas. We caught a cab and headed to the strip. I thought we were going to the hotel room. However, Angelo had other plans.

"Take us to the Grove," he said.

"The Grove? What's that?" I asked.

"Well, I did ask you to marry me. Why wait?" he replied.

"You mean we're going to get married today, right now?" I asked.

"Why not? Unless you don't want…"

"No, no, no! I do!"

"So, to the Grove then?" asked the cab driver.

"Absolutely!" I replied.

Three hours later, in a gazebo overlooking a beautifully clear pond, Angelo and I exchanged our vows and were pronounced husband and wife. After the ceremony, we shared our reception with some of the other couples that were also married there that day. Later, we took a limousine ride around Las Vegas. We then had a nice dinner at the Kit Kat Club where the incomparable Prince James was playing. After a few hours of celebrating, we retired to our room where we spent the next several hours in bed. By the time I got up, morning was on the verge of breaking. I wrapped my white robe around me and poured myself another glass of champagne. I took a few sips and walked to the balcony to think about a few things. The citrine rays of the morning sun were starting to peak from behind the eastern mountain range.

"God," I said with a sigh. "Please don't let this end. I've never been happier in my life. I have a wonderful husband and I'm in Las Vegas for our honeymoon. I wish this could last forever."

As I took another sip of champagne, I tried to soak up as much of the sights, smells and sounds of Vegas as I could. There was nothing that could compare to the joy and contentment I felt standing on that balcony. However, I couldn't help but be amazed at how my life had changed. Just two days ago, I was being chased by demons. Now, I was standing on a balcony in Las Vegas as Mrs. Vanifera Ramone. In the span of twenty four hours, my life had gone from bad to perfect. But even though this was my honeymoon night, I still had problems adjusting to all the changes.

The orange hue of the morning Vegas sky was growing brighter. The city was abuzz, filled with all sorts of things to do. The neon lights shined beautifully against the desert backdrop and people crowded the streets below. Yet, beyond the beauty and splendor of Vegas lied an uncertain future for me, a future that posed potential horrors and eventual heartache. It started to make me wonder whether I'd made the right decision in marrying Angelo. If I were all of these things that I'd been told, then my future held a great deal of pain, pain that I didn't want imparted upon Angelo.

Just as that thought entered my head, I felt a strange sensation coming over me. The feeling frightened me so much that I dropped my glass of champagne on the balcony floor. The air suddenly felt ten degrees colder. A gust of wind whipped the hem of the robe as I pulled it tighter around me. It was as if something or someone was on that balcony with me. I looked around to see if anyone was there. I saw no one, but I could still feel a presence there with me. I'd never felt this sensation before, but somehow I knew just what caused it. It was the Contravexus.

"Hello," said a voice in the wind.

"What do you want?" I asked.

"Don't play games. You know why I am here. You must come to me. You alone possess the knowledge to release our master from his imprisonment. You must give it to me," said the voice.

I began feeling frantic. I tried to back into the room, but I was too terrified to move. I folded my arms across my chest as the wind grew even colder.

"Why are you doing this? I don't know where the gate is!" I exclaimed.

"You try my patience, Gaian, by denying any knowledge of that which you guard! Beware, my tolerance with you grows thin!" said the voice.

Suddenly, I was lifted off the balcony and into the air. It was as if someone had picked me up and was dangling me over the side of the balcony. I looked down at the ground, which was twelve stories below, and began crying.

"Please, don't do this! I don't know where this gate is! I swear, I'm telling you the truth! I just want you to leave me alone!" I begged.

Suddenly, Angelo appeared on the patio, wrapping his robe around him. He jumped into the air and snatched me back onto the balcony. He hugged me in his arms and looked out into the air.

"You better get the hell out of here, right now!" he said.

I could feel the anger building inside the Contravexus. He resented Angelo's interference.

"I'm not done with you yet, Gaian, nor you, Seraph," he said.

Then, the chill was gone, and the presence of the Contravexus was gone as well. I was shaken by the experience and trembled in Angelo's arms. I sat on the balcony floor and continued crying. This had been the first time I'd ever been in the presence of this most feared being and I felt the power he possessed. There was great darkness in his spirit. It overwhelmed me so much that I was frantic with fright. I quickly tried to wipe the tears from my eyes. Angelo hugged me tightly and rocked back and forth.

"Shh, he's gone now. You're safe," he said stroking my head.

Although I could no longer sense the Contravexus, his words echoed in my head, haunting me like a phantom song. I could feel his hands wrapped around my neck as he dangled me over the edge of the balcony. It was clear that the wheels of destruction were beginning to turn, and this encounter made me wonder whether anyone could stop the awesome force that had visited me. I felt powerless and scared, like a small child cowering before its imaginary monster. I felt no emotion in him, no sense of honor or ethics. His power seemed endless and dark. I knew there was no way

I could defend myself against him and if I was the only one who could kill him, we were in serious trouble. Bitter days were ahead, and if this incident was any indication of what was to come, there would be great suffering before this ordeal was over.

"He's here, Angelo; he's in Las Vegas," I said.

"Indeed, and I'm going to find him," he replied.

"No! Please don't leave me, please," I begged.

Angelo almost seemed reluctant to comply. But then, he nodded.

"I won't leave you," he said.

We both sat motionless and silent on the balcony for a few moments.

"I felt him inside of my head, like he was looking for something, probably that damn gate's location," I said.

Angelo sighed.

"I don't think it's a good idea we stay here. He's tried to kill you and he knows where we are. There's no telling what he will do next," he said.

I turned and looked at him. He didn't seem shaken, but he was concerned.

"We are in no danger," I said as I stroked the side of his face. "If he really wanted to harm us, he would have done so. He could have dropped me if that was what he really wanted to do. But he didn't. This was only a visit."

Angelo gave me a very concerned look.

"How do you know this?" he asked.

"I'm not sure. Its like I could read his mind. I could see his thoughts, almost as if they were my own. I can't explain it, but what I do know is that this visit was his way of letting us know that there is no place we can hide from him. We're going to have to stand our ground."

"And you picked all of that up just now?"

"Yes. I just sensed that he was not going to harm me, just scare me. Don't ask me how I knew, I just did."

"Is that all you saw?"

"Yeah, I think so," I said nodding.

"I don't like this, Vanifera."

I didn't answer. Truth be known, I didn't like it either. I was sure that Angelo was thinking the same thing I was. I wondered whether the memories of the monster inside of me were starting to re-emerge. I was terrified by the thought, yet I fought to keep my composure as best I could. I didn't want my fears to show and further ruin what was supposed to be the happiest day of my life. This was not the time for confrontation. This was my honeymoon and I was determined to have at least one last happy day in my life before all hell broke loose. However, I also knew that the moment for battle was approaching quickly. Confrontation was inevitable. For now, I had to ease my and my husband's mind. I turned to him and pulled his face close to mine. I passionately kissed his mouth, then pulled back and looked into his eyes.

"This is our day, our honeymoon. Nothing is going to ruin this for us, not even the Contravexus," I said.

Angelo's scowl relaxed and he nodded his head.

"You're absolutely right," he replied.

I hugged him tightly and stared out at the sparkling city below. In my mind, this would be the last of the happy times of my life. War was coming. But for now, I wanted to make sure that we cherished these last precious moments, for they could be the last that we would ever have.

~~~

"She claims not to know where the gate is located," said a being that sat on a stool in the shadows of a corner.

"Do you think she is telling the truth?" asked a short being also hidden in the shadows.

"I don't know. When I tried to probe her mind, I sensed something blocking her subconscious thoughts. Interestingly enough, I sensed her probing my mind as well. However, I don't think it was intentional. It felt more instinctual than conscious. Perhaps the Gaian is trying to resurface."

"Maybe there *is* a block and your mind probe weakened it or distracted her concentration."

"Perhaps. But whether there is or isn't a block on the Gaian's mind, she is the only one that knows of the gates location, and if she can't remember where it is hidden on her own, then we must help her," said the seated being, who suddenly stood to his feet.

"What would you like me to do, my lord?" asked the shorter figure.

"Nothing for now. She understood the nature of my visit. I wish to allow her time to do what she must to remember. If after such time she has made no progress, then we will proceed with more persuasive tactics. Keep an eye on her though."

"As you wish, my lord."

~~~

CHAPTER FIVE

There were no further issues over the next few days. Angelo and I were able to enjoy our honeymoon, and after one week, we relocated to Seattle. Angelo began preparing for his inevitable confrontation. Each day he worked on his battle techniques, constantly trying to improve his strength, speed and stamina. His abilities were growing stronger each day. Yet, he still wasn't strong enough. I'd felt the power of the Contravexus and he was far stronger than Angelo's current state. However, my husband was rapidly making progress and it wouldn't be long before he matched the Contravexus' power.

I also had to contend with my own struggles, trying to remember my forgotten past. Those memories were the key to everything that was happening around me. Candy, Angelo, Barhim Hajj; they each were somehow connected to that forgotten past of mine, and as it would seem, their lives and many others depended on me remembering it. But I didn't have the faintest idea where to start.

One day, Angelo paused from his training and sat beside me.

"I'm going to find him, Vanifera. I'm going to hunt him down and I'm going to kill him," he said.

I knew he was talking about the Contravexus.

"What brought this on?" I asked.

"When he came to us on that balcony, he made it personal. I know the real reason why you didn't want me to go after him when we were in Vegas. I wasn't strong enough to fight him then. But I'm stronger now, and I'm going to go after him."

Angelo was indeed stronger, but he lacked the killer's heart needed to combat such an evil. I decided to use a little psychology.

"I thought you said that I was the only one who could kill him?" I asked.

Angelo looked flustered.

"You are. But I can't just sit around and wait for him to strike. I have to do something," he said.

"Then you have to come up with a plan, something that will hurt him just as badly," I suggested. "What do you know about this Contravexus?"

Angelo began telling me about certain events in history and how they connected to the Contravexus. He explained how the Contravexus manipulated and eventually came to control the minds of powerful men. He named every major catastrophe and explained how the Contravexus blinded the truth from mankind. Angelo's contempt showed in every word and gesture.

"This was not the world that my master intended for the humans. Although I despise their arrogance, the humans do not deserve the cruel game that is being played with their lives," he concluded.

"So, who is this Contravexus? Surely you must have an idea of his identity by now," I said.

"Yes, I do. His name is Dupri, Montellace Dupri."

My eyes widened and my mouth dropped.

"You mean the global financier; that Montellace Dupri?" I asked.

"Exactly."

After a few minutes of thinking, I could see how all of the events that Angelo spoke about connected to Montellace Dupri. But now, this placed a whole new light on the situation. This meant that Dupri had the financial resources as well as the god-like ability to do whatever he wanted. I felt the depth of his power and it was frightening. I also felt how cold and evil his soul was. If he was a by-product of the evil that once existed in me, I knew that there would be great suffering in the future. Nonetheless there was room for hope.

The Hierarchy, an angelic network of agents that monitored

the global operations and activities of suspected Vul Paux agents. Angelo was one of their best. If there were ever a force that could stop the Contravexus, it was them.

"So, how do you plan to hurt him? You certainly can't kill him," I asked.

"We simply have to find a way to weaken him," Angelo replied pacing.

"Seems to me that the most logical way to hurt someone like him is to hit him where it'll hurt him the most, in his pocketbook."

Angelo stopped, his eyes blooming wide.

"That's it!" he said, turning to look at me. "Vanifera, you're a genius!"

Angelo immediately contacted Hierarchy headquarters. A full-scale plan of attack was developed, targeting all of Dupri's legitimate businesses. The Hierarchy also beefed up its covert activities, raiding network terrorist cells and illegal ventures of the Contravexus. Over the course of several weeks, the plan was executed flawlessly. Like a well-oiled machine, Angelo and his comrades struck and destroyed operations in Russia, Germany, Italy, North Korea, Brazil, South Africa, Great Britain and the United States. With his global network weakening, it wouldn't be long before they got to the man himself.

I stayed at a safe house when Angelo went on his missions. It wasn't home, but until the Hierarchy could capture Montellace Dupri and crush his network, I was guarded at all times. The fear was from the possibility of his operatives getting their hands on me. If they did, they could possibly unlock my memory and locate the gateway. Sometimes I wondered if that was such a bad thing. In many ways, I wanted to remember what I'd forgotten. At least I would know what this whole thing was about.

When Angelo returned from his missions, we would go to our home in Federal Way and have some semblance of a life. For many months, that was how I lived, bouncing between my home and the safe house. But then, that fateful day came when the tables in this war were turned.

It was a cool fall evening in September when the first counter move of this war was made. Angelo had just finished another successful raid in Canada and had returned home. We decided to spend a quiet evening, cuddling beneath a fleece blanket in the bedroom while watching television. The news was on. We watched as reporter Bob Durham spoke of the bombing in Montreal and the burned bodies found in the wreckage.

"That was you guys, wasn't it?" I asked turning to look at him.

"Yep. That was one of their major cells of operation," he replied.

Suddenly, we heard footsteps in the living room. We both sat up, listening intently. The steps were slow and cautious. The floor creaked from the weight of the intruder. They drew closer and closer to the bedroom. Angelo reached under the bed and grabbed a baseball bat.

"Get into the closet," he whispered.

He stood, tiptoed to the side of the door and waited for the intruder. As he stood motionless with his bat in hand, I stood and tiptoed to the closet. I peeked through the slightly opened door and waited as the steps drew nearer.

Just then, the bedroom door was pushed open and a dark figure stood in the doorway. The sheer fact that someone had invaded our home was terrifying and a chill ran down my spine. Angelo leaped from beside the door and swung the bat with enough force to hit a homerun. But the intruder ducked and the bat lodged into the bedroom door.

"Whoa, easy there! Is this any way to treat your brother?" exclaimed the intruder.

Angelo snatched the bat from the door and held it in front of him.

"Who are you?" he asked.

Angelo backed away, forming a barrier between the dark figure and the closet I was hiding in. As the being walked toward him, the light of the television allowed us to finally see his face.

"Sariel?" said Angelo disbelievingly.

"Greetings, brother."

Angelo dropped the bat and the two embraced with joyous laughter. Then, they released each other and grasped each other's shoulders.

"Praise the father. It is good to see you again, brother," said Angelo.

"Likewise," said Sariel.

"What are you doing here?"

"Taking a little time off. After that issue in Ireland, I could use it. I heard that you were living here now and decided to come and pay you a visit."

Then, Sariel turned and looked at the closet.

"Who's in there?"

Angelo turned and called to me.

"Vanifera, you can come out now," he said.

I cautiously walked out and stood. Sariel's eyes widened and his jaw dropped.

"By my father's locks, you're here also?" he said with astonishment.

Angelo smirked. "Sariel, this is..."

"Yes. She is the vessel; the Gaian," said Sariel.

"Yes," Angelo replied.

"What is she doing here?"

"I'm watching over her."

"Watching her, huh? Somebody needs to be watching you," said Sariel with a wry smile.

He walked closer and stared at me.

"Is she safe?" he asked.

"Why don't you ask me and find out, instead of talking like I'm not here," I said.

Sariel smiled and shot Angelo a glance.

"Spunky," he said.

"Vanifera, this is my brother, Sariel. He handles the European unit of the Hierarchy."

I smirked.

"Nice to meet you," I said.

Sariel nodded.

"So, how did you get stuck with watching over the wretched vessel of the Vul Paux?" asked Sariel as he walked back to Angelo.

"Easy. Vanifera is not the same creature we fought. She has her own persona now," said Angelo.

I got very perturbed by his comment, calling me a wretched vessel. However, I could understand why he would feel that way, given the fact that I might have been somewhat destructive according to all accounts.

"Be that as it may, I still remember the devastation she caused. Has anybody come looking for her yet?" probed Sariel.

"A few. But we've done a pretty good job in keeping her hidden," said Angelo.

Sariel looked uncomfortable and fidgeted a lot. He kept glancing back at me as if I were going to do something.

"Hajj told me that the Gaian had been reanimated. I figured the Hierarchy would have placed her in a much higher level of security," said Sariel.

"Are you talking about Barhim Hajj?" I asked.

"Why yes, I am. You know him?" asked Sariel with an annoyed expression.

"Only by association," said Angelo glancing at me.

I decided that I needed to leave the room. It was apparent my presence wasn't welcome. I figured that the best way to leave was to show some hospitality by offering some refreshments.

"Would anyone like a sandwich?"

"No, thanks. I'm afraid this visit will have to be short. I have to catch a train to Spokane in the morning. But I had to come by and see how you were," said Sariel.

"I'm glad you did, brother," said Angelo.

"I'm still rather surprised to see you with the Gaian," said Sariel, glancing at me.

I was beginning to grow a little weary of Sariel's comments. He acted like I was some subspecies or a second rate entity. Angelo saw my displeasure and approached me, just as I was about to leave the room.

"Are you alright?" he asked, placing his arm around me.

"Sure, I'm okay," I said with a slightly aggravated tone.

Sariel turned and looked at me with an expression of regret.

"I'm sorry. I didn't mean to offend you. Its just that seeing you again brings back a lot of bad memories," he said.

"I understand," I replied. "But I'm not that same creature, and I don't deserve being treated like this, especially in my own home."

"Yes, you are correct. I apologize," said Sariel.

Angelo continued to comfort me despite his brother's apologies. He grabbed my hand and I placed my head on his shoulder. A scowl covered my face and I breathed heavily.

"Are you okay?" he asked.

I nodded. However, the truth was I was beginning to feel a little strange. It was like a simmering anger that I was trying to contain. I couldn't think of anything that was causing this surge of hostility. Perhaps it was Sariel's comments or the way he had treated me. But it didn't warrant this kind of emotional stirring.

"Is something wrong, brother?" asked Sariel.

"No, I just think she's a little tired," said Angelo.

Sariel was about to turn and leave, when suddenly, he did a double take at Angelo and my hands. He frowned and then looked at Angelo with a very disturbed expression.

"You married the Gaian?" asked Sariel with surprise.

I lifted my hand and showed him my wedding ring, twiddling my fingers.

"Oh my God! I don't believe this!" said Sariel. "Angelo, you are an angel, a being of God's! Vanifera is the vessel of the Anti-God! The two of you can't be married!"

"Sariel, calm down," Angelo said, waving his hands downward.

At this point, I'd had enough.

"You know what? Ever since you got here, you've been making me feel like I'm some second-class citizen simply because of my past! Now you want to insult my marriage by saying that Angelo and I shouldn't be together because of something that has nothing to do with us! I don't even know who this Vul Paux is, and I'm not going to leave my husband just because of some stupid celestial prejudices!" I said angrily.

"Whoa, I can't take anymore of this! Angelo, I'll see you later!" said Sariel.

"Where are you going?" asked Angelo.

"I'm afraid I must leave you now," he replied.

Sariel proceeded to the door with Angelo walking behind him. I started to follow when suddenly the room changed. It was as if I'd been teleported into another time. I was in my home, but it was as if time had accelerated just a little bit. I saw Angelo standing at the door. Next, I saw someone emerging from the shadows and firing a gun. I could see the blasts striking Angelo in the chest and knocking him to the ground. Then, just as quickly as it had begun, the images were gone.

I was instantly filled with fear and shock. I couldn't breathe and began trembling. I was so scared that I felt as if I were going to faint. Angelo stopped at the door and turned to look at me. He frowned and walked back toward me, grabbing me around my waist and holding me steady.

"Are you okay?" he asked with a disturbed expression.

I couldn't respond at first, probably due to the overwhelming confusion and disorientation from the vision. It happened so fast that I couldn't think at all. Shaking hands covered my mouth and widened eyes stared blankly through the veil of tears that were starting to well. I tried to compose myself, but fear's grip was tight. My eyes shifted to Angelo, who stared at me with concern. Volumes of fear were written across his face, making his thoughts easy to read. I quickly batted my eyes and loosened my expression.

"Yes, I think so," I replied.

Angelo stroked the side of my face and kissed me. He sat me down on the bed and knelt before me, still sporting a concerned look.

"Sariel didn't mean to be so rude. That's just his nature. He doesn't know how much you've changed."

I stared at Angelo, realizing that he thought my emotional episode had something to do with Sariel's comments. I wanted to tell him what just happened, but I couldn't figure it out myself. I didn't know how to explain it. Until I did, it was best that I let him continue to believe as he did.

"I'm going to walk Sariel out. You stay here and I'll be back in a couple of minutes," he said.

"Okay," I said wearily.

Angelo patted my hand, then stood and walked out of the bedroom. Chloe trotted from her normal resting place in the closet, hopped on the bed and laid in my lap.

"Hey girl," I said as I petted her.

The terrier lifted her head and began wagging her tail. For a moment, all was quiet.

"Did you hear all those nasty things that man said about me? It's a good thing he's gone, huh?" I said in my childlike tone.

Chloe looked at me, her head cocked slightly to the right. Her expression seemed to ask whether I was okay. I chuckled at the thought.

"Yes, I'm okay. But you sense something, don't you? You know something's wrong?" I asked.

Chloe gave me one of her growling whines, swiping her tongue across her lips.

"You're right. I need to tell him," I said.

I stood and walked out of the room. Chloe leaped from the bed and was on my heels. As I entered the living room, I saw Angelo standing in the doorway with a confused look on his face.

"What's wrong?" I asked.

"I don't see Sariel anywhere," he said, turning his back to the doorway.

Suddenly, a man dressed as a police officer emerged from the shadows and stepped to the entrance behind Angelo. Startled by the officer's sudden appearance, Angelo turned to look at him.

"Can I help you?" he asked.

The officer glared at my husband menacingly and I experienced a moment of déjà vu. Then, it hit me and I instantly recognized his face. He was the person I saw in my vision just moments ago. He was the one that shot Angelo. However, before I could utter a word, the officer lifted his hand in front of him. Two shots echoed and Angelo's body flinched. Then, another shot rang in the darkness.

"NO!" I exclaimed.

Angelo stumbled backwards into the house. The bullets ripped gaping holes into his chest. He fell against the kitchen counter and slumped to his knees on the ground, trembling from the pain that riveted through his body. He then fell facedown on the floor as his blood began pooling beneath him. In my shock, I stood frozen in place, watching my husband lie quivering in his own blood.

Then, the officer turned the gun toward me and fired a single shot, striking me in the left shoulder. The impact spun me into the wall of the living room. I fell to my knees, hurt and dazed. The blood began to flow from my shoulder as I grabbed beneath the point of impact. The pain was immense, as if something was burning the flesh on that side of my body. I helplessly knelt on the floor as the officer stood over me and pointed the gun's barrel directly at my forehead.

Just then, little Chloe raced toward the officer. She leaped into the air, biting the officer's hand that held the gun. Although I'd never seen her attack anyone before, I was very happy that she came to my aid. She locked her mouth and sunk her teeth into the flesh of the cop's hand. He screamed and struggled to free himself from her grip, but Chloe was locked in good. She twisted and wrenched her neck, displaying a rabid behavior I'd never seen from her before.

The officer, unable to free himself from her grip, slammed his hand into the wall, smashing Chloe's head in the process. The little white terrier released her grip and fell to the floor. She was dazed but continued to attack. I braced myself against the wall and pushed myself to stand. But as I stood to my feet, the officer, still holding the gun, squeezed the trigger again. This time the target was Chloe.

Her white coat was instantly stained with blood as she lay on her side whimpering from the shot. Her left hind leg twitched as the blood began to pool beneath her. I was still braced against the wall and stared in disbelief. On the floor before me were my husband and my dog, both viciously shot for no reason by a psychotic police officer. The sight replaced the fear and terror that filled my heart moments ago with anger so intense that I no longer felt the pain from the gunshot.

The officer seemed pleased with the situation and lowered his gun. He looked down at Angelo lying motionless on the floor. A smirk appeared across his lips and he chuckled at what he had done. Then, he lifted his gaze toward me once again. He stepped over Angelo's body and walked toward me. I'd lost a lot of blood and was growing dizzy. The increased adrenaline caused by my anger had done more damage than good. I was very weak, but I was not going to let this maniac get away with what he'd done. For all I knew, Angelo and Chloe were still alive and needed my help.

The cop drew closer and closer. I reared back my right fist and attempted to punch him in his face. I threw my blow with all the strength I could muster. But my weakened state didn't give my strike any authority. He caught my fist in his hand and tightened his grip. I grimaced even more as I fell to my knees. The cop laughed at my attempt. He knew that I was powerless to do anything at this point. I was not going to be able to save Angelo or Chloe. He lifted me up by the collar and pushed me into the wall, gripping my face in his hand.

"We can do this the easy way or the hard way," whispered the officer as he placed his face close to mine.

"You bastard! If it's the last thing I do, I'll make you pay for this!" I exclaimed panting.

The officer smiled devilishly. He relished his moment of dominance, using his body weight to press me against the wall. Then, a hand slapped down on his shoulder, burning his flesh upon touch. The officer jumped from his pinning position over me and distanced himself from the painful grip, screaming in agony. He stood on the other side of the room, brushing his smoldering shoulder to alleviate the burning. He then lifted his head. His eyes widened as he gazed at the grimacing face of Sariel. It was he who had burned the demonic officer and sent him cowering across the room. He stood between the officer and myself, almost as if he were protecting me.

The cop shook off the effects of the burning. From the look of his shoulder, he had been burned severely, so badly in fact that the wound should have caused him to go into shock. But then, something most peculiar happened. His flesh began regenerating. He quickly concluded his restoration and glared defiantly at Sariel.

"Instant Regeneration, huh? I didn't think humans could do such a thing," said Sariel sarcastically.

"I am more than what I seem," said the cop with an evil smile.

"Apparently. Let's see what you're really made of."

Sariel pulled out a small crucifix and hurled it at the cop. It whizzed through the air and lodged into his shoulder. Instantly, a red mist erupted from the mouth of the cop. It hovered over him for a moment and then the cop fell to the ground.

"You shall not have the woman this night. Leave, or you will regret being here," said Sariel.

"You have not heard the last of me. Your days are numbered and I am patient," said the mist as it dissipated.

The smell of brimstone filled the air, and the body of the police officer lay on the wooden floor. As Sariel did a quick examination around the room, I hurried to Angelo and knelt beside him. With my one good arm, I turned him over and supported his head in my lap. His chest was shredded from the bullets. He was covered with blood and panted faintly. I began crying, fearing the worst.

"Baby, please don't die on me. Hang in there," I begged.

But his eyes were wide and fixed, staring ahead unflinchingly. His hands were beginning to feel cold and his skin was turning pale in color. Just then, Sariel knelt beside me.

"Angelo, can you hear me?" asked Sariel.

"You can't leave me, not now," I pleaded to Angelo.

He gasped, coughing up blood from his throat. Then he spoke.

"V-Vanifera. You must p-protect her, Sariel," said Angelo in a grunting whisper.

I turned to Sariel and pleaded with him to not let Angelo die.

"There must be something you can do!" I cried.

"I need to get him to headquarters," said Sariel. "But I can't make any promises."

He scooped Angelo in his arms and raced through the front door. I struggled to stand and trotted to the door also. However, by the time I'd gotten there, he was gone. I braced myself against the doorframe and stood there, amazed by how quickly Sariel had departed. Now, I was alone and badly injured. The blood I'd lost from the wound on my shoulder was causing me to feel lightheaded, and I was on the verge of fainting.

I slid down the frame and laid on the floor. I murmured a prayer as I clutched my arm. The pain was immense, but lacked in comparison to the pain I felt in my heart. The ached was deep, resembling a sword being thrust into my chest. If I lost Angelo, I wouldn't know what to do. I began crying and my eyes began to close.

Just then, a hand touched me on my shoulder. I looked up and saw that it was Barhim Hajj. He knelt beside me and lifted me to sit. He placed his hand over my wound and pressed gently. I looked at him with tear-filled eyes. I wasn't sure what I should say to him, but I appreciated his presence.

"I see that they've abandoned you," he said.

I didn't have the strength to reply.

"They are a fickle sort. But no worries, I'm here," he said.

"Can you help me?" I asked panting.

"Indeed I can, Your Highness," said Hajj.

He continued to hold his hand over the wound and within moments, the bleeding had stopped. A scabbed bullet hole was all that remained and I could even feel my strength returning. After about a minute, I stood and braced myself against the counter. Hajj continued to kneel before me with a smile across his lips.

"How are you feeling now, Your Highness?" he asked.

"Much better, thank you," I replied.

Suddenly, I heard a crashing sound outside my bedroom window. I quickly walked to it and peered outside. It was the cop that had shot Angelo and me. He was running frantically down the throughway, knocking over trashcans and falling over boxes. Instantly, the taste of blood was in my mouth and all I wanted to do was kill. The swelling of anger consumed me like a hunger that had to be satisfied. Suddenly, I heard a voice inside my head.

"There is your prey, Vanifera. He tried to kill you and your precious Angelo. Chloe lies on the floor in her own blood because of him. Are you going to let this maniac get away with what he's done to you and your family?"

A cold chill raced down my spine. I looked at Barhim Hajj. "Did you just say something?" I asked.

He returned a befuddled look. "No, princess, I didn't."

I continued looking at him with a confused look on my face. In the distance, I could hear sirens. Their dual tones grew louder and louder. I assumed that they were coming here. At that moment, I didn't trust the police. It was an officer that caused all of this carnage. But I was determined that this one was not going to get away. He would pay for what he'd done, and his punishment would come by my hands.

I looked toward the front door and saw Chloe's body. The wind blew gently across her blood stained white coat. My chest tightened and a lump developed in my throat. I walked to her and knelt beside her motionless body. I gently stroked her face, tilting my head to stare into her eyes. They were still open, dark and cold. The tears rolled across the bridge of my nose. Instantly, I remembered her valiant efforts to protect me, and how her subtle look prompted me to tell Angelo about the vision I had. Yes, that's what I concluded it to be, a vision. I saw what was going to happen, yet I didn't say anything. Perhaps she knew what was about to happen also. Maybe if I'd told Angelo what I saw, they'd both be safe and unharmed right now. But I didn't, and now Chloe was dead. She died trying to protect me. If anyone deserved to die, it was me. The expression on her petite face, however, seemed to say that she had no regrets and would do it again if she had to. I knelt closer and kissed her on her nose.

"I'm sorry, Chloe. I'm so sorry," I whispered to her tearfully.

As the sirens grew nearer, I stood and walked back to the window. I wiped the tears from my eyes and gave a glance at Barhim Hajj, who sported a remorseful expression.

"I'm sorry," he said.

I looked out the window and down the alley the fleeing officer went. I reached up and unlatched it.

"Oh, hey, wait a minute. I hope you aren't planning on going after that guy?" asked Hajj.

I didn't answer. I opened the window and climbed out. I could see that the cowardly officer had made it to the end of the alley.

"Princess, I beg you to reconsider this course of action," Hajj pleaded.

My rage had consumed me and I was not about to be denied my revenge. I checked my shoulder and made sure it was okay. Then, I started running. At that moment, something inside of me was changing. I could feel the anger cruising through me, just as it did when I fought Candy. Vicious thoughts raced through my head, envisioning images of things I would do to the cop when I caught him. Gone were the virtues of mercy, pity and compassion as I raced fearlessly down the narrow pathway. Only the exhilaration of vengeance and the hunger for killing remained. As I reached the end of the alley, I could see him running down the street. I knew that no matter where he ran or how fast he fled, he would not escape my wrath.

~~~

CHAPTER SIX

As a frantic chase commenced in Federal Way, another development was taking place ten miles outside of Biloxi, Mississippi. In a dark foreboding area, another component of evil was being moved into place. A light fog covered the still marshlands as the croaking of frogs and the chirping of crickets resounded in the darkness. Slivers of moonlight seeped between the tightly entangled branches of the moss covered oak trees. It was as if the trees were hiding this place. It also gave this part of the swamp an even more sinister atmosphere. But despite its menacing vibe, an enticing aroma filled the air. It was the smell of gumbo.

The scent originated from a cluster of pots boiling over an open fire outside a dilapidated shack. A dim light shined inside the right front window. It was a candle whose flame danced atop the stick of wax like a seductive stripper. It tangoed with the wind, twisting and dipping, but never going out. In the corner of the front room, an old woman sat rocking back and forth in her rocking chair. A red smock covered her legs and her arms were crossed over her chest. She appeared to be humming a spiritual that seemed to soothe and comfort her. Her posture was slouched and her chin was tucked. She was calm and relaxed, almost as if she were well on her way to slumber. A roaring fire burned in the fireplace, and the crackling of wood gave the somewhat condemned hovel a warm and inviting atmosphere.

Suddenly, the candle's fire changed from its red-yellow color to blue green. It burned for only a few moments and then the candle exploded. The old woman slowly lifted her head and looked in the direction where the candle once burned. She leaned forward and gradually lifted herself from her wooden rocker. She walked toward the table where the pieces of the exploded candle lay, pulling the smock that had covered her legs around her shoulders. As she shuffled, her house shoes scratched the floor, echoing her struggle to make the next step.

She finally made it to the table, and with two of her fingers, swiped through the dust and wax. She raised her hand to her nose and sniffed her fingers. She placed some of the wax on her tongue, then spat on the floor. Her saliva turned acidic and burned a hole through the wood. Upon seeing this, she turned and looked out of her front window.

The wind was starting to blow and rustled the leaves in the trees. The pots began swinging as small amounts of gumbo sprayed in the wind. The moon's rays now seemed to have a tinge of red in it, casting a blood-like hue over the swamp.

Suddenly, the fire exploded from inside the fireplace behind her. The flames shot outward as if hell itself was right under her house. The old woman turned and stared in amazement. She instinctually grabbed a handful of the candle dust from the table and tossed it into the fire. The blaze's color instantly changed to the blue green color that the candle flame possessed just before it exploded. Then, the fire's intensity subsided and the color returned to normal. Upon seeing this, the old woman walked closer to the fireplace and stared into the fire.

"It has finally begun," she muttered.

~~~

From the alleys of my neighborhood to the city center of Federal Way, I continued to chase the rogue cop. I could still see his silhouetted figure hurdling the trashcans and other debris as he tried to escape. The dim streetlights gave me just enough light to see his every move. Like a cat in the night, I saw everything, sensed every object around me. I knew where everything was and each step was placed with absolute surety. I, too, hurdled the garbage cans and ducked the low hanging fire escape ladders. I even saw the bum lying in the cardboard box in the doorway. It was as if each of my senses were heightened to their peak. My movements were effortless and perfectly timed. I was a huntress, chasing the foulest of all prey.

As I approached a business complex, I'd lost track of the cop for only a moment. I looked to my right and then my left. That's when I spotted him again, attempting to disappear inside the mist that bellowed from the cracked pipes of a building. I turned and resumed the chase. He ran to the other side of the street, dodging cars that came dangerously close to hitting him.

I ran after him, being cautious not to incur the fate he so luckily dodged. I ran between the cars and made my way to the other side of the street. I saw him in the alley. He stopped for a moment and lifted his hand toward me. Then, I saw a flash of light. It was a gunshot. I'm not sure what really happened, but suddenly, everything seemed to be moving in slow motion. I was moving fine and normal, but the world around me seemed to slow to a snail's pace.

I watched as the bullet came whizzing toward me. I nonchalantly moved to the right and allowed the bullet to hurl passed me. As it did, it lodged into a wall of one of the buildings directly across the street. It was like watching a movie in slow motion. I turned to look once more at the cop, who then fired two more shots. Again, both bullets whizzed by, this time a little slower than the previous shot. As the second bullet passed me, everything suddenly returned to normal. The cop stood in awe. Perhaps he was just as shocked as I was.

"Stay away from me!" he screamed.

He turned and began running once more. I shook off my astonishment and resumed the chase. He reached a lowered ladder of a fire escape and began climbing. As he reached the second floor, he pulled up the ladder. Then, he continued up the escape to the roof. I arrived at the ladder moments later and stared as the cop ascended to the top of the building. I looked around for something to help me pull down the ladder, but there was nothing. Then, I decided to try to leap and grab it. I crouched and jumped. To my surprise, not only did I leap high enough to grab the ladder, I jumped high enough to land on the second story ledge of the fire escape. I grabbed the railing, trying not to fall backward. I stood there for a moment to compose myself. I looked back down at the ground to see how high I'd jumped.

"No way," I said with disbelief.

Something was wrong. I'd never been able to do anything like that before. My abilities had somehow increased to supernatural levels, allowing me to do some tremendous feats. I didn't understand it, but I also didn't have time to figure it out. I looked up once more at the cop, who'd finally made his way to the top of the building. I had to be careful now. By the time I got up there, he could be waiting to fire another shot at me. He had to be running low on ammunition after all the shots he'd fired, and if that were the case, it would mean that sooner or later I was going to get him.

I finally made it to the top, cautiously stepping onto the roof. I scanned the area looking for the cop. A cold wind now blew across the tarred rooftop. The crunch of the gravel under my feet echoed my ill intent. Of course, that's what I wanted him to hear. Perhaps it would draw him out, make him expose himself so I could get a clear shot at him. My heart ached, but it also pounded with anticipation. I was not going to let him get away, not after what he'd done to my husband and Chloe.

I ventured a little further onto the roof. The glow from the crescent moon provided some light. I couldn't see him, but I knew he was there; I could sense him watching me. My plan was to use myself as bait and lure him from his hiding place. All I needed to do was place myself in the open and draw him out. I took two more steps, which placed me in the middle of the roof. Now, he had a perfect opportunity to take his best shot. There was nowhere for me to hide, and he wouldn't get a better opportunity than this to finish me off.

Just then, from the corner of my right eye, I saw a slight glimmer. I didn't move my head, but instead shifted only my eyes to the right in order to see what caused the gleam. Something was moving, creeping slowly from the shadows. It was him; it had to be. I waited a few moments more, allowing him to come out into the open. Then, I turned and looked at him. He stood in the shadow of the water tower, pointing his gun at me.

"You stay away from me!" he said with a slight Irish accent.

"Why? Why did you do it? Why did you shoot my husband?" I asked angrily.

"I didn't mean to. I was forced. The voices in my head kept telling me to kill him. I couldn't stop myself," he said sniveling.

I then realized that he was not the same person he was when he shot Angelo or myself. He was different now, scared like a cornered animal. He also didn't have an accent when he spoke to me at the house. I then remembered seeing a mist escaping his body back at the house when Sariel hit him with the crucifix. It must have been a demon or some other spirit that possessed him earlier. However, just as I was starting to understand what had happened to him, the man's expression changed from fright to a scowl. His eyes became as red as fire and his demeanor became more sinister.

"It didn't have to be this way, you know. All you had to do was come with me. That was all I wanted from you," said the cop with a very deep voice.

The air suddenly became much colder and suffocating, just like it did when I was in Las Vegas. His accent was gone, sounding more like he did when he pinned me against the wall. It was clear that something else was controlling him now, and from the atmosphere I now felt, it had to be the Contravexus.

"Why are you using innocent people to get to me?" I asked.

"Does it truly matter who I use as long as I get what I want?" he retorted.

"Yes, it does. You used an innocent man to shoot my husband, and you almost killed me. What's the matter? You can't do your own dirty work?"

"Why should I, when there's all these sinful people to choose from. Besides, you cannot be killed. I only did that to get your attention."

"Well, you got it!"

"Gaian, all you had to do was come to me. But you wanted to play games. Don't blame me for your suffering. I'm only doing what I've been commanded to do and that is free our master and return you to him," he said.

"First of all, I have no master. Second, there is nothing you can say that is going to justify what you did. You can blame it on following orders all you want, but it still isn't going to change a damn thing. You tried to take something from me and now I'm going to take something from you," I said as tears rolled down my cheeks.

"We'll see," he said.

One shot. Two shots. Three shots echoed in the night. Then, silence. Although each bullet would have struck the average person, I was able to dodge them all with relative ease. He lowered his gun and looked at me with a smirk.

"Your powers are returning. Soon, your memories will be returning also," he said.

"So, that's what's happening to me," I replied.

"Isn't it obvious? Come with me and I can help speed things along."

I wiped my eyes, then snickered. "You know, I was told that I'm the only being that can kill you. Well, I'm here to inform you that I intend on doing just that."

"Bold words. Its clear you possess the abilities to take a life, but can you save one? You'll never win; and here's why," he said.

He turned and ran to the edge of the roof and stopped. I could tell that the leap to the other building was too far for him to make. There was only one thing that could happen, and the thought scared me. I calmly walked toward him and extended my hand.

"You don't have to do this. He is an innocent man and doesn't deserve to die," I said.

The cop looked back at me, then smiled. His eyes were no longer red and the panicked expression had returned. The Contravexus was no longer controlling him.

"Don't worry. Now, I can finally stop the voices," he said, once again with an Irish accent.

Then, he leaped over the edge of the roof. I lunged toward him, trying to stop his suicidal actions. But I was too late. I looked over the edge of the building with disbelief. His descent was a quick seven-story plunge. His body bounced off the pavement and blood splattered from the impact. A screaming woman quickly drew the attention of passers-by, and they huddled around the body gawking.

"Somebody call an ambulance!" screamed one of the people.

They all stared at him lying facedown on the ground. Then, almost as if someone were controlling them, they all looked simultaneously upward at me.

"Look! There's somebody up there!" exclaimed a woman.

I quickly backed away from the edge. I knew I needed to get down from here fast, so I began looking around for the quickest exit from the roof. A few feet away was a door that led downstairs. But I was certain that the bystanders were on their way up those very stairs. However, behind me was another rooftop. It was close enough for me to leap onto. I raced toward the opposite edge of the roof with all the speed I could muster and leaped. I did a tuck and roll, quickly crouching to ensure I couldn't be seen. I leaped to two more roofs and then paused to see if there was someplace I could hide.

In the corner was a storage shed. I ran to it and pulled the door open. I hurried in and closed it behind me. I struggled to quietly catch my breath. I sat on the ground and pulled my legs to my chest. I tried to slow my breathing and keep myself from panicking. In my frantic state, I couldn't think clearly. I knew I didn't kill that officer. I wanted to, but I didn't. The Contravexus made him jump. Things were quickly spiraling out of control and I didn't know what to do to stop it. All I knew right now was that Angelo was probably dead and the man that killed him had just committed suicide. People were dying all around me, and it was too much to handle. I finally broke down and began crying, clutching my legs for dear life.

~~~

Somehow during all the madness, I'd fallen asleep. When I awoke, I rubbed my eyes and looked around the shed. I braced myself against the wall and slowly stood to my feet. I didn't know how much time had passed, but it seemed like hours. I pushed open the shed door and walked out. Darkness still blanketed the sky of the city and the sound of sirens filled the air. Suddenly, a cop appeared directly in front of me. My heart raced and I began to feel panicky. *They got me*, I though.

"He can't see you," said a voice, sounding as if it came from right beside me.

I looked around, but I didn't see anyone. The cop walked passed me, as if he didn't know I was there. I frowned as I watched him walk away. I then saw a group of police officers scanning the rooftop. They, too, were seemingly oblivious to my presence.

"Leave this place, Gaian, now," said the mysterious voice.

"Who are you?" I asked.

There was no reply. I shot the officers another disturbed look, then walked to the edge of the building and looked over the side. The emergency teams were still around the building where the cop I'd chased had jumped. I decided to do as the voice said and leave the roof. I walked to the fire escape and climbed down. I quickly left the area and began walking toward home.

An hour later, I was back in my subdivision. As I approached the street my house was on, I saw that police cars and ambulances were also there. I ducked into the alley that ran parallel to the street my house was on and made my way toward my home. Luckily, the place just across the street from mine was up for sale and no one had moved into it yet. I climbed up on the roof and crouched behind the huge brick chimney. I peeked around the side and watched the flurry of activity below. A crowd had gathered behind the yellow police tape in front of my house. The flashing lights from the emergency vehicles illuminated the darkened sky as news crews clamored to gain the best positions to cover the story. Reporters stared into the cameras with their false expressions of sorrow. Their insincerity was sickening.

Suddenly, the paramedics wheeled a covered gurney from the house. It appeared to have a body on it. I frowned, wondering who it could have been. It couldn't be Angelo; I saw Sariel grab him in his arms and carry him off. Just then, I heard one of the officers giving their report.

"Yeah, a male in his early thirties. Victim's name was Angelo Ramone," he said to one of the detectives.

His words caused a knot of pain in my chest. I wanted to scream at the top of my lungs. This couldn't be happening. I couldn't have heard that Angelo was dead. It was all a mistake or some misunderstanding. My mind discredited what he said and I kept thinking that I'd heard him wrong or that this was some sort of dream that I would awaken from shortly.

The paramedics carried the stretcher to the ambulance. I just sat there watching. This wasn't supposed to happen. He couldn't be dead. My body shuddered from my fight to suppress my urge to scream. I covered my mouth, desperately trying to stifle my cries. Confusion had total control of my mind and my heart was filled with grief.

They moved the body to the rear of the ambulance, folding the wheels of the stretcher beneath it. They loaded it, then maneuvered him into position. They fastened the locking harnesses and closed the door with a slam. As the driver ran to the front of the ambulance, the police officers conversed about the scene of the murder. They attempted to piece together a motive while the forensic team dusted and examined my home. Investigators strolled in and out, bringing new items and information to the detectives that waited outside sipping their coffee. I overheard speculations that it was a botched burglary. But it wasn't. It was an assassination, plain and simple, and I knew who was responsible.

The ambulance driver climbed into the cabin and fastened the seat belt around him. He started the engine and began driving off. As I watched them swerve between the unevenly parked patrol cars, I couldn't help hoping that I would see Angelo in the crowd or that I would overhear something that indicated the body in the ambulance wasn't his.

He couldn't be dead, that was my only thought. My first impulse was to follow the ambulance and see for myself if it was him. But I didn't move. I was too heartbroken to even think straight. I was cold, confused and alone. I felt helpless and angry at the same time.

I looked back at the house once more and watched as the parade of people entered and exited. It was as if our lives were being invaded by scavengers, picking through the ruins. I felt violated. My grief was too strong and it was starting to take control. All I wanted to do was hurt someone and make them feel what I was feeling. But the best thing for me right now was to remain on the roof. Perhaps after they left, I would return to my house and see what was left of the life I once cherished.

I tucked my head and closed my eyes. I didn't feel like crying anymore. I didn't feel like thinking. I just wanted to rest for a moment. I wanted peace from the tormenting pain I felt in my heart and in my head. But, I would find no such relief. The aches were constant and showed no mercy. Their relentlessness forced me to see a bitter revelation about this world. It wasn't as cheerful or as beautiful as it once was. It now possessed a dismal and dark appearance that made me feel somewhat uncomfortable. I wanted answers as to why this was happening.

Hours passed as I sat on the roof pondering. From the chime of the church clock a couple of blocks away, it was three o'clock in the morning. I could feel the dew settling as I sat on that roof. I peeked around the edge of the chimney. Aside from a few lingering cops, everyone else was gone. There were no flashing lights and no chattering onlookers, just the murmur from the loitering officers' discussion. The rest of the world was preparing to begin another day. For me, the worst day of my life had already begun.

Suddenly, I caught a whiff of something in the air. It had a stench that I had difficulty identifying. It grew stronger by the moment and its pungency was overwhelming. At first I thought it to be garbage, or perhaps the smell from the chemical solutions the forensic team used in the house. But this wasn't a smell of rotting food or chemicals. Then, a voice whispered to me, seemingly from behind the house.

"You look confused," it said.

I turned with a start. At first, I thought it to be a police officer who'd discovered my location. For a while I didn't move. Then, I realized that if it were a cop, he would have apprehended me by now. I slid to the edge of the roof and looked over the side.

"Who's there?" I whispered.

No one answered. My first thought was that it was Angelo. I climbed down from the roof and walked toward a darkened corner just outside the kitchen door. As I drew nearer, I began to see a figure in the shadows. I couldn't make out who it was, but the voice I heard sounded masculine.

"Angelo?" I asked.

"No, not quite," the being replied.

I frowned and began backing away.

"You seem to fit right in with these monkeys. I would think someone of your stature would be in a more regal setting than this," said the being with an arrogant tone.

"What are you talking about? Who are you? Come out and show yourself," I said.

With that said, the figure began to advance slowly from the shadows. Each step seemed to possess a power that could shake the foundation of this city. A rather short man emerged, carrying a cane in his right hand. He wore a black suit with red pin stripes, a black shirt and a red necktie. In his lapel, he sported a rose whose color was the most red I'd ever seen. But for some reason, I still couldn't see his face.

"Who in the name of Heaven are you?" I asked.

"Heaven had nothing to do with me, just like they want nothing to do with you," replied the short man. "And the name's Huang!"

"Huang?" I said with a slight snicker.

"Yes. Moa Ding Huang to be exact," he said.

Suddenly, the wind became very cold. Although it blew gently, it carried a chill that I felt in my bones. I folded my arms across my chest, realizing that I wasn't properly dressed for this change in climate.

"Nice blouse," said Huang.

I figured he was referring to the bloodstains that were on my shirt. I looked at myself and instantly noticed something peculiar. The bloodstains were gone. In fact, my entire outfit had changed. When I left the house, I had on a long T-shirt and leggings. Now, I was wearing jeans, a blouse and my favorite boots that Angelo had bought for me.

"How did I..."

"Don't worry about it. You can thank me later," said Huang.

I looked at the little man, wondering how he was able to do this. But I knew now that some questions were better left unasked. I then heard some voices coming from across the street and peeked around the corner to see who it was. A small group of neighbors had returned and were conversing. I could overhear their conversations, in spite of the growing rumble of traffic. They were talking about Angelo, saying how nice he was and what a good neighbor he was. One woman even commented on how handsome he was and how she tried to set him up with her daughter. I smirked as I listened to the mini eulogy for my husband. Aside from their conniving actions, I was glad to hear he was well remembered.

"How nice!" said Huang as he too peeked around the corner. "Too bad he never took her daughter up on her offer, huh?"

I turned and glared at this short being. At that moment, I felt like punching him.

"You are beginning to annoy me," I said.

"Oh, please forgive me," he said laughingly.

"I know you're one of those demons working for the Contravexus. I should kill you for what you did to Angelo."

"I really wish you wouldn't do that."

"Why not? Why shouldn't I kill you? Why are you here?"

"By now, I'm sure you've been told who and what you are. You are an important piece of the prophecy, the reservoir of our lord's essence. There is a secret hidden inside of you, one that will help us to free our master from imprisonment. I've been sent to persuade you to return with me."

"Not interested."

"Please. You are the only being that knows the location of the Gate of Osiris. We need you."

"So?"

"So, that's why you should come back with me. With the gate, we can open the realm where he is imprisoned. His resurrection will bring a new order to all creation. You must join us and allow us to help you remember the location of the gate. The Contravexus is merely trying to reunite you and our master," said Huang.

"Is that why he killed my husband?" I asked angrily.

"It was nothing personal," said Huang laughingly. "Yet, we could not allow anything to interfere with our plans. Your husband was causing some serious problems for Lord Dupri. We had to remove all obstructions."

I grabbed Huang by the collar.

"You did the wrong thing! Tell your master that I'm coming for him! But I'm not coming to help him, I'm coming to kill him!" I said.

I snatched away from Huang and began walking away.

"How unfortunate," said Huang. "The Contravexus will be most displeased."

I suddenly stopped and turned to look back at him. A very sinister mood came over me and I glared at the little man with great contempt. He was busily straightening the crumpled collar I'd grabbed. His nonchalant attitude about what he and the Contravexus had cost me caused my anger to erupt.

"On second thought, *I'll* tell him," I said.

I leaped toward Huang and pushed him into the wall. My intent was to snap his neck. He fell backward and then disappeared into the shadows. I stumbled forward, but caught my balance just before I would have smacked against the wall. I was surprised to see that the imp had vanished. I looked around to see if he was hiding behind something. I could not find him. I stood there for a moment, then turned and began walking toward the alley that ran behind the house. I was no longer grieving. Instead, I was angry, for I knew who was responsible. Now, I was on a mission, a mission of revenge.

As I began to walk away, the voice of Huang echoed in the wind.

"We will meet again!" he said.

I paused for a moment, stunned by the threat. Then, I replied.

"I'll be waiting!"

I resumed my departure. As I got midway down the street, I thought about what Huang said about the Gate of Osiris. I still didn't know its whereabouts, but what I did know was that a lot rode on finding out the location of this gate. I was starting to figure some things out, but I still didn't have enough information to understand all of this. What I knew so far was that I was the vessel of this entity called the Vul Paux. I was created for the sole purpose of helping it to carry out its goals of destroying creation. My memories were blocked and the beings who could unlock the truth were the ones who stole my happiness from me. Everyone I had come in contact with seemed to know everything about me and what was going on. I, on the other hand, continued to wander about, devoid of the knowledge of my past and scared of my future.

My thoughts shifted back to my husband. Angelo was gone and I couldn't help feeling that it was my fault. But at least he was safe from any further harm. Now, I had to worry about myself. This was certainly not going to be the last time I saw any of the Contravexus' minions. They would haunt me until they got what they wanted. I wasn't safe anymore, and to make matters worse, I was alone. I couldn't truly trust the Hierarchy either because from what I knew, they were wary of me. They were more concerned about what I could potentially do than they were of me as an individual. I realized that if I were going to ever have peace in my life again, I had to get some answers, and I had to get them quickly. I had to somehow unlock my memories and remember my past. The real question was how.

As I made my way to the end of the street, I paused and looked back at the place where I had once lived. I couldn't go back there, at least not right now. For the second time, I had to leave my home. This time, however, I'd lost something I couldn't replace. I'd lost Angelo and Chloe.

~~~

As Vanifera walked away, Huang emerged from behind a garbage dumpster and stared at her. He then ducked into an alley between two homes and quickly punched in some numbers on his cell phone. Within moments, he was linked to his master, the Contravexus himself, Montellace Dupri.

"My lord, all went according to plan," said Huang.

"So, the ruse worked," said Dupri.

"Yes, it worked quite well. She believes that the body in the house was the Seraph named Angelo. In fact, she has vowed to come after you and avenge his murder."

"Excellent! Her emotions are getting the best of her and soon she will come to me. When she does, I will extract the location of the gate and our lord, the Vul Paux, will be freed."

"What will you have me do, my lord?"

"Perform the next phase of the plan. Are the police officers still there?"

"Yes. I am in front of her home and there are some cops still here."

"Then go and carry out your orders."

"Yes, my lord."

Huang disconnected, then strolled from the alley. His appearance instantly changed to a conservative looking white male. He walked toward Vanifera's house and directly toward the two remaining officers who were chatting.

"Excuse me, officers," he said.

"Yes, sir," one of them replied.

"Listen, I was out walking when I saw a suspicious woman coming down from the roof of that house," he said, pointing to the house that Vanifera was on.

"Suspicious? What was suspicious about her?" the officer asked.

"She had blood on her shirt. I'd heard that there was a murder in this house, and I found it quite odd that a woman with blood on her shirt would be so close to the scene of the crime," he said.

"How long ago did you see her?" asked the second cop.

"Just now. She was walking that way," Huang said pointing.

"Can you describe this woman?" the first officer asked.

"Yes. She's cinnamon skinned, about five foot eight, one hundred thirty pounds, long black hair and hazel eyes," said Huang.

The first officer pulled the radio handset from his epaulet and held it to his mouth.

"Unit twelve to base," he said.

"Base here."

"We have an alleged sighting of a possible suspect. Request assistance to our location."

"Roger."

The officer turned to the disguised Huang and nodded. "Thank you, sir. We appreciate the tip."

"No problem officer, just trying to help," Huang replied.

He turned and began walking away. The two officers watched as Huang turned the corner and disappeared. Then, they resumed their conversation.

~~~

The flames in the fireplace were starting to die. The old woman slowly knelt down and clasped her hands together. She began mumbling something unintelligible. Then, the voice of Dupri echoed within the room.

"Why have you summoned me, witch?" he asked.

"I've come to you to make a deal," said the old woman.

"I do not make deals."

"But I can help you. Please allow me to assist you in your

mission. I, too, seek vengeance on the beings that have taken my life from me and reduced me to this lowly existence."

"What use have I for the likes of you?"

"I was once the most beautiful woman that ever lived, able to bring any man to his knees before me. If my beauty were restored, I could use all my talents to serve you. I am as old as the mountains and possess the knowledge of all occult magic."

"Interesting. You are indeed decrepit. However, if you were as you say, I may have use for you. I recently lost my female servant, Caliestra, and am in need of another. I will agree to grant you the gift of renewed youth. However, beauty comes with a price. Along with the gift of youth comes the power of pestilence. You will need to hone this power, for it will be of some use to me later. Go and take the candle wax on that table and mix it with the blood of a serpent. Ingest the mixture, and you will be rejuvenated to the youthful appearance you once possessed. This I promise to you. But if I discover that your worth is not what you claim, you will know suffering as you have never known before," said Dupri.

"I understand. Thank you," said the woman.

~~~

CHAPTER SEVEN

Vancouver, British Columbia. The Hierarchy's Northwest Medical Facility. Sariel paced the hallways with his hands clasped behind his back. His head was bowed and a very worried expression etched his face. He'd been there for almost three hours, waiting to hear the condition of his brother, Angelo. Just then, a woman approached him.

"Sariel?" she asked.

He lifted his head and looked at her.

"Gabrielle. What are you doing here?" he asked.

"I had to come when I heard about Angelo. How's he doing?" she asked.

"I don't know. They're still working on him. I hope to hear something soon," he replied.

The two hugged, then Gabrielle sat in one of the waiting room chairs. Sariel, looking very exhausted, sat next to her. He wiped his face with his hands and rested his head against the back of the chair.

"I heard that a cop did this," said Gabrielle.

"Yeah, it was a cop that shot him, but he was possessed. It was Dupri," said Sariel.

"Did he get the Gaian?"

"No, not when I was there."

"Well, where is she now?"

Sariel gave her an uncomfortable look.

"Don't know."

"You don't know? What do you mean, you don't know?"

Gabrielle stared into his eyes. Her questioning expression loosened as she ascertained the answer.

"Tell me you didn't leave her there?" she asked.

Sariel stared at her blankly.

"For the love of God, Sariel..." said Gabrielle.

"Listen, when I saw Angelo lying there in his own blood, I reacted. I didn't think," Sariel replied.

"Damn right, you didn't."

Gabrielle reached into her pocket and removed her cell phone. She punched in a few numbers and was instantly connected to Hierarchy Headquarters.

"Yeah, its me. I need for you to track where the Gaian is. She was last seen in Seattle. Call me when you get a fix on her," she said.

Gabrielle disconnected and placed the phone back in her pocket. She turned to glare disappointedly at Sariel, who was noticeably embarrassed.

"Sometimes, I don't know about you," she said.

"Well, don't blame me for all this. None of this would have happened if you guys hadn't let her loose to pursue a normal life. You knew what she was and you let her go anyway. In fact, I wouldn't be surprised if she isn't responsible for what happened to Angelo. I'll bet you anything she was behind this," said Sariel.

Gabrielle's expression turned from disappointment to concern.

"I don't know about that, Sariel. When Angelo came to us and told us that he thought she had been reformed, I was a little skeptical. But then we performed tests and watched her for years. We thought she had been rehabilitated and to make sure, Angelo asked to be the one to watch her. With her memories blocked, we gave her a new identity. She seemed fine and for the last couple of years there were no problems. However, now that this has happened, I must say that I always felt a little uneasy about releasing her. After all, she was the vessel of the most vile spirit ever created. Deception is one of its strong suits," she said.

"Yeah, well, now we know," he said. "Incidentally, did you know they were married?"

"Yes."

"Figures. Why am I always the last to know these things?"

Gabrielle chuckled, then she returned to her more serious demeanor. "Do you really think the Gaian was the one that orchestrated this?"

"Yes, I do. And if Angelo doesn't pull through this, I will hunt her down and kill her myself," said Sariel.

~~~

Meanwhile, in a dark, mosquito-infested portion of the swamp, a swayed back horse pulled a ragged, wooden wagon down an unpaved path. A small lantern dangled around its neck, illuminating the way. The pace of the horse was slow and steady. The clopping of its hooves echoed within the darkened woods as the chirping of crickets serenaded the shadows of the night.

As the horse continued its trek down the path, an image of someone could be seen ever so slightly in the driver's seat. Their back was humped and the individual feebly held the reigns of the horse. It was the old woman. She was shrouded with the same red smock that she used to cover her legs by the fire.

"Thata boy, Timothy. Easy does it," said the old woman with a frail tone.

She clutched a brown tattered pouch containing a handful of the candle dust from the table. It swayed with the bouncing of the wagon as the old woman and her steed continued down the path. The dew had begun to settle in the fields and along the trail. Its moistness mixed with the sandy path, covering the trail with a thin layer of mud. The light from the crescent moon barely sliced through the moss covered limbs of the trees. The darkness of the swamp gave little hint that morning was on the verge of breaking. The gloominess of the surrounding woods would make the bravest of individuals proceed with caution. Yet, the old woman seemed un-phased by it all. She appeared to be hypnotized by the cadence of her steed and the dangling of the pouch. Her eyes stared into the darkness ahead of her without a blink. Her body swayed as the wagon rocked from side to side, surrendering to every stone and pit in the dirt road.

Suddenly, the horse stopped in its tracks. The sudden halt caused the contents in the rear of the wagon to shift forward. The old woman broke her concentrated stare and glanced at the horse.

"See something, Timothy?" she asked.

The horse grunted and nodded its head.

"Well, I guess we better take a look, eh?" she said.

She laid the pouch she had been clutching on the seat. Then, the old woman slid gingerly to the edge of the bench and began her descent. She desperately grabbed the side of the wagon, carefully planting each foot in each rung. After a few moments, she stood on the muddy path, bracing herself against the wagon. She removed a wooden cane that was securely fastened on the side. She tested it to ensure its sturdiness by placing some of her weight on the handle. Then, the old woman began walking toward the head of the horse.

As she reached its head, she patted him on his neck and removed the lantern that was attached to his harness. She turned and began walking away from Timothy, shining the light on the ground, trying to find out what made him stop in his tracks. She quickly got her answer.

A cottonmouth, coiled in an attack position, stared defiantly at the woman. It sat in the middle of the trail, almost as if it were daring them to try and pass. Hissing with all the breath contained in its deadly coiled body, the snake remained unmoved as it rebelliously leered at the advancing old woman.

"Well, hello there," she said in a grandmotherly voice. "And how are you doing tonight?"

The serpent hissed and parted its lips to reveal its beautifully cotton-like lined mouth. Its fangs dripped the ever so poisonous venom, showing its ill intent for the woman. Yet despite its threatening posture, the woman continued to approach, slowly coming closer to the snake's face. She was within striking distance, inches away from the snake's face as it tightened its coiled body.

Suddenly, the venomous serpent leaped forward. It lashed

toward the old woman with the speed of lightning. Its fanged mouth was opened to its fullest and it attempted to bury them into the old woman's eye. However, before the cottonmouth could complete its attack, the woman caught the snake in its mid air strike. She lifted it off the ground, hanging it by its scaly neck. The helpless serpent wrapped around her arm as it fruitlessly attempted to free itself from her vice-like grip. The old woman pulled the snake close to her face and examined her helpless captive. She stared into its eyes as if she were trying to understand why it defied her. Then, she pulled the snake away from her face to examine the rest of it.

"It was your kind that caused my fall from grace! How fitting that it will be your kind that will resurrect me from the clutches of time and allow me one last opportunity at redemption!" she said.

By now, the snake had wrapped its entire body around her arm in a desperate attempt to free itself. With one swift movement, the old woman shoved the head of the snake into her mouth and bit it off. The serpent's body flinched, then continued to struggle and writhe as she spat the decapitated head at the feet of her horse. The serpent's blood flowed from its neck and down her hand. Its body surrendered its remaining life in her grip. The old woman turned and looked at Timothy who had calmly observed the incident and patiently waited for her to finish. She wiped her mouth and began walking toward the wagon with her cane and lantern in one hand and the snake's body in the other. The horse snuffed in approval, almost as if he were proud that she had completed this disgusting task. She made her way back to the horse and continued to the front of the wagon. She stopped next to the driver's area and braced herself against the side in order to catch her breath.

The woman placed the lantern on the wagon bench and propped her cane against the side. She grabbed the tattered pouch of candle dust she laid on the seat. Next, she opened the pouch, placed the dripping neck of the snake inside and began squeezing blood from the snake's body into the pouch. The mixture of candle dust and blood produced a cloud of green mist accompanied by a foul stench. The old woman dropped the remains of the cottonmouth on the ground and slid her blood-covered hand into the pouch. She began mixing the two components together.

The mixture of the blood and dust created a paste-like substance. She scooped some of it on her two fingers and pulled it from the pouch. The paste emitted a trail that swirled in the air like the coiling snake whose blood helped to create it. She lifted the foul concoction to her nose and took a whiff. Her nose scrunched as the overwhelming stench caused tears to well in her eyes. The smell alone would disable a battalion of the most elite soldiers in any army. But aside from the tears, the stench seemed to have no effect on her.

She examined the texture of the paste. The foul mixture sounded as if it were hissing on her fingers. Then, without so much as a thought, the old woman shoved the paste into her mouth and slid her fingers from between her lips. She frowned from the bitterness of the paste and it burned her mouth and tongue. She began gagging instantly from the potency and flavor of the blood and wax. It caused her to jerk uncontrollably. Her cane slid down the side of the wagon and fell on the ground. She gripped the side of the wagon, attempting to steady herself and remain on her feet. The toxic blend raced through her body as she moaned and frothed at the mouth.

The poison continued to seep into every part of her anatomy, and the woman realized that she could no longer remain standing. She fell to the ground on her knees with a stunned look on her face. The poisonous concoction was taking its toll on her, making the old woman weaker by the second. She dropped the pouch on the ground and clutched her chest. Gurgling noises emitted from her throat. She began heaving in an attempt to bring up the bitter potion. Her stomach muscles contracted and her vision started to become blurry. A throbbing pain pounded in her head and traveled down her arms and trunk. The poison was contaminating every limb and every muscle.

Struggling, she attempted to stand on her feet. But by now, the toxin had seeped into every muscle in her body. She fell back to her knees and then to all fours. The poisonous mixture had begun to strip her of the life force she was fighting so desperately to keep. On the surface, it would appear that she would lose this battle. The boasting she made to the snake seemed to have backfired.

"You promised me! You promised me!" she exclaimed.

She lifted her head and released a scream that would curl the blood. Then, she attempted once more to stand to her feet and climb back into the wagon. However, her strength was gone and her body had become numb from the toxin. Near paralysis, she struggled to catch her breath, but soon found that even doing that brought extreme pain. She began shaking violently. Her motor functions were diminishing. Then, the old woman tucked her chin and collapsed to the ground.

Her body lay motionless. Her heart and breathing had stopped. Her eyes were fixed and open. It appeared that she'd been betrayed by the Contravexus, and death had claimed another soul in the darkness of the night. The bigger question was why? Whatever the reason, the old woman's body now laid prone on the muddy trail, surrounded by the darkness and silence of the woods.

~~~

Morning was on the verge of breaking. The rays were just starting to emerge behind Mt. Rainier. I'd caught a bus into downtown Seattle and had been wandering the streets all night. There was a safe house that I was instructed to go to in times like these, but for some strange reason, I was unable to locate it. I was exhausted and starving. With everything that had happened last night, it dawned on me that I hadn't eaten in hours. Though, how could I be thinking about food at a time like this? I should be thinking about how I was going to avenge the death of my husband. Nothing else was important anymore, not even eating or resting. My chest still ached with a deep pain that could only be understood by those who've experienced the loss of someone dear. I actually felt guilty for thinking of my personal needs instead of my mission.

I suddenly felt lightheaded, probably from the lack of both

food and rest. Logic started kicking in. Perhaps a meal would be the best thing right now. Besides, it would give me a place to rest briefly before I began my quest to hunt down the Contravexus. Fighting him in my current state would be a big mistake. In fact, fighting him at all was potentially a death wish. It definitely wasn't the wisest thing to do, but it was something I had to do.

I started looking for a restaurant that was open this time of morning. It was the first time I had looked up the entire night. My hunger now grew with every passing minute. It was still early, but I figured there had to be a diner or at least a convenience store open. However, every restaurant and store I came across was closed. It seemed strange that nothing was open. I continued walking the avenues and alleyways, searching for a place to eat.

As I walked down one of the alleys, I came across a man lying inside a cardboard box. He raised his head and looked at me as I approached. He was a scruffy guy with food stains on his clothes. As I drew closer, he lifted his hand toward me.

"Hey lady, you got any change?"

I knew I didn't have much money. As a matter of fact, I only had a five-dollar bill and some change. At the same time, I also knew that I couldn't ignore someone who needed help. I felt obligated, especially after hearing about my vile past. He appeared to be genuine and in much more need of the money than I. I reached into my pocket and removed the five. Then, I placed it gently into his hands.

"I hope this helps," I said.

The man looked at his hand in amazement. Then, he lifted his head and looked at me, still wearing the same amazed expression. He suddenly stood to his feet, causing me to step back and raise my arms slightly in self-defense. I sensed that I had nothing to fear, but right now, I wasn't taking any chances. He looked at me, almost as if he couldn't believe that someone actually acknowledged him and helped him. He grabbed my hand, kissing the back of it as a grateful servant would kiss the hand of his monarch.

"Thank you!" exclaimed the man with tears welling in his eyes.

I frowned as I slowly retracted my hand from his. At that moment, I found myself staring into his eyes that glistened from the streetlight overhead. They seemed to be filled with sorrow and shame, as if he were responsible for some wrong deed that caused him to be in his current state. Ironically, behind the humiliation and guilt was a familiarity to this man. I didn't recall ever seeing his face before, and yet, I somehow felt that this person was someone I'd once known. I began looking at the features of his face for clues. But I could find nothing that would help me figure out who he was.

The man suddenly performed a little dance of joy, probably from the money I'd just given to him. He completed his dance and shook my hand once more.

"You're welcome, sir," I said.

The old man smiled, showing the few teeth he had remaining. I turned and walked toward the end of the alley. I began feeling nauseous, probably due to the sight of the man's cavity ravaged mouth. I tend to think it was because I was still hungry. I knew that I had to find the safe house now because I'd just given the last bit of money I had to the old man. At a time like this, that probably wasn't the smartest thing I could have done.

"Great. Way to go, Vanifera," I said to myself.

I was beginning to feel cold in the damp dawn air. My encounter with the bum was beginning to fade from my immediate thoughts as I continued my search for the safe house. I was beginning to feel ill from the hunger and I was about ready to drop from fatigue. I needed to find someplace to rest very quickly.

As I approached the end of the alley, I heard a voice from behind me. It sounded like the bum I just walked away from.

"Just look to the right!" exclaimed the voice. "They'll take care of you!"

I was startled by his scream and halted in my tracks. I quickly turned around to look at the old man, but to my surprise, he was gone. Only the torn cardboard box remained, flapping near the doorway along with scattered debris and newspapers. The streetlight flickered and my eyes widened slightly. Only moments ago, an old tattered bum stood mere feet away from me and kissed my hand. Now, he was gone. I looked around to see if he was hiding. But this alley had nothing for him to hide behind, not even a dumpster. I frowned as I continued to survey the area. It made me wonder whether I actually saw what I thought I saw.

"I know I'm hungry now. I'm starting to hallucinate," I said.

I checked my pocket to see if my money was still there. It wasn't. My mind was weary and troubled, and my stomach was empty. I shook my head in an attempt to discard the entire affair and resumed my trek from the alley.

As I turned the corner, I saw a gleam of light about a block down the street. It was an all-night diner. The sight of the restaurant was like a beacon in the fog. This was supposed to be the seedy side of town, but at this moment I didn't care. All I wanted was some food. Then, it dawned on me. The voice I heard in the alley was guiding me to the restaurant. It was to the right when I exited the alley. But how did the old man know what I was searching for? For that matter, was there an old man?

This entire night was beginning to bother me. First, there was the encounter with Sariel, then Angelo and Chloe's deaths. Next, there was the appearance of Huang and now, the old man in the alley. I knew I needed to find some answers because it was obvious that the Contravexus' forces were at work. But were they helping me or were they leading me into harms way?

Just then, a car pulled up to the curb in front of me. A man tilted himself from the driver's side toward the lowered passenger window.

"Hey sweetheart, how much?" he asked.

I scowled at him.

"You've made a mistake! I'm not what you think I am!" I said.

"Maybe not, but I'll give you five hundred big ones if you'll let me find out!" he said with a disgusting smirk.

I walked to the passenger window where he waved the money like a flag. I bent over and looked into his lust-filled eyes. I lifted my hand and stroked the side of his face.

"Sleep!" I said.

I punched the man in the face and he fell on the front seat. I looked at him lying unconscious and then I looked at the five hundred dollars that now lay on the floor. My first instinct was to take some of it. It wasn't like I couldn't use it right now and he did offer it to me. I reached down to grab one of the one hundred dollar bills, but then I stopped. I backed away from the car, clasping my hands together. Although I knew I could use the money, I could not take any of it. It just didn't feel right.

I turned and quickly walked toward the restaurant. As I got to the doors, I gave one more glance at the car I'd just left and wondered if I'd done the right thing by leaving the money. Perhaps this was an awkwardly presented gift from the unknown and unseen forces swirling around me. Maybe the old man in the alley was a test of my generosity and I'd passed the test. But I also knew that in matters such as these, you must rely on your instincts. If it felt wrong, then it was wrong. Although the money was offered, it wasn't my money to take. With that thought, I grabbed the handle on the glass door of the restaurant and opened it.

A feeling of relief overcame me as I walked inside. The lighting in the diner was much more comforting than the dimly lit scene of the alley. I felt safe here and it seemed comfortable enough to allow me to get some much-needed rest. The décor of the diner was typical. A long counter stretched in front of the pick-up window. Napkin holders were in front of every other stool with menus propped behind them. Doughnuts and pie slices sat under pedestal cake stands covered with a domed glass top. The smell of fried grease filled the air and the crackling of something cooking on the stovetop resounded from the kitchen. The floors were covered with a waxy build-up and the leather seat cushions were covered with patches of gray duct tape. But despite the less than five star appearance, I was glad to be there. I didn't care what the place looked like at this point as long as the food was good and there were lots of lights.

As I scanned around the dingy diner, I saw a middle-aged lady standing behind the counter. At first, she looked at me with a startled expression, but then turned and continued counting her receipts. Perhaps her expression was from the way I had entered the diner. She quickly finished her count, then she turned and gave me a smile.

"Mornin' hun, what can I get ya?" she asked with a southern accent.

"I'm not sure," I replied. "Can I sit down for a moment?"

"Sure hun, have a seat!" said the woman.

With a damp dishcloth, she cleaned a booth table for me, then walked into the kitchen. The table was still damp from the rushed cleaning job. I slid into the booth and attempted to get comfortable. The hard padding of the booth seat felt as if I was sitting on a wooden bench, and it made it hard for me to get comfortable. I slid down slightly and braced my feet on the opposing seat. I released a huge sigh of relief as I tried to relax and clear my thoughts. Perhaps by focusing on something else, I would get the respite I needed.

I stared at the crumbling tile on the ceiling and thought about how disgusting and unattractive that was. Then, I wondered how long it had been that way and if there were any other crumbling roof areas, namely over the stove. I truly hoped that wasn't something I had to worry about since I didn't have the strength to look for another diner.

As I continued to stare at the ceiling, my thoughts shifted to Angelo and Chloe. I still couldn't believe they were gone. My mind kept wanting to believe that I was going to walk into the house and find the both of them waiting for me. But I had held Angelo in my arms as his body turned cold. I saw the paramedics remove a body from my house and heard the confirmation of his identity by one of the officers. I also saw Chloe's blood drenched body lying on the floor of the apartment. Sariel's attempts to save Angelo had apparently failed and the life I once knew was gone. Tears welled in my eyes once more, and the regret of leaving them began to consume me.

The empty pain returned to my chest. I kept reliving the moment in my mind, trying to see if there was something I could have done differently. But every possibility I pondered resulted in the same outcome. There was nothing I could have done. Angelo was a marked man and it was just a matter of time before they got him. Even if I had told him about the vision, I doubt that it would've done any good.

As the grim reality settled in my mind, a stream of tears rolled down my cheeks. The truth was still too hard to accept. He'd done so much to protect me and to make sure I was okay. But when it came right down to it all, he couldn't save himself. The sheer irony of it was maddening.

Suddenly, the waitress returned with a pot of coffee and a coffee cup. I sat up and quickly tried to wipe the tears from my face. I glanced up at the woman who stood there waiting for me to gather myself. She compassionately smiled, then lowered the cup onto the table and began pouring the coffee.

"You alright, suga?" she asked.

I finished wiping the tears from my face and attempted to regain some composure.

"No, but I will be," I replied.

The woman tilted her head and pursed her lips. Her look of compassion and warmth reassured me.

"I just gave my last bit of money to a guy in the alley. He looked like he needed it more than I did," I confessed.

"Did he rob you?" she asked.

"No. He just looked like he needed it more. He was living in a box in the alley," I said.

The woman looked at me with her head still tilted. It was as if she was trying to read my expression to see if I was telling the truth. I continued to wipe my face and regroup. The woman removed a napkin from the dispenser and handed it to me.

"Rough night, huh?" she asked.

"You just don't know how rough," I replied.

I removed another napkin from the dispenser. The waitress placed her hand on my shoulder.

"I'll be right back," she said.

As she walked from the table and into the kitchen, I continued wiping my eyes, trying to stop myself from crying. I didn't want to seem like I was some pity case. Just as I finished, a voice spoke from across the table.

"Sorry how things turned out, kid."

I lifted my head to see the Barhim Hajj sitting in the opposite booth.

"Where did you come from?" I asked.

"Long story! But first, we need to get you back on track," he said.

"Back on track? What do you mean, back on track?"

"Lower your voice! Remember, no one can see me but you."

"So what! You think I care if someone thinks I'm going crazy right now? To tell you the truth, I'm not so sure that I'm not! Do you know what has happened to me in the past few hours?" I asked.

"Yes, I do! But I'm here to help you because its going to get worse," said Hajj.

"Oh, well thank you for that bit of cheery news!"

"You may not realize this, but you are a very important part in the events that are taking place. Angelo's shooting was merely the beginning. You have much to learn and you don't have much time to learn it."

"Listen, Barhim Hajj, or whoever you are! I don't care about the events that are taking place or the people associated with it! My husband has just been killed! My entire life has come crumbling down around me! So, if you don't mind, I'd like to be left alone for a while! I'm sure that the universe will be fine without me!" I said in a very harsh tone.

"As you wish!" said Hajj. Then, he faded from sight.

The woman came back from the kitchen with a plate in her hand. She brought it to the table and placed it in front of me. It was a cheeseburger with all the toppings and a side of French Fries. I stared at the plate for a moment and then I looked back at her.

"I wasn't very hungry anyway," she said.

"This is for me?" I asked. "But I told you I don't have any money."

"Call it a gift. Now, you better hurry and eat before the soup line opens," she advised.

Without another word, I picked up the cheeseburger and began eating. Because of my hunger, the burger tasted better than anything I could think of. My hunger had consumed me to the point where I was eating faster than I normally did. My cheeks were stuffed and I devoured the cheeseburger ravenously.

The waitress shook her head and walked away from the table. I guess she didn't want to witness the unladylike way I was eating. Within a few minutes, the entire plate was bare. Even the coffee cup was dry. My hunger had been satisfied and now I needed a little rest before I began my hunt for Montellace Dupri.

~~~

CHAPTER EIGHT

I sat back and took a deep breath. I wiped my mouth with a napkin and stared at the ugly ceiling once more, feeling a little embarrassed for my lack of manners. Not only had I eaten the meal like a barbarian, but I also didn't thank the waitress for her kindness and generosity. I turned to look for her, but I couldn't see her. She had returned to the kitchen and hadn't been back to the table the entire time I ate, not that I could blame her. At first, I thought it would be a good time to leave. However, I didn't want her to feel that her gesture of kindness wasn't appreciated. Besides, I needed to close my eyes for a few minutes, just long enough to refresh my senses.

As I began falling to sleep, I thought about Barhim Hajj and what he'd said to me when he appeared across the table. He didn't seem the least bit concerned about Angelo or my grief over his death. I knew that things were happening as we spoke, but surely some compassion could be shown for the things I'd been through. In my dreams, all sorts of images raced in my head. I saw Angelo walking toward me and a fire blazed behind him. Sariel was walking next to him, as well as the bum I met in the alley. I also saw three shadowed images, standing in the fires behind Angelo and the others. I stood before all of them, confused, frustrated and scared. I didn't know what to do. I tried to collect my thoughts, but everything seemed so clouded and unclear. One thing I did know, they were all after me.

At that moment, the waitress returned to my table and I opened my eyes with a start.

"How you feelin', hun?" she asked.

"Fine." I answered, sitting up in the seat. "I wanted to thank you for the meal. I really appreciated it."

"Aw shucks, sweetie, it was nuthin'!" she answered. "By the way, what's your name?"

"Vanifera," I replied.

"Oh, what a lovely name. Well, Vanifera, my name is Betty. Would you like a slice of apple pie?"

"Yes, thank you."

"Alright, I'll go and heat you up a slice."

Betty turned and walked into the kitchen once again. A huge yawn caught me by surprise and I shook it off quickly. I didn't know how long I'd been asleep, but I did feel a little better. If I had a few more hours to rest, I could probably think clearer. However, my options of places to go were limited. I probably couldn't go back to the house right now and staying with friends didn't seem right either because I didn't want to place them in any danger.

I decided that I needed to get up and allow my meal to settle. I slid from the booth and stood to stretch my body. I then walked to the window next to the counter and gazed out at the sun as it began its ritualistic ascension in the sky. It was just visible, like a child peeping over the top of Mt. Rainier. It reminded me of the mornings when Angelo and I used to gaze from our bedroom window in San Francisco and watch the night slowly dissolve into morning. It was truly one of my most treasured memories.

Morning seemed to always bring such promise. However, this morning didn't seem quite as welcomed or promising as others in the past. It didn't elicit the warmth I used to feel when I watched the sun rise into the sky. In fact, it seemed cold and routine. It made me realize that regardless of what chaos or tribulation one might experience in their lives, life will continue and a new day will come. It still didn't make my pain any easier to bear. This would be the first of many sunrises I would not have Angelo there to share with me. That fact alone prompted me to close my eyes and wish this day would somehow be delayed.

The memories flooded my mind instantly. It was like a vision that had pulled me back to the house. I relived the entire ordeal again. I saw the shots from the gun explode and Angelo's limp body fall to the floor. I saw the look on the cop's face just before he jumped to his death.

"Damn it all!" I said as I grimaced from the frustration I suddenly felt.

I clenched my fists in anger and squeezed my eyes more tightly, attempting to shut out the pain. The more I tried, the more my heart ached. Was there nothing I could do to ease the pain or take it away?

I began thinking about the vision I had just before Angelo was shot. It was like a premonition, warning me of what was to come. I saw the gunman and the shots fired, as well as Angelo's body falling to the ground. However, it happened so fast that I didn't know what it was or what I was supposed to do. I'd never experienced anything like that before and the consequences of my ignorance were severe. I'd lost my husband and my dog, simply because I didn't know.

Then, I remembered what Dupri said to me just before he made that cop leap to his death. He said my powers were returning and that it wouldn't be long before my memories returned. Was he telling the truth? Although regaining my memories would answer a lot of questions, could I risk what could potentially happen if Dupri managed to get the information he needed from my memories? What kind of hell would he unleash? For that matter, what kind of monster would I become?

As I struggled with my thoughts, I heard the sound of a television. I opened my eyes and saw one at the end of the counter. The sight of the TV further worsened the pain I was already feeling. Angelo and I were watching television just before he was murdered. The flashback along with the television was too much for me to deal with. I turned and started walking back to the booth. It was time for me to leave. But then, I heard something that stopped me in my tracks. The early edition of the news was being broadcast.

"To recap this morning's breaking story, a double murder happened last night in Federal Way. One of the victims was a male in his early thirties. He was found shot to death in his home. Neighbors say they heard a scuffle and then shots were fired. This happened around nine last night. A few miles away another body was found, this time a police officer who apparently fell to his death from the roof. Investigators suspect that the officer was chasing the assailant of the first murder when he was somehow thrown off the roof. The grizzly incident has some of the local residents worried," said the reporter.

Next, they began playing the interviews of the people they spoke with. The murdered individuals were Angelo and the officer that committed suicide. I looked at the television as the reporter continued to talk about the details surrounding their murders and what the police believed to be a lead in locating the suspect. I lowered my head as the anchorman continued his report. I could still feel Angelo's cold body as I cradled him in my arms. I watched him as he gasped for breath. Yes, I remember it all. Yet, as I stood there, I began to feel anger instead of sorrow. Why did he have to die? What was the purpose to all this suffering, and when was it going to end?

As the anger swelled in my chest, I could hear in the background that the police had a description of the murder suspect. At that moment, I saw the cop's face in my mind. I could see the scar on his left cheek and the bitter disdain he displayed when he fired those shots. I could never forget his face.

As I lifted my head, I saw that Betty had returned. She was staring at me with a nervous expression. I was a little puzzled at first, until I looked at the television. I couldn't believe what I saw. They had placed the picture of the murder suspect on the screen. The suspect was me.

~~~

San Francisco, California. The Fairmont Hotel on Nob Hill, Presidential Suite. A big screen television displayed a very similar newscast to the one showing at the diner in Seattle. A scan around the room revealed the plush surroundings with all of the comforts any human could want. Expensive wine-colored tapestry donned the walls accented with hand carved molding of ivory. Gold trimming lined the furniture and the floor was covered with plush deep garnet carpeting.

In the center of the room, three naked women, one Black, one European and one Asian, entwined their bodies on the bed, grinding against and kissing one another. They fondled and caressed each other's bodies with passionate, animal-like enthusiasm. This scene of lustful indulgence would make voyeurs weak. Yet, one individual did not display a shred of interest. On the couch across the room, a naked man sat. One of his legs was propped on the edge of the leather and satin antique as he stared unblinkingly at the reporter on the fifty-inch big screen. His demeanor seemed to indicate he was hanging on every word the reporter said. He knew this story well; he actually helped create it.

As the reporter finished the points of his report, the man rose from the couch and walked towards the window, gazing at the beautiful Bay City. His silhouette against the delicate panels that decorated the window gave him a god-like appearance. He stared at the rising sun and contemplated the news he'd just heard. The European woman stopped her indulgence for a moment and looked at the man as he locked his hands behind him.

"Aren't you going to come back to bed?" she whispered to him with her thick European accent.

The man remained silent as the other women paused their activities and waited for his response. Moments passed without an answer. Realizing that he was not going to respond to the question, the women resumed their lustful exploits, hoping that they could entice the pondering stud to participate once again. But as they continued their festivities, it would come to pass that their sexually ravenous exploits would herald the last moments of their lives.

Suddenly, the three women exploded into a huge ball of flames. It happened so quickly that they didn't have a chance to scream. The flames were intense and their bodies melted within moments. After a few seconds, the flames were gone and so were the women. All that was left was a pile of ashes where the bodies used to be. The man took his stare from the outside and advanced to the bed where the luscious threesome once laid. The silk sheets showed no traces of the fire, despite the smoldering piles of ashes. In fact, the bed was virtually undamaged and a hint of roses lingered in the air.

The morning sunrise increased in intensity and further illuminated the palatial hotel room. His face could now be seen. He sported a scar on his left cheek as his baldhead reflected the glow of the rising sun. His name was known to many; yet, he was the most undetectable entity on the planet. He was the killer of worlds and the enslaver of souls. His name was Montellace Dupri, and he was the Contravexus.

He slid his hands into the pile of ashes and scooped a handful. Then, he answered the now deceased woman's question.

"Sure, I'd love to."

He stared at the pile of smoldering human remains. His eyes began to glow slightly as the rest of the broadcast played in the background. Everything was going according to plan. He'd caused the cop to leap to his death and orchestrated the shooting of Angelo. However, he knew the Seraph wasn't dead. Instead, he had Huang put a fake body in the house so that the Gaian would believe that he was dead and come after him to gain revenge. To ensure that she wouldn't be able to figure it out, he would have the police looking for her, keeping her on the run at all times. With Angelo out of the way, he had easy access to Vanifera. She would come to him and there was no one to stop her. He was now within an eyelash of discovering the location of the Gate of Osiris. Once he had found that, he could complete his mission and resurrect the Vul Paux.

He was at the threshold of victory, but he could leave nothing to chance. He had invested too much time in planning and preparing for this coup. The essence of his quest could only be understood by those who were like him. With his master defeated, he and the rest of the Vul Paux's followers were reduced to mere bottom-feeders. He had managed to use his abilities to influence the humans and attain a level of existence worthy of his god-like status. All things considered, the true reward lied in finding the gate and releasing his master.

He remembered the entire incident as if it just happened. Dupri stood by his master's side when the final blow of battle was made. The Messiah hung from the cross. The apostles all knelt before their savior as he cried and took his last breath. It was believed to be the decisive move in favor of the Vul Paux. But then, something peculiar happened. All the power contained in the vessel that the Vul Paux inhabited was removed. His master bellowed in pain as he and all the forces of sin were pulled into a huge vortex. The vessel fell to the ground, dazed and powerless. The angelic host suddenly descended and nearly annihilated the remaining members of his army. Dupri managed to escape, but the angels had captured their prize, the vessel of his master, the Gaian.

Dupri spent eons working to build his empire. When he'd finally become the most powerful entity on the planet, he began searching for the Gaian. He remembered that his master had created a gateway, which would allow him to pass between the seven realms of the universe. If the gate were opened, his master would have a portal through which he could escape the realm he was imprisoned in and return to reclaim his once powerful rule. Dupri had also managed to exponentially increase the amount of sin and evil in the world, thus providing his master with all the power he needed to defeat Jehovah. Only one piece of the puzzle remained, the gate. He believed that the knowledge of the gate's whereabouts was still locked in the mind of the Gaian. He could take her by force, but to do so would be blasphemous. To force a vessel of his God to come to him would incur a wrath too terrible to say. That's why she had to be convinced to come to him voluntarily. That way, when she was able to regain her memory, she could resume her mission without any malice toward him.

He raised the ashes of the women to his face and blew the handful of human remains into the air. The dust expanded into a cloud of gray. Before it could begin settling, the cloud suddenly began swirling in the air. An explosion of flames burst from the eye of the circle and transformed the surroundings of the once elegantly decorated suite into a realm of decaying bodies, bones and blood.

The smell of brimstone filled the air as the wails of the damned echoed around him. Dupri stood in front of the spiraling cloud that had now transformed into a dimensional portal. The image of the one known as Huang appeared.

"Have you completed your task?" asked Dupri.

"All is in readiness, my master. As we speak, the cops are out searching for the Gaian," said Huang.

"Au ru ik litrau satdu broush is tell mymutoa danya altosh," said Dupri.

The words were from the most ancient of tongues, older than any civilization. Loosely translated it means, 'The reign of the beast and the fall of the realms has arrived.'

"And what will you have me do next, my lord?" asked Huang.

"I will let you know soon, very soon," replied Dupri. "The time will be at hand shortly where we will exact revenge on those that persecuted us. We must show them no mercy, just as they've shown us."

"I will leave you now, my lord, and await further instructions," replied Huang.

As Dupri turned to walk away, the swirl of dust stopped its spiraling and cascaded to the floor. The settled ashes began to smolder and within moments erupted into an intense blaze, spreading rapidly throughout the room. Upon the eruption of the flames, clothing appeared on Dupri's body, almost as if he were never disrobed. He calmly opened the door and walked into the smoke-filled hallway. The entire building was now burning. The dark cloud of soot had already blanketed the halls. The smoke alarms blared and collapsing people cluttered Dupri's path. The clamoring of panicked humans echoed as they rumbled down the stairwell. He snickered beneath his breath, knowing that they would not escape.

Screams from inside the other rooms could be heard as he passed by them. They were the screams of the helpless souls that were trapped in their rooms. These people would be the first to incur the wrath of the Contravexus. Soon, all of mankind would suffer the same or an even worse fate. Dupri walked to the doors of the elevator and pressed the down button. The bell dinged, announcing the elevator's arrival. The doors opened and Dupri stepped onto it, turning to stare down the flaming hallway filled with unconscious people. He reached into his pocket and retrieved a cigarette. A dead man leaned against the side of the elevator cabin. The sleeve of his coat was still on fire. Dupri leaned over and lit his cigarette from the man's sleeve as the elevator doors closed. He took two puffs and pressed the lobby button. The elevator descended. Each floor he passed had the blared screams of the people that were perishing in the hellacious flames. He chuckled to himself again as he drew once more on his cigarette. He hated humans, and he despised the fact that Jehovah would favor them so. These humans broke all of his commandments, blasphemed and disrespected him. Dupri felt they were arrogant and disobedient, unworthy of the blessings they'd been given. He was a god, capable of destroying everything on the face of this planet in the blink of an eye. Yet, he was obedient to his master and followed his commands without question. He'd seen the humans break every commandment of the God they served, yet, with a simple plea of forgiveness, Jehovah would grant them redemption, a privilege that was never offered to him or his brethren. In many respects, he couldn't understand why the angels fought so hard to protect the humans. If nothing else, they should be working with him and his brethren to destroy them.

The elevator began to decelerate and finally halted at the lobby level. As the doors opened, Dupri calmly strolled off as the hotel staff raced about trying to evacuate the facility. As the patrons sprinted to the emergency exit doors, they discovered that every door in the building could not be opened. The panicked crowd began throwing chairs into windows and banging on the doors. However, their attempts for salvation proved useless. The glass would not break and the doors would not open.

Dupri surveyed the chaos. His eyes rested upon a young woman praying in the middle of the floor. She was crying, asking God to help them escape this situation. Dupri shook his head. He knew that this was the first time this woman had ever prayed and it took a catastrophe such as this to bring her to her knees. That further proved his point.

He walked to the main entrance and turned the doorknob. He opened the door and began exiting. One panic stricken patron turned to see Dupri opening the front door.

"Look, there's a door opened over there!" screamed the man.

Just as the mob attempted to stampede toward their last chance at salvation, Dupri took the cigarette from his mouth and flicked it in their direction. The smoldering blunt bounced on the floor. Suddenly, a blast of flames shot from the ignited end and engulfed the approaching mob, incinerating them into ashes instantly. The charred dust of the dead drifted in the air as the rest of the trapped patrons paused and covered their heads in horror. Dupri laughed hysterically, then turned and walked out of the door.

As he left the once plush hotel, the sound of sirens and panic filled the air. This was nothing new to Dupri, for he caused most of the major catastrophes in the world. He was the unseen instigator, the unholy shadow player. He arrogantly walked away from the flaming building. This was only the second move in the endgame for this world, and yet, the humans didn't know it. In his mind, he had actually done the people trapped in the hotel a favor. They will never know the horror that was to come.

Dupri disappeared as the crowd of onlookers gawked in amazement at the burning building. Scorched bodies were seen in the windows as the remaining patrons banged on the glass pleading for help. The flames continued their ravenous rampage, engulfing the entire structure.

Then, the hotel suddenly collapsed upon itself. The implosion happened so quickly that the smoke from the flames was pulled down with the hotel. Within moments, the once magnificent structure was gone and all that remained was a huge smoke cloud that loomed over the area where the massive hotel once stood. As the mushroom shaped cloud began to rise over the city, a burning banner dangled from one of the trees in the park. It read, 'Welcome to the First Annual Christian Leadership Conference'.

~~~

In the marsh of the bayou, morning had come. The air was still and fresh, possessing a clean smell, like that after a spring shower. The sky was painted with orange-yellow and laced with a layer of cumulonimbi. The grass blades stretched toward the heavens, and the trees that were so intimidating in the night now appeared to have an approachable nature to them. Their branches seemed to wave as a gentle breeze began to blow. It didn't seem logical that a place so dark and foreboding at night would evolve into a scene of beauty and luster during the day.

Butterflies danced in the air, celebrating their joy and appreciation for another day. Chirping birds were heard from the trees above and the dew-covered grass began relinquishing its moisture in the morning sunlight. Truly, this was a magnificent setting, one which storytellers envisioned as they reminisced about the good old days of running through fields. But this was not to be an ordinary day nor was this an ordinary field. It would become a day and place that spawned a demon that would leave an indelible mark on this world.

A wagon that once carried the body of an elderly woman stood motionless amidst a shady setting. The steed that pulled the wagon grazed on a tuft of grass. Nearby, the body of an elderly woman laid face down in the dirt. She'd been this way since the ingestion of a toxic potion a few hours ago. Her tattered garments gently flapped in the breeze, and the peaceful surroundings provided a fitting resting place. The horse raised its head from his morning grub and stared at the lifeless body that lay on the trail. He stood motionlessly for a few moments, almost as if he sensed something.

The butterflies stopped their dancing, and the birds ended their song and quickly flew away. A slight breeze rustled the leaves in the trees and possessed a hint of sweet lilac. The smell enhanced the freshness of the morning air and lingered gently amidst the dense foliage of the marsh.

Suddenly, the right hand of the old woman began to move. It trembled at first, then contracted its fingers into a fist, trapping a handful of dirt in its clutches. Slowly, the rest of the body began to move, and the woman struggled to push herself off the ground. She'd survived the deadly episode and rose from the mud to kneel on all fours.

She grunted and panted, indicating her difficulty in evading the grip of death. She then managed to sit on her legs as the smell of ammonia suddenly filled the air. Aside from the smell, there was something different about her now. She appeared to be stronger than she was before her collapse. Her breathing slowed and she became more relaxed. Her back was straight instead of humped, and she seemed less feeble. Even though her face was still cloaked by the tattered hood, it was obvious that she was somehow transformed. The woman lifted her hands and stared at them. They were no longer wrinkled and thin. They were smooth and youthful looking. Her fingernails were no longer black and cracked from age, but were healthy and perfectly manicured.

The woman began laughing at the startling discovery. Her laughter grew stronger and louder as she continued examining her hands. Then, as suddenly as her laughter began, it ended. She quickly stood to her feet and began walking toward the carriage. Normally she would require the assistance of a cane to perform this task. But her stride was strong and balanced. Each step was deliberate and poised like a model strolling down a runway. Her feet that once bore the calluses and corns of age were devoid of any blemishes. They, too, looked perfect.

She reached the wagon and began rummaging through the collection of junk in the back. Finally, she found the item she sought, a jagged sliver of a mirror. She knelt on the ground and sat on her legs once again. She laid the sliver on her lap and slowly raised her hands to the edges of the hood that covered her face. She pulled it back from over her head and picked up the sliver of mirror.

She stared into it and saw that the sunken eyes of age she once possessed were now full and expressive. Her complexion was smooth and even. Her hair shimmered a perfect shade of blonde and its texture was full and thick. Her eyes were greener than the grass and sparkled with the intensity of the night's brightest star. Her smile was warm and inviting. Her teeth were pearly white and even. She was no longer an old crone, but a beautiful and young maiden.

The woman stared at the reflection with astonishment and disbelief. It was hard for her to believe that her once cruelly wrinkled face had become this vision of beauty she saw in the mirror. She wondered whether this was truly real. Could she really be young once more?

The woman threw the sliver of glass to the ground and quickly removed all of her clothes. The tattered garments dropped to the ground in a pile around her ankles. She conducted a quick inspection of her body to see if the effects were total. As she looked, she saw that the wrinkles on her body were gone. The blue-grayish tint of her skin was now replaced with a flushing pink. The texture was as smooth as the finest silk. Her body possessed the inviting hint of the lilacs that filled the air moments ago. She was now the absolute picture of beauty reborn.

The woman continued the examination of her body, admiring every inch of her improved frame. She was perfect in every dimension. Her skin glistened in the morning air as the combination of sweat and dew gave her the aura of a goddess. Her breasts were full and firm. Her abdomen was tight and slightly etched. Her hips were perfectly curved, and her legs were strong and toned. She concluded her inspection and reveled in the glorious transformation she'd made.

It was a nearly impossible task to reverse the cruel effects of time. But somehow this woman had done just that. By swallowing the concoction, she'd reversed the effects of aging with a surprising outcome. However, the price she paid was extreme. The price was not the pain of the transformation or the near death experience from swallowing the toxic potion. It wasn't even the potential harassment she would receive for looking the way she did. Her payment came in the form of her soul. The price was high and it came with a clause. Her pact had allowed her to be reborn in the beautiful shell she now donned. It would allow her to fulfill a destiny, a destiny of revenge. Retribution was all she could think of due to the pain she had already suffered. But now, she was a slave bound to a master who had less remorse than she. Her master was the Contravexus and soon he would be summoning her.

The woman stood basking in her naked glory. Her eyes closed as she took a deep breath to inhale the morning air. As she inhaled, she detected the scent of someone nearby, someone musky. It was the scent of a man.

"Aye, someone is near. What a wonderful opportunity to test my new body," she said.

An expression of joy appeared across her face, but faded quickly into a smile that hinted her ill intent. She needed to see if she had the tools to support her claim. Failure was not an option, for she remembered the promise the Contravexus made to her should she not live up to what she promised. Besides, it had been quite some time since she'd had any physical contact. This would be a good opportunity to satisfy her curiosity and her need.

She slowly exhaled and a faint mist escaped from her mouth. It possessed the same fragrance of lilac that heralded her arrival. The wind picked up the scent and gently lifted the alluring aroma above the trees. The scent quickly spread and saturated the surrounding area. This was her beacon, like a moth releasing it's pheromones to attract her potential mate. Her intents, however, were not of procreation or companionship. Hers was to humiliate and cause unbearable suffering. Although she possessed lips that were as red as a rose and as sweet as honey, they housed the fatal toxin of the grim reaper. One kiss could steal the soul. Her victims would probably be many, and she was anxious to start killing. But first, she had to test her potential. For now, she would settle for this unsuspecting dolt and waited for him to sense her and take the bait.

~~~

CHAPTER NINE

Sariel and Gabrielle stood by a huge indoor fountain, waiting for any news of Angelo. Each possessed an expression of dismay or disturbance. Gabrielle paced while Sariel stood with his head tucked and his eyes closed. He was meditating, trying to calm his overwhelming urge to leave the confines of the Vancouver headquarters and hunt down the Gaian.

Gabrielle finally ceased her pacing and sat in one of the chairs. Just then, they both heard the sound of someone walking up the hall. The clopping of shoes caused Gabrielle to sit forward in order to see who approached. Sariel lifted his head slightly and opened his eyes, shifting them to the corners to see who was coming. To both of their surprise, Michael, the Supreme Commander, walked into the waiting area.

"Well, look what the cat dragged in," said Sariel.

"A pleasure as always, Sariel," replied Michael.

Gabrielle stood and embraced her longtime friend. Michael returned the gesture.

"How are you holding up?" asked Michael.

"Pretty good. We still haven't heard anything yet," she replied.

Sariel remained in front of the fountain with his arms folded across his chest.

"So, what brings the great Supreme Commander to this place?" asked Sariel with a tone of contempt.

Both Michael and Gabrielle turned their heads and looked at him.

"Sariel, this isn't the time," said Gabrielle.

Sariel huffed and continued staring at the fountain water.

Gabrielle sighed and turned to look at Michael once more.

"It's been a couple of hours and we still haven't heard anything yet. I just hope he's going to be okay," she said.

"I wouldn't worry too much about ole Uriel. He's one of the toughest angels I've ever known. He'll pull through," said Michael.

"And how would you know?" interjected Sariel.

Michael pulled away from Gabrielle and walked toward the brooding Sariel.

"You know, if you have something to say to me, then don't hold back," said Michael.

"I really don't. But since you're here, I do have one question. Why didn't you have more protection around the Gaian?" asked Sariel.

"I didn't feel there was a need to. Besides, it was your brother's idea to give her another chance. He convinced us that she was no longer a threat."

"And you just took his word?"

"No. We checked her out and she appeared to have been reformed," said Michael.

"Reformed? After everything we saw her do and after everything we encountered, you honestly expect me to believe that you thought she was no longer a threat to us? If you truly believed that, then you have no place being the Supreme Commander," said Sariel as he turned to stare Michael in the eyes.

Gabrielle came between the two of them.

"Listen, that's enough! Blaming anyone right now won't do any of us any good! My brother is in there fighting for his life and the only thing you two can do is argue about old history! Okay, so we made a mistake about the Gaian! But Uriel is our brother, Sariel, and no one feels worse than I do about all of this! So, if you two don't mind backing off each other for a little while, I'd greatly appreciate it," said Gabrielle.

Michael and Sariel gave each other very discerning looks. Michael turned and walked to a seat and sat down. Sariel, with arms still crossed, turned to glare once more into the waters of the fountain. Gabrielle walked to where Michael was sitting and sat beside him. He placed his arm around her and patted her shoulder.

"You know, I heard from Lucifer. He sends his regrets," said Michael.

"How's he doing?" Gabrielle asked.

"As well as expected," said a voice from around the corner.

Gabrielle and Michael sat forward to see Azreal leaning against the wall. He was clad in a black suit, a long black cashmere coat and matching hat.

"Greetings from the Consortium," said Azreal.

"What in the name of Heaven are you doing here?" asked Sariel who dropped his hands and took a defensive posture.

Michael also stood and looked at the one known as the dark angel. Azreal smirked and waved his hands trying to defuse a very uncomfortable situation.

"Calm down. I only came by to see how things are going. Besides, Uriel was once a good friend of mine," said Azreal.

He looked down at Gabrielle, who also had a very distrusting expression.

"So, how is he doing?" asked Azreal.

"We don't know. He's still in surgery. We were hoping to hear something by now, but alas..." said Gabrielle.

Azreal nodded his head.

"I'm surprised that Lucifer allowed you to come here," said Michael.

"Well, normally he wouldn't. However, after recent events, he thought it would be a good idea to touch bases with you," said Azreal.

"What recent events are you talking about?" asked Sariel.

"You mean you haven't heard?" asked Azreal with a surprised expression.

"Heard what?" asked Michael.

"The Contravexus just burned down an entire hotel of Christians," said Azreal.

"What?" exclaimed Michael.

"Good lord," said Gabrielle.

"Yep, it's true boys and girls. Looks like he's about to jumpstart this war in a major way," said Azreal.

"Indeed. Seems as though the players are preparing for the final battle," said Sariel.

"Yes, and if what Azreal said is true, I'm afraid that this time we are going to need some help. The Contravexus' power may be much stronger than I imagined," replied Michael.

"That's why I'm here. Lucifer seems to think that it's going to take the combined forces of the Hierarchy and the Consortium to defeat Dupri and his minions. From our best intelligence sources, there has been a radical increase of sin and evil in this world, conditions that make this place perfect for the Vul Paux to thrive in. Dupri has already ensnared the human's leaders into believing that he can be trusted. The United States, Russia, Great Britain and France have all given him diplomatic authority to use their forces as he deems necessary. If you combine those forces with his supernatural armies, we are going to have one hell of a fight on our hands, pardon the pun," said Azreal.

"Then it is best we begin preparing. The events of the prophecy have already begun to unfold. It won't be long before the final battle begins," Gabrielle said.

"Indeed. If we don't stop Dupri here and now, all seven realms are doomed," said Michael.

"Wait a tick. Something doesn't seem right here. Why would the Contravexus kill a bunch of Christians?" asked Sariel.

"The Contravexus is a twisted minion of the Vul Paux. It's hard to really figure out what his motives are, but I can assure you that he has a plan. One thing we do know is that he is going to try and free his master. We cannot let that happen," said Gabrielle.

Just then, a being donned in surgery scrubs walked out into the hallway where the four angels stood conversing. It was Peter. He was the operating surgeon on Angelo and from his appearance he had just completed surgery.

"Peter, how is he?" asked Gabrielle frantically.

"Well, he suffered some very serious internal injuries, but we were able to stop the bleeding. I must tell you, though, I'd thought we'd lost him a couple of time during the operation. However, I am pleased to say that he is doing okay and that we are replacing his plasma as we speak. He should be up and around in about another day or two," said Peter.

"See, what did I tell you," said Michael.

Gabrielle turned and hugged Michael. Sariel sported a look of relief and Azreal smirked and nodded.

"Thank you, Peter," said Gabrielle, who gave him a hug also.

"There was no way I was going to allow Uriel to die," he said. "Now, I'd better be getting back to my patient. If you will excuse me."

Peter turned and walked back into the operating room. The entire crowd seemed to breathe a sigh of relief.

"Well, looks like everything is going to turn out okay. At any rate, I'd better get back to HQ and go over this information that Azreal just told us. Sounds like we don't have any time to waste," said Michael.

He nodded to each of them, then turned and walked down the hall. Gabrielle sat back in the chair and braced her head in her right hand. Sariel sat next to her and patted her on the knee.

"I have to hand it to him. I didn't expect to see him here," said Sariel.

"He's not that bad, Sariel. Maybe you could lighten up on him a bit. He has a lot on his shoulders," said Gabrielle, still bracing her head in her hand.

"Perhaps, but don't count on it," he said.

"Well, since this party is coming to a close, I'll just take my leave. Speaking for the big guy, let us know if there is anything else we can do," said Azreal.

Sariel stood and looked into Azreal's eyes.

"I'm still not convinced why you came down here, but it was a very nice thing you did," said Sariel.

"Hey, don't get all mushy on me. The Consortium isn't a bad group of folks; we're just misunderstood," said Azreal with a wink.

The two angels smiled, and Azreal turned and walked away. Sariel stood there and watched as the dark angel disappeared into the shadows of the hallway. He sat next to Gabrielle once more. She patted him on his hand and sighed.

"You're a good being, Gabrielle. It's hard to believe you were married to Lucifer once," said Sariel.

"Like I said before Sariel, they aren't that bad," said Gabrielle.

~~~

A young horse rider stopped in a meadow to allow his steed a brief rest and a drink from the creek. He had ridden long and hard and decided that this clearing was a fitting place for a break. He knelt beside his drinking steed and filled his canteen with fresh water. After fastening the top and securing it around his waist, he reached down, scooped a handful and splashed it on his face. The water's brisk coldness awakened his senses and tempted him with the thought of a mid-morning swim.

Suddenly, the young rider caught the scent of lilacs and began looking around. He had ridden this trail many times but never once did he smell this fragrance.

"You smell that?" asked the young man to his steed.

The horse continued drinking.

"C'mon Spitz, let's check this out!" he said.

The horse lifted its head from the creek. It looked at the young man and seemed reluctant to obey. The young man turned and reached for the horse's reigns. The horse turned its head, distancing the reigns from him. The rider tried again. This time, the horse raced off with a start into the woods at a full gallop.

"Spitz, come back here!" yelled the young man.

But Spitz never stopped and the noble steed disappeared into the woods. The young man prepared to pursue. Before he was able to make his first step, he felt something, like someone was watching him. The feeling caused the hairs on the back of his neck to rise.

A cool breeze blew and a disturbing chill shot down his spine. He slowly turned around and saw what was causing this phenomenon.

His eyes stretched in disbelief. A naked woman was standing at the edge of the clearing leering at him. He froze in place and stared back at her. He wondered who she was and where she'd come from. He had just been looking in that direction and knew she wasn't there a moment ago. Despite her sudden appearance, never before had he seen a woman more beautiful or more perfect in his life. The more he stared at her, the more mesmerized he became.

She began walking toward him, looking as if she was gliding on the air. Her slinky walk tantalized him, making him swell with lustful passion. He hoped her movement toward him indicated an interest in him. He became uncomfortable, stretching the collar of his shirt. His body temperature suddenly became elevated, and the thought of removing his clothes was the only thing on his mind.

The woman continued to walk toward the young rider. Although her actions and appearance seemed seductive, this was just the reeling-in process. She had found her experimental subject and knew just what to do to keep him there long enough to satisfy her purposes. She continued to leer at him with eyes of lustful hunger as she gracefully walked toward him. Within mere moments, the distance between them had disappeared and the woman stood face to face with the young man who still hadn't moved since the moment he laid eyes on her. She proceeded passed him to the creek where his horse had earlier attempted to quench its thirst. The young man's eyes were glued to her as she stood at the creek's edge and dipped her toes in the water. His eyes traced every curve of her naked figure and his manly desires grew more and more uncontrollable.

The woman stepped into the creek as the coldness of the water erected her nipples, enhancing the young man's lustful thoughts. She waded to the deepest portion, which reached to her waist. She began bathing, but as she did, the faint smell of ammonia replaced the alluring scent of lilac.

The odor was a warning sign that went unnoticed by the young man. Being so entranced by her beauty, his other senses were oblivious. The hypnotic grip the woman possessed on him was powerful. He was helpless, caught in her web of infatuation and lust. Like a fish hooked on a line, she had him and there was nothing he could do about it.

As he continued to watch her in the shimmering waters of the creek, he began to disrobe in an almost frenzied fashion. His desires had taken control, and he wanted her more than anything. Within moments, he stood naked at the water's edge. The creek now possessed a sulfuric smell that still went unnoticed by the young man. She seduced him with her bathing, floating in the water and stretching her legs into the air while pointing her toes. She stroked each leg, rinsing them with the creek water while giving him seductive glances.

The young man was beside himself with excitement. He wanted to jump in, but for some reason, he was unable to move toward her. Like a statue he stood at the edge of the creek, gazing at the woman that could potentially be his. It was almost as if he had lost the ability to move any part of his body.

After a few moments, the woman concluded her bath and slowly emerged from the creek. The young man watched, filled with excitement as she approached. His manhood was at full prominence. His eyes beheld every part of her splendid form. From her wet, silken hair shimmering in the morning sunlight to her absolutely perfect figure, the woman was everything he wanted.

She walked toward him and stopped close enough to hear him breathing with anticipation. She lifted her hand and placed it on his chest. Her fingernails began to trace his pectoral muscles and abdomen. She kissed his lips and cheek, working ever so slowly down his neck to his shoulders and chest.

The young man trembled at her touch. Goose bumps began appearing on his arms and legs. The woman kneeled in front of him and continued to kiss and lick the young man's body. She paused for a moment, lifting her head and smiling at his loss of composure. He shuttered from her proximity to that one vulnerable spot on most men. She began fondling and stroking him in her hands, continuing to look up into his eyes. Her touch was exquisite, causing him to release his inhibitions and surrender to her wants.

As he began to pant from pleasure and excitement, the woman continued her erotic playfulness. She watched as his eyes rolled to the back of his head. She tasted him and drew him closer to nirvana with her mouth and hands. Although she was the giver and he was the receiver, she derived great pleasure from this. She'd gotten the answer she wanted and knew that she possessed all the tools needed to accomplish her mission. She continued to perform her pleasuring with a savageness that excited the young man more and more. He felt himself growing weak in her grasp, almost to the point of exhaustion. He tried to grab her head and steady himself, but he could not move. His body would not respond to his wants.

The young man became alarmed by the apparent paralysis, and his concern did not go unnoticed. She saw the fear in his eyes and stepped up her pace, quickening her strokes and tightening her draws. Her increased intensity caused him to disregard his paralysis and focus on the sensation that was building in his loins. Her talents were bringing him greater pleasure than he'd ever known, and he resumed his focus on the moment. He tightened his hips, trying not to end this pleasurable interlude too soon. Little did he realize, his pleasure was about to end, and it wasn't going to be the way he expected.

Suddenly, the young man felt a burning sensation on his arms and body. His mouth became dry and pasty. His heart raced faster, but not from anticipation. It felt as if he was having an allergic reaction to something. The pleasure he felt was overwhelming, but the pain he was now feeling was becoming too great to ignore. He began to panic and opened his eyes to see what was happening to him.

He struggled to raise his right arm and managed to lift it slightly. His eyes widened with fright as he stared at the back of his hand. The burning he felt wasn't his imagination. In fact, there was a very real cause to its source. His entire arm was covered with open sores. The goose bumps that were born from excitement had grown and had turned into huge lesions that spread over his entire arm. He managed to look down and examine the rest of his body. He discovered that the lesions were all over him. Blood began to ooze from the wounds, running down his arms and body as the beautiful goddess continued to perform her lustful foreplay.

"What have you done to me?" he mumbled.

His tongue had become swollen and he was unable to speak clearly. He attempted to lift his hands and push her away, but he found it increasingly harder to move. The pain raced through his body and the sores quickly became larger and more severe. He continued his struggle against his paralysis in order to pull himself away from her. His heartbeat had grown so rapid and strong that he could hear the blood rushing through his ears. His head pounded with the pain of a thousand migraines. He felt himself slipping further and further into a daze. His body began to convulse as she continued to manipulate his manhood. Blood began to spew from his mouth and his eyes once again rolled to the back of his head. His body shook and tightened, his arms flailing by his sides like limp wet towels. Then, the young man dropped his head backwards and collapsed to the ground. The impact echoed a resounding thud throughout the woods, causing the water of the creek to ripple slightly. His bloody, sore infested body trembled as he lay on the ground with his arms outstretched to the sides. His face expressed shock or maybe even pain, the result of the untimely revelation of his iniquitous companion.

The woman sat on her legs and watched as the last ounces of life faded from the young man's eyes. His breathing slowed to gasps and his body ceased its quivering. His gasps for breath diminished into lighter slurps while the whites of his eyes stared fixed into the blue morning sky. The sores on his body began to cease their bleeding and an ashen color appeared on his skin. Three more puffs were heard, then silence. His breathing stopped along with his heart.

He laid on the moistened grass, oblivious to the rationale of his fate. To him, his only crime was that he admired a beautiful woman, the very woman that now stared at his lifeless body. She showed no remorse, but instead, sported a slight smirk on her blood-smeared lips. To her, he was just a test, a hapless victim who was at the wrong place at the wrong time. He served his purpose and she discarded him like a used paper plate. She would use and abuse anyone and anything in order to serve her master, regardless of how innocent the victims were. Everyone had a sin to pay for, and she was going to make sure they all would pay for their trespasses. She thrived on this type of misery and grew stronger from it.

The woman glared at the dead body that lay before her. She stood and began brushing the dirt from her knees. She licked her lips, erasing the traces of blood from the corners of her mouth. Her choice in subjects was perfect. He had given her everything she needed. Now she was ready to assume her place aside her master and aid him in his mission.

A tingle raced through the gorgeous, sexy, cold-blooded killing machine as the remnants of the young man's soul was assimilated into hers. Her skin glistened even more in the morning light as she proudly examined her perfect figure once again. She looked down and saw the clothing of her victim lying at her feet. She knelt and lifted the shirt in the air and examined it. A look of uncertainty appeared on her face but was soon shrugged off nonchalantly. She wasn't impressed with the choice of clothing she had, but this was the best she could do for now. She gathered the items and began dressing herself.

As she donned the dead man's attire, a high shriek exploded from the woods behind her. It was quick, yet loud enough to startle the birds in the nearby trees. They erupted into flight and flew away from the area of the disturbance. Unfazed by the shrill, the woman continued to dress herself. She mumbled a quick incantation and instantly the clothes that would normally be too large for a woman of her stature began to conform to her every curve. Even the boots that were a size eleven and a half now fit her petite sized seven feet.

As she continued to dress, a figure emerged from the shadows of the woods where the sound of pain emitted moments ago. It was Timothy, the woman's steed. In his mouth was the head of the disobedient horse, Spitz, who cowardly galloped into the woods.

"I see you found a souvenir, Timothy," said the woman as she completed the finishing touches on her wardrobe.

The horse grunted and dropped the decapitated head on the ground. Timothy's mane began to change color, matching the golden locks of his mistress. His body hair darkened to the color of midnight and its sunken back straightened. Timothy stood strong and solid. He was no longer a beast of burden, but instead a magnificent stallion that was worthy of being called a thoroughbred.

The woman turned to her faithful Timothy and caressed his snout with passionate strokes. Then, she gently cupped his nose and kissed him on the brow. The horse snarled and motioned toward the bloody body behind her, as if to ask what she was going to do with this hapless fool. She glanced at the horse, then turned and walked to the body. Kneeling beside him, she looked into his still opened eyes. They almost appeared to be shouting one word, why?

The woman almost seemed regretful in having to do such a thing to him. But her look of remorse quickly disappeared. She could never know feelings of lament over her actions. If she did, she would jeopardize her mission and suffer a fate worse than death from her master. In her mind, the young man's lust brought this fate upon him. He was no different than the others who saw her only as a possession or an object to be had. The only difference between her and other women was that none who crossed her lived to brag about their conquest. Lust was a powerful sin, one of the seven deadliest in fact. It was also her most trusted weapon. It never failed her and thus has become her weapon of choice. She hovered over the young man's face and looked into his screaming eyes.

"By the way, I thought I owed you, at the very least, an introduction," said the beautiful seductress.

She leaned forward and kissed the forehead of the young man. Then, she raised her head and looked once more into his eyes.

"My name is Eve," she said with a smirk.

She turned and looked at Timothy.

"I will leave him here, as is. It will be my calling card, one of many before it is over with. Let this young man's remains be a cold and harsh reminder of what will happen to those who challenge my power. I will prove that my daughters and I are superior to Adam's breed in every aspect. No man has the ability to resist me. I am perfect, flawless in every way, and I will use my attributes to exploit all men."

Timothy snarled and shook its head.

"Ay yes, you are correct my faithful stallion. I was the accursed one, shouldered with the punishment for causing mankind's fall from immortality. I was the one forced to live a life eternal, to see the aftermath of my supposed disobedience. It was a curse that drove me to what I've become now, a woman with a vicious taste for revenge. But there is another purpose I must serve. Although I know not what that purpose is, I will face it willingly, for I have no other choice now," said Eve.

She stood and looked around her.

"You know, my life has spanned many eons. I gave birth to Kane, Seth and Abel. I was the second wife of Adam. I have seen the rise of many civilizations and the deaths of those who fought to defend their beliefs. I witnessed the rise of the Egyptian and Roman Empires, as well as their fall from power. I was present when the Star of David heralded the arrival of the Messiah and I was amongst the crowd that watched his execution. I witnessed the Renaissance and the Spanish Inquisition. I watched from the shores of the Atlantic as the new settlers from Europe arrived to a new land to escape the oppression of a tyrant. I saw the explosion of the Hindenburg and bid farewell to the people on the Titanic when it pulled from its docks for the last time. I even watched as followers ingested their fatal drinks in Jonestown, Guyana. But despite all of the tragedies I'd witnessed over my lifetime, what is to come will make the afore mentioned events look like child's play. I will make them suffer for what they did to me; they all will suffer," she said with a menacing tone.

Timothy snarled once more. She turned and began walking

away from the naked corpse on the ground. Timothy followed. Her walk was slow, like a death march. In many respects, it was. The death knell was being tolled for mankind; they just didn't know it yet. Her stare was blank and emotionless. She'd proven that she had the cold, heartless spirit to do whatever it took to aid Montellace Dupri with his mission. Eve was the quintessential feminist and the mother of all mankind. But now, she was a beautiful, cold-blooded killer with no remorse and a deep desire for destruction.

~~~

The look on Betty's face was starting to annoy me. The newscast had just flashed a picture of me on the screen and stated that I was the prime suspect in the murder of my husband, Angelo, as well as the cop that killed him. The report also stated that the police have started a citywide manhunt for me and have offered a reward for any information of my whereabouts.

In the pick-up window of the kitchen, I could see the cook on the phone attempting not to look at me. Betty walked to the edge of the counter trying to look unconcerned.

"Would you like anything else, suga?" she asked.

"I didn't do it, Betty!" I exclaimed.

Betty looked at me with a disbelieving yet concerned expression.

"He was my husband and I loved him more than my own life!" I said.

Betty sighed.

"If you didn't do it, then tell the cops! Let them handle it!" she pleaded.

I looked at Betty and realized that she had no idea how disturbing of a statement she had just made to me. If I explained what really happened, she'd really think I was a nut. I could tell that she was a person who tried to see only the best in people. To tell her that the dead cop was responsible for Angelo's murder, along with the circumstances surrounding his death, would be difficult for anyone to believe.

"The police won't catch this guy! They can't help in this matter!" I retorted.

"You can try," she urged.

I just stared at her not really knowing what to say. In my mind, she was too naïve to understand. She glanced over her shoulder toward the kitchen and then whispered.

"I think you need to get out of here. Johnny is on the phone with the police right now," she said.

The news of the police approaching didn't concern me. I was determined that they were not going to take me in, no matter what the cost. Still, I didn't want the loss of any more human lives on my hands. I knew that in order to prevent anyone else from getting hurt, I had to do as Betty suggested. I had to leave now.

"Thank you for everything, Betty!" I said as I turned toward the door.

Just then, two police officers emerged through the diner door. The cook, Johnny, erupted from the kitchen and pointed toward me.

"There she is, officers!" he said.

The officers placed their hands on their guns.

"Ma'am, would you please slowly place your hands above your head!" stated one of the officers.

Johnny stared at me with a smug look, clutching a meat cleaver in his right hand. In his eyes, I was already guilty. But he didn't matter. It was Betty that mattered to me. I looked at her and saw the concern on her face. I felt as if she believed me and wanted me to cooperate because she didn't want anything to happen to me.

"I think you better do what they say, hun," Betty pleaded.

Given the circumstances, I didn't think I had a choice. I knew if I resisted, someone was going to get hurt. I could feel the swell of anger building in my chest and the taste for vengeance in my mouth. But then, I remembered what Dupri said. If, in fact, that monster was trying to reemerge, I had to do my best to stop it. I stared at the two officers with great contempt. Even though I had a tremendous hatred for the police right now, I had to suppress my urge to attack.

I'd seen enough death and suffering in the last twenty-four hours to last me a lifetime. I didn't want anyone else to suffer by my hands and I didn't want to feed the monster that was trying to resurface. I slowly lifted my arms and placed my hands on top of my head.

"I didn't do anything," I said.

My comment was ignored. It was apparent that they weren't going to listen to a word I said. One officer walked behind me and began placing handcuffs on my wrists. All the while, I couldn't believe that I was being arrested as the prime suspect for murdering my husband. Something didn't make sense, and this whole situation reeked with the smell of the Contravexus. Even so, I was going to get him, that much was certain. I closed my eyes as the other officer began reading me my rights.

~~~

CHAPTER TEN

As the murmuring of my rights continued, so did my struggle to suppress the urge to hurt the police officers. My mind kept shifting to murderous thoughts and I fought with all the concentration I could muster to push them out of my mind. But the struggle was becoming increasingly hard. My anger toward them was feeding my deadly desires. I was a time bomb whose fuse was growing shorter by the moment. Unless I found a way to defuse my anger, something bad was going to happen. I decided that I needed to get away from them. I couldn't let them take me in and if I were going to flee, I needed to do it soon. In fact, judging from my current state of mind, it may already be too late. I could feel myself loosing control. I could hear my heartbeat and I felt a slight pain in my head. I couldn't wait any longer. For the good of everyone, I had to get away now.

As I was about to make my move, a thought popped into my head. Perhaps these officers worked for the Contravexus. If that were the case, they would lead me right to him. He was the one who truly deserved my scorn and if my hunch was right, he would be brought to me on a silver platter. The thought of getting my hands on him lessened my hostility. It was like an acceptance of fate. I instantly became calm and a sigh of relief flowed from my lips. Although I still had my apprehensions about letting the cops take me in, it was a necessary evil in order to get my revenge.

As my aggression lessened, I suddenly realized that the officer had stopped reading me my rights. I opened my eyes to see what was going on. A chill ran up my spine as I looked down. There, lying on the floor were the two police officers. They weren't moving, and it appeared that they weren't breathing either.

I neither heard anything nor was I sure what happened to them. All I knew was that I didn't do anything to them. I quickly looked around the room and found everyone lying on the floor: the police officers, the cook and even Betty.

Whatever happened occurred so quickly that the officer didn't have time to place the handcuffs on me. I knelt down and checked the officer closest to me. His body looked as if he had starved to death. His flesh was shriveled and barely clung to his skeleton. It looked like wet clothing draped over a garment rack.

"Good lord! What happened to them?" I mumbled.

Suddenly, another voice blurted from behind me.

"They were killed!"

I turned around and saw that there was someone sitting on the counter eating a piece of apple pie. It was the guy I spoke to a few hours ago, Huang.

"It's funny, but I never knew that the fruit from the tree of knowledge could taste so good! These humans, what will they think of next?" said the cocky little imp.

"Did you do this?" I asked.

"You can say I had a hand in it", said Huang as he stuck his finger into the slice and licked it. "Have you been thinking about what we discussed?"

The horror of the moment overwhelmed me, and his nonchalant attitude infuriated me once again. I stood, attempting to keep myself composed. I looked at Betty lying facedown on the floor behind the counter. I walked toward her and then knelt beside her. I turned her on her back. Her skin was withered and wrinkled. The lovely 'joie de vivre' expression that effortlessly covered her face was gone. Now, her skin also clung desperately to her skull and her hazel eyes were sunken and lifeless. I held her in my arms, trying desperately not to cry. Despite my thoughts of keeping her out of harms way, she had become a victim after all.

The revelation of her demise added to the pain and sadness that already existed inside of me. I stood and walked to Huang, grabbing him by the collar. I lifted him in the air and glared at him. My heart was filled with all the anger I tried to suppress earlier.

"Why did you do this? You didn't have to kill these people!" I said.

Huang looked disturbed that I had grabbed him and his jovial demeanor quickly turned sour.

"Take your damn hands off of me!" he replied.

I lowered him to eye level. "Or what? You gonna try and kill me like you did them? Give it your best shot!" I said.

I glared at him and was filled with an overwhelming urge to kill him. He seemed a little unsure as to what he was going to do next. He lifted the slice of pie back to his face and took another bite, still watching me. Infuriated as I was, I drew back my fist and prepared to take his head off his shoulders. The flood of pain and hatred had driven me to the point of concentrated insanity. I was giddy from the thought of killing him and a chuckle escaped from my lips.

"That's it! Let yourself go! Take that last step!" he said taunting.

Instantly, reality and sanity returned. Huang's comment made me realize what he was trying to do. He wanted me to loose my composure; it's what fed the monster inside of me. Giving in to my killing urges would make the monster grow stronger. I knew now that it needed hatred and pain. In fact, I realized at that moment that everything that I'd experienced over the last several hours was done to increase my pain and anger. Even now, I found it hard to control my urge to kill him. The revelation frightened me. I'd almost given them what they wanted. Fear suddenly gripped my heart. I released his collar and slowly backed away.

"What are you doing? This isn't in the freakin' script. Attack me!" he said.

"No." I said fearfully.

I turned and walked out of the diner. I needed to distance myself from him. I was still trying to fight the anger, and the struggle was making me tremble. This was the third murder scene

I'd been affiliated with since last night and now I understood why. Each of them were killed for the single purpose of making me feel anger or pain. These emotions fed the creature inside of me. Dupri killed Angelo and the cop in order to create enough trauma to feed the Gaian and make it reemerge. It was equally apparent to me that the killing of innocent people would continue until he got what he wanted. But I still didn't know where the gate was. Until I could figure out what I needed to do next, I decided that it would be best to keep my distance from anyone. That way no one would get hurt. It was getting harder to think or keep my focus. I needed to find someplace I could go to get away from the madness that seemed to be following me around. As I walked away from the diner, I heard the voice of Huang yelling behind me.

"Hey, stop her! She just killed these people in this diner!" he screamed.

At first, I was shocked by the comment. Then, I became infuriated. As I turned to confront the little imp, I saw a mob of people slowly moving toward me. They glared at me with expressions of pure hatred. Their eyes were glazed and in their hands they clutched clubs, knives, scissors and any other weapon they could get their hands on. Somehow Huang was controlling them. If I fought them, I would be doing the same thing he was. I would be hurting more innocent people. So, I did the only thing I could do, I fled.

I ran for a couple of blocks, and then ducked into the alley. Their angry words echoed amidst the streets as they followed me into the alley. I ran as fast as I could, but the mob wasn't far behind. I exited that alley and ducked into another. I found an empty garbage dumpster and hid behind it. This was so cliché, but it was the only thing I could think of at the moment. The crowd rushed by the alley and continued up the street. I slumped to the ground, trying to breathe as quietly as I could. The noisy maniacal roar soon diminished, but I remained in the alley, waiting for the right moment to emerge.

I looked around trying to find another way out, just in case

I was discovered. In the far corner of the filthy throughway, I discovered a hole in the fence. It wasn't very big, but it was just large enough for me to get through. If I was going to escape, I needed to do it now. I peeked over the top of the dumpster to ensure it was safe to come out. Then, I scurried to the hole and attempted to squeeze through.

Just then, a drunken bum lying next to the fence awakened.

"Hey, you mind closing my door. You're letting in a draft!" yelled the man.

I turned and glared at him. He screamed so loudly that someone was bound to hear him.

"Go back to sleep," I said in a whisper.

The man fluffed his makeshift pillow and fell back to sleep. I quickly realized that the hole in the fence was too small. I backed out and gave a yank on the wooden plank, popping a chunk of it loose. I knelt and prepared to crawl through once again. At that moment, one of the lingering mob members peeked around the corner just as I was about to squeeze through the fence.

"She's over here!" he screamed.

I looked up to see the lone vigilante lunging toward me with a butcher's knife. I had only seconds to get to safety. I squeezed into the hole and pushed with all my strength. He raised the blade and prepared to bring it down. With one last effort, I lunged through the hole just as the knife lodged into the ground where my legs had been.

Once I was on the other side of the fence, I turned to see the knife-wielding maniac attempting to come through also. Fortunately, he was too large and couldn't get through the opening. However, I could see his face. His scowl displayed the pure hatred he possessed toward me. It was the same look of disdain the cop had when he shot Angelo. But that wasn't the only thing I saw. On his forehead, there appeared to be a symbol in the shape of the number six, except it was sideways. This was the mark of the beast, the mark of the Contravexus' property. The man continued his attempts to lunge through the fence, making every effort possible to get to me. I knew he wouldn't make it through, but to be on the safe side, I wasn't going to stick around to find out otherwise. I turned and continued my escape down the adjoining alley, running as fast as I could. I was certain that the rest of the crowd would be here in moments, so I did my best to get out of that alley before they got there.

Just then, the mob returned and rushed to the other side of the fence where the butcher knife wielding man was still trying to dig his way through the fence. They began pounding unmercifully on the wooden structure. The fence rumbled and shook as the maniacal crowd tried to push it down. I continued running toward the opening of the alley, for my life depended on it.

As I neared the end, I noticed that the screaming and banging had stopped. I glanced back to see if they had gotten through. The fence was in tact. In fact, no one was at the fence nor were they in the alley. All was still and quiet. It was as if the mob had disappeared. This could or could not be a good thing, I thought. I paused for a second and listened to hear if they truly left or if they were circling the block to attack me from the side I was on. I could not sense anything. The possibility crossed my mind that the mob could be waiting for me to exit the alley. In any case, I had to take that chance. If I stayed there, they would surely get me.

I crept to the corner of the alleyway and peeked. There were people walking the streets, but none of them were members of the group that was just after me. I checked in both directions and even above my head. It appeared to be safe to leave. I stepped out and swiftly made my exit from the alley.

It dawned on me that I needed to get off of the streets, but I didn't know where to go. I couldn't go back home, and I couldn't get close to any of my friends without putting them in danger. To make matters worse, it appeared that I was now public enemy number one. Everything was happening so fast that I couldn't absorb it all. From Angelo's death to this mob, I felt truly overwhelmed. Despite it all, I was determined that I was going to survive. I had to.

At that moment, I looked up and saw the steeple of a church.

The sign by the front door read, 'The First Church of God'. The sight of the church brought some relief to my mind. If there was any place on this planet where I could find refuge, this was the place.

Just then, I felt a familiar presence near me and I knew exactly who it was. From out of the shadows of the alley stepped the Barhim Hajj. I turned and looked at him.

"What the hell is going on?" I exclaimed.

"No time to explain. We need to get you off the streets. Go over to that church and enter. You will be safe there," said Hajj.

I looked at the Barhim Hajj with doubtful eyes. With everything that had happened, I wasn't sure who I could trust. But so far, he seemed to be the only being that was concerned about me, and he hadn't given me any bad advise yet. I quickly checked around me to see if the coast was clear, then ran to the church. I jogged up the cracked marble steps and stopped at the entrance. The doors were ten feet tall and made of heavy cherry oak. The handles were pure gold and the entryway was decorated with beautiful carvings of saints and other angelic figures. I quickly pulled open the doors and entered.

A huge sigh exploded out of me as I braced my back against the door. I took a moment to collect myself, then slowly made my way into the main chamber. As I walked down the aisle, I saw the sculptures of angelic beings, representing guardian angels and patron saints. The stained glass panes cast the multicolored shades of sunlight throughout the chamber. The pews made of cherry oak were symmetrically lined with cushioned backs and soft matching seat pads. Above the pulpit, a huge crucifix stretched across the entire front stage. It was more intimidating than it was comforting.

As I looked around the church, sorrowful faces were scattered amongst the pews. People were praying or reading their bibles. Their sad expressions made me instantly think about all the suffering I'd witnessed. It seemed like everywhere I turned, someone was dealing with a debilitating pain. Even in this house of worship, misery seemed to abound. It made me wonder if comfort could be found anywhere. I was beginning to doubt it. Soft cushioned seats and a lot of elaborate artwork decorated the chamber. It was truly one of the more beautiful churches. However, amidst all the trappings of evangelical wealth, I found no serenity or fountains of encouragement and hope. I did not feel the presence of God here and I began thinking that Barhim Hajj had lied to me. I was about to turn and walk out when suddenly, I felt a strong presence in the church that wasn't there a moment ago. There was something different in the air now, and it enveloped the entire chamber. The people in the pews suddenly started crying and bellowing. The sun began shining a little brighter through the stained glass, and the church suddenly had a warm, inviting atmosphere. I didn't know what caused this change, but it gave me a sense of peace and security, something I'd been longing to feel since my entire ordeal began. I, too, began crying. As the tears fell, the pain and anger that was in my heart lessened. A warm sensation filled my chest. I sat down, leaned back and rested my head on the back of the pew, moaning as the tears continued to roll down my cheeks. It was then I realized what this presence was. The Holy Spirit was in the church. It touched me as well as everyone else, allowing us to release our debilitating agony. For fifteen minutes, I cried and moaned. My wails were mixed with the others who released their pains. I laid my head on the cushioned seat and began sobbing quietly.

When I opened my eyes, I realized that somehow during my mourning, I'd fallen asleep. I didn't know how long I had been out. I looked at one of the stained glass windows and could tell by the lessening sunlight that it was well into the evening. Apparently, I'd slept through the entire day. I sat up and looked around the church. The place was virtually empty, except for the front altar where a group of people were praying. One of the clergy was ministering to them, apparently trying to comfort them. As I continued watching, I couldn't help noticing that they were upset. The man was sobbing and the clergyman was holding the woman upright. She seemed as if she was on the verge of fainting. It was then I heard that they'd lost one of their children after a long illness. I wanted to go over and help, but something wouldn't let me leave my seat. I sat there wondering about their sorrows and compared them to those of my own. As rough as things were for me, my troubles seemed to pale in comparison to theirs.

The first thing I thought about doing was praying for them, but then I began thinking of the reasons why people pray. Most prayed for strength, understanding or some other miracle that would remove the turmoil they were experiencing. Some even tried bargaining with God. They all seemed to be looking for something, some sort of answer or relief. Regardless of what they were looking for or why they prayed, their fortune or misfortune was God's will, and there was nothing I could do to change that. I, too, was looking for something. I wanted answers. I looked at the kneeling couple once more and said the only prayer I could. I prayed for them to have the strength to handle the turmoil that brought such pain to their lives.

A few moments later, the couple and the clergyman walked through a door at the side of the pulpit. I stood and attempted to follow them. As I got to the pulpit, the door was closed. I stood at the front of the church and looked around the huge main chamber, wondering what I should do next. Then, my eyes rested upon the huge cross that stretched overhead. I wondered whether I should do as the others I'd seen in the church and pray to God for answers. If the monster inside of me was trying to reemerge, I, more than anyone, needed help. I'd been told that I was the vessel of the ultimate evil. But I had no memory of this nor did I wish to harm anyone. The more I tried to prove that point, the more people were dying around me. Angelo, the cop, even Betty; they were all dead because of me. I'd run out of options and this was the last place I could go to find the answers and the strength I sought. I knelt before the altar and bowed my head.

"God, what have I done to deserve this? Why must I go through all of this, and what am I to gain from my suffering? I don't know what to do and I need your help."

I paused for a moment and began crying once again. I was overwhelmed and frustrated. It all seemed so wrong and unjust, and the burden was too much for me to handle. As I continued to wallow in my self-pity, I began to feel anger and resentment for the trials I was enduring. I clenched my fists and squeezed my eyes closed in an attempt to shut out the pain. My heart swelled with a wrath-like anger that almost seemed uncontrollable. It consumed me and almost drove me to the brink of screaming. Hadn't I suffered enough or was there more torment to come? Where was *my* fairytale ending? When was all of this going to be over, and what was going to be my reward? I sat on the floor before the cross, doing the same thing as those I observed when I entered the church. I was consumed with pity and doubt. I was forgetting how to maintain my faith. I wanted to believe that through it all, somehow it was going to be okay. Right now, however, believing in that fairytale was the hardest thing to do.

Suddenly, I felt a pulsating vibration jolting the floor of the church. I lifted my head and looked around. I began hearing the sound of something pounding the ground. At first, I thought it was some form of construction on the street outside. But the more I listened, the more I realized it felt and sounded like a ball being bounced.

I wiped the tears from my eyes and looked around me to locate where the source of the bouncing was coming from. Then, I saw in a distant doorway, a young boy bouncing a basketball. He couldn't have been any older than twelve. I thought it to be very odd that someone would be bouncing a basketball in the church. Perhaps he was the child of one of the mourning patrons. I noticed that other people had entered the church and were sitting in the pews. None of them seemed to notice him or the incessant bouncing of the ball. I turned and looked at him once again. The pounding grew louder and louder. The noise echoed off the gothic carvings that decorated the walls. The sound was almost deafening. Yet, I seemed to be the only one who heard it.

His presence intrigued me, and the fact that he went unnoticed piqued my curiosity even more. Was he an apparition or perhaps another form of the visions I'd had earlier? Perhaps he was another demon that had been sent to trick or torment me. Either way, I felt compelled to go to him.

I stood and walked toward the door where the boy was. As I got closer to him, he turned and walked into the chamber. I wasn't sure if I should follow him, but I couldn't stop myself. I felt drawn to him, if for nothing else than to find out why he was bouncing the ball in the church. I walked through the doorway and into the chamber. Inside, I could see his silhouette against the setting sunlight through the far window. He'd stopped bouncing the basketball and sat atop some covered boxes staring at the world outside.

He tossed the ball into the air and caught it without looking. Then, he began fiddling with it, passing it from hand to hand. The drab plaid long-sleeved shirt he wore was much too large for him, as well as the jeans he wore. But that didn't seem to bother him. He looked comfortably adjusted to his baggy attire, continuing to shift the ball from hand to hand while staring out of the window.

Although his childlike appearance led me to believe that he was a pre-teenager, I couldn't help noticing that he also possessed an older demeanor than his age suggested. His posture was erect and his head was tilted upward. There was a regal air about him despite his dowdy attire and youthfulness. I was even more intrigued by this prodigy and wanted to find out more about him. Without a word, I walked to where he was and stood in the diminishing light of the evening sun. He bounced the ball on the ground once and caught it. He then tucked it under his arm, remarkably without relinquishing his stare from the view outside. My eyes widened and my brow lifted. I recognized him.

"Hey, I know you. You're the boy that bumped into me at the BART station," I said.

He didn't respond. In fact, he never took his eyes from staring out the window. I frowned, thinking that it was quite rude for him to ignore my remarks. I began wondering what was so interesting outside that window. I decided to see what captured his attention.

My eyes widened with amazement. The view totally surprised

me. Somehow we had ascended above the skyline, staring down on the city from a thirtieth floor perch. The height would require the use of stairs or an elevator, but I didn't use either. As I looked through the dirt-covered window, I saw people, cars, trains, buildings, airplanes, and bridges. I saw everything the city had to offer, and it was right outside this window. I saw Seahawks Stadium and the Space Needle. I saw Safeco Field and the Public Market. It was all right there, seemingly at my fingertips.

The sun was setting behind the far hills, and the lights were beginning to come on. I smiled in amazement and turned to the young man who was still perched atop the boxes. I would have thought the view would spark some pleasant response from him as it did from me. His expression, however, was not of happiness or admiration. Instead, his face displayed a look of pain and despair. It was as if he saw something I was missing.

"Are you okay?" I asked.

He sighed and continued to stare at the world outside, like he was looking for something. I felt snubbed by his silence. The least he could have done was answer me or acknowledge my question. I almost spoke in anger, ready to chastise the youth for his rudeness. But I kept my composure. I didn't know this child, and perhaps there was a reason he didn't answer. I decided not to judge hastily and turned to look once more out of the window.

Moments passed and the young man remained silent, continuing to stare at the world outside. I wanted to say something, but it was apparent from my earlier attempts that he didn't feel like talking. His expression remained sad and troubled. He, too, appeared to be attempting to deal with some issue of suffering. If he didn't want to talk, I wasn't going to force the issue.

I continued gazing at the magnificent view of the city. The panorama allowed me to focus on something other than the pain that haunted me since yesterday. This was the first place since leaving my home where I truly felt safe. I could relax and think about everything that transpired over the last day or so without worrying about mobs or people getting killed around me. It wasn't home, but at least it was sanctuary.

I relinquished my view of the city and slumped on the floor. I rested my head against the wall, stared at the ceiling and released a huge sigh. It was quiet, the most quiet I'd had in quite some time. The sun had set and the cloak of night now blanketed the city. Although it only seemed like a few moments, hours had actually passed. The young boy sat atop the stacked boxes the entire time, staring unflinchingly out of the window. He never made a sound. No glances were given in my direction and no gestures were made. Yet, I felt great just sitting there. It was hard to describe, but despite the silence, I enjoyed not having to move or do anything but rest and think. It allowed me the opportunity to get a lot sorted out. But I couldn't stay here forever. Eventually, I had to resume my mission. I would find the Contravexus and make him pay for what he'd done.

I suddenly decided that I needed to get going. I stood to my feet and stretched the kinks out of my back. I turned and looked out of the window once more. This time, the view was different. It wasn't the same twinkling, pre-evening gem I saw earlier. Now, I saw lives and situations I hadn't noticed before. I saw an old man getting robbed on the street corner. I saw the hooker having sex with the married businessman in the hotel room across the street. I saw a drug deal and an attempted murder. I saw a mother that left her child with a stranger and another child that had been born and left in a garbage can in the alley. This was a different world than the one I saw earlier today. I was now looking into the lives of some of the people that lived in this city. It was strange watching these moments unfold right before my eyes. The entire city was being exposed to me. Everything, the good and the bad, I witnessed without leaving this one spot.

It was nine forty-six according to the clock on the bank across the street. The city was winding down from the evening rush period, but it still possessed a degree of liveliness. The sun was gone and the crescent moon gleamed in the frosty night sky. The young lad, who had been literally motionless the entire time, suddenly jumped down from the mountain of boxes and resumed bouncing the basketball. He started walking toward the door of the chamber. I turned to watch him leave, still unaware as to who he was.

He never said a word as he continued his exit from the room. The bouncing of the basketball echoed throughout the main chamber of the church. He'd left the room, leaving me standing next to the window. Suddenly, the bouncing stopped. Dead silence was all I could hear. I quickly walked to the chamber door to see if something had happened to him. My first thought was that the mob that was chasing me earlier had somehow made their way into the church. When I got to the doorway, however, I beheld a sight far more frightening than the presumed mob.

The chamber was covered with cobwebs and dust. Beams from the streetlights outside cast gothic silhouettes within the main chamber. The pews were cracked, splintered or totally destroyed. The statues that were in perfect condition when I had entered were now crumbled or smashed. Huge holes riddled the ceiling, and the rotted support beams barely held the fragmented roof intact. The podium on the pulpit had been destroyed, resembling a stack of firewood. Slivers of stained glass littered the aisles and a moldy smell lingered in the air. This church that was so pretentiously beautiful when I first arrived had now been destroyed.

I stood in the doorway consumed with shock and disbelief. All of this couldn't have happened during the time I was in here. I questioned my own sanity, wondering whether I was going mad or if I was experiencing another vision. I knew what I saw when I arrived, and it was nothing like what I was seeing now. I heard nothing and could not explain what had happened. It was inconceivable that this much devastation could happen without me hearing it. In fact, judging from the condition of the church, no one had been here for decades.

A numb feeling began to overtake me. This was a place that had brought me some comfort and refuge. I actually felt safe here, the safest I'd felt since last night. Now, it also had suffered the same fate that everything else around me had. The peace I felt when I arrived was now replaced with more confusion and an even greater sense of frustration.

I slowly walked into the main chamber and toward the building's entrance. The light from the street lamps outside shined through the broken windows, providing the only light inside the church. I shuffled my feet, trying to make sure I didn't bump into anything. As I approached the front doors, my feet bumped into something blocking my path on the floor. The light from outside shined directly on that one spot and revealed that it was a basketball. In fact, it was the very one the boy had been bouncing. I looked around to see where he might be and called to him.

"Hello? Little boy are you in here?"

There was no response. I looked once more at the ball as it sat motionless on the floor. There was no dust or spider webbing on it. It looked as if it was just played with. I knelt down and picked it up, feeling a little disturbed as I held it in my hands. The dust on the floor around the ball was undisturbed. I thought that perhaps his footprints would give me a clue to his whereabouts. However, there were none. It was as if he'd vanished into thin air.

I stood and passed the ball between my hands a couple of times. Then, I looked up. Over the door was a huge crucifix with the body of Christ hanging from it. It was the same one that had hung over the pulpit when I arrived. Only this time, the body of the Messiah was attached. His eyes stared directly into mine. They possessed the same pain and sorrow I saw in the kid's eyes as he stared out of the window. The basketball was laid directly beneath the crucifix. Was it possible that the boy who sat atop the boxes was the Messiah? If he was, why was he here? I stood transfixed, my eyes staring into his as the possibilities raced through my head.

As I looked up at the cross, I realized that some very powerful hands were manipulating my life. But at least I knew now that some of them were trying to help me. My time here allowed me to get the rest I needed. It also gave me shelter from the raging hell storm outside. Perhaps I'd been wrong about this place. Maybe, there was a fountain of hope here after all. As I drew that conclusion, the surroundings slowly changed back to their regal and elegant state. The cobwebs were gone and the pews, windows and pulpit were restored to their original state. I looked around at the palatial chamber and chuckled beneath my breath. Then, I turned and looked at the crucifix. I could almost swear I saw a smile on the lips of the Messiah.

"Thank you," I said.

I placed the ball back on the floor and walked out of the front door of the church.

~~~

CHAPTER ELEVEN

The Bank of America Tower, one of the largest skyscrapers in the city of San Francisco. Atop this dark yet magnificent structure stood an equally dark figure. His long black coat flapped in the turbulent winds as he stared over the city in a disdainful god-like manner. The city lights twinkled below and the sounds of civilization echoed from the streets.

A helicopter circled the top of the building and began its decent. The dark figure maintained his menacing stare. As the helicopter landed on the launching pad behind him, the lights from the chopper revealed a glimpse of this ominous figure that stood waiting. It was the Contravexus himself, Montellace Dupri.

He stood unaffected by the winds from the spinning blades of the helicopter. His coattail flapped like a flag behind him as he continued to scan the entire city from his lofty perch. It was as if he was searching for something or someone. The blades of the chopper began to decelerate and soon ceased their spiraling.

The door of the helicopter opened, and a pair of two-toned black and white wing-tipped shoes touched the turf. The dubious demon, Mao Ding Huang had arrived. He was dressed in a double-breasted virgin white silk suit with a black shirt and a red silk necktie. He completed the ensemble with a matching white Cashmere coat. He exited the helicopter and strolled to the conservatively clad Montellace Dupri.

"Nice view!" said Huang.

"The time is near. What do you have to report?" asked Dupri.

"She was rather distraught over the Seraph's death. I lost track of her when she left her house so I listened to the police scanner. I figured she'd be spotted sooner or later, especially after I dropped that little tip about her. Sure enough, the cops got a report of a woman matching her description in downtown Seattle. When I got there, the cops were trying to arrest her."

"What did you do?"

"What else? I killed them, as well as everyone else in the diner. I thought for sure that another murder scene would drive her over the edge."

"Did it?"

"No. She was a little shaken up, though, and tried to leave. Surprisingly, she still didn't break. I sent my minions after her, but for some strange reason, we lost her. It was as if she vanished into thin air," explained Huang.

"The Messiah. It had to be him. I thought I sensed his annoying presence. He's hiding her, probably thinking that he's helping her. What he doesn't realize is that no matter what he does, I will find the gate, even if I have to kill every last being in the process," said Dupri.

"My lord, perhaps it's time we increased the heat? We can no longer afford to allow her the time to come to us willingly. We must act now and bring her in, even if it is done forcefully. If you sense the Messiah as you say, then surely they will do all they can to keep her hidden," said Huang.

Dupri sighed and tightened his clenched fist.

"We've destroyed millions of lives, sent trillions upon trillions of souls to Hell. We are so close to victory that I can see our master's radiance once again. Yet, it seems strange that it can all be ruined because of one annoying little brat and a vessel who can't remember its past nor its purpose," said Dupri.

"If only we had gotten to her before they did," stated Huang.

"Yes, the Hierarchy did a good job in keeping her whereabouts a secret. However, their interference will cost them dearly. There will be another war. But this war will be different. This time the Hierarchy will fall. The only force that has ever opposed us has been the Hierarchy. Well, not anymore. I will watch their bones and flesh burn on the altar, and the Messiah's billions of followers will watch their beloved savior perish once and for all. This time, we will succeed. This time, we will take over this realm and rebuild this entire universe the way our master, the Vul Paux, sees fit!" Dupri retorted.

"Shall I retrieve the Gaian then?"

"Yes. Find her and bring her to me, by any means necessary."

"Very well."

Suddenly, a third person appeared on the roof.

"So, is this an all-male fashion show or can a girl get in on the fun?" asked a soft voice from the shadows.

Dupri and Huang turned to acknowledge the intruder.

"Eve?" asked Dupri.

Eve smirked and struck a pose.

"Most impressive," Dupri said.

Eve's silky golden hair blew in the crosswinds. A red sequin, thigh high dress with a plunging V-shaped neckline complimented her perfectly sculpted and buxom figure. Her shapely legs were accented with a pair of fishnet pantyhose and her feet were graced with a pair of matching sequin pumps. Draping her silken shoulders was a pure white mink shawl. Her neck and wrists were accented with diamonds, and her fragrance was an enticing lilac scent. She walked toward the two men and stood next to them.

"Huang, I'd like for you to meet Eve," said Dupri.

The two looked at one another. Eve smiled, Huang scowled.

"This is who you chose to replace Caliestra?" asked Huang turning to Dupri.

"You sound as if you disapprove," said Eve.

"I do. You're a human, and what's worse, a woman," said Huang.

"Not just a woman, *the* woman. She was the one who gave birth to this race," said Dupri.

Huang gave Dupri a very disapproving look.

"My lord, I mean no disrespect. But if this is the person you say she is, she couldn't follow the commandments of her God. She couldn't possibly do us any good. I strongly oppose this plan of action," said Huang.

"Sorry to hear that, Huang, but she will be helping us," said Dupri.

"Yes, my lord," Huang replied, tucking his head.

Eve turned and looked at Dupri. "And what is your opinion, Lord Dupri? Do you approve?"

"If I didn't, you wouldn't be here," Dupri replied, tracing a lock of her hair.

"I hear that you are planning a going away party for a friend. Mind if I help with the plans?" Eve asked.

"Why not? Man cannot suffer without a woman's touch," said Huang.

Eve turned and gave the three-foot tall imp a look of disgust.

"Okay, Huang, that's enough. We have a gate to find," stated Dupri.

"Any word yet as to where it may be?" asked Eve.

"No. And it's beginning to annoy me. The vessel has no memory of where it is and the governments of the world aren't having any success in locating it either," retorted Dupri.

"I don't understand why we are allowing the little princess to wander about freely? If you need the information, why not take it from her?" queried Eve.

"It's not that simple. The princess, as you call her, is the only one that knows the location of the gate. However, her memories have been sealed, thus preventing us from finding the gate's location. I figured that if enough drama occurred in her life, she would somehow break the bonds that bind her memory. Then, she could lead us to the gate and we could free the Vul Paux. Unfortunately, the bonds are much stronger than we thought," explained Dupri.

"Do we really need her? I mean, you have control of the entire world's armies. Can't they locate the gate?" asked Eve.

"We've tried that. I've had the Russians, the Germans, the Brits and the Americans searching this entire planet for the last millennia; they've all been unsuccessful in locating it. I do not wish to wait another thousand years when the being that can hand me the gate on a silver platter is within my grasp," answered Dupri.

"So why not abduct her and force her to tell you where the gate is? I'm sure your methods of persuasion could cause enough trauma to break the bonds," said Eve.

"Unlike you humans, we have great respect for things we deem holy. We wanted to try and coax her to remember by causing certain traumatic events in her life. However, our tactics have proven unsuccessful," said Huang.

"But now we see no other choice. Things have reached crucial levels now and we have no other alternative but to forcefully bring her in," said Dupri.

"What of the Hierarchy? Aren't you worried about their interference?" asked Eve.

"I don't think that they will be much of a problem," said Dupri.

"Why wouldn't they be?" questioned Eve.

"That's where you are going to come in. You are that one piece of the puzzle they don't know about. Have you mastered the toxin that cruises through your veins?" asked Dupri.

"Yes, I have."

"Good. You will use that toxin to take out their top man, Michael. Without him, they will all be lost," explained Dupri.

Huang looked surprised. "She is going to kill Michael? My lord, that should be a privilege reserved for a god, not a human."

"That is exactly the kind of thinking one would expect from a celestial being. However, history has taught us well. Remember the Trojan Horse? I believe Eve fits that part very well," said Dupri.

Eve looked stunned. "Lord Dupri, are you certain about this?"

"Whom better to cripple the Hierarchy than the person who has been forever cursed by them? They say that you were the being that brought down mankind. They placed a punishment upon you that was cruel and unjust. Well now, you will have your revenge. When we get the gate, we can create a new world. We will restore order, wiping the slate clean of all sins, yours included. You will finally be able to live as freely as the rest of humanity has done. Imagine it, Eve. No more suffering; no more pain," explained Dupri.

Eve looked distressed and uncertain, but quickly nodded her head to show her commitment to Dupri's plan. She realized that her association with him could possibly give her a chance at redemption. It would also free her soul from the guilt she's had to carry since the beginning of mankind. It was the only chance she had.

"So, what do we do now?" she asked.

"Phase two begins. We need to build up our forces. If we are going to face Jehovah and his armies, we need more souls," said Dupri.

Eve flashed him a surprised look. "So what do you plan to do, start killing people?"

"Exactly!" exclaimed Huang.

Eve was noticeably disturbed at first, then a smile slowly bloomed across her lips.

"You do realize this means destroying everything you helped to create?" asked Dupri.

Eve nodded. "Let's do it."

Suddenly, the distant roar of thunder was heard.

"Hmm, even the planet is bracing for the war. C'mon, let's get out of here," said Dupri.

He turned and began walking to the exit door with Eve and Huang following closely. As they left their lofty meeting location, the wind began to gust and swirl on the roof. The thunder boomed and rattled the foundation of the building. Dupri was correct. The spirit of the planet did indeed feel the impending battle and tried it's best to alert its inhabitants. But mankind was oblivious to the various ways nature attempted to communicate. Mother Earth's warnings went unheard and would later be explained as anomalies in the weather. However, those who knew the various tongues of the universe heard the warnings and began their preparation for the tribulations to come.

After the three individuals departed the roof, leaves and trash that had somehow drifted to this high perch began to swirl and dance on the launching pad. The flashes of lightning grew brighter and the crash of the thunder became louder. In the shadows of a corner, a pair of eyes stared from the darkness. Their glowing presence went unnoticed by the three individuals. However, the being those eyes belonged to heard every word that was spoken.

As the lightning continued to illuminate the sky, the outline of the figure's face became clearer. It was that of a young boy. He squatted motionlessly in the corner with his knees brought to his chest and his arms enwrapping them. A look of pain and sorrow deeply engraved his face as he stared from his secluded location. His eyes lacked the fire that one so small would normally have. He unlocked his hands from around his legs and stood to his feet. The residual lightning burned its last bit of energy as the young man faded into the shadows, leaving behind the haunting echo of a basketball being bounced.

~~~

His eyes fluttered open, but his vision was still blurry. He'd been unconscious for two days and now, he was opening his eyes for the first time since his injury. Angelo Ramone, known to his angelic brethren as Uriel, looked around the room and tried to focus his eyes. He lifted his hand to his face and pinched the bridge of his nose. Just then, he felt someone grabbing his other arm.

"Welcome back," said a soft voice.

Angelo saw a face, but it was still too fuzzy to recognize.

"Who's there?" he asked.

"Its me, Gabrielle."

"Gabby? Is that really you?"

Angelo patted her hands and she cupped his.

"How are you feeling?" she asked.

"Everything is blurry, like my eyesight is bad," he said.

"Yeah, Peter said this might happen. But don't worry, it's just your body trying to adjust from the trauma you underwent," said Gabrielle.

"Trauma? What trauma?"

"You were shot several times in the chest. You nearly died," said another voice from the corner.

It was Sariel. He was sitting in a chair across the room.

"Sariel!" said Angelo, lifting his hands toward the direction of the voice.

Sariel stood and walked to the bed. He leaned over and hugged Angelo firmly.

"We almost lost you there," he said.

"Was it that bad?" Angelo asked.

"Yes, it was pretty bad. If Sariel hadn't gotten to you when he did, you would be dead," said Gabrielle.

"Then I'm glad he did. Thank you," said Angelo.

"Nah, no need to thank me. That's what we do," said Sariel.

Angelo relaxed in his bed and sighed.

"Peter said that your blurred vision should last for about another ten minutes, then you should have your full sight back. In about another three hours, he said that you should be in physical therapy, and by tomorrow, you can leave the facility," said Gabrielle.

"That sounds great," said Angelo.

"It's a good thing we angels heal quickly," said Gabrielle.

Sariel sighed deeply.

"What's the matter, brother? You sound disgruntled," said Angelo.

"I am. If it hadn't been for that damn vessel, you wouldn't be in this predicament," said Sariel.

Right then, Angelo remembered Vanifera.

"Where is she? Where's my wife?"

"Who knows, and to be honest with you, who cares," said Sariel.

"Sariel, stop that," said Gabrielle.

"What do you mean you don't know?" asked Angelo with a slightly agitated tone.

"Angelo, calm down. Michael has some agents out looking for her as we speak. When they find her, they'll bring her in. In the meantime, I suggest you get some rest. You have a lot of therapy to go through before you are released," said Gabrielle.

Suddenly, Angelo remembered what happened to him.

"Oh God! I remember now. I saw a guy with a gun and he shot me. I can see it like it just happened," he said.

Gabrielle frowned. "It's all over now. Just rest..."

"Does she know I'm still alive?"

"I don't think so."

"Gabrielle, find her. She's probably out there wandering around thinking I'm dead."

"Why do you think she cares? She probably hired the gunman to shoot you in the first place," said Sariel.

"You're wrong! She isn't like that. She *is* reformed, and I'd stake my life on that!" said Angelo.

"Oh really? Well, I hate to break it to you, bub, but you already staked your life on it and she nearly took it from you. She was the vessel of the Vul Paux! Do you remember who that was? She is evil, pure and simple," said Sariel.

"You're wrong, brother. She isn't evil at all. She's not the monster you think she is. She loves me and I love her. You must find her. Please, do this one thing for me, please," begged Angelo.

Sariel sighed and glanced at Gabrielle.

"Very well, Uriel, I will find her," said Sariel.

"Thank you," said Angelo with a sigh.

"Okay, now that that's been settled, get some rest," said Gabrielle.

Sariel and Gabrielle turned and walked out of the room. In the hallway, stood Azreal, waiting.

"What are you doing here again?" asked Sariel.

"I came to give you an update. It seems that a body has been found on the edge of a swamp this morning," said Azreal.

"Yeah? So?" asked Gabrielle.

"The body was covered with lesions. It was leprosy. The wounds were fresh, like they'd just been made," said Azreal.

"I still don't get it," said Gabrielle.

"You folks amaze me sometimes," said Azreal shaking his head.

"Just get to the point, Azreal!" said Gabrielle.

"The lesions found today haven't been in existence for over four thousand years. Whoever inflicted these fresh wounds knew of the toxin strain to bring about this kind of misery," said Azreal.

"You think it was the Gaian?" asked Sariel.

"Who else would it be? She is the only unchecked entity running around. The bonds must be weakening and she's probably regaining her memory," said Gabrielle.

"This is bad. If her memory comes back, she will remember where the gate is hidden. If that happens, she is going to release the Vul Paux. We have to stop her, now," said Sariel.

"The Consortium is already on it. Lucifer has dispatched the royal guards led by none other than his own son," said Azreal.

"Lorimar?" asked Gabrielle.

"Yes, Gabrielle, your son is leading the search from our end. I suggest you two get with Michael and get something started on your side. Time is up, and if we don't find the Gaian soon, we are going to be in for one hell of a time," said Azreal.

Just then, Gabrielle's cell phone began ringing. She quickly flipped it open.

"Yes, Michael?" she answered.

"I just received some very disturbing news. Seems that a body has been identified as Angelo Ramone. It was taken from his home on the night he was shot. Someone is playing a very interesting game. Agents have checked out the body and found it to be a man that had been murdered earlier that day, some homeless person. Whoever put that body there knows that Uriel isn't dead. I suspect that they want the world to believe he's dead. On top of that, the Gaian is wanted for his murder, as well as the murder of a police officer and a diner full of people," said Michael.

"Good lord!" said Gabrielle.

She relayed the information she just received to Sariel and Azreal.

"Azreal has also informed us that a body was found on the outskirts of a swamp. Seems as though the body has a strain of leprosy dating back four thousand years," said Gabrielle.

"Really?" queried Michael.

"We think she might be getting her memory back. Her killing instincts may also be returning. She may even be trying to locate the gate," said Gabrielle.

"That's possible," said Michael.

"The Consortium has already begun their search for the Gaian. What do you want us to do?" asked Gabrielle.

"Go to threat-level Omega. Although all of this sounds convincing, I don't believe the Gaian is behind these deaths. However, we can't take any chances. Start searching for her. I suspect she is still in Seattle. We've been trying to find her using the Sky Eye, but we haven't been successful. Find her and bring her in. Let's just hope that our worse fears haven't come to pass," said Michael.

"Roger! Out!" said Gabrielle as she flipped closed her phone.

"Roger? Out? What is this, Sergeant Bilko's army?" asked Sariel.

Gabrielle pursed her lips.

"Alright, you heard the man. Let's get out there and find us a vessel," said Gabrielle.

Azreal had slipped away during the conversation with Michael. Sariel turned and began walking away without saying a word. Gabrielle stood in the middle of the hallway and watched the white haired Sariel depart. She sighed and then began following him.

Sariel was seething. He remembered the destruction the Vul Paux brought when it was here last. Now, through the mishandling of the Hierarchy, the single greatest threat to all of creation was on the verge of being released from the pit called the Omega Realm.

"Yeah. I'll bring her in alright, in a body bag," said Sariel.

~~~

Portland, Oregon. A young man donned in tan khakis pants, a black oxford shirt, a speckled tan and dark brown sports coat and black tasseled Nunn Bush loafers stood in front of the Rose Garden, watching the famed Rose Quarter water fountain oscillate its water jets from its brick floor. He was fascinated by the spectacle and continued to marvel at it. However, he was no mere spectator, but a being whose power rivaled his father's. His name is Lorimar and he is the Prince of Hell. As he continued to watch the water shoot into the air, an old man scurried toward the suave looking prince.

"Prince Lorimar, sir, our readings indicated that she was in this part of the country, but now her signal has gone dead. We assume that she has moved to a protected location. But she is close, sir, very close," said the man.

"Not close enough, I'm afraid. I, too, sense the Gaian is near. Unfortunately, she is not in this city. Since we can't pinpoint her, we should hold our positions. Have your men fan out and report to me as soon as you find something. Time is of the essence and we haven't a moment to spare," said Lorimar.

"Yes sir," said the man.

He quickly scurried off and disappeared into the shadows. Lorimar continued to watch the shooting fountain and a smile came to his face.

"So amused by the small things, eh, Lorimar?" said a feminine voice from behind.

Lorimar didn't turn around. His expression turned from delight to a scowl.

"*What* are you doing here?" he asked.

"Just doing my part in the search for the unholy grail," the voice continued.

"Father would be most upset if he were to find out that you were here, my dear sister," said Lorimar.

"Father would be a lot of things if these were settled times, but they aren't. Therefore, my antics aren't his primary concern, my dear brother," said the voice.

"So, why are you hiding in the shadows? Why don't you come out and be the devil-spawn that you are? Or are you afraid you might get busted?" asked Lorimar.

Just then, a woman dressed in an ankle-length, blood-red chiffon gown emerged. Her dress had a waist-high slit, revealing her shapely long legs. Her long hair was jet black with faint streaks of red. She was a perfect size seven with an attitude to match. She was the Princess of Hell, daddy's little girl and Lorimar's pain-in-the-ass sister. Her name was Kitana.

"So tell me, why have you come to bother me?" asked Lorimar.

"Just thought I'd let you know some information we just found out about your illusive target," said Kitana.

"What is it?" asked Lorimar.

"She's still in Seattle. You missed your mark by just a little bit," she said squeezing her index finger and thumb together.

"You came all this way to tell me this? Kitana, spare me the bullshit. You didn't come here to tell me that. You came here for Azreal," said Lorimar, who now turned to look her in her eyes.

"What? Me? I would *never* do anything like that," she said playfully.

"I'm not sure what you're thinking, but this is not a game. If you're not going to help, then you're going back home," said Lorimar, pulling his right hand from his pocket.

Suddenly, two demons appeared on both sides of Kitana. They grabbed her arms and waited for their commands.

"Take my sister back to Consortium Headquarters," said Lorimar.

Kitana turned and glared at one of the demons. "Get your filthy hands off me!"

Neither complied. She then opened her mouth slightly and released a high-pitched tone that caused the ground to start shaking. Lorimar squeezed his eyes closed as his little sister continued with her mild tantrum. The windows on the Rose Garden started cracking and sparks flew from the illuminated marquee, causing the lights on it to go dead. The two demons on both sides began vibrating until they shattered into piles of dust. Then, as suddenly as she began, she stopped. The rumbling ceased and all was calm.

Lorimar peeked one eye open and then the other. Kitana stood there smiling at him.

"I sure hate when you do that," he said.

"Next time, keep your filthy little monsters' paws off me. They shouldn't be touching me anyway," said Kitana.

"And you shouldn't be here! This is an important operation, and I can't allow you to treat it as if it's some childish game!" exclaimed Lorimar.

"That's your problem. You always think you can handle everything, like you don't need anyone's help. I may not be the commander of the Royal Guards, but I can help. For instance, you're looking in the wrong place. The Gaian isn't here. You need to go to Seattle; that's where she is. The Hierarchy is on their way there also, so I'm told. If you want to continue to look good and save your precious reputation, I'd advise you to stop sitting here lecturing me and go get your target," said Kitana.

Lorimar was seething. He hated when she tried to tell him what to do, and he hated it even more when she had a point.

"One day, you will push me too far, my dear sister," he said.

"I'll worry about that when that day comes. As for now, you need to go to Seattle," said Kitana.

"Yes, I heard you the first time. Now, if there isn't any other information you need to give me, please leave."

"Well, there is one little, teeny-weeny piece of info you might want to know."

"What's that?" asked Lorimar with an annoyed expression.

"There is a good chance you'll run into...mother," she said.

~~~

CHAPTER TWELVE

Seattle. In a small room at the rear of The First Church of God, a young boy sat on the floor clutching a basketball in his arms. His head was bowed, staring at the floor in deep thought. His facial expression was somber and his body was tense. He appeared troubled, as if he'd received some disturbing news and was pondering his next course of action.

As the boy sat contemplating, a man walked through the doorway and glanced at the young lad on the floor. He carried a bag of groceries and had a newspaper tucked under his arm. He walked passed the boy to a counter near the window. The man placed the bag down along with the newspaper and began unpacking the groceries. He stored the items into a pantry and closed the doors. Then, he folded the bag and packed it into a gap between the cabinet and the counter. He braced himself on the tabletop and bowed his head.

"She's very beautiful," said the boy.

The man lifted his head and looked at the boy. His response was surprising, particularly since the lad hadn't spoken in days.

"How is she holding up?" he asked.

The lad lifted his head and looked at the man. He paused for a moment, debating on whether to give him additional information. He looked at the man's face and saw the urgency he displayed in knowing more. The boy sighed and continued.

"She spent most of the evening with me. The Contravexus was trying to overwhelm her. Barhim Hajj guided her here and I managed to protect her by concealing this place. It took all of my concentration just to hide this location. She tried to talk to me, but I couldn't answer right then. I'm sure she thinks I was being rude.

But I didn't want them to find her. She appears to be doing fine right now. However, I fear that she may not be ready for the return of her memories just yet," he replied.

The man sighed deeply and bowed his head in disappointment. The boy stood to his feet and tucked the ball under his right arm. He walked to where the man was standing and patted his shoulder.

"That's not to say we can't help prepare her," the boy continued.

The man lifted his head and looked into the compassionate eyes of the young man. "Is she that close to regaining her memories?"

"I'm not sure," the boy replied.

"You know the news reports are saying she is the one who murdered the Seraph, the cop and those people in the diner."

"Yes, but I don't think she did it. In fact, I'm certain of it."

"Why would you say that?"

"If she were responsible for those deaths, then that would mean she has reverted to her former self. The synaptic connection inside the Gaian that's blocking her memories would have been destroyed. If that were the case, she would have remembered the location of the gate and resurrected the Vul Paux by now. That is her prime directive, not going on a killing spree."

"What makes you think she hasn't already resurrected him?"

"If the Vul Paux were released, you think we would still be on this planet?" asked the boy wryly.

"I see your point. The Paux would have destroyed this planet by now."

"Exactly."

"So what do we do now?"

"We watch her and we wait. So far my observations have shown that the synaptic bond is holding. But with all the trauma she's been through, I'm not sure how much longer it will last."

"You sound worried."

"I have good reason to be, old friend. I believe the Contravexus is the one behind all this turmoil pointing to the Gaian. He wants her to become mentally unstable. Perhaps doing so would break the bond that has kept her memories suppressed."

"How do you know this?"

"I tracked him down. He was in San Francisco just last night. I placed myself in a trance and teleported my spirit to his location. I happened to overhear him on the roof of a skyscraper discussing his plans with his demon aide. He has even managed to enlist the services of the first woman. I'm afraid that the moment of confrontation is close at hand."

"He got to Eve? Damn him! He certainly isn't playing around, is he?"

"No, he isn't, and neither should we. With Eve's mastery of the occult crafts, he is an even greater threat. There is a lot at stake, and if we wish to survive this battle, we must get to work. I overheard them saying something about increasing their armies. That's probably what all these other murders are about. They're harvesting souls. I've got to find some way of saving as many souls as I can."

"Do you think you are up to the task?"

"I don't know. But I will give it everything I have."

"Do you still think we'll have to kill her?"

"If her memories remain sealed, I may not have to. But we cannot allow Dupri to get his hands on the gate. His truest intentions are to eradicate all of creation. If all goes well, I will let her live. However, if I'm forced to kill her, I will not hesitate."

"It's amazing. You are the savior of souls, the bringer of peace. It seems ironic that you have the ability to kill her."

"Yes. I don't believe that even the Vul Paux's minions know of my ability to do that. The Gaian was seemingly indestructible. It feeds off sin and evil. However, removing those things it needs to survive makes it weak. That's its Achilles' heal."

"Indeed. Should I go to the Hierarchy and find out what they know so far?"

"No, not just yet. I want to see what the Contravexus' next move will be. He knows that we have her and I suspect he will retaliate, trying to smoke her out. We just need to keep her safe and out of sight for a while."

The old man nodded. "I'd like to see her."

"She's up on the roof. Why don't you go up and say hi," said the boy.

~~~

Inside the Bank of America building, bodies lay on the floor and dangled over the tops of the cubicles. Headless and impaled carcasses littered the offices with pools of blood beneath them. The pungent odor of death filled the entire building. They were the second group of unsuspecting casualties in this Holy War. The path of bodies led to the main boardroom. Traces of blood were smeared on the half-opened door, marking the concluding location of the massacre. The individuals responsible for this wake of destruction were inside, lounging.

Dupri sat in the CEO's board chair, staring out of the window. He could view the entire city from his position. He sat in the seat of a man who was once one of his chief rivals in the city. Now, the man that once controlled this company was a corpse, lying on the floor beneath the table.

Eve reclined on the couch. Her shoes were off and her feet rested on the arm of the plush sofa. She twirled a golden cross medallion attached to a gold chain. It was a memento she snared from one of the victims in the other room. It was a reminder to her of the mission ahead. Although she appeared calm on the outside, Eve was the most anxious to start her duties. She had the taste of revenge in her mouth and it permeated every cell in her body. She hated God for punishing her for being human. Now, after all this time, she would have vengeance. She would make those who betrayed her pay for their deceit. But for now, she had to wait until the time was right, just like the rest of her compatriots.

On the other side of the room, Huang played with a dagger as he sat on the windowsill. It was a beautifully crafted blade with a serrated edge and a hooking tip. The handle was made of pure ivory

182

and onyx, perfectly crafted to fit his deadly hand. On the point of the blade was an impaled eyeball. It, too, was a souvenir from the killfest that happened on his way to the boardroom. A smudge of blood now stained his pure white silk suit. Normally, this would be something that would infuriate the demonic playboy. But today wasn't the average day. It was the day he, Eve and Dupri prepared for.

The three killers continued to lounge in the palatial office. This rampage was not just an effort to gather souls for their army, but was also a message to the Hierarchy, letting them know that their patience at this point was running thin. In their minds, the people they killed were already dead. It was just a matter of hours. The three of them were the beings that would bring the end of this world. From their varied perspectives, it was a job they couldn't wait to perform.

"That was a nice little killing spree. Those souls will make excellent additions to our army," said Huang.

"Yeah, but now I'm really getting bored!" exclaimed Eve.

"Go find something to do! Perhaps there's still someone alive in the offices who could really use a good lap dance right about now!" retorted Huang.

"You know, you are really working my last nerve," said Eve disturbingly calm.

"Like I give a ..."

Suddenly, Eve grabbed a sword that was attached to a display above the couch. She stood to her feet and lifted the sword, pointing it toward Huang.

"So you want to play, do you?" asked Huang.

"I've had enough of you and your comments! I'm going to kill you right here and right now!" threatened Eve.

Huang leaped off the sill and whipped his blade, dislodging the eyeball from the tip. Then he lifted his knife and prepared to defend himself. Dupri appeared unconcerned about the battle that was about to take place behind him. He continued to stare out of the window while Eve and Huang circled one another.

Eve attacked with a series of overhead sword swings. Huang and his knife deflected each one of them. But he knew that this was only a test. Huang had heard that Eve was one of the greatest sword wielders ever. It was rumored that the Archangel Michael himself trained her before her expulsion from Eden. Despite the rumors, Huang still wanted to see what she could do.

After successfully deflecting her attacks, Huang charged toward Eve with his knife pointed directly at her chest. Huang was known for cutting out the hearts of his victims and devouring them. However, it was the very move Eve anticipated. She gracefully sidestepped Huang's attack and countered with a vicious swipe across the back of the pint-sized demon. The blade of her sword sliced through the silk suit and lacerated his flesh. Huang bellowed in pain as Eve completed her follow through.

"Damn it, that hurt!" said Huang as he reached behind him to survey his injury.

Eve stood with a smile on her face. She lifted the sword and saluted Huang, then gracefully returned to her defensive posture. Huang removed his hand from his wound and looked at it. A yellow fluid coated his palm. The sight of his own injury infuriated him. He was a demon. How could she inflict this type of damage to him?

"You are going to pay for that!" threatened Huang.

"I'm shaking!" said Eve with sarcasm.

"You know, killing you will be almost as sweet as watching this pathetic world end!" professed Huang.

Eve puckered her lips and blew the angered demon a kiss. She sensed that Huang was out of his element in this battle. However, she also realized that he wasn't giving his all. Huang was a very powerful demon, one that she could not underestimate. Even though she was given the sentence of eternal life to forever walk this planet and view the aftermath of her supposed disobedience, it didn't mean she couldn't be killed. There was but one way that Eve could lose her immortality, decapitation. However, that was not her concern right now. She was determined to teach the obnoxious imp some respect for her.

Huang leaped into the air and dove on top of Eve, knocking her to the ground. His weight was placed on her shoulders, pinning her beneath him. He placed the jagged blade of the knife across her neck and began pressing it into her throat. Huang knew that Eve could be killed the same way he could be killed. He had to cut her head off.

He was about to rake the blade across her neck when he heard a whistling sound. Huang looked up as Eve's sword pierced through his forehead. The blade impaled his skull and the point erupted through the back of his head. The impact knocked the demon from Eve's chest and into the far wall of the boardroom. Huang hit with a crash and slid down the wall to the floor. The yellow fluid that oozed from the gash on his back now gushed from his head.

Eve quickly stood to her feet. She checked her neck, finding only a small cut where Huang pressed his knife. Luckily, she was able to mount her attack before the demon's blade could inflict any serious damage. Eve's mastery of the sword was just one of her strong suits. She was the original occult priestess. She could control the sword without having to touch it. That was how she managed to get Huang off of her.

The sword protruded from Huang's head as he attempted to stand. His body trembled from the pain. Eve watched as the demon rose from the floor and braced himself against the wall. Huang reached up, grasped the sword's handle and slowly extracted it from his skull. The blade eased from his head as the slurping sound of wet brain tissue echoed in the room.

He concluded the extraction with one final yank of the sword. The act sent a shockwave of pain through his body and he dropped the sword to the ground. Huang fell to one knee and placed his hands on the open wound on his head. Eve folded her arms and continued to stare at Huang. She sported a confident smirk, feeling that she'd taught the arrogant demon a lesson. However, her smugness quickly disappeared.

The wound on Huang's head began closing and healing. It was reforming right before her eyes. Cells turned into tissue and tissue into skin. Within moments, the gaping hole that once spewed a yellow fluid was now a mere scratch on his forehead. Eve had witnessed firsthand one of the benefits to being a demon: regeneration. She lifted her hand and recalled the sword to her. It floated into the air and rested in her palm.

Having completed his regeneration, the fury of Hell was now captured in Huang's eyes, lifting his head to stare at the voluptuous vixen of voodoo. He opened his mouth and released a roar that shattered the floor-to-ceiling windows of the boardroom. Eve was knocked sliding across the floor, stopping just shy of falling out of the building. The shockwave blew her to the edge, her head sticking outside of the window frame. She pulled herself back in and quickly stood to her feet.

As she faced Huang, Eve noticed that he had changed. She'd heard that each demon had the ability to transform into a more powerful version of themselves. Huang had done just that. He had metamorphosed into his second level of demonhood. His height had increased to three times his pint-size. Huge horns had grown from his shoulders and his skin had become crimson in color. His eyes glared with a foul green color, and his huge, dark butterfly-like wings stretched across the length of the boardroom. His deep breaths made a growling sound, and his mouth dripped saliva in anticipation of round two of the battle. He had transformed into a first level Raksasha, an upper level demon of Hell.

Eve raised her sword and prepared to defend herself. She knew that playtime was over, and now she would be dealing with Huang in his most powerful state. The two combatants began circling one another, sizing up each other to see who would strike first. A mistake at this point would prove fatal to the being that made it. Huang released another roar and Eve also released her battle cry. The two began charging toward one another.

Suddenly, a ball of fire crashed to the floor between them and exploded into a hellacious flame. Eve and Huang stopped in their tracks, startled by the blast. The intensity of the fire singed their flesh. They both backed away from the mini inferno, as well as distancing themselves from one another. They shielded themselves with their hands, attempting to lessen the effects of the heat. As they grimaced from the burning of their flesh, the fire suddenly disappeared.

Eve, opening her eyes, slowly lowered her arms and peeked cautiously over them. Huang performed the same action. Across the smoke-filled room, they looked at one another, quickly realizing that neither of them caused that explosion. Then, Dupri slowly emerged from the cloud of soot and stood before them.

"Now, let me make this crystal clear to the both of you! I could give a damn about your petty differences and much less about your existence! However, we have a mission to fulfill! After that has been completed, you can kill each other for all I care! But should either of you choose this course of action before the mission has been completed, I'll kill you myself!" stated Dupri in a calm yet deliberate tone.

Eve and Huang looked at Dupri, then turned and glared at one another in silent hatred. They weren't able to challenge his power. He was the right hand being of the Vul Paux. Their powers were no match for his. The blast of fire was only the tip of the enormous capabilities he possessed. They knew he meant what he said. He would kill them without a second thought. For now, they would do as Dupri commanded and work together.

"Hear me, witch, when this is over with, I will have your head and your heart in my hand! It will be a fitting exclamation to our victory!" threatened Huang.

Eve shoved the tip of the sword into the floor as Huang changed back to his former form. Dupri watched as they returned to opposite sides of the room. Eve slipped her feet back into her shoes. Just then, a phone rang. She reached into her purse and removed a small cellular phone.

"What is it?" she answered angrily.

Dupri turned and resumed his stare upon the city as Eve took her call. As he looked at the street below, he could see a hoard of police cars surrounding the building. *No doubt they are on their way up here,* he thought.

Eve continued taking her call. "Hmm, that's interesting. Hold on for a moment."

She walked to the boardroom table phone, pushing a deceased female executive to the floor whose hand was covering it. She pressed a few buttons and instantly her call was connected to the speakerphone.

"Go ahead, he's listening," she said.

"My lord, this is Amir Fawan," said the voice on the speaker.

"Well, hello Secretary-General," said Dupri. "Have you found something for me?"

"Yes, lord, their coordinates are being sent to you as we speak. We have had the full cooperation from the President and the Prime Minister. They are both with me right now," said Fawan.

"Excellent! Then I will see you gentlemen later," said Dupri.

"Yes, sir!"

The speakerphone clicked, indicating that Fawan had hung up. Eve pressed a button and turned off the speaker.

"What was that about?" asked Huang.

Both he and Eve looked at Dupri with a degree of uncertainty.

"That was the other half of the equation. In order to bring our lord, the Vul Paux, from the Omega Realm, we need the gate. However, we also require the altar so that he can be reunited with the Gaian. Fawan has found the altar," Dupri explained.

"Where was it?" questioned Eve.

"In different locations. The first piece was located in a church outside San Francisco. The other two's locations are being faxed to us now. However, seeing that things are starting to come together rather quickly, I have a job for each of you," said Dupri.

"Anything boss," said Huang.

"Eve, I want you to pay a little visit to Toronto, Ontario. It is time for you to take out the Seraph called Michael. With him out of the way, they won't be able to function very well," Dupri stated sadistically.

"As you wish," Eve replied.

"You remember the plan?"

"Yes. It should be fun."

Dupri then turned to Huang.

"Huang, I have an equally important job for you. Find the Gaian and bring her back to me, even if you must do it by force. Do you understand?" Dupri asked.

"Yes, my lord," he replied. "But what if she becomes hostile?"

Dupri returned a very stolid look. Huang tucked his head. Eve turned to Dupri.

"What will *you* do?" she asked.

"I shall return to Rome. I have a taste for some Italian food. I figured I'd better get some before I destroyed this world."

A strong gust of wind blew through the shattered windows of the boardroom, ruffling the curtains that barely clung on their rods. The wind howled inside the room filled with bodies and blood. Suddenly, a voice blared through a bullhorn.

"You in there! Come out with your hands up!"

Dupri snickered. He turned to Huang and Eve. "Do you believe this?"

They both smirked. He walked to the doors of the boardroom and opened them abruptly. He stared into the barrels of several guns pointed directly at him. Unflinchingly, he looked at each of the police officers with a smirk. Bewildered expressions began to bloom across their faces and each of them slowly lowered their guns. The officers then reached for their heads, as if they'd suddenly became dizzy or confused. A few of them even slumped to one knee.

"You do not see me or my associates," said Dupri. "All you see is a room filled with dead executives. You will suspect this is the act of terrorists, namely members of a Muslim group from Iraq. You will radio this information to the officers below, then detonate several grenades and sacrifice yourselves."

Blank expressions covered each of the officers' faces as Huang,

Eve and Dupri exited the boardroom and walked to the elevators. One of the officers radioed what Dupri had told them to the police chief below. Ten minutes later, a massive explosion occurred at the top of the building. Five minutes after that, the entire building collapsed.

~~~

I could never tell what each day held, for it kept its secrets well until the time was right. It was this factor of each day that I could never get used to. As the world slept, the troubles of that day faded into dreams only to reappear with great vividness at dawn. This was the irony of daybreak. It brought the illusion of hope, as well as the reality of anguish.

I gazed from the rooftop of the church where I spent the night. I kept thinking about the little boy bouncing the basketball and the crowd of possessed humans that tried to kill me. I remembered the markings on the man's head and the little Asian-looking imp that harassed me everytime I turned around. I remembered Betty and the people in the diner, as well as the cop who committed suicide after killing my husband. Each of these images replayed in my head, adding to the depression that already consumed me.

The most painful thoughts were those concerning Angelo. I missed him terribly and my heart still carried a profound ache. I couldn't help feeling that perhaps I'd caused all of this. If it weren't for me, none of this would've happened. I tried to rationalize things, saying that everything that had happened to me over the last few days was done to make my life as miserable as possible. At one point, the events were happening so fast that I couldn't think straight. I'd grown frustrated and confused, acting on instincts alone. But I now knew that Dupri was doing everything possible to break me. It was like some twisted game being played with my life and it made me mad as hell. However, things were about to change.

Dupri was unaware that I now knew what he was up to. I began thinking of ways to use this to my advantage. The police were still after me, and sooner or later, they would probably catch up to me. I couldn't stay at this church forever and even if I could, I didn't want to. I didn't feel like hiding anymore. I was now ready to fight. While I was in the diner, a thought had come to mind. I suspected that the police were working for Dupri and I was going to use them to help me get to him. My plan had been to let them take me in, that way they would lead me right to him. However, Huang screwed that up. Regardless, it was the best plan I could think of and I began psyching myself up to resume carrying out my plan.

"You can do this, Vanifera," I said to myself. "Just let them take you in and they'll lead you right to him. They can't kill you, so there's nothing to worry about."

"So, you're going to turn yourself in, huh?" said a voice behind me.

I didn't turn to acknowledge him, but I knew it was the Barhim Hajj.

"You're eavesdropping on conversations now?" I asked.

"I can't believe you'd consider such a thing," he continued.

"Why shouldn't I?"

"Because you will be walking right into their hands, princess, don't you see that?"

"Maybe that's what I want. Maybe I want the Contravexus to find me. Then I could have my revenge for what he did to Angelo," I said still staring at the city.

I decided that this was the time Barhim Hajj needed to look into my eyes, so he could see just how I felt when I spoke. I turned and stared at him. He hunched his brows.

"Angelo didn't deserve to die. He was a good man and I will not let Dupri get away with what he did. I want to look into his eyes as I rip his heart out of his chest. I want him to feel what I felt and if that means I must turn myself in to get my revenge, then so be it," I said calmly.

I could tell Barhim Hajj was taken aback with my comments and my calm demeanor. He sighed and shook his head.

"You would be sacrificing yourself in vain," he said.

"What do you mean?"

"Angelo isn't dead."

I was stunned.

"Not dead? What do you mean he's not dead?" I asked flatly.

"The Seraph was taken to the headquarters in Vancouver, British Columbia," said Hajj.

"You're lying."

"No, princess, I'm not."

The tears began to well in my eyes and roll down my cheeks. I didn't know whether I was crying from joy or relief. Maybe it was both. I leaped up and walked toward Barhim Hajj.

"Why didn't you tell me this before?" I asked, stopping in front of him.

"I didn't know. I just found out about this a little while ago. That was the reason why I came here. It's a good thing I did. Otherwise you would've handed yourself and the universe over to Dupri on a silver platter," said Hajj.

"Where is this place? Do you know where it is? You must take me there!"

"Princess, please try to keep your perspective on this. I know you're excited by this news, but there is very little I can do to aid you. This is a very dangerous time for you. The Hierarchy as well as the Consortium are looking for you and I'm afraid that if they find you, they will try to kill you."

"The Consortium? Who are they?"

"They are a deadly organization, a group of assassins led by the Satan himself, Lucifer."

"Why are they looking for me?"

"They are the ones who wish to kill you. Events are starting to happen and the Contravexus is making his move. You, as well as I, know that everything that has happened to you so far has been his doing. He's even been killing innocent people. With all this activity, Lucifer and his agency are not going to take any chances. You are now considered a threat and the Consortium will do everything possible to prevent the Gate of Osiris from falling into the Contravexus' hands. They intend to stop this conflict before it starts. That's why it is imperative that you remain out of sight right now," said Hajj.

"But I thought only the Vul Paux could kill me?" I asked.

"Kill you, yes. But there is more than one way to die. Lucifer can inflict suffering in ways that will make you beg for death. This is a fate I do not wish to happen to you," said Hajj.

"But I want to see my husband," I said.

"I understand and I will see what I can arrange. But for now, please remain out of sight."

I shot Barhim Hajj a frustrated look.

"I'm tired of running and I don't want to hide anymore!" I said.

"If you knew the horror we are trying to prevent, you'd stay hidden for as long as you could," said Hajj.

I frowned. "You look scared."

"Terrified, more than you could ever imagine."

The look on Hajj's face showed a fear I'd never before seen in him. I knew that the Vul Paux was bad, but I obviously underestimated the depth of his cruelty. He had to be the most sinister being ever created. To have someone like Hajj scared, as well as having the Hierarchy and the Consortium looking for me was proof of that fact.

"Did I ever hurt you?" I asked.

Hajj raised his eyebrows. Then, a deep pained look came to his face. He slowly nodded, then tucked his head.

"I'm sorry. I don't remember what I did to you, but I wish I could make up for it," I said.

"It's not your fault. It wasn't you that did the wrongs and you don't deserve what's happening to you. You were just a pawn, like I was," said Hajj.

"If I was half as bad as I'm led to believe, don't you think I deserve this?"

"Not really. Many don't know you because they don't see what I see. Take the Seraph, Sariel, for instance. If he would've looked a little more closely, he would've seen the love that exists between you and your husband. He would see the joy each of you bring to the other's life. Far be it for me to judge, but when someone loves another as deeply and as purely as you love Angelo, you cannot be all evil."

"Is that why you're helping me?"

"Partly. The other reason is because I feel you will be instrumental in defeating the powers that wish to destroy all of creation."

"So, you're calling me a savior?"

"Indeed."

His words were very comforting and were just what I needed to hear. I leaned toward Barhim Hajj and kissed him on the cheek.

"Thank you," I said. "Its nice to hear that someone doesn't think I'm a monster."

"You're welcome," he replied with a smile.

"Very well, I will keep out of sight. But I want you to do me a favor. If there is anyway you can get a message to Angelo and let him know where I am, please do."

"That might not be wise. He's a member of the Hierarchy and might try to capture you."

"That's a chance I have to take. Please do this for me, please?" I begged.

Hajj tucked his head and pondered for a moment. Then he looked at me and released a sigh.

"Very well, princess, I will let him know," Hajj replied.

"Thank you."

"Well, I'd better be getting out of here. You take care of yourself, Vanifera."

"I will."

The air had dried the tears on my cheeks and I was beginning to feel a little better about things. Barhim Hajj quietly left the roof. I turned and looked at the city once more. As I became absorbed in my thoughts, several minutes had passed. I was snapped out of my trance by the sound of footsteps approaching from behind. In my mind, I thought it was Barhim Hajj coming to bring me more news.

"Forget something?" I asked.

He did not respond. I turned to look at him. However, it was not Barhim Hajj. Instead, I saw a raggedly dressed man staring back at me. His appearance startled me at first. I cautiously turned to face him.

"Who are you? What do you want?" I asked.

The man just stared at me with a stunned look on his face. As I stared back at him, I realized he looked very familiar. Suddenly, it hit me. I did know him. He was the old man from the BART station in San Francisco.

~~~

CHAPTER THIRTEEN

W hat the hell are you doing here?" I asked.

The old man seemed startled by my question and my actions. He backed up slightly, which allowed me to get a good look at him. His clothes were tattered and dirty. His hair was ratty and nasty. His beard was stained from food he'd spilled on it. There was no question about it; he was the same old man from the BART station. Come to think of it, he sort of looked like the bum in the alley who directed me to the diner yesterday morning.

"Well, I saw you sitting up here all night, and I was wondering if you'd like some coffee?" he asked.

I looked at his hands and saw that he was holding two cups of coffee. I shot him a glance and then I looked back at the cups in his hands. I lowered my fists, but continued to give him a very distrusting look. I wanted to believe he was being genuine, but after the past few days as well as what Barhim Hajj just told me, I was skeptical of everyone. However, seeing him holding the coffee was actually a welcomed sight. It was a little chilly and something warm to drink sounded very appealing.

I looked at the man's face once more. I couldn't explain it, but it felt eerie to see him standing there. Even so, instead of following my instincts and keeping my guard up, I decided not to be rude and give him the benefit of the doubt. He held out the cup and I accepted it.

"Thank you," I replied warily.

"Sorry if I startled you. I just thought that by being up here all night, you might be getting a little chilly," he said.

The man sat down on the roof, leaned against one of the skylights and began drinking his coffee.

"That was very thoughtful. I want to apologize if I seemed defensive. I thought you were somebody else," I said.

"That's okay. You seem to have a lot on your mind," he said taking another sip.

"I do."

The old man nodded his head understandingly and continued sipping his coffee. The warmth from my cup radiated throughout my body. It felt good and momentarily took my mind off my worries.

"You should try to drink it before it gets cold," he said.

I glanced at him and then took a sip. As I attempted to swallow, the bitter taste of three-day-old coffee saturated my mouth. My face scrunched and I pursed my lip. Undoubtedly, this was the worst tasting coffee I'd ever had. I shivered as it traveled down my throat. I rubbed my tongue across the roof of my mouth, trying to erase the taste of the burnt coffee. As I regrouped from this awful tasting experience, I heard the old man snickering.

"It's a might strong, but you'll get use to it by the time you get to the bottom. One things for sure, it'll kill germs and is great for stripping floors," he said.

"What is this? This can't be coffee," I probed.

"If I told you, then you wouldn't drink it. Why don't you take another sip? I promise this time it will taste better."

"No way! I don't know what you gave me, but this sure as hell ain't coffee."

"Well, I guess it is a little strong. Some folks actually think it's got some whiskey in it. All I do is add my filter, put in a few scoops and add the water. But I guess if you aren't used to the taste, it can be a bit overwhelming."

Of course, I didn't believe him. With a smirk, I turned to look back out on the city.

"Hey, I know what you need," said the man.

He reached into his pocket and pulled out a brown bag. He

turned the bag upside down and began shaking it until the contents fell in his hands.

"Take a look at these. Ain't these the finest things you ever seen?" he said boastingly.

I turned to see what the old man was raving about. In his hands he held an assortment of nuts: cashews, pistachios and pecans.

"My friend Ethel says I have the firmest nuts in town. Would you like to feel my nuts?" he asked.

At first, I didn't know whether to be offended or amused. However, I sensed he was harmless.

"No, thank you," I replied, trying not to laugh at his poorly asked question.

"Well, if you ever want to, they'll be right here in my bag" he replied.

"I'm sure they will be," I said with an embarrassing chuckle.

The old man then carefully placed the nuts back into the bag and tucked it into one of his coat pockets. Then, he looked up at the skyline of the city. With a startled look on his face, he pointed to an old, condemned building a few blocks over.

"I used to go to that place all the time when I was younger. That was the old Fairmont Hotel. They used to have the best prime rib there. All the high falutent types used to go there all the time. That was one hoppin' spot; too bad it caught fire," he explained.

I looked at the building, or should I say what was left of it. The smoke-stained shell was the only darkened area in the entire city. The fire seemed to have burned every room on every floor. As I stared at the building, I began to hear distant screams. They sounded as if they were coming from the building itself. The more I gazed at the burnt structure, the louder the screams became.

Then, almost as if I was sucked into a vortex, I found myself no longer on the roof with the old man. Instead, I was in the building at the time of the fire. I stood in the middle of the lobby floor as panic-stricken patrons dashed around me trying to escape the burning hotel. The flames engulfed the walls and furniture. Bodies covered the floor as their flesh began to sizzle and burn. The stench of the dead filled the room and the sound of sirens could be heard outside. The horror of the vision was overwhelming. Suddenly, a woman fell at my feet. I reached down to assist her, but my hands went right through her, as if I was a ghost. I instantly became anxious, staring at my hands with disbelief.

"This must be another vision," I said beneath my breath.

I looked around at the chaos, watching people die from smoke inhalation or burning to death. I began trying to suppress the images. I could not bear to watch more innocent people die. However, the more I tried to stifle the vision, the stronger it became. I began to panic, frightened by the images I saw. What was the purpose of this? Everyone was burning to death and there was nothing I could do to help. I knew that somehow I had to control this vision. Perhaps if I found a way out of here, I could end this madness. I quickly began looking around the room for a way out. I spotted a door a few feet away and ran toward it. But as I approached the exit, I saw something that chilled me to the core.

A dark figure stood between the doorway and me. His presence was powerful and intimidating. He had an aura that was more overpowering than the inferno that blazed around us. It was the same powerful presence I felt when I was in Las Vegas. It was then I realized who he was. It was the Contravexus, Montellace Dupri.

I stood motionless, staring at him as the entire hotel crumbled around me. My morbid curiosity wanted to see the face of the being that was responsible for all of my suffering. Fire exploded all around me, yet I remained there, looking at him. This was what I wanted, to confront the being who'd tried to kill my husband. At first, I was terrified. But just as the fear rushed through my body, so did the rage. His baldhead gleamed from the fires and a smirk donned his lips. Before I could catch myself, my anger got the better of me and I darted toward him, attempting to exact my revenge.

As I got to within arms reach of the smirking Contravexus, I reared my fist back and prepared to throw the hardest punch I'd ever delivered. Then, just as I was about to strike his face, I felt something grab my shoulder. In that instant, I found that I was back on the roof. The sudden change disoriented me and I looked around with bewilderment. The old man was kneeling next to me with his hand on my shoulder, looking quite concerned.

My eyes were wide with confusion and anger. A few seconds ago, I was in a flaming hotel, preparing to battle the Contravexus. Now I was back on the roof, still holding that cup of nasty coffee. I wasn't sure what took place while I was engulfed in that vision, but the old man's concerned look indicated that he saw me do something unexpected or strange.

"You okay?" he asked.

Still feeling very disorientated, I looked around to assure myself of my whereabouts. I rubbed my left temple, trying to collect my thoughts before I replied. I looked at the place where the building was and found that it wasn't there anymore. The revelation made me very uncomfortable. I turned to the old man.

"Wasn't there a hotel over there a few minutes ago?" I asked.

The old man shook his head.

"No, that's the Space Needle," he said with a befuddled expression. "You sure you're okay?"

I didn't know what to make of what just happened. To avoid looking like I completely lost my mind, I decided to drop it.

"Yes, I'm fine," I said with a degree of uncertainty.

As I tried to regroup, I realized that what just happened was not a figment of my imagination. I had just experienced what happened to some people that were in a hotel. I saw the horror and the death. I saw the flames and the demon that caused the whole thing. I turned and looked at the old man.

"Do you know if Seattle ever had a Fairmont Hotel?" I asked.

"Can't say that I do. I'm not from this city. I'm just visiting," said the man.

I decided to try my luck and ask him the question that was on my mind from the moment I recognized him.

"Are you from San Francisco?" I asked.

"Why yes," he replied.

A chill went down my spine.

"Why are you here?" I asked.

"I'm homeless. I move around from place to place," he said.

I turned and pondered for a few moments. Then, I looked at him once more.

"I remember you from the BART station. You bumped into me and gave me a very nasty stare," I said.

"I did?"

"Yes."

"Well, I apologize for…"

"And now you just happen to be in Seattle, and you just happen to be here with me on this roof."

"Some coincidence, huh?" he said.

"Yes," I replied suspiciously. "Who are you?"

"Just a simple bum."

"Well, Mr. Bum, I don't know whose side you're on, but I've had all I can take for right now," I said.

I dropped the cup on the roof and stood up. As I walked to the roof door, the old man started rocking back and forth.

"There's a strange wind blowing today," he said as I reached the door.

"Indeed," I replied.

The old man smiled. I opened the door and walked down the stairs.

~~~

Everett, Washington. A Mercedes SUV pulled into a rest area. It parked in a space reserved for a Winnebago. After a few seconds, Gabrielle and Sariel stepped out of the SUV and took a few moments to stretch their bodies. Gabrielle pulled out a cell phone and punched in the number for headquarters. She paced back and forth waiting for her party to pick up while Sariel walked to the water fountain near the restrooms. After three rings, Michael picked up.

"What 'chu got?" he asked.

"Well, she's still in town. Her bio readings indicate she's in downtown Seattle," Gabrielle replied.

"Good. That means that Dupri hasn't gotten to her yet," said Michael.

"We stopped off for a few moments to stretch our legs. I don't know how these humans can ride in these things; they are so bloody uncomfortable," said Gabrielle.

"Yeah, well when in Rome..." said Michael.

"Are you sure it was wise to allow Sariel to come with me? You know he would rather kill the Gaian than to bring her in."

"I didn't want you trying to bring in the Gaian by yourself, especially when we don't know her mental state. If she is getting her memory back, she might become volatile and dangerous. If that happens, you'll thank me for allowing Sariel to come."

"Perhaps you're right. I just wish there was another way."

Just then, Sariel walked back to where she was.

"Have you located my son?" asked Gabrielle.

"Not yet. But we believe he's in Portland. We've detected a lot of activity there," said Michael.

"Let me know the moment you find something concrete."

"I will. I know it's been hard on you all these millennia not seeing your family."

"You have no idea. To this day, I still do not know why I was summoned to serve at this post. Still, as a good soldier to the throne, I did what I was told, no questions asked. Nevertheless, I've regretted my decision from the moment I made it. Not a day goes by when I don't think about Lorimar and Kitana, my children. How I agonized over the fact that they've had to exist without me, simply because I am doing what I've been commanded to do. It doesn't seem fair, Michael; it never has," said Gabrielle.

"That's why it is important that we complete this mission. Soon, you will be able to see your loved ones again. I am setting up arrangements for you to spend some time with them while they are on Earth. But first, we must get the Gaian back to headquarters, that's the primary mission," said Michael.

"How's Angelo?"

"Better. He should be up and around in a few minutes."

"You know he's going to come here looking for her."

"Yes, I do. But I have other plans for him."

Gabrielle sighed. "In some respects, I envy him."

"I know this has taken a toll on you. But hang in there, Gabrielle. You *will* see your children," said Michael

"Thank you. I appreciate everything you're doing, Michael," said Gabrielle.

"Steady your heart, my beloved sister, for the time draws close. Now, go bring me that Gaian."

"Okay."

Gabrielle disconnected and turned to look at Sariel.

"So, the old blowhard giving you the old song and dance?" asked Sariel.

Gabrielle sighed.

"Not really. C'mon, we better get moving," she said.

Gabrielle and Sariel got back in the SUV. Gabrielle cranked it and pulled off.

"So, you trying to see the little hellions?" asked Sariel.

Gabrielle screeched the Mercedes to a stop and turned to glare at Sariel.

"Don't ever make the mistake of calling my children out of their names," she said in a very sinister tone.

Sariel looked surprised.

"Okay, sorry," he said.

Gabrielle continued to glare at him for a few moments more. Then, she turned and resumed driving. Sariel was surprised by the way she snapped at him. He turned and silently looked out his window as they headed toward downtown Seattle.

~~~

San Francisco. Eleven fifteen a.m. That was the time on the clock when Denise Terrence heard her phone ringing. She looked to see if her husband, Sidney, was still in the bed. He wasn't. She quickly rubbed her eyes and looked around for her glasses. She grabbed them from the nightstand and placed them on her face. She slowly propped herself up in her bed and picked up the phone.

"Hello?"

"It's me, Denise, Vanifera."

"Vannie? Where are you?"

"I'm still in Seattle."

Denise quickly scrambled to sit up straight.

"Girl, I've been so worried about you," said Denise with a trill in her voice. "Are you okay?"

"Yes, I'm fine, or as well as I can be."

"Sidney and I heard about Angelo. We're so sorry."

"He's not dead, Denise."

"He's not? But I heard that…"

"You heard wrong. Anyway, that's not why I called you. I just needed to hear a friendly voice."

"Where have you been? We've been worried sick about you! We tried calling your house and everything."

"I've been wandering."

"Wandering? Do you realize your name is all over the news?"

"Not really. Can't say I've been watching too much television."

"Vannie, the police have been here a couple of times, asking us questions about you and Angelo."

"What did you tell them?"

"Nothing really. What's going on?"

"If I told you what was really going on, you wouldn't believe me."

"Well, who tried to kill Angelo? Was it an old boyfriend? Have you been having an affair?"

"No, nothing like that. I could never cheat on Angelo. It was a cop."

"A cop?"

"Yes."

"Vannie listen, the news is saying they suspect that you killed a cop. They say witnesses saw you at the scene where a cop was thrown from a seven story building."

"I didn't throw him off the building; he jumped."

"He jumped?" said Denise with a disbelieving tone. "Is this the same cop that tried to kill Angelo?"

"Yep."

"Oh my God, this is unbelievable," said Denise.

"See, I told you."

"Vannie, I'm not saying I don't believe you. But why haven't you gone to the police and explained all of this?"

"Do you think they would believe me? Do you really think I could convince anyone that I didn't do any of this? Look at the evidence and listen to the witnesses, then tell me if anyone in their right mind would believe me?"

"Well, I believe you."

"Yeah, but you're just as crazy as I am."

Denise sighed.

"My only hope of proving myself innocent was that cop, and he jumped! Now everyone is looking for me for committing two murders that I had nothing to do with!"

"What are you going to do now?" Denise asked.

"I don't know."

"Do you need some money?"

"No, I'll be okay. I just wanted to say hi. Listen, I better go, I'll call you later."

"Vannie, be careful."

"I will, and thanks, Denise."

"You're welcome, hun."

Denise placed the phone back in its cradle. She sat in the bed thinking about her best friend and what she must be going through right now.

"Oh Vannie, may God watch over you," she said.

~~~

Vancouver, B.C. A weary Angelo knelt on the floor after an extensive rehabilitative session with his therapist, Raphael.

"You're doing quite well," said Raphael as he helped Angelo to his feet. "You're getting stronger by the moment."

"I just need a few more hours and I'll be back to my old self," said Angelo as he took a moment to catch his breath.

"Well, you don't have to break your neck to rush anything. You've already made achievements that have surpassed anyone else who'd been in less serious conditions."

"Thanks, but I need to get back up to speed as soon as possible. Time is running short, and I need to get out there and help the others."

"The others are doing fine. They can handle things for the next day or so if need be. However, you won't be of any use to them if you aren't at one hundred percent. Let's try to get you healthy once again, and then we'll worry about the rest," said Raphael.

Angelo nodded. He tested his balance to see if he were ready to try another session.

"I'm ready when you are," he said.

"I think we need to take a break. C'mon over here and sit down," said Raphael as he ushered Angelo to a chair.

"Any word from Gabrielle?"

"Not yet. They're out there looking for her. Don't worry, they'll find her."

Just then, Peter walked into the room.

"So, how's the patient?" he asked.

"Progressing nicely. In fact, he's exceeding expectations," said Raphael.

"Good."

"Give me a couple of hours and I'll be ready to get back out there," said Angelo.

"Whoa, slow down there, son. This isn't a race," said Peter.

"I beg to differ, Peter; this is a race. The Contravexus is trying to restore Vanifera's memory and locate the Gate of Osiris. We both know that can't happen. So, it is imperative that I get well as quickly as possible. I can't let anything happen to her."

Peter tucked his head and pinched the bridge of his nose.

"Raphael, could you give us a moment alone?" he asked.

"Sure."

Raphael left the room, closing the door behind him. Peter walked to where Angelo was sitting and squatted next to him.

"Listen, Angelo, I need to talk to you. Do you remember anything about the war that took place with the Vul Paux?" asked Peter.

"Yes, I do," Angelo replied.

"The Gaian isn't some entity we can reason with. It is a vile creation with no conscience or remorse. During the war, when the Vul Paux inhabited the vessel, there was a degree of control and purpose in the Gaian. But when the Messiah was sacrificed and the Vul Paux's essence was extracted from the vessel, it went on a killing spree the likes never before witnessed. It had no control or reasoning. It just killed for the sake of killing. If that creature is reanimated here on Earth, it will resume its killing spree and perhaps wipe out the entire planet's population before we can stop it, if we can stop it," said Peter.

"I know what the Gaian is capable of. However, if you remember, there is another persona to this creature; the one it merged with that has prevented it from committing the horrors you speak of," said Angelo.

"Yes, I do know this."

"That's the part I'm trying to save, and if there is a chance to keep that part alive, I will do whatever I must."

"That's why Gabrielle and Sariel are out trying to find her now. The Contravexus is trying to break her and it may already be too late to prevent the seal binding her past memories from breaking. I know that you're trying to help this woman, but I don't want you to misunderstand the situation. Vanifera and the Gaian are one being now. If she has somehow regained her memory, we are going to have to do whatever we can to destroy her. There may come a point where you're going to have to choose, and right now, I'm not sure if I trust your judgment," said Peter.

"If Vanifera must be destroyed, than I'd rather it be by my hands. I know that if there were no other way to save her, I would kill her in a heartbeat. But the Gaian is not just a vessel anymore, nor is it an easy entity to kill. As you recall, it is damn near indestructible. But it was stopped before by the woman it is now merged with, the woman I now call my wife. If she could stop it, surely we as the Angelic host can stop it."

"I admire your optimism, my dear comrade. However, some of us do not share your hopeful expectations," said Peter.

"What are you saying?"

"There are others who are searching for her, others who do not have her best interests in mind."

"You don't mean..."

"Yes, I do. The Consortium has begun searching for Vanifera and if they find her, their orders are to kill her on sight."

~~~

Portland, Oregon. Atop the US Bank tower, Prince Lorimar stood gazing at the city below. His arms were folded and his posture was regal and arrogant. A figure approached from behind, stopping approximately twenty feet from him.

"Prince Lorimar!" said the being.

"What have you to report?" he asked.

"We have located the Gaian. She apparently is in Seattle as your sister stated. We have troops already in route there now," said the informant.

"Very good. Make sure she does not live another day."

"As you wish, my lord."

The being exited the rooftop while Lorimar continued to stare at the Rose City. Suddenly, his phone rang. He reached into his pocket and removed it.

"Yes?" he answered.

"My son, is the Gaian dead?" asked the voice on the other end.

"Not yet, father. But my forces are converging on her location as we speak. The Gaian will be dead by morning," said Lorimar.

"Do not underestimate this creature, Lorimar. It cannot be easily defeated. I wish for you to go there and ensure its death.

The Hierarchy is already on its way there, but their intentions are containment. This is no longer a diplomatic issue. The Gaian must not be allowed to live. The chances of it being reunited with the Vul Paux are great. We must prevent this from happening at all costs."

"I understand, father," said Lorimar. "By the way, I just wanted to inform you that Kitana is here."

"I know. But she may be of some assistance to you. Utilize her services and destroy the Gaian."

"As you command."

Lorimar disconnected and sighed in disgust. He then placed the phone back into his pocket.

"I don't know how much use you will be to me, but father states that I might need you," said Lorimar.

Just then, Kitana emerged from the shadows.

"How did you know I was here?" she asked.

"I am the son of the Satan, the prince of Hell. There isn't much I don't know."

"Well, I don't know about all that, but I do know that we should be making our way to Seattle. Every moment we waste here allows the Hierarchy or the Contravexus to get that much closer to the Gaian," said Kitana.

"You have a point," Lorimar replied.

The two siblings exited the roof of the forty-four story building and prepare to head to Seattle.

~~~

CHAPTER FOURTEEN

Although Hajj warned me to keep out of sight, I couldn't get Angelo off my mind. Like a moth, I was naturally drawn to the one place where the flame of our love burned the brightest. I was extremely tired after I got off the bus near my home in Federal Way. I wasn't sure why, but I had a burning desire to go back. Perhaps it was because I was subconsciously hoping that Angelo might come back here looking for me. The news that he wasn't dead was making me very anxious. I wanted to see him again, despite the instructions Barhim Hajj gave to me. He warned me to be on my guard, but I truly believed that Angelo wouldn't harm me. However, I wasn't so sure about the rest of the Hierarchy, and I definitely knew that the Consortium wasn't interested in bringing me in.

As I got closer to the house, a strange feeling came over me. I felt as if I was being watched or followed. I paused for a moment and quickly looked behind me. A few people were walking up the street to the bus stop, but none of them seemed to notice me at all nor did they seem suspicious. I shrugged off the feeling, blaming it on being paranoid about what Barhim Hajj had said.

I continued walking, thinking only about Angelo and seeing him again. I hadn't ruled out going to Vancouver B.C. and looking for this place that Hajj spoke of. First, I needed to get cleaned up. A shower, a nap and a change of clothes would be just the thing to make me feel better and help me to think clearer. By now, I was sure that all of the investigators were gone and I could enter my home without any problems.

I suddenly became nervous. My stomach had butterflies and at times, I hesitated taking the next step. My reluctance wasn't so much from the possibility of encountering the police, but from re-entering the house for the first time since Angelo's shooting. There was still a great deal of mental anguish I was dealing with.

Somehow, I found the strength to continue. Only a few more blocks separated me from my answers. I kept my head low so that no one would recognize me. But that did not ease my growing nervousness. The more I walked, the more uneasy I felt. I sensed the frustration and anxiety building with each breath. My chest tightened, and I wanted so badly to stop and walk the other way. But I stayed on my path, growing closer by the moment. My mind was beginning to play with me, pushing me to consider the slim possibility that Angelo might be there waiting for me.

Finally, I reached my destination. The emotions gripped me and I almost broke into tears from the sight of my home. This was my moment of truth. The police tape was gone and no one seemed to be around. I looked at the window of the front room. It was the room where we used to eat dinner every night. As I stared at my house, it was different now. It was once so lively. Now, it was dark and empty.

I turned and started to walk away. It was obvious that Angelo wasn't there, and I couldn't handle the memories popping into my mind. Instead of leaving, though, I stood there. I'd come all this way and I couldn't leave now. I wanted to see, one more time, the life we once had. I turned and looked at the house. My heart and my mind wrestled with one another. The questions batted back and forth in my head until I could handle it no longer. I inhaled deeply, attempting to control my emotions and not allow any second-guessing. I needed to go in, although my logic was still trying to convince me otherwise. I slowly began walking toward the front door. Each step brought anxiety. Yet, in those same steps came a catharsis. Angelo wasn't gone, and even if he wasn't in this house, I knew I was going to see him again. I finally reached the door and stood before it for a moment, contemplating once more whether to open it or not. I looked at the automated lock and paused for a moment, trying to remember the key code. I punched it in, closed my eyes and turned the doorknob.

As I walked in, I felt a breeze blowing across the back of my neck. The room was dimly lit from the afternoon sunlight and the stench of blood could still be detected. The walls had been cleaned, repaired and painted with a fresh coat to cover what couldn't be cleaned. It was obviously the work of the Hierarchy's clean-up crew. I cautiously walked through the door and closed it behind me. It was weird being back here. I could almost feel Angelo's presence.

I walked through the living room looking at everything. This was my home, but it didn't feel the same. I glanced around the room, instantly recalling the joy that used to abound here. Then, I looked at the floor where Angelo laid in my arms. My eyes were fixed on that one spot and I couldn't pull myself from staring at it. I still remembered the look on his face as he struggled to catch his breath. Visions of the entire ordeal replayed in my mind, forcing me to relive the moment as if it just happened. From the appearance of Sariel to the bastard cop that killed him, I saw it all.

The memories began to overwhelm me. I shook my head, attempting to block out the pain. I knew this would be difficult, but I never knew just how much. I walked toward the bedroom, trying to fight the tears that were starting to well in my eyes. Still the memories kept coming. They flooded my mind, pushing me toward an emotional breakdown. Just then, I looked at one of the corners of the room. I was unsure why this particular corner grabbed my attention, but as I looked at it, the corner seemed darker than the rest of the room. It had a sinister air, almost as if someone or something was there. I walked to the nightstand and turned on a lamp to examine the corner. I glared at it and then walked toward it. As I drew closer, I detected a faint odor. It was there for a moment, then it dissipated. The smell was musky at first, then turned burnt smelling. The odor was familiar, but I couldn't remember where I'd smelled it before. Perhaps I was hallucinating from the stress I'd been under. After what I'd been through the last few days, I didn't rule anything out.

"Easy there, Vanifera, you're starting to lose it," I said beneath my breath.

I took a deep breath and calmed myself. I walked into the bedroom and to my dresser. I pulled out some new underwear and laid them on the bed. Then, I went to the closet. When I opened the door, I saw Angelo's shirts, pants and other articles of clothing hanging on his side, right where he left them. I stood in the doorway, tucking my head and sighing. My visit back here was proving tougher than I thought.

I gathered myself and proceeded to pull out a white button front blouse and another pair of jeans. I threw them on the bed and walked toward the bathroom. As I was unbuttoning my blouse, I glanced at the clock. It was seventeen minutes after two in the afternoon. I quickly took off my clothes and placed them in a pile by the bathroom door. I reached into the shower and turned the water to its hottest setting. The steam began to rise and filter throughout the entire bathroom. The smell of hot, clean air filled my lungs and it felt good to be taking a shower again. I opened the curtains and stepped in. The water sprayed against my body and flowed down to the tub floor. The hot water seemed to relax not only my body, but also my mind and soul. I picked up the bar of soap and lathered it in my hands. Then, I began to soap every part of my body.

Suddenly, I heard a loud noise in the next room, like something had fallen over. I turned the shower off, grabbed a towel and wrapped it around me. I stood silently for a moment, trying to hear if someone was in the house. As I continued to listen, I quietly pulled back the curtains and scanned the bathroom looking for something to defend myself with. I spotted a lead pipe in the corner. It was used to prop the window open during the summer. I tiptoed to the corner and grabbed the pipe, clutching it tightly in my hands. Then, I opened the bathroom door and slowly made my way through the bedroom and toward the living room.

The house was quiet, but I could still sense that something wasn't right. I then felt a draft blowing through the room. I crept into the living room to find that the front window was open. I was spooked by the discovery because it wasn't open when I had arrived. I looked around the room to see if anyone was there. I checked the entire place, including the kitchen and every closet. No one appeared to be in the house.

I walked to the window and pulled it closed. I started feeling a little scared because this was the second strange occurrence that had happened since I arrived. I rationalized that perhaps the window was slightly opened and a gust of wind pushed it open further. But this was not a lightweight window, which made its opening even more puzzling. No sooner than that thought entered my head, I detected that burnt smell once again. This time it was stronger. It was then I remembered where I'd smelled the odor before I detected it in the corner of the room. I smelled it when I'd crawled from the roof of the house across the street. That could only mean one thing.

"I must say that you have the nicest set of legs I've ever seen. Since you're already dressed for the occasion, what do ya say you and I do the wild thing!" said a voice behind me.

I knew the voice. It startled me at first, but I quickly grew angered by his intrusion. I slowly turned to discover that the little imp from the roof had returned, Huang.

"What are you doing in here?" I asked, fighting to keep my calm.

"Well, if you must know, I'm here to see you. I've been sent to bring you home," he replied.

"As I already told you, not interested. Now, get out!" I said.

"No can do, princess. Boss said that I have to bring you back, even if I have to use force," he said as he started moving toward me.

"You take another step and I'll knock your head off," I replied.

Huang didn't say a word, but kept coming toward me. It was obvious there would be no reasoning with him. I lifted the pipe in the air and prepared to swing.

"Ya know, I wouldn't do that if I were you," he said.

I tightened my grip around the pipe. He would have to kill me before I would allow him to touch me. If he wanted a fight, I was going to give him one.

"Ah, I see you like it rough," he said.

Then, without warning, he lunged toward me headfirst. I swung the pipe with everything I had. The pipe connected to the left side of his head and neck. The impact would have killed the average man. However, much like what happened with Candy when I hit her with the lamp, he didn't budge. In fact, he smiled as I raised the pipe and prepared for another swing. He then swung his fist and knocked the pipe from my hands. He grabbed me by my arm and tossed me across the room. I crashed headfirst into the wall by the fireplace. The impact busted a hole in the wall and opened a gash on my head. I fell to the floor stunned from the impact. I was on the verge of passing out, but somehow I fought it and remained conscious. I knew I could not allow myself to black out.

"Your powers are still dormant. If your memories and powers were to be released, I wouldn't have been able to lay a finger on you," said Huang.

My vision was blurry, but I could still see him continuing to stalk me. I attempted to rise to my feet, stumbling into the fireplace accessories and knocking them over. I fell on top of them, struggling to gather my bearings as Huang continued his approach. During my panic to distance myself, I realized something. One of my hands had the poker from the fireplace accessories beneath it. I looked up to see him preparing for another charge. I wrapped my hands around the poker and waited for him to make his move. He snorted and then charged toward me again. I lifted the poker and aimed it for his chest. As he lunged, the poker went through his abdomen and exited out his back.

A look of astonishment came across his face as he bellowed an inhuman scream of pain. I scrambled to my feet and stood there to see if I had hurt him enough to get away. The short imp stepped back three paces and looked down at the protruding object sticking through his stomach. Then, he reached down, grabbed the poker and ripped it from his body with one yank.

The yellow ooze that flowed from the gaping wound began to disappear within moments until both the blood and the wound were gone. Huang dropped the poker to the ground. Then, he lifted his head and stared at me with a sinister look.

"Naughty, Naughty," he said with a demonic smile.

He reared back and swung again, this time punching me on the side of my face and knocking me to the ground. The blow from this swing stunned me to the point of near unconsciousness. I lay on the floor, unable to move. I tried desperately to gather my bearings and crawl away, but I was too disoriented to really see straight.

"You stay away from me, you bastard," I said breathlessly.

"Gaian, we can do this the easy way or the hard way. It's your choice," said Huang.

Then, through the very window I'd closed, a beam of light exploded through and nailed Huang in the chest, knocking him through the wall and into the tub in the bathroom. Plaster and sheetrock cascaded to the floor, creating a cloud of white dust. The tremors from the impact shook the entire house and it felt as if it was going to collapse any moment.

Amidst the chaos, I noticed a sublime golden glow surrounded me. It felt warm and I could see through it. It was deflecting the debris from falling on top of me. The gash on my head healed and I began getting my bearings. I then saw the silhouettes of two figures standing in front of the window. One was tall and the other much shorter.

The glow slowly dissipated and the room became dark. I braced myself against the wall as Huang rose to his feet and stepped out of the tub. He crashed through the remnants of the wall and stared at his two assailants with disdain.

"So, Messiah, I see you finally showed yourself!" said Huang.

The taller figure reached over his shoulder and unsheathed what appeared to be a jeweled sword. The blade of the sword appeared to be made of pure light. Two curved spikes projected from the base of the blade. The grip was accented with a cup-shaped hand guard whose inner lining was a blood-red coating.

Suddenly, I was able to identify one of the two figures. The taller one was the old man from the roof. However, he seemed different now. He stood more upright and regal. His presence was that of a knight or a warrior. He was the one wielding the sword. The smaller being's face was hidden. The sunlight was behind him, and all I could see was his silhouette. However, I heard Huang refer to one of them as the Messiah. Was one of these beings the illusive Son of God? I stood to my feet and attempted to slide along the wall to distance myself from the impending battle.

"Behold, creature. I am the Valkydine called Desmond Christi," said the old man pointing the sword at Huang. "You shall not take the woman."

"Christi, huh? Well, you're going to have to kill me to stop me," said Huang.

"Then it is time for you to die, demon! Come and meet your fate!" said the old man.

"Do you really think you can defeat me by yourself? The sheer thought of that suggests madness! However, a lesson must be taught and an example made! Unfortunately, this is a lesson you won't live to learn from!" said Huang.

Then with a snarl, Huang began to change. His neck stretched and his eyes turned blood red. Scales began to appear over him and he began increasing in size. His face changed in appearance, taking on the characteristics of a shark. The house began to rumble as he continued to grow. The walls cracked and crumbled around us.

Suddenly, his head erupted through the ceiling. The old man gracefully dodged the chunks of debris that fell as my home was being demolished. I, too, ducked and dodged the falling debris, but I needed to get out of there. The front door was open due to Huang's destructive actions. I covered my head and ran through the doorway. The house continued to break apart around me. I turned and noticed the old man still standing in the middle of the floor.

"C'mon, let's go!" I yelled.

He didn't move. He defiantly stood there as the crumbling house continued to fall around him. I noticed that the smaller figure that was with him was now gone. I took a moment to see if he had fallen victim to the debris, but it was hard to see through the cloud of dust. I wanted to save them, but by now, the rumblings were too strong. I glanced once more at the old warrior, then dashed out of the front door and raced across the street to the vacant house that faced mine. I ran behind a bush and covered my head.

"What the hell is going on?" I asked terrifyingly.

I peeked around the bush at my home. It was completely destroyed, however, that wasn't what caught my attention. My eyes widened as they panned up into the sky. Huang had grown to at least fifty feet and towered over the trees and houses like a monolith. He completed his transformation with a strain and a bellow. His head then divided into two separate heads attached to long, serpent-like necks. The act caused an explosion that leveled the rest of the house. Debris flew for blocks as the hideous beast stood amidst the fallout of the rubble. The explosion erupted small fires. Open gas lines fed the flames that quickly towered into the sky and spread to some of the neighbors' houses. The scene was the epitome of what Hell on Earth would look like. The apocalyptic scene should have killed all of them. Yet, there they were, the beast and the old man, glaring at one another amidst the havoc and destruction.

"Now, Valkydine, you will die!" exclaimed the beast-like Huang.

~~~

Downtown Seattle. Gabrielle and Sariel were standing in the top row of Safeco Field Stadium. Suddenly, a slight rumble was heard. They both turned to the south to see a huge cloud of smoke rising into the sky.

"I think we may have found our girl," said Sariel.

"I think you're right," said Gabrielle. Let's move!"

~~~

Tacoma, Washington. Another group of eyes noticed a cloud of smoke ascending over the trees. Lorimar and Kitana peered from the windows of their Cadillac Escalade at the black and gray mushroom-shaped cloud.

"What is that?" asked Kitana.

"Just an educated guess, but I think it's smoke," said Lorimar.

"Funny," said Kitana giving him a sneer. "But where there's smoke, there's sure to be destruction."

"Driver, proceed to the location where that smoke is coming from!" commanded Lorimar.

"Yes, sir," replied the driver.

~~~

Huang raised his foot in the air and brought it down right where the old man named Desmond Christi stood. Christi did not move. As the huge beast's foot crashed to the ground, it appeared he had crushed the old warrior beneath it. The beast then began grinding and twisting his foot, attempting to snub any remaining life out of the valiant opposition. Then, the beast lifted his foot to admire his handiwork. What he saw shocked him. The old man was gone.

The beast looked bewildered and frantically started scanning the area for his illusive opponent. His heads went in separate directions as he attempted to locate Christi.

"Clever trick, Valkydine. But you can't hide from me!" he said.

Suddenly, the ground began to shake, as if an earthquake were taking place. The remaining rubble of the house crumbled and crashed to the ground, fanning the flames of the surrounding fires. It felt as if the entire earth was about to shake apart.

At that moment, the sword of light erupted from the ground beneath the beast and lodged into its chest. The beast let out a mighty roar. It stumbled backwards as it attempted to distance itself from the piercing blade. However, the more he retreated, the more the sword embedded itself into its chest. Then, the image of Desmond Christi ascended from beneath the ground. He was grasping the handle, continuing to push the sword deeper into the chest of the monster. Its blood flowed like a river from its open gash. The beast bellowed and writhed in pain.

The old man then crouched and lifted the beast, who was still lodged on the end of the sword, into the air. The monster struggled to free itself. It screamed in pain as the sword opened the wound wider. The crimson flow pooled on the ground beneath the man. The old warrior, covered with blood, tilted his blade to the right and swiftly withdrew the sword from the chest of the demon dragon. The mighty beast crashed to the ground and writhed in its own blood.

"H-How dare you!" exclaimed the beast Huang.

"I dare," replied Desmond Christi.

The Valkydine raised the sword over his head and readied himself for a final attack. He stared at the suffering demon as it writhed on the ground. He paused to see if any further attacks were necessary. Christi, like most warriors, lived by a code. He would not senselessly or needlessly inflict more pain on his enemy than needed to subdue him. Huang was incapacitated and seemed to no longer be a threat. But even though it didn't seem necessary to inflict any further injuries, Desmond Christi knew that he could never trust a demon, and Huang was one of the highest-ranking disciples of the Contravexus. In spite of his code, Christi realized that he had to finish him off. He raised the sword as high as he could and brought it down swiftly.

Just then, the beast launched an attack of desperation. It whipped its tail toward the striking warrior, knocking the sword from the old man's hand and lodging it into a chunk of debris. Christi crashed to the ground with a thud and slid to a stop. He quickly tried to stand, but the blow from the beast was apparently more powerful than he thought. He dropped to his knees and shook his head, trying to regain his bearings. Then, he scanned the area, looking for his sword. It was at least fifty feet away. He attempted to stand once again and retrieve his weapon. But before he could, the beast slammed its foot on top of him, pinning Christi on the ground. The impact crushed his lower anatomy and Christi bellowed in pain as the beast lowered its heads to his face.

"Did you really think I would lose to the likes of you? You are pathetic! Your time to rule is over! It's our time now! After I kill you, I will take the woman to my master and a new reign will begin! Now, it is time for you to die!" said Huang.

The mouth of the left head opened wider and the fangs grew longer. The beast coiled its neck and readied itself to strike. The old man was in intense pain, pinned beneath the massive claw of Huang. However, he stared defiantly into the beast's eyes, waiting for the killing blow to be struck.

~~~

I stood there watching the gruesome scene unfurl. Huang came here to capture me and now one of the individuals that had come to help me was at his mercy. I couldn't let this happen, and I wasn't going to let him take me without a fight. I looked around for something to attack him with. I knew from my previous encounter that I may not hurt him, but perhaps I could distract him long enough for the old man to mount some sort of attack. That's when my eyes fell upon the sword that was still lodged in the chunk of debris. Without thinking, I sprinted to it and extracted it from the slab.

Huang's head charged toward the old man. I raced toward him and lifted the sword above my head. As Huang's gaping mouth came within inches of the old man's face, I swung the sword. The beast stood motionless, almost frozen in its mid-strike pose. Suddenly, traces of blood could be seen around the neckline of the attacking head. That was the area I'd sliced him. The flow of crimson increased until the head separated from the rest of the neck and crashed to the ground. The giant monster backed away, releasing its grip on his trapped victim. It stumbled and then fell on its side. The elderly warrior struggled to tuck his head. His eyes widened when he saw me standing before him, holding his sword in my hands.

I was shocked as well from my actions, trembling as I watched the beast wallowing in its own blood. My shaking wasn't from fear or even from being cold because I was improperly dressed, but from exhilaration. It was like a dark mood was descending upon me. I felt strong and confident. I was no longer the helpless woman that cowered in the corner, but instead a predator stalking its prey. I looked at the monster as the feeling of anger grew in my chest. I wanted him to pay for what he tried to do. Fueled by my pain, the rush of vengeance was now surging inside of me. I became blinded of all rational thoughts. The feeling of contempt was intoxicating as I tightened my grip on the sword's handle. To have been previously at the mercy of this vile creature was unnerving. But now, to have it at my mercy was such poetic justice. I stood there glaring at the beast. I felt the anger increasing with each passing moment, and the yearning to kill was all consuming.

Suddenly, the beast began to shrink and return to its human-like form. I made my way to his head and stood over him. I raised the sword into the air and prepared to deliver the final blow. As I looked down at Huang, I could see that the left side of his face was severed off. Only the fleshy remains of a once complete head remained. However, this only strengthened my resolve. I had reached a point where I could barely contain my rage. I released a scream and brought the sword down with all my might.

"Stop!" screamed a voice behind me.

At the last instant, I diverted the blade's path, causing it to embed itself into the ground just above Huang's head. I'm not sure how I made such an adjustment that quickly and effortlessly, but it seemed that somehow the blade could read my thoughts and obeyed me without question. Curiously, I lifted my head to see who shouted the command that stopped me from killing Huang.

Just then, the smaller figure that originally stood next to the old man in my house emerged from a shadowy area of the rubble. As he came into the light, I could see his face clearly. It was the kid from the church. He continued to approach me, finally standing next to me and staring down at the fallen demon.

"Let him live to tell his master what he has seen here today!" said the boy.

"Curse you!" exclaimed Huang as he continued to spew blood from his half face.

Then, Huang turned toward me.

"Finish it. Finish me now!" he gurgled.

I looked down at him, still shivering with contempt. Like Candy, Huang was begging me to end his life. I wanted to kill him so badly that I could almost taste blood in my mouth. But I didn't. For reasons that were beyond me, my anger began subsiding. My breathing slowed and I began feeling tired. The stench of Huang's open wound began to fill the air. Then, without warning, Huang faded away right before my eyes.

"Where'd he go?" I asked looking around.

"Back to his master," said the boy.

I frowned as I stared at the boy. I felt I'd somehow been cheated out of my revenge.

"You allowed him to escape? Why did you do that?" I asked.

"Your thirst for vengeance needs to be controlled. His punishment will be far greater now that he has been allowed to live. I did let him get away, but he will wish that you had killed him before it's over," said the boy.

"You should've let me," I said.

Although I was upset over the fact that I wasn't able to exact revenge on Huang, I did see the strategy that the boy explained. Huang had been sent here for a purpose. The Contravexus did not tolerate failure, this much I was certain. Huang would be punished by his master and it would be far worse than anything I would have done to him here.

The boy walked toward the injured old man. He knelt beside him and placed his hands on his forehead and chest. I extracted the sword from the ground and hoisted it over my shoulder. I followed the boy and knelt beside him as he tended to the old man.

Suddenly, I detected the sound of sirens. Their distant howl grew closer by the moment and I was certain they were on their way to this location. I looked around at the shambled remains of my and my neighbors' homes. There was nowhere for me to hide and the sirens sounded as if they were mere blocks away. Despite Hajj's urgings, I hadn't done a good job in keeping out of sight. I could hear the squad cars screeching around the corner and it seemed I had no choice but to let them take me in. I turned to say goodbye to the young lad.

"I hate to leave you at a time like this, but I'm afraid that I must go!"

The boy did not acknowledge me. Once again I felt he was ignoring me. I shrugged it off and stood to make my departure.

"There is no need for you to leave," he said.

His response surprised me. I looked at him curiously.

"I don't think you understand. I'm wanted by the police. When they arrive, they are going to arrest me," I retorted.

"The police are no longer of any concern, and if you want to learn your past, you will do as I say," the boy replied.

"My past? You can help me regain my memory?"

"Just stay. I assure you it will be worth your while."

I looked at the boy, feeling a little hesitant at first. From what I understood, unlocking my memories was a bad thing. I was skeptical. With everything that had happened to me, I had every reason to be. I didn't really know who this boy was, although I had my suspicions. He, like Huang and the old man, suddenly appeared at my home. For all I knew, he was just another psycho demon who was trying to either kill me or take me to the Contravexus. But then, something happened. As if some force reached into my heart and pulled out all my fears, I felt compelled to stay. It was as if an inner voice was speaking to me, telling me to trust him and give him a chance. I wasn't sure what he could do, but if he were truly trying to help me, I was willing to give him the benefit of the doubt. I knelt once more beside him as he continued to tend to the injured old man.

"How is he?" I asked.

"He's badly hurt."

Suddenly, the old man lifted his head and spoke.

"My Lord, I'm sorry I failed you!" he said struggling.

"You have not failed me, old friend. Rest. It will be alright," said the lad.

A golden glow began to appear around the boy and the old man. It was the same glow that surrounded me when I lay on the floor after Huang's attack. The glow was magnificent and warm. It had the color of a sunrise and the warmth of a loving hug. The man laid his head back and closed his eyes. He was motionless for several seconds. During this time, I noticed that his wounds were healing themselves. After about thirty seconds, the glow dissipated and the boy stood to his feet.

At first, I thought the old man was dead. Although his injuries had vanished, he was still and his breathing appeared to have stopped. Then, his eyes opened with a start and he turned his head and looked at me. I was startled by his reanimation, and I jumped up and raised the sword in self-defense. The old man struggled to sit upright. Then, he stood to his feet and balanced himself against a nearby boulder. He began coughing as he brushed the dirt off his clothing. Then, he turned and looked at me once again. He scanned me up and down, as if he were looking for flaws. It was then that I realized that I still had the towel wrapped about me.

The police cars screeched to a halt where the front of my house used to be. The old man lifted his right hand and it appeared that the entire world stopped. Nothing moved, not even an inch. Only he, the boy and I appeared to be moving. The old man walked closer to me and looked me in the eyes. I still held the sword in front of me, just in case I needed to defend myself.

"I do believe that belongs to me!" he stated.

Suddenly, the sword erupted from my hands and levitated toward his. It gently rested in his palm and he secured his grip around the handle. He quickly inspected the sword to insure that it wasn't damaged. Then, he sheathed it into its holster that was draped across his left shoulder. I felt a little uneasy. Beside the fact that I was barely clothed, I was now defenseless as well.

"Are you ready?" he asked.

"Am I ready for what?" I retorted.

"You've been wandering these streets for the last few days trying to figure out what's going on. We are offering you an opportunity to learn the truth about yourself and your past," he replied.

I frowned. "So, now you're ready to tell me the truth. What made you change your mind? Lord knows you could have told me the truth when I was at the church. Why didn't you tell me the truth then?" I asked angrily.

"Valid questions," said the boy standing. "However, this is not the time for such discussions. Desmond has stopped time for only a moment. If you want to know the truth, then I suggest you follow us. Or you can stay here and attempt to explain this to the police."

I shot the both of them a very nasty look.

"Very well, I'll go with you," I said calmly.

The old man took off his overcoat and wrapped it around me.

"Don't want you to catch cold," he said.

The two began walking away. I was still a little hesitant, but I didn't want to stay here. I trotted behind them. As we made our way to the next street, I glanced back and noticed that the pause in time that the old man created had worn off and everything was returning back to normal.

~~~

CHAPTER FIFTEEN

For one square block, houses were either totally destroyed or were raging infernos. Emergency teams scurried to help the individuals that were either trapped beneath rubble or lying injured. Sariel stood with his hands in his pockets while Gabrielle calmly surveyed the chaos through a pair of binoculars.

"This is terrible," said Gabrielle.

"Don't get soft on me. I'm not about to go over there and start helping these people," said Sariel.

Gabrielle ignored the comment.

"Do you see her?" he asked.

"No, but I know she was here."

Sariel pulled out a pen-shaped device and lifted it into the air. The tip glowed red.

"I'm also detecting that someone else was here and it wasn't the Consortium. You think it was an abduction attempt?" asked Sariel.

"Perhaps. But by the look of things it didn't go so well," said Gabrielle.

"So, where to now?"

Gabrielle sighed.

"Let's check the area. We might get lucky."

The two agents turned and began walking back to where their vehicle was parked. However, unbeknownst to them, another pair of eyes watched from the wooded area near the burning homes. Kitana stared menacingly as Gabrielle and Sariel walked away. As they disappeared around the corner, she folded her arms across her chest and pursed her lips.

"Nice to see you again, mother," she said.

She turned and walked back to the Escalade which was parked

around the corner. The driver opened the door and she slumped into the seat next to her brother.

"Well, what did you see?" he asked.

"The place was a mess. It was the Gaian alright. She must be close by," she said.

"Then let's start searching. She couldn't have gotten far," said Lorimar.

~~~

Vancouver, B.C. Angelo was dressed in a collarless black suit with a colorless white shirt. He walked toward Peter and Raphael, who were standing by the water fountain.

"Ah, Angelo, how are you feeling?" asked Peter.

"Okay, I guess," he replied, stopping in front of them.

"Ready to go back and make the realms safe once more?" asked Raphael.

"As ready as I'll ever be," said Angelo.

Peter nodded. He then pulled out a passport and handed it to Angelo.

"This came from Michael," said Peter.

Angelo opened the passport and found its destination was Rome, Italy.

"Dupri has returned to the Vatican. That seems to be his base of operation. Michael wants you to go there and render it inoperative," said Peter.

"So, I'm being separated from my wife?" said Angelo glaring at the passport.

"Politics of Hierarchy operations, Angelo. You know the drill. You're too close to the issue right now," said Peter.

"Yeah," replied Angelo sarcastically.

Raphael pulled out a copy of orders and handed them to Angelo.

"Your plane leaves in one hour," he said.

"Thanks."

Angelo turned and walked down the hallway. Peter and

Raphael stood there for a moment, watching their disheartened brethren depart.

"You know he's going to come back here and look for the woman," said Raphael.

"Yeah, I know. I just hope he doesn't allow his heart to fool him into making the wrong decision should the moment of reckoning come," said Peter.

~~~

New York. Michael was in his office looking over some surveillance footage. The phone on his desk rang. He picked up the receiver and answered.

"Yes?"

"I know you know who this is," said a female voice on the other end.

"Eve?" he asked.

"Yes. I have a little package for you. It will be at the Four Seasons Hotel in Toronto. Try not to take too long."

"Eve wait, why are you doing this? Why have you aligned yourself with the Contravexus?"

"I'm trying to help you. I've infiltrated Dupri's network and I have something you might find interesting. But we can sit here and talk, or you can find out what I left you. You better act fast. Time is running out."

Michael sighed.

"Very well, I'm on my way," he said.

"Come alone," she said.

The phone clicked.

Michael hung up the phone. He hurried out of his office, grabbing his coat as he exited. He shot passed Augustine and Mary, two of the administrative agents who were chatting in the hall.

"Where's the fire, Michael?" asked Augustine noticing Michael's hurried pace.

Michael stopped and walked back to them.

"Do me a favor," said Michael. "I have to go to Toronto. I want you to use the Sky Eye to keep track of me."

The Sky Eye was the Hierarchy's surveillance satellite system that could see everything on the planet.

"Toronto?" asked Augustine.

"Yes. I don't have time to explain, but just watch my back," said Michael.

"Will do. You want us to contact anyone?" asked Mary.

"No," said Michael.

He then turned and walked down the hall.

~~~

A private 767 airliner was just beginning to fly above Israeli airspace when the phone in the main cabin beeped. Amir Fawan answered it.

"Yes. Yes, he is here. One moment," he said.

He walked toward the front of the extravagant cabin that surpassed the luxurious Air Force One. He stood beside a swiveling chair and handed the phone to Dupri.

"It's the Russian President, Mr. Dupri," said Fawan.

"Put him on speakerphone, then leave me," said Dupri.

Fawan did what he was told and hurried away.

"What is it President Smirnoff?"

"Sir, sorry to bother you, but we just received word from the Prime Minister that British Intelligence detected a temporal disturbance somewhere around the Sinai. Its frequency matches the one you asked us to look for. We've dispatched a team to investigate. We may have found it, sir," said Smirnoff.

"And you are certain of this?" asked Dupri.

"Very certain."

"Excellent! I am on my way to the Vatican. Keep me posted."

He pressed a button on his chair's control panel and disconnected the call. Then, he sat back in his chair and tilted his head upward.

"The Sinai, huh? Interesting."

Fawan walked toward Dupri.

"Is everything okay?" he asked.

Dupri nodded.

"Yes. I just got word that a temporal disturbance was detected in the Sinai. I'm wondering if we found the gate," said Dupri.

"Why would you suspect that?" asked Fawan.

"It was my theory that if the Gaian were to be placed under extreme levels of stress, it might cause the bonds blocking her memory to erode and eventually break. If that were to happen, she would regain her memory and the gate would instantly activate. This would release a frequency that would guide the Gaian to the gate. But this frequency could also be activated intermittently if the Gaian were placed under extreme stress. I orchestrated a series of misfortunes to occur to the Gaian, thus creating stress. The temporal disturbance that President Smirnoff just reported to me possesses the same frequency as those emitted by the gate," explained Dupri.

"Interesting," said Fawan.

"Indeed. The Gaian must be undergoing a tremendous amount of anger or stress. No doubt, Huang has really pissed her off. She is unknowingly triggering a reaction in the gate, which also means that the bonds blocking her memory are weakening."

"My lord, if I understand you correctly, she has inadvertently shown us where the gate is located. Why do we still need her?"

"Because our master needs her body. The three pieces of the puzzle are falling into place. We have the altar, and if this turns out to be what I hope, we'll have the gate. Now all we need to do is wait for Huang to bring the Gaian to me. Then, our master will be reborn."

"My apologies for my ignorance," said Fawan.

"No need. It was a part of my plan not to reveal this information. See, the Hierarchy didn't know that the Gaian's mental frequencies are linked to the gate. By helping her, they were, in fact, helping me."

"How so?"

"Despite their less than honorable intentions, I knew that eventually they would try to kill her. She would begin to distrust the Hierarchy and become frustrated and confused. That same doubt and confusion would also weakened the bonds that confined the true Gaian's mind, thus triggering a reaction in the gate."

"You make her sound as if she were some kind of machine."

"In part, she is. The Gaian is nothing more than a vessel, a shell that our master uses to accomplish his objectives. It can't think for itself, but merely exists for the single purpose of serving my master. The frequency is like a homing signal."

"How sad. It would almost make one feel sorry for her."

Dupri shot him a dirty look.

"I will be taking my leave, sir," said Fawan, tucking his head.

Dupri nodded.

~~~

It seemed like we'd been walking forever. We were now on the outskirts of Seattle, probably near one of the stadiums. I was beginning to tire and it was getting cold. Darkness was falling and I had no idea where we were going. The boy was silent the entire time. The old man kept checking on me to ensure I was alright.

"I believe I know your answer to the question I'm about to ask, but I'll ask it anyway. How much further?" I asked, pulling the coat tighter about me.

"Almost there," replied the old man.

"You said that two hours ago," I retorted.

Suddenly, the boy stopped and we each followed suit. We stood inside a dismal, dingy alley. The smell of fish permeated the air and trash cluttered the entire alley. The boy walked to a doorway and pushed it open.

"This is it," he said.

"This is what?" I asked.

"The safe house," replied the old man.

I scrunched my nose and gave a disapproving scowl. It was

a dump. Trash cluttered the entrance and mold was along the threshold.

"You can't be serious," I said.

The boy walked in without saying another word. The old man followed. I stood there looking once more at the disgusting entrance and questioned whether I should go in or leave. Suddenly, a crash of thunder echoed. I looked up, puzzled. The sky had been clear during our entire trip and this part of the country wasn't known for such storms. But now, there were thick patches of dark cumuli in the sky. It looked like a downpour could occur any minute. With the storm on the verge of beginning, I had no choice. I walked to the door, stepping over the garbage in front of it. As I stood in the entrance, I peeked inside to see if it was safe.

The old man sat on a wooden bench before a fireplace, trying to get a fire started. I slowly walked in, still a little unsure about all of this. There was a bucket that had been turned upside down. I walked to it and sat, relieved that I could finally rest for a moment. He managed to get the fire started, and within moments, it was a hearty flame.

"It will be a while before dinner is ready, but you can rest a while if you like," he offered.

He walked to the near wall and pulled out a cot. He dragged it closer to the fire, then turned to me.

"Well, are you waiting for an invitation?" he asked.

I stood and walked to it, still clutching the coat about me. I sat on the edge of the cot and stared at the flames as the popping of the wood echoed within the chamber.

"Rest. You'll be needing your strength," he said.

I nodded.

The old man disappeared into the shadows of the room. I sat there, staring at the flames as they danced inside the fireplace. I was anxious for answers, but I was also very fatigued. It had been a very exhausting day and I could barely keep my eyes opened. I laid my head on the cot and wondered what would happen next.

~~~

235

Morning had come to Rome. All was calm and still. A gentle breeze blew from the east and dark clouds were on the horizon. The clean smell of the air hinted that rain was on the way.

Montellace Dupri deplaned and walked to his limousine. Amir Fawan closed the door after Dupri stepped in. Then, Fawan stepped back as the white stretch limo pulled off. Inside, Dupri chuckled beneath his breath. Delilah, his assistant, began briefing him on the business events that had happened while he'd been gone. Dupri was not concerned with what she was saying. He held up his hand, indicating that he did not wish to hear anymore. Delilah apologized in Italian. Dupri looked at the young woman. She was a stunning creature with a slim body. Her eyes sparkled, and her crop-cut hairstyle was always neat and shiny.

"Delilah, take off your clothes," said Dupri.

"Excuse me?" she replied with her thick accent.

"You heard me, take off your clothes."

The woman was shocked by his request. He'd always shown her respect and professionalism. She was puzzled that he would ask her to do such a thing and had every intention of refusing to do what he asked. Then, she looked into his eyes. Without saying a word, she began unbuttoning her blouse, almost as if she'd been placed under a trance. As the last one was unfastened, she slid her top off and laid it on the seat.

"Now your skirt," he said.

She reached behind her, unfastened the button and unzipped it. She slid the skirt off and laid it on top of the silk blouse. Then, she took off her remaining undergarments and placed them in a pile on the floor. Dupri got undressed also and laid the woman on the floor of the limousine. As he lowered himself on top of her, the limo driver buzzed his cabin.

"What the hell do you want?" he asked.

"Sorry sir, but there is an urgent call from the British Ministry," said the driver.

Dupri sat back on the seat and snatched the phone from its cradle.

"This had better be good," he said angrily.

"My lord, I apologize, but I just wanted to let you know that we have the altar," said the voice on the other end.

"Good!"

"I don't have any further information concerning the temporal disturbance yet, but we are working on it."

"Don't call me until you have something and that had better be soon!" said Dupri.

"Another thing, sir. Mr. Huang has been looking for you. He says it's urgent."

"I'll contact him later," said Dupri.

He slammed the phone back on its cradle and pondered for a moment. He looked down at Delilah, who was still lying naked on the floor. He looked once more out his window and saw that they were nearing the Vatican.

"Get dressed; we're here," he said as the limousine pulled into St. Peter's Square.

~~~

"Damn the rotten luck!" Angelo exclaimed.

He was still angry about the assignment he'd received. He knew that the only reason why Michael had given him this assignment was because he felt that Angelo wasn't reliable enough to carry out his post. What Michael failed to realize was that there was more to Vanifera than just a simple beast who cared about nothing else except killing. Part of her was human and that was the part that kept her Gaian half in check. That was the part he loved and had to save. But first, he needed to complete this mission. Then, he'd find her. He marched out of the airport to a cab and got in.

"I need to get to the Vatican."

"Sorry, sir, but I'm on me break for a few more ticks," the man retorted with a Scottish accent.

Angelo looked at the man. He revealed the rage that lay just behind his deep eyes of brown. Within seconds, the man's will was gone. He'd taken over his mind and now the man was nothing more than a simple servant.

"Now, get me to the Vatican!" said Angelo.

"Yes sir, right away," replied the man.

~~~

Two people sat in a booth of a restaurant just outside of Federal Way, Washington. Sariel tapped his spoon against the side of his water glass while Gabrielle typed on her laptop. She paused, looking at him with an annoyed expression. Sariel stared out of the window next to him, totally oblivious of his actions.

"Do you mind knocking that off," she said with a hint of suppressed frustration.

Sariel looked at her and instantly ceased tapping. He placed the spoon down and folded his hands, resting them on the table. Gabrielle took a deep breath and resumed her typing.

"So what 'chu typing?" asked Sariel, trying to sound chipper.

"I'm just writing my report and sending it to Michael," said Gabrielle.

"Why don't you call him?"

"I tried. He's not answering."

Sariel nodded. Just then, the waitress brought over two cups of coffee, a slice of chocolate-layered cake and a bowl of peach cobbler. She sat them on the table and walked off. Sariel looked at his cake, but Gabrielle continued typing.

"This is the only thing I like about the humans, dessert," said Sariel.

"Yeah, well I have to hand it to them, they can make some good sweets," Gabrielle replied.

She finished typing and sent her report. Then, she closed her laptop and pulled her peach cobbler to her.

"I'm a little disturbed that we haven't been able to pick up the Gaian's trail," said Gabrielle.

"Indeed. I know she was the one who caused that destruction. That was Uriel and her house. But, why would she do that?" asked Sariel.

"Good question. You said you picked up some other bio

signals while you were there," said Gabrielle as she took a bite of her cobbler.

"Yeah, I did. But they weren't angelic signals. I detected a demon bio signature as well as the Gaian's. But there were a couple others. I couldn't determine what they were."

"Seems as though we may have some shadow players."

"Could be."

Suddenly, they were joined by an unexpected guest, Azreal.

"Did you order me one, too?" he asked.

"What do you want?" asked Gabrielle.

Azreal slid next to her. Gabrielle scooted over to give him a little more room to sit, obviously annoyed by his intrusion.

"Just thought I'd let you know, Gabrielle, that your children are here in the city," said Azreal.

An emotional expression suddenly bloomed on Gabrielle's face. Sariel looked surprised.

"Where are they?" she asked.

"Just look out of your window," said Azreal.

Gabrielle raked open the curtains and stared outside. There, stepping out of the massive vehicle were her daughter, Kitana, and her son, Lorimar.

~~~

Toronto, Ontario. A cloud of smoke emerged from the exhaust pipe of a late model car. Its tires screeched as the car sped from the parking lot of the hotel. A few automobiles were scattered about, yet, one vehicle stood out from all the rest. An expensive late model BMW was parked in a reserved parking space. The tags read "Blessed 1". Inside the luxurious hotel, the "Do Not Disturb" sign dangled from the doorknob of Room 169.

Inside the room, a gentle breeze danced with the curtains as the sound of grunting, panting and moaning could be heard. The rhythmic cracking of the bed frame echoed off the walls. The temperature in the room was like a sauna or a Turkish bath.

Candlelight cast the shadows of two lovers against the far wall.

The naked woman was straddled atop the man as she purred with satisfaction. Her grinding motion was deliberate and firm, bringing her lover closer to his climax. He fondled her breasts and massaged her firm and curvaceous body. His lust for her was uncontrollable as she magnificently maneuvered her body on top of his.

She continued with her pace, tightening her inner muscles in an attempt to draw him closer to ecstasy. The man responded to her actions, flexing his muscles and arching his back. He strained in an attempt to lengthen this moment, but his efforts were futile. His eyes rolled to the back of his head, his breathing grew short and shallow. His hands moved from her breast and gripped her sides as his body tightened and shuddered. The sensation in his loins grew and grew, to the point where he had to surrender.

Her pace quickened ever slightly as she panted and cooed. She felt him losing control, fighting to stop the inevitable. The pressure mounted higher and higher. Their bodies pounded faster and faster until...

The intensity of his release sent tremors throughout his entire body. The woman was filled with the satisfying warmth for her efforts. The man tightened his grip around her waist and continued to stretch his body to enhance his release. The woman arched her back and slowly grinded atop her lover. As the last of his strength escaped from his body, he began to relax and allow the tingling pulsations to subside.

The woman leaned closer to him and gently kissed his mouth. They stroked and caressed each other, mixing the sweat from their bodies as they enjoyed the final moments of their lustful interlude. The man took a deep breath and relaxed on the pillows with his hands outstretched.

The woman ceased her grinding and dismounted. Her body glistened in the candlelight as the flickering flames revealed the definition of her magnificent frame. From her hair to her feet, she was flawless. The light enhanced the tightness and tone of her body, showcasing her muscularity.

The man glared at the woman he just finished making love

to as she quietly strolled to the mirror in the bathroom and began fluffing her hair. In his mind, he couldn't believe he had been with such a beautiful creature. The pride of conquest began to swell in his chest. This was truly an accomplishment worth bragging about. He was mesmerized by her beauty and grace, and he couldn't take his eyes off of her. She was truly the most gorgeous being he'd ever seen, and he wanted more.

The woman continued primping, never once turning around to acknowledge her lover.

"I hope I made you feel good," said the woman seductively.

The man locked his fingers behind his head and stretched out on the bed.

"Oh yes, my dear, you've made this man feel quite good!" he replied.

The woman turned and slinked back to the bed. She stopped at the foot and stared at the man seductively.

"So, Pastor Roberts, what would you like for me to do now?" asked the woman.

Suddenly, the lights from the candles began to brighten slightly, totally illuminating the woman's face. It was Eve. She bent down and began crawling on the bed toward the good reverend. Her crawl was like that of a tigress stalking her prey. She moved over his legs and stopped with her face above his pelvic area. Eve glanced quickly at the face of the reverend, who smiled at her non-verbal suggestion. Then, she began playing as only she could. The reverend quickly surrendered to her charms.

After about a minute, she stopped and looked up at the pastor.

"Tell me, Jerry, will this save me?" questioned Eve.

Pastor Roberts struggled to focus on her question.

"I don't see how it can't," he responded with a trembling voice.

Eve smiled coyly and lowered her head to continue. Another minute passed and once more, she stopped to ask another question.

"How will I be saved?" asked Eve.

The reverend began feeling anxious from her tactics. He wanted her to continue, but now her questions had a religious tone.

In a slight pant he said, "Just repent, my dear. You will be forgiven and you will be saved."

Eve lowered her head once more and continued. Then, she stopped once again to ask another question.

"When will I be saved?" she asked.

Roberts lifted his head with a frown. Her teasing was becoming annoying and her questions were aggravating.

"Why are you asking so many questions?" probed Roberts.

Eve tilted her head and posed yet another question.

"Does that bother you?" she asked, completely stopping her pleasures.

Reverend Roberts sat up and stared into the deep green eyes of his enchantress. They seemed to hold a sorrow he could not fathom. He felt guilty for being so gruff with her and decided to try a more patient approach.

"Not at all," he said. "But I'm not sure when all will be forgiven. All I know is we must continue to pray. The Lord hears our prayers and he will forgive us."

"Then, you don't know if I will be forgiven?" asked Eve.

Reverend Roberts saw that a very serious look had come across the face of Eve. Her eyes had turned ice cold. Her demeanor was more sturdy and authoritative. She was no longer the obedient sex goddess he had been with a few moments ago.

Eve slid from the bed and turned to where her clothes lay. Roberts stared at her, totally confused by her change in attitude. In his mind, he thought that she was merely a prostitute, but it was clear she was a tormented woman seeking redemption or guidance. He slid to the edge of the bed and tried to talk to her.

"My child, are you in some sort of trouble?" he asked.

Eve began snickering.

"Tell me, reverend, are you saved?" she asked softly.

Suddenly, the reverend felt a burning sensation in his loins. He cupped himself, hoping that it was a reaction to the intense sexual interlude he had just encountered. He began to inspect himself as the pain intensified. Then without warning, the reverend's pelvic area was riddled with sores within seconds. He quickly jumped up and ran to the shower in an attempt to douse the lesions with water. He screamed in agony, turning the faucet handle to the fully opened position. However, no water would come out.

The burning increased and the lesions began spreading across his entire body. The pain grew too intense for him to stand and he dropped to his knees. Within moments, he was entirely covered by the lesions and a foul odor filled the room.

Eve was almost completely dressed by this time. The reverend writhed on the floor near the sink. He looked above his head to see the toilet in the bathroom. He had now lost feeling in his legs. His arms and chest burned as the discharge began oozing from the sores. He crawled to the bowl, struggling to stay conscious. He grabbed the sides of the toilet and with a lunge submerged his head inside. The water splashed and doused most of his body. Then, Roberts collapsed to the bathroom floor. His body hissed and smoked almost as if he'd been set on fire.

A pair of white pumps strolled toward the barely alive man. Eve knelt down and stared at him.

"You're not going to die, or at least not yet. I have a purpose for you. A certain Seraph will arrive here shortly. When he does, I want you to give him something," said Eve as she slid her hand across the smoldering man's chest.

Roberts in an attempt to speak, coughed, spewing blood from his mouth. Eve bent over and kissed the pastor on the mouth. Then, she lifted his hands and kissed his palm. She wiped the corners of her mouth, then stood and looked down at the reverend once more before turning to walk to the door.

"Make sure you give him what I gave you," she said.

She walked out and closed the door behind her, laughing hysterically. The lingering scent of lilacs drifted in the air. The room was dark. The candles were all burned out. All was silent. On the floor near the toilet, the Reverend Jerry Roberts laid near death.

His body was riddled with lesions of sores and his mind was in shock. His eyes were fixated on the textured ceiling as he struggled to remain alive. Now, he waited for his visitor that Eve spoke of to arrive, praying silently that he could remain alive long enough to possibly be saved.

~~~

CHAPTER SIXTEEN

The statues surrounding St. Peter's Square represented the ever watchful sentinels of this most holy of places. As the morning sun began peaking from behind the dense layer of clouds, a cab pulled up and the rear door opened. A pair of brown wing-tipped shoes were planted firmly on the curb and an elderly man lifted himself out of the cab. He shuffled forward a few steps, then turned to assist his wife from the cab. She clutched his arm for support and balance, pulling herself from the back seat. She turned and closed the door as the man stepped to the passenger window and paid the driver, rewarding him with a hefty tip for his safe delivery. A few Italian phrases were exchanged. Then, the cab pulled off and the couple proceeded toward the inner courtyard of St. Peter's.

The pigeons fluttered about in front of the elderly pair. It seemed as if they were happy to see the couple. The man paused for a moment and began pulling from his coat pocket a small brown bag. He opened the bag and pulled out a handful of breadcrumbs, allowing them to drop delicately to the ground. The pigeons flapped their wings as they scrambled and fought for food. The woman reached into the bag and pulled a handful also. She slowly knelt down to allow the birds to eat from her hand. The elderly man slowly descended to his knees and watched as the birds enjoyed their meal. He placed his arm lightly around the woman and smiled. To him, this was Heaven.

The elderly couple weren't the only ones who enjoyed the harmonious calmness that existed here. Only in this place could the rigors of life be cancelled out and allow those who visited to once again be reconnected to the soothing whisper of tranquility. This was the most picturesque place in all of Rome. It was serene and relaxing, a veritable garden of sculptures and architecture. Children ran, giggling as their parents pretended to chase them. As far as the eye could see, there were no unhappy faces. There were no frowns, no grimaces.

Suddenly, an explosive boom erupted from inside the St Peter's Basilica. The domed roof burst outward, as if someone had detonated a bomb. The outer shell of the foundation cracked as the blast projected objects through the air. The ground rumbled and shook as the square patrons ran for cover. Some ran toward the basilica to assist those closest to the blast to safety. Slivers of glass had pierced their clothing like needles and the hurled rubble left many bruised.

The steps of the basilica were cracked and crumbled, and the huge doors to the church were blasted off their hinges. Small fires burned around the entrance and along the inner halls. Statues of saints were leveled to dust and the furniture was nothing more than expensive firewood. Every window had been shattered, and the sounds of moaning could be heard amidst the rubble.

A thick layer of dust blanketed the air, and the figure of a man was seen emerging from the inner chambers. He stepped over the mounds of concrete and wood that littered the floors. The figure quickly surveyed the area and noticed a man struggling to free himself from beneath a large pillar. He walked toward the man's location and stood over him. He watched him struggle for a moment, then, he leaned over and placed his hand under the crushing slab of marble that pinned him. With a slight flip of his wrist, the large pillar was raised off the injured man and tossed to the other side of the room. He reached down, grabbed the man by his collar and lifted him in the air. By his clothing, it was clear that the injured man was one of the cardinals.

"Please, don't hurt us anymore!" pleaded the cardinal in Italian. "Why are you doing this?"

"You have soiled yourselves with the mark of the unbegotten. For years, you've preached to the people about goodness and mercy. Yet, you give sanctuary to the unjust and the merciless. It is judgment day, cardinal, and I am here to pass sentence!" said the figure.

As the dust cleared, the avenging man's face could be seen more clearly. It was the face of an Archangel. It was Angelo.

"I have been sent by my superiors to purge this place of its impurities! This will be your only opportunity to redeem yourself! I would not waste it if I were you!" said Angelo.

"You have been sent by God?" asked the cardinal. "No, this cannot be!"

Suddenly, Angelo's eyes began to glow and radiate a heat that was intense. The cardinal began to feel his flesh burn as the light in the Archangel's eyes intensified.

"Feel the torment of the billions of souls that were lied to! Feel the hell they now endure! Tell me cardinal, do you believe now?" asked Angelo.

The cardinal screamed in agony as he felt a pain he had never known. It was the pain of billions of tortured souls intensified. It permeated every part of his body. It was like a fire burning its way to the outside. The pain debilitated him, crippling him like a disease. He curled in the clutches of the Archangel, sobbing uncontrollably.

"Now you know the hell that awaits you! But, before I take your soul and send you to a damnable existence for eternity, I will give you one last chance at redemption!" said Angelo.

The cardinal continued to cry in agony as he struggled to listen to the question that could save his soul. Angelo released the man of the cloth and he flopped to the ground clutching his chest. Angelo knelt in front of the writhing man.

"Where is Montellace Dupri?" he asked.

As the words flowed from Angelo's lips, the pain began to subside inside the cardinal. He stopped clutching his chest and began breathing deeply, struggling to regain the precious breath he had lost. The cardinal realized that he needed to answer his torturer or he would suffer the agony of torment again. He quickly gasped and shouted as loudly as he could.

"I don't know where he is! But if I did, why should I tell you?

You've brought great pain to my body and you say you're sent from God! Our teachings tell us that God is merciful to his children! Yet, you destroy his temple and desecrate his holy house! You aren't a follower of God, for he resides with us and he will surely make you pay for your impudence!" exclaimed the cardinal.

Angelo frowned at the cardinal's answer. He glanced to the right and saw a copy of the Holy Bible.

"Your words are nothing but foolish jargon spewed from the mouth of a misguided fool!" said Angelo as he grabbed the holy book. "You do not follow the word of God."

"That's a lie! We do!" said the cardinal.

"The hell you do! From the beginning, you assisted in twisting the simple minds of mankind to believe in the necessity of performing evil deeds for a good cause. You and the rest of your religious cults brainwashed your brethren with contradictions and visions of grandeur. The murdering of innocent lives, all done in the name of God. Does this sound familiar? The blood that was spilled is nothing but a testament to the vile actions that you and the Contravexus have stooped to in order to ripen this world for eventual destruction!" said Angelo.

"We did not!" interrupted the cardinal. "We were loyal to God and his word. These wars were necessary in order to maintain peace!"

"Peace? Forcing a world to live by your rules is no one's idea of peace," said Angelo as he stood and began walking around the ravaged basilica. "You build your churches and your temples, claiming that these were done for the glory of God when all along they were nothing more than glorified dens of iniquity. You fed off the sins of this world, pretending to give comfort to those you cared nothing about. Then, you used this information to force these beings who sought your help to do unspeakable horrors in the name of God. Well now, father, the preverbal swallows have returned to roost. The time has come for you and the rest of your kind to pay for your blasphemy."

"You are no messenger of God's. You are a demon. Any person

who would say such things and destroy a house of worship can be nothing more than that!" said the cardinal with disdain.

"You sorely tempt my wrath, father! My Master doesn't care about your temples or your marble statues. He doesn't care about your robes or even the way you manipulate the Messiah's teachings. You parade around with your high and mighty noses in the air, capitalizing on the misfortunes of the weak. They come to you looking for answers and you mislead them with pretentiously sorrowful words. But alas, your fate will come not by my hands, but by the hands of your master," said Angelo.

"What are you talking about?" asked the cardinal.

"There is an evil that is coming; one whose very being was born from the purest of the pure. This evil possesses levels of destruction you could never imagine. You are harboring the one person who will unleash the evil. So, I will ask you this question just one more time. Where is Montellace Dupri?" asked Angelo.

"I-I, I don't know! As God is my witness, I don't know!" stammered the cardinal.

The Archangel dropped the Bible in the lap of the cardinal, who now had pulled himself to a sitting position. The cardinal looked down at the hallowed book lying in his lap. Angelo stood over him and pitifully looked at the cardinal as he sat with a stunned expression from the revelation that had been stated by Angelo.

"You're... you're lying, right? This can't be true," said the cardinal with a whimper.

"I never lie. That is a human trait. But I do pity you. May God have mercy on your soul," said Angelo.

Just then, footsteps were heard approaching from the darkened hallway. The cadence was slow and deliberate and gave the indication that the approaching individual was not anxious to emerge from the shadows. Angelo waited as the intruder drew closer. Then from out of the dust-filled hallway, a figure emerged and stood amidst the debris.

"I'm afraid he's right, cardinal!" said the figure.

Angelo's eyes widened as he glared at the being to see who dared to validate his words. It was Montellace Dupri.

JAMES GORDON

"YOU!" exclaimed Angelo.

"You look surprised to see me, Archangel! I hope I didn't interrupt your quality time with the cardinal! He looks like you really shagged him well!" said Dupri with cockiness.

With the blink of an eye, Angelo created a concentrated ball of light in the palm of his hand and hurled it toward Dupri. The ball struck the Contravexus in the chest, knocking him through a wall of marble. The cardinal, still in shock, scrambled to get away as Angelo walked toward the huge hole in the wall. As he drew closer, the dust cleared from in front of him, as if a huge fan was blowing before him. He reached the hole and peered through it. To his surprise, he found that Dupri was gone.

Angelo walked through the hole. He scanned the entire area only to discover that the Contravexus was nowhere to be found. Just then, a blast of fire-red erupted from beneath the floor where Angelo stood. It knocked the Archangel through the ceiling into the room above. His body flipped in the air and he landed face down on the hard wooden floor. Dupri slowly ascended through the huge hole as Angelo attempted to shake off the blast. His full-length leather coat still smoldered from Angelo's attack. The prideful Archangel rose to his feet, shaking off the effects of the Contravexus' blast. He looked at Dupri with an unflinching glare of hatred.

"I'm not here to fight you, Archangel!" said Dupri.

"I care not why you are here, beast! You were responsible for trying to end my life! I'm here to return the favor!" replied Angelo.

Angelo's eyes began to glow bright like the sun. Suddenly, Dupri found himself lifted from the floor and thrust against the far wall. His arms were extended outward from his sides. He helplessly dangled in the same position the Messiah did on Calvary. Sharp slivers of light pierced Dupri's hands and the mighty Contravexus grimaced in pain. After several moments of anguish, Dupri dropped his head from exhaustion and looked at the Archangel. The stare of Angelo's was sinister and piercing. It showed the very hatred he had for Dupri. Suddenly, the Contravexus thought of a scheme.

"I know where your wife is," he said straining.

"What?" Angelo asked.

"The Hierarchy doesn't have your wife. She is out there still, and I know where she is. I can bring her to you and restore her to her old self," bargained Dupri.

"That's impossible. The Gaian merged with Vanifera and the fusion is permanent," said Angelo.

"No, it isn't. I know of a way to reverse the absorption of Vanifera. But you must release me," begged Dupri.

Angelo paused for a moment, then increased the power of his spikes of light.

"You're lying!" he exclaimed.

"NO! I swear!" screamed Dupri.

"If we couldn't do it, how can you?"

"You nor your master created the Gaian. But my master did. He embedded certain failsafe commands and entrusted this information to me. He also gave me the information on how to perform the same separation process Jehovah used to separate himself from my master. I can use the ritual to save your wife."

"Tell me what this ritual is!"

"It will do you little good. You must have the altar and the Gaian in order to perform the ritual. I have the altar. If you let me go, I promise I'll help your wife."

If there was one thing Angelo wanted more than anything, it was to save Vanifera. The only way he could do that was by separating the Gaian from her. If there was a way to do it, he would take that chance. He thought for a few moments more and then looked up at Dupri.

"Do you swear to me on your life that you can reverse the effects of the fusion?" asked Angelo.

"I swear to you on the life of not only myself, but also that of my master!" wailed Dupri.

Suddenly, Dupri discovered that the forces that nailed him to the wall were beginning to lessen. He quickly jerked himself from the crucified positioning and fell to the floor. He landed directly in front of Angelo, who stared at him menacingly. Dupri snarled beneath his breath, angry at the fact he'd been so easily overtaken. He shook off the effects of his torture and raised his head to glare into Angelo's eyes. He realized that the Archangel was stronger now, much stronger. The pure hatred that Angelo possessed toward him showed in his eyes. It was that same hatred that made him powerful enough to defeat Dupri, perhaps powerful enough to even kill him. That angered the Contravexus most of all. Then Dupri smiled, almost as if an idea had come to him.

"I'm sure the temptation of killing me was almost too much for you. I applaud your restraint," said Dupri.

Angelo stared back into Dupri's eyes. He knew Dupri was trying to egg him on.

"If you do not do what you say, I will kill you," said Angelo.

Dupri adjusted himself. Then, his phone rang. He reached into his coat pocket and removed it. He pressed the button and held it to his ear.

"Yeah?" he said. "Good. I'll be right there."

He hung up and placed the phone back in his pocket.

"That was one of my people. Seems as though we've found your wife. They have her at my chateau across town. Shall we?"

In truth, the call was from Huang who had been trying to contact Dupri. He stated that he'd been injured, but Dupri made misleading comments during the call in order to throw Angelo off. Dupri had thrown a hook and waited to see if Angelo would bite. If he did, he would either kill him when the opportunity presented itself, or he would escape. Dupri knew that he didn't have any information about the location of Angelo's wife, and if he didn't get away soon, Angelo would figure it out.

Angelo wasn't sure what Dupri was trying to pull and he didn't really believe what he said. It was too coincidental that he would get a call about his wife while he was there. However, if he was telling the truth, it might be the only opportunity for him to save Vanifera. Angelo knew that the Consortium was after her also, and if they found her, they would try and kill her.

"Alright, lead the way!" said Angelo.

"Let me call my limo," said Dupri.

"No, I will not ride in one of your vehicles. We'll walk."

Angelo lifted his hand and created another ball of light. Seeing that the exits were blocked by rubble, Angelo would create his own exit. He released the ball of light, blasting a hole in the wall. He then turned and looked at Dupri.

"After you."

Dupri looked a little surprised by his suggestion, but quickly shook it off and resumed his normal smug expression.

"You don't actually expect me to walk, do you?" he asked wryly.

"Get moving," replied Angelo deliberately.

A resentful look bloomed across Dupri's face. Realizing that he didn't have much of a choice, he walked to the hole and leaped through it, descending to the ground below. Glass and wood covered the ground as Dupri waited for Angelo to arrive. Angelo levitated through the hole and glided to the ground like a feather. Upon landing, they began walking from the Basilica and within thirty minutes were outside of Vatican City. Soon after, they came across a car dealership and Dupri got another idea.

"Since you won't ride in one of my vehicles, why don't you let me get one you *will* ride in? It sure as hell beats walking," he said.

Angelo was a little uncertain, but the walk was becoming a little tiring.

"Fine," he replied.

Dupri walked toward the establishment and strolled into the showroom. He found a silver Ferrari and headed toward it. The salesman anxiously scurried to him.

"It's a beauty, isn't she?" asked the salesman.

Dupri turned and looked at the man.

"Why yes, she is. But you know, you can never be sure by the way a car looks. Why the guts of the vehicle could be totally shot," he retorted.

"Not this baby! She purrs like a kitten and runs like a cheetah!" said the salesman.

"Well, there is only one way to be sure," said Dupri.

The salesman pulled a set of keys from his pocket.

"Why don't you crank that baby up!" he said.

Dupri grabbed the keys.

Angelo walked into the showroom and stood in the corner, glaring at Dupri as he sat in the car.

"This guy is wasting my time," said Angelo under his breath.

Dupri opened the door and sat in the driver's seat. He slid the key into the ignition switch and cranked the car. It was sheer perfection. Dupri revved the motor, testing the power of the Ferrari.

"You're right, it does sound good!" he said.

Suddenly, he slammed the door and shifted the car into first gear. The movement was so quick that it startled the salesman. Then, Dupri slammed his foot on the gas.

"See you at the finish line, Archangel!" he exclaimed as he barreled toward the showroom window.

The car exploded from the showroom in a waterfall of glass. Dupri and the car flew through the air and landed on the ground as sparks and burned rubber smoke exploded behind him. Angelo was even surprised by the action and quickly looked around the showroom for another car like Dupri's. He saw a red one in the far corner and quickly raced toward it.

The remaining salesmen raced toward the Archangel, attempting to prevent another vehicle from being stolen. Angelo lifted his hand, sending the men flying into the air in different directions. They crashed into other vehicles or to the floor. He leaped into the air and landed into the driver's seat of the red Ferrari. There were no keys in the ignition. He pulled down the visor and a set dropped into his hands.

"I don't believe it. They actually kept keys under the visor," he said.

The Archangel cranked the engine and revved the motor. He shifted the car into first gear and pressed the accelerator. The car exploded from the showroom in much the same manner as Dupri's vehicle. It landed on the street, shooting smoke and sparks into the air.

Dupri raced through the streets without a care in the world. Although he wasn't trying to hit anyone, he didn't try to avoid them either. Pedestrians leaped to safety as the silver bullet-like vehicle hurled down the road at a deadly speed. Humans were of no concern to the Contravexus. To him, they were expendable obstacles that added excitement to the race. The only thing that mattered to him was getting away.

Angelo possessed the same fury in his driving as Dupri. His only concern was catching the lying Contravexus and finding the whereabouts of his wife, or beating the crap out of him. He glanced down at his speedometer that now read one hundred and ninety miles per hour. He looked up to see if he was closing in on his opponent. His trail wasn't hard to pickup. The people that littered the sides of the street, attempting to regroup from their near death encounter with the silver automobile, was evidence enough that he'd been that way.

Dupri downshifted and spun around the corner, then accelerated back to a killing speed down a one-way street. Moments later, Angelo swerved around the same corner and followed in close pursuit. He was closing in on Dupri, and soon, he would catch him.

Dupri jetted passed a truck that was backing up to unload. His speed startled the men as they ducked and ran for safety. However, the truck continued to back up and soon blocked the road.

Angelo barreled up the street. He saw the truck and knew that there was no way for him to stop the vehicle in time. Then, he saw a loading ramp on the right side of the street. He turned the car toward it and drove up the ramp, propelling the car into the air. The Ferrari flew over the top of the truck, but at this height, the car would explode upon impact with the ground.

Angelo could not risk allowing the car to land at this speed, nor could he allow Dupri to get away. The Seraph squatted between the two seats, clutched both door's sides and in a moment of desperation did the only thing he could do. He revealed his wings.

They were a beautiful shade of silver. As the sunlight struck each feather, the Archangel's wings shimmered with the colors of a rainbow. They expanded beyond the width of the car, allowing him to float the automobile gently to the ground. Once on the ground, the Archangel retracted his wings and they disappeared from sight, almost as if they were never there. He returned to a seated position in the car, revved the motor once more and resumed his chase. The men who were working in the area stared in disbelief. Their jaws dropped as the red Ferrari sped away in a cloud of black smoke.

Dupri looked into his rearview mirror and noticed that the Archangel was nowhere in sight. He huffed to himself, delighted by his driving ability. Perhaps the truck had taken him out, which would have been very disappointing. Surely the Archangel wasn't so easily defeated. He slowed down a bit to see if his assumption was correct. He didn't have to wait long for his answer. Just then, he heard the sound of something approaching very quickly. He looked to his right toward the next street over. A red Ferrari spun around the corner and headed straight toward him. Dupri smiled once more. He was happy to see that his adversary was still in the game and was extremely and recklessly persistent. He quickly shifted into gear and pressed the accelerator.

Angelo turned the wheel to the right and followed the Contravexus, who was only a few feet in front of him. Their speed was above two hundred and ten miles per hour as they rocketed down the streets of the waterfront. Angelo pressed the pedal to the floor and pulled along the right side of his opponent. Now, they were neck and neck as they raced down the bumpy road. The howl of sirens was heard in the distance as they closed in on the end of their little excursion.

Dupri looked at Angelo and smiled. He was having fun, but it was time to end this little race. Angelo looked up and saw that the street they traveled was connected to a bridge that was incomplete. The road was about to end. He turned to look quickly at Dupri who was standing in his seat and waving goodbye. Then, he leaped into the air as his vehicle raced toward its doomed destination. They were ten feet from the end of the bridge. The drop was steep. The bridge ended midway across the huge river. Angelo stood in his seat, preparing to perform the same escape as Dupri. However, the road ended before he could leap.

The cars jetted off the unfinished bridge and plummeted toward the river below. Angelo jumped and dove in the air as the two cars crashed into the river with a huge splash. The Archangel made a perfect swan dive into the water. He quickly surfaced and looked at the slowly sinking vehicles. Anger then consumed him as the cars continued to sink beneath the water.

"Damn it! How did I allow myself to be suckered like that?" he asked.

It was clear to him now that Dupri had no knowledge of his wife's whereabouts. He'd allowed his emotions to place him in a very unsettling predicament. It was a mistake he would not allow to happen again. He looked back at the bridge where he saw Dupri giving him a half-hearted salute. Then, the Contravexus disappeared into the shadows.

Angelo sighed from disgust and began swimming toward shore. Dupri would pay for this, but Angelo would have to wait for another time to get his revenge. As the sirens approached, he made it to the opposite shore and trotted into the bushes. In a moment, he would do the same thing that Dupri had done, disappear. He waited for a few moments, then darted from the bank and into the nearby village. For now, he could only hope that Vanifera was okay, and if it was the last thing he ever did, he was going to find her.

Meanwhile, from the shadows at the base of the bridge, Dupri watched as the Archangel departed. Pride filled his soulless insides as he lit a cigarette and spoke toward his defeated opponent.

"It's all over, ya know! It's just a matter of time! Victory is mine!" he said as he watched the automobiles sink beneath the surface of the rippling water.

~~~

San Francisco. A very palatial mansion secluded by dense woods.

It was a place built during the turn of the century. Everything was handcrafted. The construction and composition was astonishing. Each brick, carving and accessory was made on site. Its marbled outer walls and ivory trimmings defied the futuristic appearance of the other homes nearby. Within this charming structure, the walls were covered with tapestry and the doors were made of mahogany. Each room had its own personality and everything matched, from the carpet, to the tapestry, to the pattern on the furniture. The scent of roses filled the air inside the dimly lit rooms.

But amidst the luxurious trappings, a figure slumped in the corner of one of the rooms. A trail of crimson stained the floor and smeared the walls the figure leaned against. A small pool of the blood surrounded the being as it clung desperately to its remaining existence.

"How dare he hang up on me," snarled the wounded individual.

The being in the corner sat up slightly, mustering all of the strength it had just to do that. It was Huang. He had survived the battle with Desmond Christi and Vanifera, but he was badly wounded. The light from outside showed that half his head was missing.

The task of regenerating was proving more difficult than he thought. The loss of fluid and the severity of his injury placed the demon in a very compromising position. Huang had neither the strength nor the bearings to defend himself. His injuries debilitated him, reducing him to nothing more than a cripple.

"She will pay for this. Somehow I am going to make her pay," he snarled.

Huang braced himself against the wall and pushed himself to stand. His pain made him ponder his reasoning for following Dupri and enduring the kind of agony he currently experienced. He was not a creation of the Vul Paux like Dupri, or an eternal human like Eve. Huang was a demon who escaped the pits of Hell. Even though the Fallen Cast of the Consortium were considered outcasts, assassins and vigilantes by the Hierarchy, the demon clan was viewed as being even lower. They were scorned by the Fallen Cast and considered peons or low-level subordinates. They were treated like insignificant beings whose only purpose was to serve the ranking members of the Consortium. Huang's defection was his opportunity to prove that he and his kind deserved to be treated with respect and not like simple foot soldiers. He would prove his worthiness and show once and for all that his kind were not second-class servants to the Fallen angels. If he assisted Dupri in succeeding in his quest, he would be elevated from the role of servant in Hell to a chief god in the new Celestial Order.

"I will not fail," stated Huang. "I will show them all that I am a being to be reckoned with. The demon clan will no longer be pathetic servants anymore. Dupri will bring down the realms, and the Vul Paux will create a new order. Finally, I will claim my rights and my respect."

Huang reached up and touched his face. He traced his hand across the open wound where the other half once was.

"There must be some way to get that woman back for what she did to me," said Huang.

His dilemma was simple. He wanted to gain revenge on the being that his master was extremely interested in. To harm her directly would bring upon him a wrath worse than anything he would ever receive from Lucifer. He looked at the window as the dimming rays of the evening sun shone through the panels. Anger surged in his heart. Huang reared back his fist and punched out a pane of glass in the window. The slivers cascaded to the ground like rain. Huang retracted his hand and stared through the hole he'd just created. Then, he had an epiphany.

"Wait a minute. Didn't she have a friend living somewhere in this town?" stated Huang beneath his breath. "Yes, I do seem to remember a woman, Denise."

The demon looked toward the setting sun in the sky. Then, he looked to the right and noticed that the moon was starting to become visible. He turned and began walking into an adjacent room. Although he was nowhere near the level of strength he was when he fought Desmond Christi, he was, however, strong enough to carry out the plan he now formulated in his mind. He had the perfect way of getting the Gaian back for what she did to his face, and there was nothing she could do about it.

~~~

CHAPTER SEVENTEEN

Cobwebs were everywhere and the smell of mold was almost as strong as the other stenches that filled the air. I lay on a cot inside of a dingy room trying to gather my thoughts. The place was huge and cold. I grabbed the blanket that was on the cot and wrapped it around me. After the destruction of my home, I had nothing: no clothes, no food and no place to go.

I could feel that I was losing my grip. My emotions were numb and I was developing a great disdain for the life I now had. I didn't care anymore, especially since everything that mattered to me was gone. I didn't know where Angelo was and it was doubtful that I would ever see him again. I lost my home and all my possessions. I was naked, penniless, hungry, tired and dirty. I was once a very well respected nurse. Now I was a pauper, all because of who I was supposed to be.

I stood and looked around the huge, dark room. I spied a chair in the shadows and walked toward it. It had an unusual design. The seat was U-shaped and it had a very high back. The cushions were deep purple and the frame of the chair appeared to be made of pure gold. The carvings had an Egyptian design to them. It was in perfect condition, almost as if it were just made. Suddenly, the old man emerged from the shadows. He carried in his arms some clothes and what appeared to be a basin and a towel.

"What do you say we get you cleaned up, huh?" he asked as he placed the items on the floor before me. "I'll leave these things right here and when you're finished, come through that chamber door and I'll have some food prepared."

He pointed toward the rear of the darkened chamber. I squinted my eyes and began to see a faint image of an arched entryway. I glanced down at the items he brought and then looked at the old man.

"Thank you," I said half-heartedly.

He winked and walked toward the arch. I stood there for a moment and waited for him to distance himself from me before I started washing up. When I was sure he was gone, I walked to the basin and removed the coat and towel. The water was a perfect temperature. It was hot but not too hot. I lifted the towel and dipped it into the soapy water. I cleaned all of the grime and dirt from my body. I rinsed the towel in the basin and watched the water turn to a grimy pool. I quickly finished washing and got dressed. The old man brought me some jeans, a body shirt and a pair of shin-high roper boots. As I dressed, I couldn't help feeling that there was something familiar about the old man. I knew he was the one from the BART station, the alley and the one on the roof of the church. However, there was something else about him that seemed more familiar. He acted as if he knew me also. Even the fit of the clothing he brought me was perfect. But was I on the right track with this thought, or was this some flighty possibility I had suddenly latched on to in order to make myself feel better? Regardless of what spawned this surge of curiosity, I suddenly felt the urge to quickly finish dressing and proceed to the other chamber. Things were growing stranger by the moment. However, I knew that the only one who had the answers to my questions was through the arched entryway.

I checked myself and ensured that I was properly dressed. Then, I started walking to the arched entrance. I was barely able to see due to the darkness of the corridor. There were no lights, not even a torch. So, I kept staring at the faint light that illuminated from inside the adjoining room.

I walked to the doorway and peeked inside. A fire burned in a huge fireplace and a long dining table stretched before it. The table was lined with high back chairs whose design appeared to be from medieval England. It was a very authoritative setting. I scanned the room attempting to locate the old man, but I didn't see him. I proceeded into the massive chamber cautiously. I walked to the fireplace and stood.

Suddenly, I heard a cough. It startled me and I put up my hands in defense.

"We can fight if you like, but your food is going to get cold," said a voice.

I lowered my hands and looked around the room.

"Are you talking to me?" I asked.

"There's no one else here," the voice replied.

The voice wasn't the old man's. Then, someone stood from a chair in the corner closest to the fireplace. It was the kid. He stood there staring at me as if I'd done something wrong. His eyes examined me from the top of my head to the shoes on my feet. I checked myself to ensure there was nothing wrong with how I looked.

"Come closer," he said.

I looked at him, slightly cutting my eyes. I didn't know him, and after everything I'd been through, I had a dozen reasons to be a bit distrusting. I wasn't about to walk toward him until I got some questions answered first.

"Who are you?" I asked.

"My name is Raiel," said the boy.

"What do you want from me?"

"I want nothing. However, you desire something I have."

"What's that?"

"Knowledge. Knowledge of your past and of your identity."

Suddenly, the boy began to glow and transform right before my eyes. He grew in size until he was the height of an adult. His features changed to an older, more mature figure. Scars began to appear on his forehead and visible puncture holes appeared on his hands and feet. He glowed like a star in Heaven, brighter than the fire behind him.

As he stood before me, I felt something reaching into my soul and melting away all my sorrow and pain. It was a warm feeling, one I'd long forgotten existed. Tears welled in my eyes and I wanted to cry aloud. I tried to suppress my building emotions, but it was no use. I couldn't hold it any longer. I tilted my head upward and released a cry of agony. My tears rolled down my face and my pain erupted from my chest as I wailed. My screams were long and loud, shaking the very foundation of the building. After several moments, I slumped to the ground, exhausted, but totally drained of all my pain. Through all the turmoil I'd endured and all the agony I suffered over the last few days, I finally felt relief.

The adult image of the boy looked at me compassionately. It was the kind of look that reassured me that everything was going to be fine. His hair was shoulder length, black in color and wavy in texture. His skin was cinnamon colored and his eyes were a deep shade of brown. As I looked at him through widened eyes unclouded by pain and agony, I realized who the boy was. He was the Messiah.

The warming glow began to dissipate and the image of the adult savior returned to his childlike state. I was astonished by the fact that I was in the presence of the Messiah. My path of turmoil and despair led directly to him. It seemed so poetic, but when I was lost in this world and had nowhere to go, I tried to find my own way, wandering the streets looking for answers. Then, just when I was helpless and had lost all hope, he appeared. It sounded like a hokey Sunday morning sermon, but it actually happened.

I felt the tears welling in my eyes again. However, these weren't tears of pain or sorrow, but of joy. I felt something inside of me breaking down the walls of anger and hatred. He lifted and stretched his hands toward me. I knew now that I could trust him, and I couldn't help but move toward him.

I stood to my feet and approached him, placing my hands into his. His touch was gentle and his hands were soft and warm. The wounds in his palms were gone and the scars across his forehead had vanished. I looked into his eyes. His stare possessed one of innocence, patience and love. It was like a child staring into the eyes of his mother, delivering the nonverbal message that he would be with me until the end of time. Although he had reverted back to his childlike form, I felt safe and protected around him.

Just as I was getting comfortable, I sensed a surge of energy inside me. I felt jittery, like I'd had too much coffee. My insides felt warm, like an internal fire that was intensifying by the moment. I looked at Raiel, who now had a dim shimmer of gold around his hands. The surge intensified until I was ready to burst from the inside. I shuddered in anxiousness as an aura of light appeared around me as well. It was every bit as bright as the one that engulfed him during his transformation. I was frightened, but I kept my hands in his. As the glow diminished, I felt different. He released his grip of my hands and I lifted them before me. They were still glowing. I felt intense relief, like a burden had been taken off me. I felt relaxed, as though all the worries and fears that shrouded my spirit were gone.

"How do you feel?" he asked.

"I've never felt like this in all my life. What did you do to me?" I probed.

"I simply took your burdens from you," he replied.

At that moment, the glow began to fade from around me, but I still felt energized. Then, I heard the sound of footsteps coming up behind me. It was the old man.

"Vanifera, this is my companion. His name is Desmond Christi," said Raiel.

"Pleasure," he said.

"Same here," I replied

"There is much to tell you and very little time. Please, sit in this chair and I will try to explain," said Raiel.

He pointed to the throne-like chair he had been sitting in when I entered the chamber. Desmond walked behind the young lad and stood patiently. I walked to the chair and sat. The Messiah stood in front of me.

"There is darkness in your past that is trying to reunite with you. It is a reunion we cannot allow," he said.

"Yes, I already know about the Vul Paux and that I'm its vessel, but I don't remember any of that," I said.

"Well, there's a reason why you don't remember. Perhaps it is best that we start at the beginning in order for you to understand the full story," replied Raiel.

"That would help."

"In the vast universe of creation, there are Seven Realms: The Phantom Realm, The Living Realm, The Shadow Realm, The Realm of Time and Space, The Realm of Hell, The Realm of Heaven and The Omega Realm. Each has their various inhabitants. Some are considered good and some aren't so good. I am the ruler of the Second Realm; Heaven," said Raiel.

"Interesting," I said. "But..."

"Patience, my lady," said Christi, holding up his hand.

"Long ago, the Master, our creator, was comprised of both a malevolent and benevolent spirit. But controlling these two essences proved most difficult and he excised the evil from his being, thinking it would perish without a host. However, instead of perishing, the evil created a vessel and poured itself into it. It then called itself the Vul Paux. Now that it assumed a physical form, the Vul Paux performed vicious acts, wreaking unspeakable havoc on the universe. Countless civilizations were destroyed, and unless the evil was stopped, it would have destroyed all of creation. The angelic host was dispatched to stop the threat, but the Vul Paux had other plans. It created beings called the First Centines, or gods, to combat the angels. Even here on this very planet, the evil created creatures like trolls, dwarfs, elves and other beasts to torment mankind. When the Great War was waged, the Vul Paux was defeated and our master banished the creatures that he made to a place called the Shadow Realm. The Paux was stripped from his vessel and imprisoned in the Omega Realm, a realm of infinite space and darkness," explained Raiel.

"Yes, Angelo told me all of this already. However, it still begs the question, why can't I remember any of this?"

"The vessel managed to escape. It still possessed the instinctual evil habits of the Vul Paux. However, it was believed that it would eventually die since the essence had been removed. In a last ditch effort to avenge its master, the vessel, called the Gaian, attacked a mighty kingdom on the Earth. A young woman with a special psychokinetic gift opposed the Gaian, attacking its mental functions. She was on the verge of defeating the Gaian when it performed a most unexpected act. It formed a mental link with the woman and absorbed her essence. The two were merged and the once hideously disfigured Gaian took on the appearance of its vanquisher, which is you, Vanifera," said Raiel.

I sat there shocked beyond words. I didn't know what to say or how to feel. It was like a bad dream. How could this happen to me?

"I-I don't believe this," I said.

Raiel tucked his head and sighed.

"Many attempts were made to separate you from the creature, but nothing worked. However, the mental link forged between you and the Gaian sealed its memories. Unfortunately, it blocked all your past memories as well. We watched you for eons, hoping that the seal would be permanent. We finally felt confident that it would and decided to give you a new life. You were allowed to keep your name, but we gave you a new identity. The one you call Angelo is really an angel named Uriel who was sent here to keep an eye on you," said Raiel.

I bowed my head at the mentioning of Angelo's name.

"I know this already. I know about the gate and what it can do. That's why everyone's trying to kill me."

"Partially. The Consortium are the ones trying to kill you. You see, they sort of have a grudge against you," said Christi.

"Grudge? Why?"

"Shortly after the Great War, the Master created Heaven, also called the Sanctuary, as a reward for his angels. When you were brought to the Sanctuary, some of the Vul Paux's essence was still in the Gaian and infected the individuals who examined you, namely Lucifer and some of his associates. It took over Lucifer's mind, causing him to believe that he was the Master's equal, and thus started the great revolt in Heaven," said Christi.

"When it was all over, the Master banished Lucifer and his associates to a new realm he created, Hell," said Raiel.

"This one entity did all of this?" I asked.

Raiel and Desmond looked at one another.

"Yes, it did. When the master saw that there might be the possibility that the evil might spread to the rest of creation, he sent me back here to stop it. When I arrived, I saw that the evil had contaminated the entire population. I tried to save as many as I could," said Raiel.

"But I thought you were crucified?"

"I was. That's what caused the Vul Paux's defeat. When I was resurrected, I returned to this world in order to save as many lives as I could."

"So, you died to stop me and the grudge that Lucifer and his gang have against me is in fact because I got them kicked out of Heaven, is that it?"

"Yes."

"So why are you telling me all of this? If I am the cause of all this sorrow, why are you helping me?"

"Let's just say that a friend of mine asked me to. Logic would state that I get rid of you. But there are some people who care about you, Vanifera, and they believe you can be saved."

"Do you think I can be saved?"

"Yes...yes I do," said Raiel nodding.

I sat and pondered for a few moments. I was on the verge of tears, but I struggled to keep it together. I understood some of what was going on, enough to know who wanted to harm me.

"So, what do you know about the gate?" asked Christi.

"Well, the Gate of Osiris is a dimensional gateway that the Vul Paux created to travel between realms. He hid it just before he was defeated. If Dupri finds the gate, he can open a portal that will release the Vul Paux from the Omega Realm. Then he'll come looking for me," I said.

"Very good."

"Honestly, this sounds like a very bad comic book story."

The boy turned and stared into the fire.

"Alas, I wish it were. I brought you here in hopes that by keeping you secluded, he will not find the gate. Yet it seems that the Contravexus is more resourceful than we thought," said Raiel.

"How so?" I asked.

"He has managed to elicit the assistance of the world governments and has located a strange energy frequency. Supposedly, the gate reacts to your emotional patterns; the more emotionally stressed you are, the weaker the bond suppressing the Gaian's thoughts become. Somehow, we missed that. However, he was able to cause you enough pain to allow the Gaian's mind to release a frequency that could pinpoint the location of the gate. I know this all seems a bit confusing, but to make a long story short, by making you angry or upset, he was able to find the gate," said Raiel.

"So all of this was a ploy," I said.

"It would seem that way," said Raiel with a sigh.

Desmond Christi came closer.

"Please tell me this is a dream or a really bad joke! Please tell me that this isn't real!" I begged.

"I'm sorry," said Desmond.

I bowed and grabbed the sides of my head, trying to dismiss what I'd just been told.

"Don't be disheartened, Vanifera. You are a hero. You saved a lot of lives with your actions on that fateful day. Because of your kind heart, others live," said Raiel.

"Then why aren't I happy about it?" I asked.

I sat back in the chair with a huff and covered my face with my hands. Raiel came and knelt before me.

"I don't want this. I didn't ask for this. Why didn't you just kill me when you had the chance?" I said.

"I know how you feel," he said.

I dropped my hands and stared at him with astonishment.

"You! You know how I feel! You, the Son of God, knows how I feel!" I said slapping my hands on my lap. "How would you know how I feel? You aren't some by-product of a foul spirit! You are the Master's child! How in the hell would you know how I feel?!"

He tucked his head.

"Well, I may not know exactly how you feel, but I can relate."

"You can relate! Boy, I'd love to hear this!" I said as I sat forward in the chair.

I pouted like a spoiled child. The Messiah sat before me in yoga style squat.

"Let me tell you a little story," he began as I rolled my eyes. "One day, an angel came to me and informed me of the responsibilities that had been placed on my shoulders and how the very people I tried to save would eventually kill me. I, too, tried to deny what I was told, believing that such atrocities couldn't happen on this planet. I made blind men see and sick people well. But when I started to heal people, things changed. I was shunned and lied about. People began to treat me as if I were some diseased creature. They hurt those who followed my teachings and even threatened me if I didn't stop preaching. From that moment, I knew that despite the attempts I made to deny my destiny, I couldn't deny the effects I had on those lives I'd touched or didn't touch. So, eventually I accepted my plight. It was the hardest thing I'd ever done," explained Raiel.

"So, I'm supposed to accept this? Is that what you're saying?" I asked.

"There are some things we can change and there are some things that are beyond our control," he replied.

His comment wasn't very encouraging. In fact, I felt helpless and broken once again. That's when Desmond Christi walked to me and continued where Raiel left off.

"We all have our destinies. I am the Valkydine, the sworn protector of the Messiah. My purpose is to ensure that no harm comes to him. It was a duty I rejected at first also. But for the last five thousand years, I've been by his side," he explained.

"So now, if I understand this correctly, you're saying that we all have our places and there is nothing we can do about it?" I asked.

"It's like he said, some things we can change and some we can't. The power comes in knowing the difference between the two. However, there is more to your destiny than simple acceptance. Already, your actions have started certain events," said Desmond.

"My actions?"

"Yes."

"You know what, I've had about enough of this! I'm tired of

the riddles and the mind twisting! I'm tired of running and I'm tired of the games! I don't care what happens to you, me or anyone else on this planet! I'm ready to die! So, go ahead! Kill me! End my life! I'm giving you a free shot right now!" I exclaimed as tears rolled down my cheeks.

Desmond Christi approached me and laid his hand on my shoulder.

"It's okay. No one is going to hurt you," he said.

A confused look appeared across my face.

"You don't get it, do you? I *want* to die! I don't want to be some evil spirit's outer garment and I DON'T WANT THIS LIFE ANYMORE!" I screamed.

Then, I felt a sharp pain in my head, like someone had stuck a knife in it. I grabbed my head and fell forward out of my chair, kneeling on the floor. It felt like an intense migraine. I felt dizzy and my vision was blurry.

"Vanifera, what's wrong?" asked Christi.

"My head...hurts," I mumbled.

"Desmond, get her to the cot," said Raiel.

Christi lifted me up and carried me to the cot in the other room. I felt as if I was going to black out. My head was spinning and I felt nauseous. He laid me on the cot and Raiel knelt beside me, placing his hand over my forehead.

"She has a fever," he said.

I did feel warm and uncomfortable. But, a few moments later, I was cold and shivering. Raiel held his hands on top of my head for a few more moments and then stood.

"She's not well. Her mental bonds are starting to weaken. It must have been her tantrum a few moments ago. We need to do something to calm her down. Go get me some fresh water and some food," said Raiel.

"Yes, sire," said Christi.

Christi ran off to get the items. But there was a bigger problem than what Raiel had said. Although his words sounded echoed, I heard and understood every one. The mental bonds that kept the

Gaian part of me in hibernation were beginning to rupture. My shaking, fever and chills were caused by my mental attempts to suppress that part of me. The truth was that I was starting to remember. Little by little, portions of my memory were starting to seep out. I remembered images of my parents and I recalled the evil Gaian that took their lives. It burned our village and killed my friends. It laughed as it exterminated those I cared for and loved. I recalled standing before the mammoth vessel, armed only with the psychokinetic powers given to me by my God. I engaged the creature in mental warfare. I recalled how taxing it was. The confrontation almost killed me. Yet, I was able to gain an advantage, and soon, I was able to break the creature's mind. It was like I was pushing it into a deep dark hole and almost had it in. But in an act of desperation, it latched on to my mental abilities, binding me to its mind and pulling me into the hole with it. My essence was absorbed into the monster, and for eons, I kept that hole secure, banishing all recall, including my own. Now, however, I remembered everything and didn't want to. Not because of what happened that fateful day, but because I knew that if my memory was returning, the Gaian's would also be returning.

Desmond returned with the items he was asked to bring and laid them on the ground next to the cot. Although my vision was blurry, I could see his face and finally recognized him. But it wasn't from the dock at the BART station or from the alley or from the roof. I knew him, and now I remembered why he was so familiar. I lifted my head and summoned the courage to say my thoughts out loud.

"Daddy?"

~~~

The figure of a man stood atop a building overlooking the city of Rome. The wind blew from the west as the streetlights began coming on. He was as still as a mountain, absorbing the activity of the evening. The honking of the horns from the traffic echoed along the boardwalk. The smell of the salty air filled his nostrils, and the birds hovered in the amethyst sky.

Two hours ago, Angelo was involved in a race with Montellace Dupri. It was a decision he regretted because it allowed Dupri to get away. Now, he stood contemplating his actions and wondered what the results of his actions would be. He gazed at the city's majesty standing proudly along the shoreline. He searched his mind for some profound thought to make him feel better. But he could not find one. Despite his efforts to focus on his mission and the possible consequences of his actions, his mind kept wandering to thoughts of his wife. He couldn't help thinking of how much he missed Vanifera. His heart still carried an intense love for her. In all the eons of existence he'd experienced, he'd never known love. This was the first time anyone had ever touched his heart and he longed to see her once again. To him, life was complete with her. Now, she was lost to him, a ghost in his memories.

He wanted terribly to delay his mission in order to find her. However, if he did, he ran the risk of losing the war and more importantly, Vanifera as well. He remembered the terror called the Vul Paux and the destructive capabilities of the Gaian. If there were a way to save her, he would find it. To see her again would be his fondest dream.

Angelo realized that Dupri had done more damage to him than any physical attack he could have executed. Angelo was prepared for matters of spiritual and physical combat. But Dupri managed to attack the one place that Angelo had not guarded well, his heart.

The Archangel bowed his head.

"I'm sorry, Vanifera. I wish I could still be there for you. I just hope that one day I will be able to see you again. I miss you so much," Angelo mumbled to himself.

Just then, he heard footsteps approaching from behind.

"Figured I'd find you here," said the approaching being.

Angelo didn't recognize whom the voice belonged to. He turned his head to acknowledge his visitor. The man was dressed in a quarter-length cowhide coat with a fleece lining, black sweater and jeans.

"Hajj?" asked Angelo.

"Hello, Angelo," said the Barhim Hajj as he stopped alongside of him.

"What are you doing here?" Angelo asked.

"Just visiting. What are you doing?" asked Hajj.

"Thought I'd get a glimpse of the city before all hell breaks loose."

"I see."

The two beings were silent for a moment.

"This is one of the more beautiful cities of this world, so exciting and full of life. It's sad to think that a civilization that could create such beauty is on the verge of destruction," stated Hajj.

Angelo glanced at Barhim Hajj, then returned his view to the city once more.

"Yes, it is indeed a pity," he retorted.

The two beings stood for another few moments in silence. It was as if they were attempting to absorb as much of this moment as possible.

"You said you were visiting. Somehow I don't quite buy that," said Angelo.

Hajj sighed deeply.

"I'm actually here to help you. Have you seen your wife lately?" he asked.

"Do you know where she is?" asked Angelo anxiously.

"She's not here," replied Hajj.

Hajj's expression instantly turned from contentment to a scowl. He then backhanded Angelo across his face. A stunned Angelo shook his head, then looked at Hajj with fire in his eyes.

"I hope your soul is right because you're about to die," he replied.

Hajj stepped back as Angelo raised his fist.

"Angelo, I beg you to hold your temper for just one moment and I will tell you why I struck you?"

"I'm listening," Angelo replied with a growl.

"It is because you showed weakness! You are allowing your emotions to get the best of you! There is a power out there right now waiting to end everything that's been created! Don't think it won't exploit your weakness as I just did! You must forget about her, Angelo; she's as good as dead!" shouted Hajj.

Angelo rubbed the side of his face.

"As long as the part of her I love still lives, I will never give up on her!" Angelo replied.

"Then you are a fool! This war isn't about love; it's about death and preventing it! Don't think for one second that the Vul Paux wouldn't use her to get to you. He is a vile creature, and if the Gaian regains her memory, she will use your emotions to her advantage. Never forget that, Seraph!" said Hajj.

Angelo grabbed Barhim Hajj by the collar and lifted him off the ground.

"I forget nothing, Hajj. It would serve you well to remember that the next time you raise your hand to me," said Angelo.

He then shoved Hajj stumbling backward. Hajj caught his balance, then gave a regretful look at Angelo.

"Listen, I am very fond of Vanifera, and she has been through hell since you've been gone. Right now, I'm sure she could use some happiness," said Hajj.

"And just how would you suggest we give her this happiness?" Angelo asked.

"Perhaps a visit from you would do the trick."

"I'd have to know where she is in order to do that."

"Then consider this my way of apologizing for my insult earlier. She is still in Seattle, the safe house. She's with the Messiah and the Valkydine. You should go there tonight."

"Why are you doing this?"

"She's a good woman, and I can see that there has never been a deeper love than the one that exists between the two of you. I'd hate to see something like that destroyed. The Hierarchy and the Consortium are looking for her. You could very well be the only thing that saves her. I will go make the arrangements for you to leave Rome. Wouldn't want you to go and get yourself banished from the Hierarchy for disobedience."

Angelo shot Hajj a distrusting look. Then, Barhim Hajj walked away. Although the sun was gone from the sky and dusk had fallen around him, there was a warm sunrise in Angelo's heart. He'd gotten the lead he wanted, and now, he was mere hours from seeing his beloved once again. Next stop, Seattle.

~~~

CHAPTER EIGHTEEN

Oakland, California. Two joggers, Denise and Sidney Terrence, were nearing the completion of their evening routine. Their pace was strong and rhythmically in cadence. They turned the corner on their last pass before they headed back to their apartment.

As they passed under the streetlight, a shadowy figure observed them. It had been following them the entire run, making sure to stay within visual contact. The duo finally ended their jog in front of their apartment door. They paused for a moment to catch their breath and cool down before they entered. Beads of sweat rolled down their faces and arms. Denise pulled a hand towel from her side pack and wiped her face and arms. Sidney, using his wristbands, did likewise. He lifted his watch and pressed a button, turning off the stopwatch.

"That was a good run!" he said, panting heavily.

"Yeah, I could really feel the burn on that one," Denise replied.

As they continued cooling down, the dark figure quietly circled around them, ensuring that his presence remained undetected. A dog in the neighboring apartment began barking feverishly. Like all animals, it detected that something wasn't right. It sensed the dark figure lurking in the darkness. The dog continued barking as its owner came to the window to retrieve it and to ensure that all was well.

"Quiet!" said the woman.

She peered out her second story window clad in a housedress and a scarf wrapped around her head. She saw the couple as they simultaneously looked up at her.

"Good evening, Ms. Baxter!" exclaimed Denise.

The homely woman waved to the couple and closed her window to avoid any more attention being brought on them due to her pup's barking. Sidney reached into his pocket and removed the house key. Denise began to affectionately caress his shoulders.

The dark figure coiled itself in the shadows. The time had come for it to strike. With the speed of a cobra, the figure leaped from the darkness. As Sidney turned the key and opened the door, he felt that Denise's caressing had ceased. Without turning around, Sidney attempted to make fun of the situation.

"Ah, don't stop now. We're just getting started," he said jesting.

There was no response. Sidney turned to see what she was doing behind his back. He discovered that she was no longer there. Sidney frowned at first. Then, he chuckled and began scanning the area, thinking she was playing some sort of kinky cat and mouse game. He looked around the furniture on the porch. Then, he walked down the steps of the porch to see if she were hiding by the stoop. But she wasn't in either of those places. There were no signs of her anywhere.

He laughed and said, "Okay, babe, I'm coming to get you!"

He jumped off of the last step and began rummaging through the bushes.

"Come out, Come out, wherever you are!" he joked.

Still there was no response from Denise.

He pulled a flashlight from his waist pouch and shined it in the shrubs that surrounded the building. In his mind, he realized that this was unusual behavior for her, but the change was exciting and different from the norm. He continued to scan the general vicinity, only to find that she was nowhere to be found.

Sidney, still thinking this was a prank, began walking around to the back of the building. He shined his light on the ground looking for footprints. He looked in the bushes hoping to find her squatting within them, waiting for him in some newfound secluded spot. However, his search was fruitless, and Sidney's once playful attitude was beginning to turn serious.

"Babe? Where are you? This is getting a little weird now! Come on out!" he said.

As his light illuminated the backyard, his eyes detected something dangling in the tree above their patio area. He raised the light and shined it overhead. He was unsure what it was at first. But as he drew closer, he realized that it was a strip of fabric from Denise's sweat suit.

He walked to the tree and pulled the swatch from the branch. He examined it closely. He wondered how it got in the tree. Anxiety began to mount inside of Sidney as his mind raced with ill possibilities.

"Denise?" he exclaimed.

He continued his search at a more frantic pace. The beam of the flashlight swept across the lawn like a spotlight, combing every area of possibility. Sidney scoured the grounds and the trees looking for some sign of her presence. Everywhere he looked, his search resulted the same. The tension began to mount and he feared the worst had happened to his wife. He retraced his path again and again, yielding the same outcome. He screamed out her name once more in hopes she would respond.

"Denise! Denise, where are you?"

His hopes lessened more and more each time she didn't respond. Fear now gripped his chest. Something was wrong and he didn't know what to do. For that matter, he didn't even know what happened to her. He did know that he needed help.

He turned and began walking toward the front door of his residence to call the police. As he walked back onto the porch, he glanced down to see something that stopped him in his tracks. It was on the very spot where he saw his wife last. He knelt to examine it, lifting his flashlight and shining it on the item.

It didn't appear to have a shape. However, it was in the form of some sort of gel or glob. Sidney leaned closer to examine the substance. It was unlike anything he'd seen before. Suddenly, the substance began melting into a puddle. It had a greenish tint that reflected the various colors of light from the beam of the flashlight.

Sidney shined the light overhead to see if there was any more of the substance. There wasn't. As he scanned the porch, he spotted another object from the corner of his eye. He quickly shined his light on it. It was a shoe. In fact, it was one of Denise's shoes, the ones she had on moments ago. Sidney picked up the footwear and began to examine it, trying to glean some sort of understanding as to what happened to his wife. As he continued his analysis, a faint voice began to call in distress.

"Sidney, help me!"

Sidney quickly lifted his head and whisked his light around in order to locate the direction of the plea.

"Denise?" he said as he tried to locate the origin of her cry.

Sidney flashed his light in the bushes again and all around the porch, but he still could not locate her. Then, he heard her call again, but this time, it sounded like it was coming from right beside him.

"Sidney, please help me, please!" screamed the voice.

Sidney was certain that the voice was Denise's. He called to her, hoping that she would answer again.

"Denise, where are you?" he exclaimed.

Sidney waited to see if she would answer one more time. If she did, he was positive that he was going to find her. Seconds passed, but for Sidney it seemed like an eternity. Then, he received a final plea.

"Oh God, Sidney! Help me, please!" screamed Denise.

Sidney was certain that the voice was right next to him. He shined the light on the porch floor. All that he saw were the shoe and the puddle that used to be a blob. Sidney knelt down again, but this time, he shined his light into the puddle. As the light refracted inside, Sidney began to see images. At first, he thought it was the light playing tricks with his eyes, but after a few blinks and resuming his stare into the liquefied substance, Sidney knew that this was no illusion. He could see Denise reaching out to him. She was naked and she wasn't alone.

Behind her appeared to be a figure, but it wasn't human. It

was grotesque and had only half a face. It seemed to have wings, but not like anything he had ever seen before. Scales covered the creature's body as its hands caressed Denise's body. The creature was moving in such a fashion that suggested it was having sex with her. It fondled and played with her, tracing its hands across her body. Its long tongue flickered and wrapped around her face, tasting every droplet of sweat as she continued to reach for Sidney. She appeared to be in some euphoric trance as the beast continued its posturing.

Then, the grotesque monster grabbed Denise by her ponytail and gently pulled her head back. Her expression was that of fulfillment as she continued to call for Sidney to save her. The demon lifted its hand and used his long fingernails to stroke Denise's neck and breasts. He firmly cupped her in his scaly hands as his long tongue flickered at Sidney.

Sidney cringed and screamed to Denise in an attempt to awaken her from this nightmare. He tried to place his hands into the slime, only to feel his flesh burn when he touched it. He quickly retracted his hand and gripped it, trying to ease the pain.

"Denise! Denise!" screamed Sidney into the puddle.

Denise didn't respond. She was well into the moment and was quickening her rhythm against the creature. The demon then stopped its seduction and stared at Sidney with disdain. He snarled as he defiantly slid his hand down between her legs and began fondling her. Denise moaned in ecstasy as she continued to plead for Sidney to save her.

"Take your Goddamn hands off of her, you son of a bitch!" he exclaimed.

The demon grinned and slid his hand up Denise's waist and traced her shoulders until his hands were around her neck. The movement made Sidney hold his breath, hoping that this monster wasn't about to do what he thought. Sidney clenched the discarded shoe in his hands, trying to think of some way to stop this abomination.

The creature gently turned Denise's head to the right. He stared into her eyes as she returned a look of helplessness. The creature paused and gave Sidney another glance. Then with one quick move, the creature twisted her head and snapped Denise's neck. Her body dropped to the floor as her eyes stared up into Sidney's. He screamed in horror. He couldn't believe what he saw. The shock drove him beyond the edge of sanity.

"Denise! No!" he exclaimed tearfully.

Emotions of disbelief rushed over Sidney. He couldn't believe that the woman he loved had been killed right before his eyes. What was worse was that there was nothing he could do to stop it. The sheer spitefulness of the beast was maddening. The heartbreak was overwhelming. The anger began to swell in his chest as he attempted once more to try and get into the puddle. He scratched and punched, but his efforts were painfully unsuccessful. His fingers bled from his attempts to reach the image in the puddle. He picked up Denise's shoe and began banging the puddle. Inside, the creature laughed at Sidney's pain, mocking him and his efforts for vengeance. The laugh echoed as Sidney continued to pound on the porch floor.

Suddenly, a flash of light appeared. Sidney stopped his rampage and looked up to find that he was now in his bedroom. The room was dimly lit by candles that lined the furniture, creating a very seductive atmosphere. Sidney was at the foot of his bed, kneeling on the floor. He looked around the room trying to regain his bearings. He wondered how he got there. Moments ago, he was on the porch attempting to kill a demon in a puddle of slime. He'd witnessed his beautiful wife being killed by this beast that sodomized her. Now, he found himself in his bedroom.

He raised his hand to wipe the sweat from his face. As he did, he noticed that it was covered in blood. His eyes widened from the discovery, and he quickly performed a self-examination to see if he had been injured. He examined his hands for cuts or abrasions, but there were none. He checked the rest of his body to see if the blood could have come from another injury. Although his T-shirt was smeared with blood, he, however, had no injuries. Then, he began to wonder where the blood had come from.

He looked down on the floor and discovered a hammer coated

in the very blood that covered his hands. Sidney jumped up and backed away from the bloodstained object. He noticed that it was his hammer, but he couldn't figure out how it got into his bedroom or how it got covered in blood.

He looked around the room and noticed a maroon towel lying on the floor by the door. He picked it up and began wiping the blood from his hands. The ease of the cleaning made him realize that the blood was fresh. He walked into the hallway and yelled to Denise in hopes for a response.

"Denise! Baby! You in here?" he asked.

To his shock, there still was no response. He slowly walked down the hallway. He headed toward the living room where he saw a faint light emitting. As he approached, Sidney saw that the room was filled with candles, just like the bedroom. Then, he looked down to see a trail of blood on the floor and smears of red on the wall. He paused for a moment, confused and scared. A chill ran down his back as he stood at the entrance.

Sidney scanned the living room. Nothing appeared to be out of place. He continued further into the room and decided to call once more to Denise.

"Denise! You in here?" he asked.

This time, a faint whimper was heard from inside the room. Sidney's chest filled with anticipation. He walked around the couch and found Denise lying in a pool of blood on the floor. He quickly jumped over the couch arm and cradled her in his arms. Her head had depressions, as if she were struck with a blunt object. Blood poured from her injuries, and her eyes were fixed and dilated. She was near death.

Sidney sobbed as he held his beloved in his arms. He tried to get Denise to talk.

"Denise? Can you hear me? Denise, baby! Say something!" he pleaded.

Denise struggled to speak. She coughed and cleared her throat. Her stare remained fixed. Her body was growing colder and her heartbeat had begun to slow. However, she managed to summon enough strength to speak. Sidney lowered his head in an attempt to hear what she had to say.

"Why, Sidney?" she asked as she exhaled.

Then, Denise's body slumped in Sidney's arms. She was dead.

Sidney cradled his lady. Her last breath was taken while he held her. The helplessness he felt at that moment was overwhelming as her last words rang in his ears. He couldn't think; he couldn't breathe. He clutched her tightly and sobbed uncontrollably. Just then, the front door of the apartment burst open and police officers stormed into the room.

"Freeze!" said the officers as they entered with weapons drawn.

Sidney remained on the floor, holding Denise and rocking back and forth. The cops ordered Sidney to back away from the body. But Sidney didn't move.

"Sir, please back away from the body and place your hands over your head!" ordered the officer once again.

Sidney still remained unmoved.

Another officer circled behind him in an attempt to pull Sidney away.

Distraught and confused, emotions began to build inside of Sidney. All he wanted to do was hold his love in his arms, hoping that she would somehow awaken. Her body was still slightly warm as he tried to imagine that she was only sleeping. The circling officer readied himself for the lunge. From the corner of his eye, Sidney saw the officer. He turned and looked at him with a confused expression. He wondered why they couldn't give him a moment to hold her one more time. He didn't do anything wrong and he resented their actions.

Suddenly, the officer began transforming. Sidney watched in amazement as the officer changed into the hideous creature Sidney witnessed killing Denise in the puddle. The rage exploded in Sidney. He relived the entire episode in an instant, and now, his thirst for vengeance consumed him.

"You!" he exclaimed. "You are responsible for this!"

Sidney lowered Denise's head and rested it gently on the floor. Then, he stood slowly and glared at the beast that stood laughing at him. His emotions exploded inside and he lifted his hand and clenched it into a fist. He leaped across the sofa and charged toward the beast. His intent was to kill the creature that had killed his beloved Denise.

Suddenly, two shots were fired from behind Sidney, striking him in the back. Sidney's body stiffened from the instantaneous pain. He couldn't move at first, but then slowly turned to face the individuals that had fired the shots. To his surprise, he saw two more beast-like creatures standing behind him, mocking and laughing at him.

The pain that raced through his body was incredible. However, he was intent on making each of them pay for what they did to Denise. His love for her was stronger than the pain he felt. Sidney summoned his remaining strength and attempted to lunge once more. However, before he could execute his attempt, two more bullets whizzed through the air, striking him in the chest. His body twitched from the impact. He stood erect, trying to fight the disabling pain. His eyes focused on the ceiling.

Riddled with pain, Sidney fell to his knees and then face first to the ground. The smoke swirled from the bullet holes in his back. Sidney attempted to maintain his defiant resistance to defeat. But he was losing blood by the second. His body began to grow cold as the monsters scurried toward him and hovered. He could hear them, but he couldn't understand what they were saying. Their voices were echoed and muffled. The pain in his body lessened by the moment due to the loss of more and more blood.

Finally, he lifted his head slightly to see that he had landed next to his beloved Denise. He stared into her blue eyes, which appeared to be staring back into his. It was then he realized that the time had come to let it go. He had done all that he could. But his efforts weren't enough to gain the vengeance he desired. His body no longer felt the pain, and the warm life-sustaining fluid oozed from his body and pooled beneath him.

"I'm sorry!" he whispered to Denise.

Then, with one big exhale, Sidney died. His hand had landed on top of Denise's.

Outside, police cars flooded the front of the apartment. The lights illuminated the neighborhood. The surrounding neighbors gawked from behind the yellow streamer tape. Mumbled messages were sent through walkie-talkies as a police sergeant blurted out the results over the police radio.

"OK, he's down; we got him!" said the husky voice.

The congregated neighbors began conversing amongst themselves, trying to piece together any information that would give them some idea as to what had happened. Paramedics and forensic teams scurried about performing their duties at the scene.

Amongst all the chaos, a dark figure stood in the shadows observing the entire chaotic ballet. With all the drama in the condo, no one noticed him, yet he was the key player in all of this. He stepped from the shadows. It was Huang.

His face was whole and healed, and the horrible scene that unfolded here was his doing. He'd successfully killed Denise by using her own man to do so. He invaded his mind, making him see what he wanted him to see. He'd clouded Sidney's mind, fooling him into seeing the creatures. When he pounded the puddle with the shoe, he'd actually attacked Denise with the hammer. Then, when the cops arrived, Huang caused Sidney to see them as monsters, which provoked the officers to shoot him when he attacked. Now, it was all over. He'd gotten his revenge on the Gaian and no one was alive to implicate him. He saw an older gentleman standing near one of the patrol cars. He calmly strolled toward the man and tapped him on the shoulder.

"Excuse me, sir. What's happening here?" Huang asked with concern.

The man turned and looked at Huang.

"Well, they say that the guy who lived in that house killed his wife by beating her to death with a hammer," said the man.

"No!" replied Huang with a false hint of shock.

"Yep!" replied the old man. "But they got him though. He tried to attack the cops when they went in and they had to shoot him!"

"Is he dead?" asked Huang.

"Yep!" said the man. "Odd though, they were such nice people. They were always together and never seemed to have any problems. I wonder what would make him do such a thing?"

"What, indeed," answered Huang as he turned and departed from the senseless and grim crime scene.

~~~

Rome, Italy. Barhim Hajj held a cell phone to his ear, waiting for Angelo to answer.

"Yes?"

"Angelo, its me, Hajj. Everything is in order. You'll leave in twenty minutes on flight 1775. It will fly directly into Portland and you can catch the Amtrak up to Seattle."

"You sure didn't give me much time, did you?"

"Figured you'd be anxious to leave. Was I wrong?"

"Don't be absurd. Anyway, thanks."

"Don't mention it. May God's spirit go with you."

Hajj hung up the phone and placed it in his pocket. He sighed deeply, then looked at the house he now stood in front of. It was a modest home surrounded by a fifteen-foot high iron fence. It was the residence of one of the cardinals who worked at the Vatican. He walked through the gate and made his way to the front door of the house. He knocked twice and took a step back, clasping his hands in front of him. Moments later, a young woman answered. After an exchange of greetings in Italian, Hajj asked the young woman if the cardinal were present and if he could speak to him. She nodded and allowed him to enter. As he stood in the foyer, Barhim Hajj couldn't help but admire the beautiful floral arrangements that decorated the waiting area. He enjoyed things of beauty, and these flowers were some of the most dazzling he'd ever seen.

The woman returned, followed closely by Father Xavier Wright.

"Ah, brother Hajj. How good to see you again," he said with a deep Italian accent.

"Father Wright," said Hajj as they performed the customary kissing of cheeks.

"To what do I owe this honor?" asked Wright.

"Well, I simply wanted to let you know that the evil one has been removed from the Vatican."

"I heard. My thanks to you and your associates. I can't possibly tell you what this means to my brethren and I. The evil one soiled our halls and our faith. He hurt so many people and took so much from us. Finally, we can start to rebuild our church."

"The Basilica was destroyed. It will take a lot to rebuild it."

"A small price to pay for salvation. I'm just glad that we were able to get rid of that monster. He has poisoned the minds of many of our brethren, making them do unspeakable things. The molestation issues have hit us the hardest. But finally, we can get our house in order, all thanks to you," said Wright.

Hajj sighed and tucked his head.

"What is wrong? You do not look happy. Is this not a time of celebration?" asked Wright.

"Not really, father. I'm afraid that things have actually gotten worse," said Hajj.

Wright's face changed from the jubilant expression to one of stern seriousness.

"It is the Gaian. She is starting to remember, yes?" he asked.

"I don't know yet. But I fear we need to prepare," said Hajj.

Wright folded his arms across his chest and sighed.

"Has the gate been found?" he asked.

"Not yet," replied Hajj.

"Then, there's hope, yes?" asked Wright.

"Maybe. There's always hope, father. I just wonder if it will be enough," said Hajj.

~~~

The Vatican. Dupri had made his way back and sat in a

boardroom seething at his recent run-in with Angelo. His assistant, Delilah, sat across from him working on some letters.

"That damned Seraph. Who the hell does he think he is? If it's the last thing I ever do, I'm going to make him pay for what he's done," said Dupri beneath his breath.

The phone rang.

"Hello?" answered Delilah with her thick accent.

She quickly handed the phone to Dupri.

"Yes," he answered.

"It's Eve. I'm in position. The trap has been set."

"Very good. I'll see you shortly."

Dupri hung up the phone and turned to look at the huge television screen. Delilah continued to sort through paperwork and make notations. Then, the phone rang once more.

"Hello?" she said. "One moment."

She turned to Dupri, covering the mouthpiece of the phone.

"It's the President," she whispered.

Dupri motioned for her to place him on speakerphone.

"Yes, President Davidson. What news do you have to report?" he asked.

"We've found the gate! It was buried just south of the Sinai!" said Davidson.

"Excellent! I guess that little war you started with Iraq paid off. It provided the right camouflage needed to carry out your mission. You've done well. Have everything brought to Seattle and prepared. I'll be there in a few hours," said Dupri.

"Very well," replied Davidson.

They disconnected.

"Shall I prepare your plane?" asked Delilah.

"Yes," Dupri replied.

Delilah picked up the phone and made the preparations. Then, she sat quietly, looking at the television screen. Dupri glanced at her and then stood from his seat. He walked toward the double doors of the boardroom.

"If you have anyone you'd like to say good-bye to, I'd do it quickly. In a few hours, everything ends," said Dupri as he turned the knob.

Delilah tucked her head as Dupri exited the room. She played with a paperclip as the tears welled in her eyes. Then, she buried her head in her arms and sobbed on the boardroom table.

~~~

Toronto. Michael stood at the roof's edge of a twelve-story building. Just then, his cell phone rang. It was Augustine.

"Michael, we just intercepted a phone call from President Davidson to the Vatican. According to the conversation, it appears that U.S. intelligence has located the gate."

Michael sighed.

"Get everything in order and have all agents go to Level 7 alert status. I'll be back shortly," he said.

He closed his flip phone, then leaped from the building and floated to the ground below. In the distance, he detected the sound of sirens. It was coming from the direction he needed to go.

"Better check this out!" he said.

Then like a bullet, he leaped into the air, landing on the rooftop of another building. He jumped from roof to roof with the grace of a gazelle until he reached his destination. He walked to the edge of the Four Seasons' rooftop and stared at the collection of police cars and ambulances below. Then, a sore infested body of a nearly dead man was pulled from the building. Michael crouched on the edge of the roof trying to remain undetected. He wanted to see if he could identify the victim. However, due to the flurry of madness by the emergency personnel, it was too busy to get a good view.

Michael stood and leaped into the air once more and floated behind the bushes. He emerged and walked to where the ambulance was parked. A paramedic attempted to insert an IV into a locatable vein. The sore infested man's skin clung to his body like wet tissue paper. The lesions on his body were so severe that the paramedics had difficulty controlling the bleeding.

In Michael's mind, he thought their efforts were useless; it would be more merciful to allow him to die. He looked at the man's face. The pain was severe and it showed in his expression. One of the paramedics looked up at the Archangel.

"Hey buddy, you need to leave!" said the paramedic.

Michael waved his hand in front of the paramedic's face. Using his powers to cloud the mind, Michael prevented the man from seeing him, thus allowing him to continue examining the victim. He grabbed the lesion-ridden man's hand. Then, he placed his other hand on his forehead.

The Archangel began to see images from the victim's mind. His thoughts became Michael's as the horrors causing his injuries unfolded. He saw visions of a woman and recognized her in an instant. It was Eve. He saw how she had made love to him and then torturously riddled his flesh with lesions. He saw the sheer madness in her eyes and he felt the pain in the reverend's body. After a few moments, Michael had seen enough. He removed his hand from the pastor's forehead.

"May your soul rest in peace," he said.

Then, Michael turned and walked away from Reverend Roberts. The reverend took his last breath. The blips on the defibrillator flat lined and his spirit passed to the next realm. The paramedics began their futile attempts to save the reverend. Michael, however, walked into the crowd of onlookers and never looked back.

The Supreme Commander of the Hierarchy was puzzled. On the phone, Eve sounded as if she was trying to bring down the Contravexus. But the visions he saw in the reverend's mind made him realize that he'd been mislead. The real question was why.

As he continued to distance himself from the scene, Michael felt a pain in his chest. It appeared so suddenly that it took his breath away. Each time he tried to inhale, the pain grew worse. He knelt to the ground and clutched his chest. The pain was intensifying by the moment. He tried to take shorter breaths, but even that proved difficult. Then, Michael sensed something else, the presence of a vile spirit. Its source emanated from his left side. He turned slightly to see a woman dressed in a red pantsuit with a white blouse. It was Eve.

"What have you done to me?" asked Michael grunting.

Eve lifted one eyebrow.

"Do you really need to ask? I poisoned you, you fool," she replied.

Michael squinted. His vision was getting blurry, and he felt as if he were going to pass out any second.

"Did you like the way I handled the good reverend back there?" she asked coyly.

"I see now. You weren't trying to stop Dupri. This was an elaborate trick."

"Bingo!"

"I should have known. You're an evil woman, who needlessly abuses others for her own twisted pleasure!" exclaimed Michael.

"Oh, it wasn't just for my pleasure; although, I did have fun! The old regime had its fun with me and then discarded me like garbage! Dupri will find the gate and the Vul Paux will be released! No matter what you do, Archangel, this is one war you will not win!" professed Eve.

"We will see about that!" retorted Michael.

Eve rolled her eyes and sighed deeply.

"Just so you know, I planted a special poison on the good reverend, one specifically designed to affect angels. It's a fast acting toxin, one that will break down your immune system and leave you a vegetable in a matter of minutes. Your time is up, Michael," she said.

"Perhaps. But I am not the last angel. The others will hunt you down and you will pay for your treason," said Michael, who gasped between words.

"You see, that's where you're wrong! I've already paid for all my past and future sins! My name has been cursed since the beginning of mankind's existence for an act that has been distorted beyond repair! I was not the one that brought the plight of death to mankind! I was given free will and then I was punished for utilizing it! However, I will be the one to ensure its annihilation! Now, it all comes full circle! I will be revered as the woman that recreated the earth, the queen mother of mankind!" she said with a sneer.

Michael smiled and shook his head.

"You're insane!" he said.

Eve pouted.

"And you're dead," she replied.

"Still the child, eh, harlot? Poor little Eve, the woman who's been forever cursed. If it's pity you want, then you have it," said Michael.

He then collapsed on the ground face first. He'd passed out from the pain. Eve stood over him, seething from his comment. She despised the fact that he made jest of her misfortunes and sensitivities.

"I don't want your pity. All I've ever wanted was respect. But you and your kind were too good to give that to me. You treated me like trash, throwing me to the harsh cruelty of an eternal life. Well, now you're going to die, Michael, and I'm glad I was the one who brought you down," she said.

The scent of lilacs filled the air once more. Eve turned and began walking away, leaving Michael lying face down on the ground. Her job was done. The toxin had a firm grip on the Seraph and he would no longer be a factor. He was in a coma, and soon, he would be dead.

~~~

Mary, who'd been monitoring Michael by using the Sky Eye, saw something peculiar on one of her display panels.

"Augustine, take a look at this," she said.

Augustine walked over and looked at the reading.

"Well that can't be right. According to this, Michael's in a coma. His bio readings are all off," he said.

He lifted the command phone. It rang Michael's line, but he never answered. After about a minute, Augustine hung up, displaying a very worried expression.

"Something's wrong," he said.

"I'll dispatch someone to his location," said Mary.

She quickly placed an emergency call to several agents.

Augustine glared at the readings. He bit his nails, trying to think of what this meant.

"Michael, what have you gotten yourself into?" he asked beneath his breath.

~~~

CHAPTER NINETEEN

Gabrielle waited anxiously outside the restaurant. She clasped her hands before her as her children finally made eye contact with her. It had been a long time since she'd seen either of them and she couldn't believe how mature they were. Lorimar wore the imperial shield of the Consortium on his left lapel. He instantly marched toward her and stopped just in front of her. He stared unflinchingly at Gabrielle, almost as if he was unsure of what to do next.

"Lorimar?" asked Gabrielle.

The young commander began breathing heavily, trying to maintain control. He glanced at Kitana, who stood with her arms folded across her chest. He then looked back at Gabrielle with an expression of anticipation.

"Mother?" he asked.

Gabrielle smiled with joy and pride. She embraced her son tightly. He returned the gesture, hugging her as if his life depended on it. Gabrielle and Lorimar then sat on a bench and held each other's hand. She was impressed with her son and how he had become such a strong warrior.

"It's good to see you again, Mother," said Lorimar.

Gabrielle did all she could to keep from crying. She looked into Lorimar's eyes and saw the emptiness that filled his heart due to her absence.

"I've missed you greatly," said Gabrielle.

Lorimar bowed his head. Although he tried to fight his surge of emotions, he was deeply touched by his mother's words. Gabrielle continued holding his hand for support. Then, she turned to see a young woman with stunning eyes of hazel standing before her. Her hair was jet black with red highlight streaks, and it was braided in a long ponytail that extended midway down her back. Her skin had an ashen-caramel color and her body was sleek and toned.

"Hello, Kitana," said Gabrielle.

Kitana stared menacingly at Gabrielle.

"Hello, Gabby," she said.

Gabrielle pursed her lips and tucked her head.

"Kitana, do not embarrass me with your disrespect!" barked Lorimar.

She looked at her brother and then turned to stare at Gabrielle once more.

"Sorry, Mother," she retorted.

Gabrielle cleared her throat and attempted to be cordial once more.

"So, how have you been?"

"Peachy," replied Kitana, stretching out the pronunciation of the word.

"That's good," said Gabrielle.

One of the agents approached Kitana and whispered something to her. She frowned, then turned to look at her brother.

"Bandores just called in. He said that earlier today they detected a quantum disturbance in the Sinai. They dispatched a team there and found an excavation taking place," said Kitana.

"Does he believe the gate was found?" asked Lorimar.

"Yes," she replied hesitantly.

"Where is it now?"

"He doesn't know. It was gone by the time he and his agents arrived. He's trying to find it as we speak."

Lorimar bowed his head.

"They're probably taking it to wherever Dupri is. If we find him, we may find the gate," said Gabrielle.

Lorimar nodded in agreement. Kitana sneered and rolled her eyes.

"See if we can find out where he is," Lorimar said as he stood.

"As you wish," said Kitana.

"Wait, I have another idea. The Hierarchy has a system called the Sky Eye. If we tune it into Dupri's biorhythms, we might be able to see where he is," said Gabrielle.

Sariel was stunned that Gabrielle had divulged this level of information and quickly leaned toward her.

"Do you think it's wise to say such secrets around them?" he asked in a whisper.

"Listen, Sariel, this isn't a game. We may be on the verge of extinction, and this may be our last chance to stop it. Besides, these are my children. If I can't trust them, then who?"

"Need I remind you that they are still members of the Consortium."

"Don't worry, Seraph, I won't tell anyone about your precious eye," said Lorimar.

Sariel turned and stared at the young commander.

"If I were worried, you'd be dead," Sariel replied.

"Now, now, everybody needs to calm down," said Azreal, who finally exited the restaurant and strolled toward them.

"Azreal!" exclaimed Kitana, who darted to him, giving him a huge hug.

Gabrielle, Sariel and Lorimar stood staring at the two. Gabrielle and Sariel turned and looked at Lorimar.

"They're seeing one another," he said embarrassingly.

Gabrielle shrugged.

"Well then, I guess we better get things started," she said.

Gabrielle reached into her pocket and pulled out her phone. She dialed a few numbers and was soon connected to headquarters.

"This is Gabrielle. I need the assistance of the Eye," she said.

"I'm glad you called, Gabrielle. This is Augustine. Peter needs to speak to you. Hold on for a moment," he said.

"Wait! Before you do that, I need you to track the Contravexus for me. Lock onto his biorhythms and let me know where he is located," she said.

"Will do. Here's Peter," said Augustine.

Suddenly, Gabrielle's tri-dimensional image projector in her phone showed the image of Peter standing before her.

"Gabrielle," he said.

"What's this about?" she asked.

"I have some distressing news. Michael has been incapacitated."

"Incapacitated? How?"

"It appears he's been exposed to a very unusual and deadly viral strain. It has attacked his central nervous system. He's being transported back to headquarters as we speak," said Peter.

"Who did this to him?" asked Gabrielle.

"We suspect it was Eve. Michael told Augustine and Mary that he was going to Toronto and that they should track him using the Eye. When he got there, we detected that Eve was there also. Shortly after they met, he collapsed," said Peter.

Gabrielle was noticeable disturbed.

"Do what you can for him, Peter," she said.

"You know I will. Be careful out there," said Peter.

The transmission ended and Gabrielle sat on the bench totally in shock. Sariel walked to her side and placed his hand on her shoulder.

"Sariel," she said with a sigh. "We are out of time."

"Indeed," he replied.

Lorimar looked at Kitana and Azreal. They both nodded. He turned and looked at his mother.

"If there is anything you need, let me know. You'll have the full cooperation of the Consortium," said Lorimar.

Gabrielle and Sariel turned and looked at the threesome.

"That's good, because I fear we are going to need everyone's help to fight this war," said Gabrielle

~~~

I clung to my father, as if my life depended on it. Tears of joy filled both our eyes and our embrace seemed to last for an eternity. He pulled back, cupping my hands in his. I looked down at our hands and smiled.

"Why didn't you tell me who you were when we first met?" I asked.

My father looked into my eyes.

"I wanted to, but it meant risking you regaining your memory," he answered.

My eyes welled with even more tears. My father's voice brought a comfort that I seriously needed. I dropped my head and leaned against his chest.

"I have so many questions, so many questions! I don't know where to begin," I said.

My father cupped my chin and lifted my head.

"Why don't you get some more rest," he said. "We'll talk later."

I nodded and laid down once more on the cot. My mind was racing with thoughts. However, the massive migraine I'd just had made me feel very tired. I laid my head on the pillow and, within moments, was fast asleep.

~~~

Raiel and Christi walked out of the room and huddled.

"She remembered you," said Raiel. "That isn't a good sign."

"Yes, but she still seems to be in control. I beg you to please wait and see how she is after she awakens," said Christi.

"Desmond, you have been my guardian for eons and have saved my life on numerous occasions. It is because of that I've spared her life thus far. I figured as long as she didn't get her memories back, she was no threat. But now that they have started to return, I'm not so sure that we shouldn't go ahead and kill her while we have the chance. You know as well as I do that she may turn hostile."

"Yes, I understand."

Christi lowered his head. For an instant in time, his daughter remembered him. They connected as only father and daughter could. After all these years of praying, he was finally reunited with her. Since that fateful day she sacrificed herself for the sake of their kingdom, Christi prayed that she would regain her memories without releasing those of the Gaian. He wished to have his child back. After all these years, it seemed that his prayers were answered.

But as is the case with most wishes, there is a catch. Even though she showed no signs that the Gaian's memories had been released, she'd become an even greater risk, a risk that Raiel could not allow. For the sake of all creation, Vanifera had to die.

The young Messiah saw the pain etched on his protector's face. He knew the decision that needed to be made was one of ultimate sacrifice and ultimate pain. What parent could feel anything but sorrow and anguish when it involved the sacrifice of their child? No matter how justified the reasoning is, no parent should outlive their children.

"Will you at least allow me to say goodbye?" Christi asked.

"Yes." Raiel nodded.

~~~

The sands of time passed quickly. As minutes turned into hours, the stage was now set and the final pieces were being moved into place. At Sea-Tac airport outside of Seattle, a massive Boeing 767 had been on the ground for twenty minutes and its passengers were about to deplane. Montellace Dupri walked down the steps of his private aircraft and strolled to his limousine. Inside the vehicle sat Eve. She had a huge smile on her face. Dupri got in and the door was secured.

"Well, this is it. Now all we need is the woman," said Eve.

"And where is Huang?" asked Dupri.

"Don't know."

"Find him! I'm too close to victory to have anything screw it up now."

~~~

Angelo had also made it to Seattle. He'd taken the train and exited Union Station. He looked into the sky, overjoyed to be back. However, he felt a very disturbing vibe in the air. He knew something was happening, but he didn't know what. He snapped the collar of his coat and began his trek to the safe house.

~~~

"Here, eat this," said a voice that awakened me from my sleep. My eyes fluttered open, instantly squinting as my vision adjusted. I sat up and rubbed my eyes. As they adjusted, I could see Raiel lifting a bowl toward me.

"Its soup," he said.

I took the bowl and began sipping the soup. The warm broth felt good going down my throat. I looked around the room and noticed a small radio in the corner.

"Could I listen to some music?" I asked nodding toward it.

"Sure," my father said. "But I'm afraid that all you're going to get are the news channels. The reception isn't all that great in here."

"That's fine," I replied.

He turned it on and then walked back to me. Raiel stood, walked to the throne-like chair by the wall and sat. My father placed a few more logs on the fire while we listened to the news. The weatherman was discussing the unusual thunderstorm that occurred earlier. Then, the sports came on. Although I wasn't truly interested in any of that, it was nice to hear what was going on in the human world for a change. All this time I'd been dealing with these supernatural issues, I'd forgotten what it was like to be human. My father stoked the logs, then turned to look at me.

"You okay?" he asked.

"Yes."

"How's your head?"

"Better. At least the pain is gone."

"Do you feel any different?"

"At first I did when I saw images from my past. I saw the battle I had with the Gaian and I remembered what happened. Is that thing really inside of me?" I asked.

"It is a part of you and you a part of it," said Raiel from the shadows.

"So, I'm stuck like this forever?" I asked.

My father tucked his head. I sighed deeply as the news about the Seattle Mariners' recent victory echoed in the background. It diverted my attention for a moment and I chuckled. The Mariners were one of Angelo's favorite teams. I looked once more at my father. He kept stoking the fire, keeping his back turned to me the entire time. It was almost as if he were trying to avoid looking at me. Perhaps the return of my memories disturbed him. I decided to try and make him talk.

"How is it that you're still alive?" I asked.

He poked the fire some more. "The Messiah gave me another chance at life. He needed a guardian while he was on Earth. I volunteered."

"So, you *were* dead?" I asked.

"Yes, but I was reborn, thanks to Raiel."

"Humph."

"Does that bother you, child?" asked Raiel.

"Nothing bothers me anymore," I replied.

I lifted the bowl of soup and took another sip. Then, I heard something on the radio that caught my attention.

"Police are describing it as a ritualistic murder. It happened in Oakland, California at about eight thirty last night as a man bludgeoned his wife to death with a hammer. A call came into 911 around eight-fifteen about a disturbance and screaming coming from one of the apartments at the Oak Forrest Apartment complex."

My ears perked up when I heard the name of the apartment complex. It was where my friend Denise lived.

"Police say when they arrived, they found a man clutching the body of a young woman. The man then attacked the officers, forcing them to open fire. He was pronounced dead at the scene."

Fear began to heighten in my chest. I waited to hear if they were going to mention the names.

"The female victim was twenty-nine year old Denise Terrence."

The bowl fell from my hands and smashed on the floor. I sat there stunned by what I'd just heard. I began shaking and I grabbed my head. My father came to me and placed his arm around me.

"Vanifera, what's wrong?" he alarmingly asked.

"They killed them. They made Sidney kill her and then they killed him," I said in a near panicked tone.

Raiel stood and quickly raced toward me. I began shaking once more and the pain in my head returned. This time it was worse. I started going into convulsions as the news of Denise and Sidney's deaths sank in.

"Lay her down quickly," said Raiel.

~~~

In a seemingly condemned building, Eve descended a flight of spiral stairs. She made her way to Dupri, who stared into a huge pit in the floor. She, too, began to peer down the hole, curious as to what he was looking at. Dupri turned to look at her.

"Did you contact Huang?" he asked.

"Yes, he should be here any minute," she replied.

"I'm here now," said a voice from the shadows.

Huang emerged and walked toward a smirking Eve and scowling Dupri. His new face was completely healed.

"You wanted to see me, my lord?" he asked.

"Where is the Gaian?" asked Dupri.

"Well, there was a little problem," replied Huang, stopping next to Eve.

Just then, Dupri grabbed him by the neck and lifted him off the ground. He turned and dangled him over the pit. Eve stepped back, surprised by Dupri's actions.

"Give me one reason why I shouldn't drop you into this pit," growled Dupri.

Huang gasped as Dupri began crushing his throat. He grabbed Dupri's hand and wrist, trying to lessen his master's constricting grip.

"Please, Dupri, don't drop me!" he begged, wiggling like a worm on a hook.

"Where is the woman?" he asked.

"I tried to get her, sire. But the Messiah and the Valkydine got there just as I was about to retrieve her. They sliced off half my face.

I had to retreat and heal myself before I went back after her. I was about to do so when you called," said Huang gurgling.

Dupri held him for a few more seconds over the void. Then, he threw him across the room with an effortless toss. Huang landed on the floor with a thud and slid to a stop against the far wall. He scrambled to pick himself up from the cold, hard concrete as the Contravexus turned his head and looked at him.

"Get out of my sight and do not return without the Gaian," said Dupri.

"Yes, sire," said Huang as he stood.

Suddenly, Eve sensed something. She looked up at the roof of the building, as if she were scanning the heavens.

"Dupri, hold on for a moment. I'm detecting something. There is a surge of energy in the air. It is unlike anything I've ever sensed," said Eve.

Dupri turned and looked at her.

"I don't have time for your little voodoo games, Eve," he said.

"I assure you, this is no voodoo game. Something is out there, something very evil. I can feel it," she said.

Dupri continued to stare at Eve, as did Huang. A look of fear began to appear on her face.

"It's a very dark presence, the most evil presence I've ever felt," she said.

Dupri turned and looked at Huang.

"Prepare the gate and the altar. I think our Gaian is about to come to us," he said.

~~~

Vanifera had gone into a full seizure. Her eyes had rolled back into her head and she shook violently on the cot. Desmond Christi and Raiel held her down as best they could. Raiel tried to use his powers to calm her, but nothing was working.

"We're losing her," said Christi.

"I know. I'm doing everything in my power, but nothing's working," said Raiel.

The two of them struggled for a few more moments. Then suddenly, Vanifera stopped shaking. She lay motionless on the cot and panted heavily. Raiel and Christi continued to hold her just in case she started up again.

"You think it's over?' asked Christi.

"I don't know," replied Raiel.

"What happened?"

Raiel stood and walked to a table. He removed a small wooden crucifix, clutching it around the top. The lower half was shaved into a point, mimicking a stake. He turned and began walking back toward Vanifera.

"She reacted to that news report about the woman in California. She said something about someone killing them. I think she was referring to the Contravexus. They may have killed her friends in order to get to her," said Raiel.

"Do you really think the bonds were severed?" asked Christi looking at the stake.

"I'm not sure. But I can't take any more risks. Go turn that radio off."

Desmond Christi stood, trotted to the radio and switched it off. As he walked back, Vanifera began moaning. She lifted her hand to her head and held it for a few moments. Raiel leaned closer to talk to her and lifted the stake.

"Vanifera? Can you hear me?" he asked.

"Messiah," she whispered.

"Yes, I'm here," said Raiel.

Vanifera nodded her head. Raiel raised the stake high in the air and prepared to bring it down. Christi bit his bottom lip and turned his head slightly to avoid seeing his daughter's life being taken. Suddenly, Vanifera reached up and grabbed Raiel by the neck with a grip so powerful that it took his breath away. The stake fell to the floor and splintered into several pieces. She lifted the young boy off the ground as she stood from the cot. Desmond was momentarily shocked by the move, but quickly unsheathed his sword and held it before him. Vanifera turned to look at Desmond Christi. Her eyes were blood red and an evil grin was on her mouth. She looked back at Raiel, pulling him close to her face. He struggled to free himself from her grip, but she was much too powerful. She snarled, pulling him to within inches of her face.

She looked into Raiel's eyes as she growled, "I'm free!"

~~~

Gabrielle, Sariel and the members of the Consortium had all convened at a park on the north side of Seattle. They were going over search plans, when suddenly, she stood from the bench and looked toward the west side of the city. Simultaneously, Azreal, Kitana, Lorimar and Sariel did also. They all felt a sudden change in the atmosphere, like a shockwave had been released.

"Did any of you just feel that?" asked Gabrielle.

"Indeed. Something is happening," said Azreal as Kitana grabbed his arm.

"I don't know about the rest of you, but I have a bad feeling about this," said Sariel.

"I share your fear, Sariel. I'm not sure what that was, but I know it wasn't good," said Lorimar.

Gabrielle turned and looked at Sariel. They knew what caused that surge of energy. They'd felt it before, and the fact that they were feeling it now could only mean one thing. Gabrielle then looked at Azreal and her children.

"I'm afraid our worse fears have come to pass. The Gaian has been released," she said.

~~~

Angelo froze in his tracks as the dark surge of energy passed through him. He shivered and instantly recognized what he felt. It was the same energy that he'd battle in eons past. He tucked his head as the realization of what this meant began to sink in.

"Damn it! Damn it! This can't be happening," he said. "Vanifera, no! You can't leave me now!"

~~~

"YES!" exclaimed Dupri. "She finally broke!"

Eve smiled as Dupri showed joy for the first time since her association with him.

"It would appear that the Gaian is back," she said.

Huang continued to massage his neck as an assistant whispered in his ear. He then turned and spoke to Dupri.

"My lord, the gate and the altar are prepared," he said.

"Excellent. Now all we need to do is bring her to us. Eve, locate the Gaian. Trace that energy surge to its source. Huang, summon the troops. We have a Gaian to pick up," said Dupri.

~~~

Raiel dangled by his neck in Vanifera's clutches. Desmond Christi clutched his sword and stared disturbingly at his daughter.

"Vanifera, what are you doing? Put him down," said Christi.

She turned and looked at the Valkydine.

"The one you called Vanifera no longer exists. For eons, I've been locked in her mind, floating in suspended animation. This woman's mental abilities have kept me trapped in the bowels of her subconscious. But now, I am free and I will have my revenge on the ones who once challenged my master, and I will start with the one responsible for my master's downfall. You, Messiah!" said the Gaian.

"Don't force me to hurt you," said Christi.

"Go ahead, strike me! I doubt you have the guts to lift your sword against your own daughter," said the Gaian.

Christi paused in thought for a moment. Then, he raised his sword and charged. He swung and slashed the arm of the Gaian, causing it to release Raiel and clutch the area that had been injured. Raiel fell to the ground gasping for breath. Christi knelt and assisted the young Messiah away from the bellowing image of his daughter. The Gaian removed its hand and looked at the area where Christi sliced it. A deep gash oozed blood. The Gaian turned and looked at Desmond.

"Father, how could you do this? How could you attack your own daughter?" spoke the normal voice of Vanifera.

"You are no longer my daughter. You are that creature who stole my daughter's body. Somehow, someway, I will destroy you for what you've done," said Christi.

"But I am Vanifera. I am your daughter," she said as she began walking toward them.

"Stay back, or I swear I will kill you where you stand," said Christi.

"Father, please," she said as she continued to grow closer.

Desmond whispered to Raiel, who was still gasping for air.

"Are you well enough to get away?" he asked.

"Yes, I think so," Raiel replied.

Christi stood to his feet and swung his sword once again. This time, the Gaian ducked and swung a backhanded blow, knocking Christi into the far wall of the room. The Valkydine warrior fell to the ground. The sword dropped from his hand and clanged on the concrete floor. The Gaian snickered and slowly began walking toward its fallen opponent.

"How predictable. I would have thought you to be a much better challenge to me. But since you aren't, I will make an example out of you," said the Gaian.

She stood over Christi, who struggled to regain his bearings and stand to his feet. The Gaian reached down and lifted him up by his collar. Christi dangled in her clutches like a wet towel.

"How appropriate that you should die by the hands of your own daughter," said the Gaian.

She reared back her fist and prepared for the killing blow. Just then, she felt something grabbing her drawn fist. It burned her flesh, causing her to drop Christi and back away, shaking her hand to calm the pain. Her skin smoldered and the pain was excruciating. After a few moments, the burning subsided and the Gaian looked up to see who dared to inflict such a burn. It was Raiel.

"This is not right. I am not supposed to feel pain like this," she hissed.

Raiel assisted Christi to his feet. Christi grabbed his sword and raised it once again, wiping the blood that trickled from the corner of his mouth.

"She's lost her invulnerability. Perhaps she can be killed now," Christi whispered to Raiel.

"It would seem. However, she is still a very dangerous opponent. We need to be careful," said Raiel.

Desmond stood a little straighter and Raiel took a couple of steps toward the Gaian.

"If it is a fight you want, beast, then a fight you shall have," said Raiel.

The Gaian ceased shaking her hand and stood glaring at her two opponents. She was confused by the fact that she could be hurt, a symptom that she didn't have before the merger with Vanifera. In this state, she realized that she could not fight either Christi or Raiel. She had to get away and figure out how to restore her invulnerability. Suddenly, a smile came to her lips. She stood erect and began mumbling what appeared to be a chant. Desmond and Raiel were befuddled by the Gaian's antics.

"What do you think she's doing?" asked Raiel.

"I'm not sure. But whatever it is, you can bet that it won't be good," said Christi.

"She seems distracted. I suggest you strike right now."

"Good idea."

Desmond Christi was about to make another charge, when suddenly, the Gaian spat a glob of gel on the floor. Seconds later, the glob began melting, spreading across the floor like syrup over pancakes. It released a hissing sound, as if it were burning the stone floor beneath it. A strange stench filled the air and the room was blanketed with a thick cloud of smoke.

The gel continued to bubble and smolder as it spread. Then, it began to stiffen and hints of something inside the gel began to rise. Faces appeared and slowly ascended from the goop. Moans echoed in the hollow halls of the building and bodies formed beneath the now risen faces. As the creatures concluded their ascension from the muddy gel-like substance, they stepped from the sludge and congregated in a darkened corner of the room. The gel continued to bubble, and soon, hoards of these creatures were popping up from the slime. Within a matter of moments, several dozen had been made and they surrounded Raiel and Christi.

"I figured that since I am not yet ready to fight you, I'd give you a few playmates to keep you busy," said the Gaian.

The battalion leered at Raiel and Desmond Christi with eyes of resentment. They were mindless creatures created for one purpose, to kill. As the last of the minions shuffled to their respective spots, the Gaian jumped up to the top of a stack of boxes and squatted to stare at her massive army of soldiers. A creature in the middle of the crowd lifted its head and bellowed out a cry.

"Yes! Yes! That's the kind of spunk I like to hear!" exclaimed the Gaian.

"This is sick. You're too weak to fight us, so you send these pitiful creatures to do your dirty work," said Christi.

"Sorry, but I don't believe in that heroic, going-down-fighting motto you seem to have," said the Gaian.

"You will pay for this, Gaian. I will see to it," said Christi.

"I doubt it." said the Gaian as she turned to face her army of creatures. "Now…go! Tear them to shreds!"

~~~

CHAPTER TWENTY

The demonoids roared with enthusiasm as they leered at Raiel and Desmond Christi with a look of blood-lust. The two angelic figures stood poised for battle, studying their massive opposition. They were outnumbered and without backup. However, Raiel and Desmond realized that the demonoids were simple pawns in this battle. The real villain stood atop a stack of boxes, cloaked in the body of an innocent woman.

Desmond stared disdainfully at the Gaian. He resented how it had invaded the body of his daughter and used her likeness as a shield. He also remembered what it had done ages ago. It was a killing machine and now, the despicable creature had returned. Desmond was determined to make it pay for what it had done.

A screech exploded from the mob as the creatures rushed toward the two warriors. A single demonoid dove into the air attempting a leaping attack. Desmond swung the blade, slicing the hellion in half. He continued the rotation of his swing and decapitated the three demonoids closest to him. A sublime golden glow began to appear around Raiel and permeated the ground beneath him. Suddenly, the ground began rumbling and shaking, growing in strength by the moment. The demonoids struggled to maintain their balance, gripping and clinging to each other. Lightning bolts shot across the ground, striking the entire first wave of demonoids and instantly frying them where they stood. The unearthly power of the Messiah quickly reduced them into pillars of ash, and their burnt remains crumbled to the ground into piles of dust.

As the second wave advanced, Desmond buried the point of the sword into the ground. The hellions rushed to overtake the Valkydine. Just as they were within arms reach of the guardian, he twisted the buried blade. The ground in front of him crumbled and a huge hole opened beneath the hellions. The demonoids tumbled into the void and disappeared into the darkness of a bottomless pit. Their screams echoed from the crevice as the last of the advancing squadron disappeared. Desmond swiftly withdrew the sword from the earth and the ground rumbled and merged, sealing the minions within. Desmond stood and surveyed the surroundings. Raiel stood by his side. There were still a few more creatures left and they waited for them to attack.

"You must stop this, Gaian! These creatures are innocent souls who do not deserve this! If you want a fight, then wage the battle yourself," said Raiel.

"I will not soil my hands with the likes of you!" said the Gaian.

"How long do you plan to hide behind these pawns, you accursed creature? Can you not fight your own battle, or is that something you aren't used to?" exclaimed Christi.

"This is simply the preliminary! The main event is yet to come!" retorted the Gaian.

Just then, the next band of demonoids charged. Raiel knew that he had to stop this, and he had to do it now. He lifted his hand to reveal a small ball of light, which hovered just above his palm. It shimmered like a tiny crystal with thousands of glittering sparkles inside. He hurled it toward the charging creatures. The ball instantly burst into flames, consuming the creatures with a massive plume of fire. The flames engulfed the remainder of the mob like a wave. The demonoids were incinerated and reduced to dust in a matter of seconds.

Desmond and Raiel looked up at the Gaian, who was now seething with anger.

"We've beaten your creatures. Now, it's your turn," said Christi.

The Gaian grimaced with clenched teeth. It slowly relaxed its scowl and began snickering, then bursting into hysterical laughter.

"You pitiful, pathetic creatures! You don't get it, do you?

You cannot challenge me! I possess powers that are far beyond your realm of understanding! This was only a mild yawn, perhaps encompassing about two percent of my abilities! But since you are so eager to die, then allow me to grant your wishes!" said the Gaian.

She lifted her hands, like she were conducting an orchestra. Then, small spikes appeared from the floor, walls and the ceiling of the room. Raiel and Desmond looked around and pondered what the Gaian was doing. They quickly got their answer. She swiped her hands through the air and the spikes suddenly began shooting from the walls.

Desmond formed a block between the spikes and Raiel, swinging his sword and deflecting the first several shots. The Gaian continued her symphony and fired several more shots at her stationary targets. Desmond deflected her second round of shots but the intensity and speed of her attack was increasing. He turned and whispered to Raiel.

"My lord, it might be a good idea if you got out of here," said a winding Christi.

"You cannot fight her alone, Valkydine. She is far too powerful," said Raiel.

"Better for her to just kill me, then to kill you as well," said Christi.

Just then, a spike from beneath the floor shot up and struck Raiel on his right arm. The young Messiah shrieked in pain.

"Messiah!" exclaimed Christi as he turned toward the wounded Raiel.

Another spike ejected from the wall and stabbed Desmond Christi in his back. Raiel grabbed the stumbling Valkydine just before he would have fallen on another protruding spike in the floor. Raiel lifted his other hand and formed a golden sphere of light that surrounded he and Desmond. The Gaian continued to shoot the spikes, but Raiel's shield was staving off the attack. Raiel was injured and so was Desmond Christi. The Gaian ceased her attack for a moment to gloat.

"Nice try, Messiah! But you've only managed to prolong the

inevitable! You're injured, and it will be only a matter of time before you weaken," said the Gaian.

"S-She's right, my lord. You need to save yourself. Without you, w-we will not be able to defeat this creature," said a heavily panting Christi.

Raiel could see that the wound on Desmond's back was quite severe. He could heal him, but he couldn't maintain the shield simultaneously.

"I can see the wheels turning in your head, Messiah. Should you maintain the shield or save the Valkydine? Tisk, tisk," said the Gaian.

She fired a few more powerful shots at the shield and paused once more.

"I can feel that you're starting to weaken. Just a few more blows and it will be all over," she said.

Raiel knew that she was right; he was starting to weaken. He'd lost quite a bit of blood from the wound to his arm, and it was just a matter of time before the integrity of the sphere would collapse. The Gaian fired another flurry of spikes and they were more powerful than any previously. Finally, one of the spears penetrated the sphere and struck Raiel in the thigh. The Messiah screamed as the golden protective orb vanished.

"Ah, now we're getting somewhere," said the Gaian.

"Messiah, leave now!" exclaimed Christi.

"I'm afraid the window of opportunity to flee has now closed. I've waited a long time for this, Messiah. For eons, I sat waiting for the moment when I would have my revenge on you. Now, the time has come for you to die," said the Gaian.

She raised her hand and prepared to launch another spike.

"Vanifera!" exclaimed a voice in the shadows.

The Gaian froze in place. Then, she turned and looked in the direction where the voice emanated. From the darkness emerged the one being she didn't expect. It was Angelo.

"You must stop this, Vanifera. I know that you're still in there and you can hear me. You must fight this creature," said Angelo.

The Gaian's eyes widened and she stared at the Seraph.

"Angelo?" she asked.

"Yes, Vanifera, I'm here," he said.

In that moment, the essence of Vanifera seemed to have returned. The sinister red glow in her eyes faded and the scowl on her face loosened. She looked at Angelo as if she remembered him. Angelo slowly walked toward her. She turned to face him and stared into his eyes as he halted in front of her. She lifted her hand and stroked the side of his face. He grabbed her hand and kissed her palm.

"Angelo," she said softly.

The two embraced. Tears welled in Vanifera's eyes and rolled down her cheeks. She clutched her beloved husband as if her life depended on it. The spikes began disappearing from the walls, floor and ceiling as the two lovers continued to hug one another.

"I've missed you so much," she said tearfully.

"And I've missed you, too," he replied.

She lifted her head and they kissed.

During this distraction, Raiel managed to partially heal Desmond. The Valkydine stood to his feet and lifted his sword.

"Now is our moment to strike. This distraction may be our only chance," said Raiel.

Desmond nodded. He charged toward the two lovers with his sword. Just as Desmond thrust his sword toward Vanifera, Angelo opened his eyes. He saw the attack and instinctually pushed Vanifera out of the way. The sword impaled the Archangel through the abdomen. Vanifera fell to the ground and slid against the far wall.

Desmond was stunned that he'd missed his true target. He quickly extracted the sword and Angelo fell to his knees with a shocked expression on his face. He clutched his stomach as a stream of blood poured from the wound. Desmond backed away as Raiel stood his feet. He rushed passed the stunned Valkydine and knelt beside Angelo.

"Easy there, Angelo, you're going to be alright," said Raiel.

Angelo looked at the Messiah and struggled to speak.

"She is not evil. D-don't hurt h-her," he said.

"Just lie still. Everything is going to be alright," said Raiel.

Desmond watched as Raiel began trying to heal Angelo. He couldn't believe that he'd missed or that Angelo had made such a move in order to save this vile creature. Then, his eyes turned toward Vanifera, who now sat in the corner with her head tucked and her arms wrapped about her pulled-in knees. She rocked back and forth, like someone trying to control a fit of hysteria.

"You tried to kill my husband. You tried to kill me. Now, I will kill you," she said as she finally lifted her head.

Vanifera's eyes were blood red once more and a look of contempt covered her face. It was clear that the Gaian had regained control. She stared at Desmond Christi, then leapt to her feet. She charged at him and with one backhanded swipe, knocked him into the far wall. Christi fell to the floor with a thud and was apparently unconscious. The Gaian then walked toward the fallen Valkydine. Her fingernails grew into claws and she prepared to deliver the killing blow.

"Don't take another step!" exclaimed a voice from behind.

The Gaian turned. Standing behind her were Sariel and Gabrielle. A few seconds later, Azreal, Kitana and Lorimar appeared and stood next to them. The Gaian snarled and then completely turned to face them.

"Well, it looks like the gang's all here," she said.

Azreal lifted a gun resembling a magnum. Sariel lifted a nine millimeter and Gabrielle lifted an Uzi. They pointed them at the Gaian.

"Oh please, don't tell me you plan to shoot me," she said.

Angelo lifted his head.

"Please, don't harm her. Vanifera is still in there," he pleaded.

"Sorry, Ange, but we can't afford to let this go any further," said Sariel.

"The Gaian has lost her invulnerability! Shoot her now!" exclaimed Raiel.

Then, an explosion of gunfire rang. Azreal, Gabrielle and Sariel unloaded a rain of gunshots that was deafening, and their aim was perfect. The Gaian shook violently as each bullet tore gaping holes in her body. After all of the bullets had been exhausted, a deafening silence fell in the room. The click of the triggers continuing to be pulled was the only sounds to be heard. The Gaian's bullet ravaged-body swayed and then collapsed face first on the ground. A pool of blood formed beneath her as she lay motionless. Sariel, Gabrielle and Azreal lowered their weapons and glared at her.

"It's over," said Kitana.

Angelo, with tears in his eyes, dropped his head. He was unable to convince his peers not to harm Vanifera, and now she was dead. For an instant, he'd been able to bring that part of her out of the creature, and he truly believed that she could have been saved. But because of his injury, he could not stop them.

"Vanifera, I'm sorry," he said.

Raiel, who continued to heal Angelo, saw his grief.

"It was for the best, Angelo. She was too far gone," he said.

"Was she? For a moment, she held me, and when we kissed, I felt her love and the desire she had to overcome that demon," said Angelo.

Raiel finished doing what he could to heal the Seraph. Angelo stood to his feet as did Raiel. Gabrielle and Sariel walked to their brethren's side. Azreal, Kitana and Lorimar all stood glaring at the corpse that lay on the floor.

"How are you feeling?" asked Gabrielle.

"How should I be feeling? There lies the woman I love, and the beings who took her life now ask me how I feel?" replied Angelo.

"We had no choice, Angelo. Either we took this opportunity while we had it, or we might not be standing here right now," said Sariel.

"There's always a choice, Sariel. You made yours..." said Angelo as he walked away from them and toward Vanifera's body.

Angelo knelt beside her. She lay face down on the ground. He grabbed her and rolled her over, cradling her head in his hands. He looked at her blood-covered face and began sobbing as he removed the hair from covering it. Raiel bowed his head, then went to revive Desmond Christi. Lorimar released his stare from Vanifera and turned to face his mother. Kitana did likewise.

"Well, mother, it appears that this little crisis is over," said Lorimar.

"It appears so," she replied.

He walked to her and they exchanged hugs. Kitana crossed her arms, refusing to relinquish her hatred and contempt for her mother's abandonment. Azreal walked to her side and placed his hand on her shoulder. She glanced at him, then reached up and cupped his hand.

"Don't feel bad. Maybe one day you two will find a way to talk," he said.

Kitana glanced at him.

"Don't count on it," she said.

She turned and walked into the darkness. Azreal watched her until she vanished, then turned to Sariel and Gabrielle.

"Nice working with you," he said.

Sariel flipped his head in acknowledgement. Gabrielle and Lorimar concluded their embrace, then he backed away and began walking in the same direction as Kitana. Gabrielle appeared touched by the moment and struggled to keep her composure. Azreal turned and followed Lorimar. Sariel walked next to Gabrielle, who gave him a quick glance and turned to watch her departing children.

"Perhaps it's time we departed also," said Sariel.

Batting her eyelids to fight her tears, Gabrielle nodded.

"Perhaps," she replied.

Raiel completed healing Desmond Christi. The Valkydine warrior rose to his feet and braced himself against the wall.

"Steady there," said Raiel helping to stabilize him.

"Thanks, I'm okay," said Christi.

"That was some blow you took," said Raiel.

"I've taken worse," Christi replied.

~~~

Outside the safe house, Dupri stood glaring, his arms folded across his chest. Huang stood next to him.

"Are the troops ready?" asked Dupri.

"Ready and waiting," said Huang menacingly.

Just then, Lorimar, Kitana and Azreal exited the building.

"Here they come. Release them," Dupri commanded.

Huang placed his fingers between his lips and whistled. Suddenly the sound of moans erupted and an army of zombie-like creatures crept toward the exiting Consortium members.

~~~

As Lorimar walked out of the building, he detected something he didn't like.

"Wait! Did you guys hear that?" he asked, extending his arm to halt Azreal and Kitana.

They all paused and listened intently. They soon heard what Lorimar was talking about. It sounded like moans of suffering. Just then, a creature grabbed Lorimar on the shoulder. He stared into the corpse-like face, its mouth opening wide.

"What the hell is that?" asked Kitana as she began backing up.

Lorimar quickly snatched away and distanced himself from the creature.

"I have no clue," said Lorimar.

Suddenly, they were surrounded by the zombies. They appeared suddenly and all seemed to be coming after the Consortium members.

"Whatever they are, they picked the wrong day to screw with me," said Azreal pulling his gun from its holster.

"I'm with you, babe," said Kitana as she lifted her gun.

~~~

The sound of gunfire suddenly echoed inside the building. It sounded as if it were coming from the outside. Everyone quickly glanced at each other, then darted toward the sound of the commotion. The only one who remained was Angelo, who clutched the body of his deceased wife.

Within moments, Gabrielle, Sariel, Desmond Christi and Raiel were outside. What they saw surprised them as well as horrified them. Azreal, Kitana and Lorimar were barricaded behind their Escalade SUV firing rounds of shots at hundreds of zombie-like corpses walking toward them. It was as if the entire area was covered with these hideously deformed creatures. Some were decaying vessels oozing a dark fluid and festering maggots. Others looked as if they'd just been killed.

"In the name of Heaven..." said Christi.

"This is bad. This is really bad," said Sariel.

Just then, a group of them reached the SUV and began lifting the side, trying to tip it over. Kitana, Azreal and Lorimar quickly backed away as the massive vehicle crashed to its side. They continued firing as they backed their way toward the building.

"Quick, into the building!" exclaimed Raiel.

The group quickly rushed back into the building and began barricading the door.

"What are those things?" asked Christi.

"I'm not sure; they appeared from nowhere. We were walking back to the car, when suddenly, they surrounded us. Each one we shot got right back up. It's like they are the walking dead," said Lorimar.

"That's exactly what they are," said Raiel.

"You mean those things out there are the bodies of dead people," asked Kitana.

"Exactly. Vessels with no soul."

The sound of the creatures banging on the door echoed inside the hollow chamber. The group had placed everything they could find behind the door. But with the massive size of the army of zombies that were outside, it wouldn't be long before they would get through the door.

"How much ammunition do you have left?" asked Sariel.

"I have two clips," said Lorimar.

"Maybe a half," said Kitana.

"I've got about one and a half," said Azreal.

"Gabrielle, what about you?" asked Sariel.

"I'm out," she said.

Sariel checked his pockets and found one full clip for his nine millimeter.

"We don't have enough," he said.

"Then we'll just have to make it enough," said Christi.

~~~

Angelo clutched Vanifera's body as the stream of tears rolled down his cheeks. Even though he mourned for his wife, he also detected another presence in the room. He lifted his head and stared into the eyes of Dupri.

"I figured you'd show up sooner or later. I'm glad you did. You've saved me the trouble of hunting you down. Like I promised you, this time there will be no mercy," said Angelo.

"I just came for the woman, Archangel, that's all," said Dupri.

"What do you want with her now? Can't you see that she's dead?"

"Looks can be deceiving."

"You'll have to kill me before I allow you to touch her!" said Angelo as he gently laid Vanifera down and stood to his feet.

"I was hoping you'd be reasonable. However, it is clear you do not understand just how hopelessly in peril you really are," Dupri replied.

Just then, Huang leaped from the shadows and attacked Angelo. He swung his claws and sliced a gash in his chest. Angelo stumbled backward, bracing himself against the wall in order to catch his balance. He reached down and clutched the area that Huang attacked. He hadn't totally recovered from the wound inadvertently inflicted by Christi, and now he was beginning to bleed once more.

"I will make pâté out of you," said Huang as he prepared for another charge.

"Then you're going to have to do better than that," replied Angelo.

Huang leaped and tried to perform another attack. Angelo caught him in mid air and slammed him face first to the ground. Angelo then pounded the face and body of Huang, reducing him to a bloody mess in a matter of seconds. Just then, Dupri attempted an attack. He lifted a dagger and swung it toward Angelo's head. But the Archangel delivered his own attack, swinging his fist and knocking the dagger from Dupri's hand. The Contravexus grabbed his wrist and backed away from the Seraph. He realized that in Angelo's enraged state, he was clearly outmatched. Angelo stood over Huang, who was barely able to move. Having lost his reasons to restrain his anger, he glared at Dupri with one thought in mind.

"It's time for you to die, Contravexus!" he said.

Dupri showed a look of horror. Then, a smirk appeared on his lips.

"I'm afraid not, my friend," he replied.

Angelo suddenly felt an unbearable pain in his back that paralyzed him. He was unable to move and stared at the smirking face of Dupri. His body went numb and his head dropped, allowing him to see a hand protruding from his chest. Instantly, he knew who it was. The hand retracted from his body and the Archangel fell forward on the ground. He could barely breathe, and his body was beginning to grow cold. However, with his last bit of energy, he craned his neck to look into the eyes of the one who'd injured him. It was his wife, Vanifera. With one last sigh, Angelo fell into unconsciousness.

Dupri looked at Vanifera, still sporting his devious smirk.

"Well done, Gaian," he said.

Just then, Vanifera collapsed into Dupri's arms. Huang managed to regenerate enough to stand.

"She is weakened. Send some of your creatures in here and have them take her to the stronghold," said Dupri.

"Not so fast, Dupri," said a voice from the shadows.

The Contravexus craned his neck to see a pair of blood-red

eyes staring at him from the shadows. Both Dupri and Huang's jaws dropped as the being emerged from the darkness. He was tall with a long streak of gray accenting the left side of his long black hair, which dangled down his back. He wore a black suit with a black, collarless shirt. It was the Supreme Commander of the Consortium, Lucifer.

"Well, will you look at what the cat dragged in," said Dupri as he handed the limp body of the Gaian over to Huang.

"Hand over the woman," said Lucifer.

"Afraid not, ole bean."

"Very well."

One second passed. Dupri and Huang felt sharp pains across their throats. Another second passed. They fell to the ground clutching their necks. A third second passed. Vanifera was being supported in the arms of Lucifer. In those three seconds, Lucifer managed to incapacitate both Dupri and Huang and capture the Gaian.

"Those were merely flesh wounds to your neck. Now it's time to finish the job," said Lucifer.

He clutched Vanifera close to him and prepared for the final attack. Huang and Dupri still clutched their neck, trying to quicken their regeneration process. As Lucifer lunged, the Gaian's eyes opened. With one swift move, she drove her hand into the left side of Lucifer. He bellowed in pain and fell to the floor, dropping the Gaian in the process. As they both collided with the concrete, Eve suddenly appeared and raced to Dupri's side.

"Are you okay?" she asked.

"Quickly, get us out of here!" gurgled Dupri.

Eve lifted her hands and began murmuring a spell. Within seconds, she, Dupri, Huang and Vanifera had vanished. Lucifer struggled to sit up, bracing himself against the wall. He clutched his side, glancing down at the moderate gash. He grimaced, then scanned the room looking for the Contravexus and his crew. But they were nowhere to be found. He looked down at Angelo, then banged his hands against the wall and released a deep bloodcurdling bellow. The release caused the windows in the room to shatter.

"Damn it! We failed!" he exclaimed.

~~~

Lucifer's cry and the sound of breaking glass resounded in the main chamber.

"What the hell was that?" asked Lorimar.

"I don't know. Azreal, you and Sariel check it out," said Raiel.

As they prepared to race down the hall, Lucifer emerged from the darkness, carrying a body in his arms. As he approached the group, everyone's eyes widened with shock.

"Father?" asked Lorimar.

As the shock of seeing the being called the Satan sunk in, Sariel noticed that Lucifer was carrying Angelo.

"What the hell did you do to him?" asked Sariel.

Lucifer knelt and laid Angelo on the ground.

"I did nothing to him," said Lucifer.

"Then what happened?" asked Raiel.

"While the rest of you were out fighting the corpses, Huang and Dupri attacked. The zombies were merely a diversion. I happened to be monitoring the entire thing. When I saw Angelo in trouble, I decided to intervene," said Lucifer.

Sariel and Raiel knelt beside Angelo, quickly noticing the huge wound in his chest.

"He's been hurt pretty bad," said Raiel.

"Can you help him?" asked Christi.

"I don't know. I'm still weakened from healing you two earlier," he replied.

Lucifer backed away as Raiel attempted to restore Angelo back to health. Then, his eyes caught sight of Gabrielle, who still stared at him in shock.

"It's been a long time," he said in his deep husky voice.

"Yes, it has," she replied starry eyed.

Kitana, Azreal and Lorimar approached Lucifer and performed their customary bows and curtsies.

"May I ask what happened to the Gaian?" Lorimar probed.

Lucifer sighed. He seemed a little reluctant to answer.

"Despite what you thought, you did not kill the Gaian. It was still alive, and it was the one who did this to Angelo," he said.

"Where is it now?" asked Christi.

Lucifer grimaced and clutched his abdomen. Kitana then noticed that his suit had been ripped and he was bleeding.

"Father, you're hurt," she said.

"It's nothing," he replied.

She helped him to a chair. Christi approached him and repeated his question.

"I understand you're hurt, but where is the Gaian?"

"The Contravexus has her," he replied with a grunt.

Sariel shot Lucifer a surprised look, then stood and glared at him.

"You mean to tell me you allowed Dupri to get his hands on the Gaian?" he asked.

"I didn't allow anything! Had you been thinking and doing your job..."

"Oh, so you're saying this is my fault?" said Sariel, walking toward Lucifer.

"Guys, please," Gabrielle interrupted as she came between them.

Lucifer and Sariel leered at one another. Raiel stood from the floor.

"That's all I can do for now. He should be fine in a couple of hours," he said.

Azreal shook his head in disbelief.

"Frankly, I don't think we have a couple of hours. We are in serious trouble. Lucifer and Angelo are hurt, Dupri has the Gaian, and there are hundreds of zombies outside who want to kill us. And if that weren't enough, we are low on ammunition," he said.

"Indeed, things do not look well," said Sariel as he and the rest of the group turned to stare at the rumbling door being pounded upon by the walking dead.

~~~

Barhim Hajj looked at Cardinal Xavier Wright with a hint of regret. Father Wright was a member of the Genesis Warriors. The sole purpose of this group was to defend the world of the humans when the prophecy of the final battle came to pass. The cardinal dialed a few numbers on his desk phone and pressed the number six. This generated a broadcast message to all of the Genesis warriors, alerting them that the time had come for battle.

"There," said Cardinal Wright with his thick accent. "All is done. I've alerted everyone and they should be converging in Venice in a matter of hours."

Just then, the woman who answered the door when Hajj arrived re-entered the room with a worried expression. She called to Wright and quickly whispered something in his ear. Wright looked at her and instantly garnered the same expression. Then, he turned and looked at Hajj.

"There is something I think you should see," he said.

Hajj shot Wright a suspicious look.

"What is it?" he asked.

Wright motioned for the woman to lead the way and for Barhim Hajj to follow. They left the office area and proceeded into a huge room with a big screen television set against the far wall. The volume was low, however, the unmistakable sound of screaming could be detected. They walked to the television and stood before it. The images they saw were quite disturbing.

Bodies littered the ground. The cameraperson panned back and forth between the corpses and a woman reporter crouched behind a barricade. With pale shaking hands, she clutched the base of the microphone. Her eyes were wide, filled with tearful fear. Smudges of dirt stained her clothes and her right shirtsleeve had been ripped. With a trembling voice, she described the events that led to this grizzly scene.

"It was the most horrible thing I'd ever seen! Just moments ago, a mob of creatures stormed the park and began killing everyone! The celebration that took place here was to commemorate the lives of those lost during the September 11th attacks! But now this peaceful gathering of humanity has turned into another holocaust as hundreds of people were literally ripped apart and left for dead! No one seems to know what these creatures are or where they came from! All that we know now is that no one is safe!"

She paused for a moment to fight back the swell of emotions overcoming her. She brushed away a tear that had rolled down her cheek and exhaled deeply.

"Even as we speak, these creatures are roaming the city and killing anyone they come across! What's also terrifying is that as each creature kills someone, the victims also turn into zombies! Police officials are asking everyone to stay indoors and to secure themselves as best they can! However, from what I've seen here today, that may be impossible! The creatures seem unstoppable! Some of the fleeing participants of this gathering attempted to drive over some of them while trying to escape! But they just got right back up! People are calling this the Day of Revelation! The dead have risen and are walking the face of the earth!"

Just then, the muffled voice of the cameraperson could be heard. The woman slowly turned. The picture suddenly went black, but the voice of the woman could still be heard.

"Oh my God, they're coming back!" she shrieked.

As the screaming woman's voice continued to broadcast, Cardinal Wright motionlessly stood with a look of horror. Barhim Hajj also stood frozen sporting a similar expression. They both knew what was happening and the woman reporter had called it succinctly. This *was* the Day of Revelation, the Apocalypse, and it heralded the end of all creation. Cardinal Wright turned and looked at Hajj.

"Dear God! It's started!" he said wide-eyed.

"Yes, Father, it has and it doesn't look good. May God help us all," replied Hajj.

Barhim Hajj continued watching the television. Although the picture was now dark, the images he saw were burned into his memory. The bodies of men, women and children littered the park and the streets. He knew that despite their best efforts to protect themselves, no one was safe. Within a few hours, very few humans would be left alive, if any. Time had run out. Even the well-trained battalion that Wright belonged to would have very little impact. Hajj looked over and saw Wright kneeling to the floor. At that moment, Hajj also felt the need to do the same. He knelt beside his longtime friend and began praying as the frantic voice of the woman reporter continued to emanate from the television.

~~~

"The world...is mine!" exclaimed Dupri, followed with a menacing snicker.

He stood before a huge golden altar, as the body of Vanifera lay motionless upon it.

"At long last, our moment of triumph has arrived," said Eve.

"Yes, and now the time has come to free our master," he replied.

Dupri, Eve and Huang all began laughing as they stared at the Gaian, the woman named Vanifera.

~~~~~~~~~~~~~~~~~To Be Continued~~~~~~~~~~~~~~~~~~

The exciting saga continues in "The Unbegotten: Sacrifices"